ELIZABETH ⚶ STEPHENS

D0861248

IMMORTAL
WITH SCARS

POPULATION SERIES· BOOK THREE

Table of Contents

To you.

E.S.

Chapter One

It is seven-thirteen. It is the evening, I suppose, though the sky betrays no difference in color. On Sistylea, it would be bright pink by now, perhaps deep purple should the clouds have resumed their cover, failing to burn off entirely before the night renders the world dark.

Here, in this world, there is no dark. There is no fluorescent pink. There is no indigo. There is only a flat red-orange that is not so much red or orange as it is grey. There are only the clocks that the Notare Abel and her *council* have elected to simultaneously set, describing a time that they have agreed upon that makes no sense to me and the time that I have long since learned to live without. Or perhaps, the time that has learned to live without me.

These numbers continue to count up and then down and then begin again in a ceaseless rhythm. *Strange, though functional.*

I rise from my seat and stride slowly to the door to my study. At precisely hour twenty the Notare Abel dismisses her council and retires to the comfort of her home with the Notare Kane.

She is heavy with child now, but she still seems intent to perform the inspections herself and she continues, despite protest from said council, from her mate, and from all other humans and Others unanimously — including from myself — to perform manual labor. Each watch she takes is strain to Notare Kane.

His affections for the female intrigue me and I have spent much *time* contemplating it.

Time.

No, I have spent much of my own *energy* devoted to thinking about their relationship. His fascination with her is fascinating in itself. He has existed for hundreds of their earth years, while she has existed for very few. She is penetrable in ways he is not. So quick to temper. Easily riled. Impetuous. Impulsive. Passionate.

Yet, he cherishes her as if she were an extension of himself.

It is a funny thing and reminds me again that Heztoichen are as different from humans as I am different to Heztoichen. A momentary grief flutters through me, one I have not devoted much of my energies to until the recent whispers reached me that there may be one of my own kind on this planet — a *female*. It is a pity that she is among these impassioned rebels who seek to destroy the Notare Abel, despite the fact that she carries true Tare. Were she not, I would have most certainly considered seeking her out. Together, we could continue our species, at least for one more generation, had we together the stomach for it.

I straighten up where I stand at the window, looking out. The clock now reads twenty-one forty-eight. Much time has passed. Time, this inconsequential thing. As inconsequential a concept as grief.

"No, the rebels must be rooted out and slaughtered." I say the words out loud. Hearing them always serves as a means of solidifying truth, lest my mind attempt to stray. "They have lost their way."

It is with a certain...acceptance that I exhale that fleeting, ephemeral desire and return to a truth that is as lonely as I am: I am the last and the last, I must remain. For my kind was doomed from the moment we sacrificed ourselves when Sistylea fell. We chose to stay behind, all but one. Myself. I wonder every so often were my purpose here not so necessary, if it were perhaps, not too great a sacrifice not to die alongside the rest.

Instead, I must remain here, in this wretched world, as the last of my kind, dedicated to my purpose until the Tare shifts again and life itself fades. I will watch these Notare fall as I have watched them fall for the past three millennia until, some millennia from now, I too return to dust.

And that will be the end of the role of the Lahve.

Three thirty-four. I move back to my desk and continue to pour over the correspondence I have received from the Notare around the world. Seven regions. The Diera. Brianna. Carata. Hviya. Molthanithra. Strentara. All regions are functioning as well as predicted, short of Carata, across the ocean, where Notare Tanen continues to pillage and burn and destroy. I attempt to reach him on one of the few communication devices still functional in this new world — a thing the humans call *computer* — but the connection does not go through. I do not believe he uses this or any other technology born of this world, unless it is to destroy.

And I understand why he has chosen this path, even if I do not approve.

I wrinkle my nose in distaste at the thought of returning to that part of this globe to negotiate with Tanen directly. His region holds the manufacturing plants necessary to create these communication technologies — as well as other life-saving harvesting equipment — that other regions do not. If the humans fall beneath his attacks as he advances further and further east, then it will all be lost. And, if these humans here in Brianna do not get their small, frail hands on those technologies soon, they may no longer have enough food to sustain their rapidly increasing human population. They are a species much like a virus. How greedily they consume.

I sigh and repeat my thoughts out loud, "Tanen will need to be dealt with soon."

Yet, before I can cross the world, I will need to root out the rebels here who disgrace the Tare with their attacks on Notare Abel. That it was given to her, a human, matters not. They disgrace themselves by attempting to interfere, forcing the Tare's hand as if it were a mortal.

No. The Tare chose and it chose a human called Abel and though I myself never dwelled much on the matters of humans — the primitive, brutal race that occupied this planet before our arrival — I am merely the Tare's incarnate. Neutral, above all else.

Five fifty-four. Night has long descended as I have ruminated at my desk. I leave the brick structure I have claimed for my manor and walk the streets of Brianna alone, members of my guard lurking at a respectful distance. The sky remains light, even through the night. A longing for our home world sweeps me — the sprawling violet fields, the luminous cities that spiraled high among the clouds, the rural dwellings carved directly into the mountainsides...

Here, I pass by squat homes, mostly brick, though some are constructed of wood. Stars mark the front doors of the houses where, only a few weeks ago, Elise and her Heztoichen supporters kept and tortured humans for their own perverse pleasure.

It angers both Notare Kane and Abel that this practice was undertaken, however, what they do not know is that it is a common practice among several of the other regions as well. That, however, remains the problem of those Notare. It is not my place to give voice to the Notare on how to govern themselves, merely on how they must interact with one another. I will intercede only when Notare Abel summons her humans back home, for it is certain that many other Notare will not be so willing to lose their blood supply. It will..create friction. It already has. Through these gangs of defilers and betrayers that dare to call themselves Heztoichen, it has already begun.

That however, is a matter for another day. Another *time*.

The suburban streets come together in a cul-de-sac at the end of a road marked *Starlight*. Here, a marketplace already begins to see its earliest activity, with those that harvest bringing their fruits and vegetables to long wooden tables. Bakers have stands where they keep bread. The aroma is pleasing.

Other humans have begun crafting — creating plates and cups from fired clay, weaving baskets from dried reed grasses, even concocting soaps and perfumes from animal fats and herbs.

Primitive though they may be, they are resourceful and inventive, these creatures.

As there is no coin here, goods and services are often bartered. When they are not, paper tickets are exchanged for more valuable goods, however this system is badly flawed. Alcohol, above all else, is the greatest currency. People have begun concocting all manner of foul beverage to trade with one another only to drink themselves into glut on the days labeled "weekends." Often, on these weekend days I find men and women passed out on the lawns surrounding each house, or occupying one of several buildings at the end of Starlight called *bars* and *restaurants*, though these restaurants are distant relatives of Sisylean restaurants, at best.

I remember what it was like walking through wide archways in all the trappings of glamour. Eyes roaming my body yes, but never touching. They know better than to attempt to touch their Lahve.

It is eight-twelve and I find myself passing through Brianna's steel gates. Four humans attend the gates at all times, while twenty-two additional humans stand as sentries at intervals along the steel walls that surround Abel's territory.

The territory is tight, the need to expand strong, particularly given the rise in attacks...

While the compound itself has not been raided, groups attempting to travel to Brianna often find themselves under siege. Survivors have told us of bleak attacks by humans *and* Hezoichen. Families have been lost that Notare Abel would have saved. Discussion has commenced over whether or not the humans of Brianna are prepared to build outposts, however, there is doubt over their ability to adequately protect them...

Hmm.

I still. Up ahead, a tree catches my eye. I advance towards it, changing my trajectory by a few degrees, my swordstick held lightly in my fists behind my back. My shin-length coat flutters with my steps, but there is no wind out here beyond the perimeter in what the humans call Population. Though this territory is still classified as Brianna according to my maps, there is no marker for it and too many feral humans reside outside of the walls in these cannibalized cities, in these forgotten woods.

Coming to a stop before the tree, I tilt my head to the side and inspect the sign carved into the bark. I narrow my gaze, flipping through a long list of languages both old and newly acquired, but there is no meaning in this sign that comes to me. My fingers twitch around my swordstick.

My gaze pans out, widening and absorbing everything rapidly. I take in the entirety of the woods before me clearly, precisely and in the blink of an eye, I spot three other signs nearly one hundred paces away, all equally foreign.

Alien.

Nine forty-two. The Notare will be awake by now.

I close my eyes and seek out her husband. Using my rheach, I prod into him. I cannot speak to him telepathically, but I can alert him to the fact that I seek him. I feel his conscience ping in acknowledgement.

Out loud, I say, "Yours and the Notare Abel's assistance in the woods is requested." It is not a request and he does not treat it as such.

Some moments later, I hear the loud crunching of feet through the undergrowth and moments after that, the Notare of Brianna and the Diera appear flanked by a small battalion of soldiers.

Notare Abel's stomach proceeds her as she walks — waddles — behind it, grumbling grumpily under her breath, "This is ridiculous. We don't need forty guards accompanying us wherever we go."

"Correct." Notare Kane nods. "That is why we only have fourteen."

Notare Abel growls, "It's too many. They're crowding me."

"They wouldn't be able to guard you properly if they were far away."

"I don't need guards."

"Of course not. They're here for me."

He looks down at his wife with a grin that disorients me. Standing together as they are, I can feel their love as a tangible body between them. When we arrived on this planet, I had no expectation to ever see such attachment between one of our kind and one of theirs yet here it is, in defiance of my predictions. I am rarely wrong. Never.

Only once.

Because of the human that stands before me, golden light beaming from her chest like a torch in the Antillian desert right at sunset. The lights of the sky would reflect off of marbled sands, turning the dunes to a charred black — but if one held a torch or light a flame right at that moment — the contrasting reflection would send rays of light scattering in every direction, in millions of colors. It was…incredible.

And now it is lost and the only beauty to be found here is none at all for, in Population, beauty itself is a foreign concept to these humans. There is only survival.

"You're a liar, Notare." Abel throws her hands up in the air and when they land, they land on her belly, drawing eyes from several of the guards flanking her. Mine as well. Fascinating. My curiosity to see the first child born of an inter-species union is strong and helps to break up this thing called *time's* perpetual monotony.

"To you, Notare? Never." He turns to face her and tips her chin up with just his fingertips. Her eyelids flutter and she leans in. Before they can partake in their embrace, I clear my throat gently, to alert them of my presence.

"Lahve," Abel says, stiffening and spinning to face me, her pronunciation aggressively horrible. She says my name like the human word for *lava,* rather than LAHH-vey, as it should be correctly said.

Kane must hear it as well, for he manages some contrition as he bows from his waist. "Lahve," he repeats, correctly emphasizing the *h.*

I bow to each of them in return. "Notare. Notare."

"What's going on? Why are you out here?"

Brash as ever, I have learned to accept this unfortunate style of communication as I have learned to accept the faults of many other Notare before her. "I make it a habit to patrol the perimeter daily."

"By yourself? Out here? You could get ambushed."

The thought is amusing. As is her concern for my well-being. It is…quite nearly…endearing.

"I do not think the Lahve is in any position of risk out here alone, Sistana," Kane says, tucking a strand of unruly hair behind her ear. "And he isn't even alone. His guard is two hundred paces behind us. We passed them." He kisses the top of her head.

"We did?" Heat rises in her cheeks that I can feel even from where I stand, so many feet separating us. "Alright. Well, we still could send patrols out here. You don't have to do this. I know you have a lot on your plate."

"The safety and wellbeing of Brianna is within the scope of my charge, Notare." I give her a slight bow, to let her know that I am not offended by her remarks. Her eyes grow large.

"Oh. Yeah of course. Shit. I mean shit. Fuck." She stammers.

Her mate cracks with light laughter. "We appreciate your assistance, Lahve. Did you find something?"

"I did, indeed." I turn from them and gesture at the tree and the marking decorating it. "At nine forty-one, I came across something I have not seen before. I had hoped you could correctly identify this marking and let me know if one of your own people had made it and, if so, for what purpose. Further, should this be a mark made by one of your scouts or under your direction, I will need to rheach through the one responsible so that I may have a thorough understanding of all marks. I do not wish to alert you each time I encounter one." *I do not want to rely on humans for anything, not even a Notare. I am Lahve. I must know all.*

Notare Abel shifts uncomfortably as she speaks, gaze flashing to my sharpened teeth. She blinks many times before switching her gaze past me and strutting towards the tree carved with that alien carving that unfortunately eludes me. Her face scrunches up, emotions so easily betrayed as they often are for these humans, who are paper thin in every way.

"No, that's not one of mine. We don't leave signs like that. We use the radios — the six that actually work, " she snorts. "Either that or the council just shares info by word of mouth with the guards that need to know. Only gangs use marks like these. Sometimes as warnings. Sometimes as a way to communicate within the gang. Sometimes to communicate with other gangs."

"And can you read them?"

"No. I never spent time in any gangs and I never paid attention to the markings when I was out there by myself with Ashlyn and Becks." I do not miss the way Kane's fingers tighten on his Sistana's neck. "Can one of y'all go back and get Diego? He's one of the best at this stuff."

"One of, Notare? Should we not procure *the* best among your people? These signs could be drawn with malicious intent."

"Of course they're drawn with malicious intent," she snaps, then blanches when she meets my eye. "Sorry. It's the baby, I swear. I'm not usually so irritable." I do not believe her, but I offer her a conciliatory nod nonetheless. With that small creature in her stomach, she is afforded every liberty.

"I think…I mean, Diego will be fine. He's the second best. He lived his whole life in a gang."

Second best. I find this phrasing curious in its precision and her deflection. But no matter. I nod.

Time. Too much of it is needed for the human male Diego to be retrieved. He watches me warily as he approaches the group and, atop his jacket, I notice his sling is covered in weapons fit for battle. I also do not miss that his left hand reaches for the nearest among them as he eyes me.

"W-w-what's up?" He says, his speech distorted for some reason. As is his face. He bears gruesome, painful-looking scars. And then I remember rheaching through members of that wretched human gang and reliving the spliced hallucinations from so many memories accompanied by so many sensations…

Throat pain as a man is stabbed. Pain lancing up his side as he's stabbed again. His eyes fluttering as he struggles to his knees. He watches as Diego — with his pale brown skin and eyes the color of the crystal ice caves on my home world — circles another man who looks remarkably like Kane.

Jack.

I know of Jack. I know of him through this rheach and many others. He still haunts this weary world even though he is dead.

The knife in Jack's hand as it comes down across Diego's face. He is unable to avoid the strike as he's outnumbered and surrounded. I occupy the body of the man as he moves onto his feet. He fights Diego and they nearly lose, all four of them. But they don't. Not when Jack cuts Diego down.

How, with Diego's injuries, he was able to flee from this and survive is a story I learned from other witnesses, but I am...*impressed*. It is not a sentiment I experience often toward these humans. But from this battle, both Diego and Abel proved remarkably brave and alarmingly resilient. I doubt many other humans would have survived such assaults. *Any* other humans. And from the account that I witnessed myself through a read of the Notare Abel, I know that this male received these scars in defense of her. For this, and no other reason, I hold him in slight elevation from the other human creatures crawling this camp.

"Can you read this?" Abel says, pointing up at the tree.

He approaches with his head cocked and I find myself momentarily forgotten as the two humans debate this sign.

"Could it be the sign for refuge?"

He shakes his head. "Nnnno. That's got a hhhhook at the top. This is three st-st-straight lines and an X above them. It could be a w-w-w-warning."

Abel grunts and shouts at me over her shoulder. "Did you see any others?"

Sometimes, I believe she forgets that I am not human and that we are not friends.

She looks at me when I do not answer immediately and her cheeks heat once more. She curses under her breath then stutters almost as badly as Diego does, "Sorry. Didn't mean to uh...shout."

I nod, accepting her contrition, and lead her one hundred paces further around the perimeter wall where three thin trees stand clustered together, each one bearing a different marking carved at eye-level — a human's eyes, not my own.

Diego curses when he is within sight of them. "I d-d-d-don't know these, b-but you can see here that this one matches the one b-b-b-back th-th-th..." He cannot finish his sentence, at least, not right away. A moment later the word bellows out of him. "There." Other than the way his pulse beats slightly quicker, he gives no indication that this speech bothers him. Curious.

I look him over once, from his scarred face, to his sling stacked with weapons, to his build which suggests he knows how to use them. Perhaps, confidence then, can explain it.

There is a long silence, one that is filled with a tension whose provenance I cannot place, before Abel finally says, "Should we..."

"*Nnnnno.*" His voice is laden with emphasis, communicating a meaning that frustrates me as I do not understand it. On my home world of Sistylea, there were no things I did not understand. Here, in Population, there are a few. And that is far, far too many.

Her fingers twist together. Abel huffs, "This seems kind of important and she's the best. She has a better shot than the rest of Brianna combined."

"Sh-sh-she won't come," Diego hisses.

"If you go get her..."

"You-you want me to ab-ab-abuse our rrrrelationship like that?"

Abel's eyes widen, but her tone does not betray the racing of her heart. "If it means ten minutes of her being uncomfortable against her being ripped from her bed by a bad guy looking to take Brianna, then I'm going with the latter. The former, I mean. Ugh. Whichever it is." She stomps her foot. There it is. The childlike stubbornness that both reminds me exactly why she is leader of her humans, and confounds me in equal measure.

But I am not here to judge. At least, not out loud.

Another long silence stretches, while Diego seems to weigh a decision on a scale that's tipping towards no. Then Kane says, "Pia lives in Brianna too, Diego."

Diego stiffens and levels an icy glare at the Notare — one that would have gotten him flayed had it been up to me, and had we lived in an earlier era. "That's llllow."

"It's true."

Diego groans, "Ffffuck. I'll need human g-g-g..." He struggles through the word. It comes out in a bluster. "... guards."

"Whatever you need."

Diego trudges away and again, time passes. I stand immobile, looking at the carvings in the trees while my guards push forward into Population. They hear it, too. Far, Teera and Nethral. Just over six miles away, the sound of humans speaking with one another is clear, though their words are muted and mumbled at this distance. Still, their presence is significant.

I ask my guard under my breath to confirm their numbers and, finding them in line with my estimates, I return to the present with a lurch and inform Notare Abel of the presence of two humans. She diligently makes notes in the small pad she carries with her everywhere to combat an affliction of the memory that she calls "pregnancy brain," though I have yet to investigate the validity of such a diagnosis.

She speaks with Notare Kane and some of the guards, attempting to devise a plan to retrieve these humans. I remind her gently that, perhaps they could be retrieved in combination with a plan to build the first outpost and she hastily agrees and thanks me many times for the part I've played in this recovery and many others. She comes towards me, she stumbles, trips and catches herself on my arm and, even though there is fabric between us, I still catch a glimpse of a memory — *her* memory — I would rather not have.

Cold. The sensation comes over me quickly and I shiver all over, even though my body has never felt true chill before. *Desperate. Looking at two faces — both women, one older and one very young — debating leaving a building that had running water while chewing on the fetid, stale remains of dog food. Then going out onto the street and having to run.*

"Oh my god, I am so so sorry!" She wrenches away from me and I extract myself from her thoughts.

With great pain.

I straighten and say nothing at all. I merely clench my lips together and allow her memories to slough off of my skin like an oiled shield under the rain, worn down but not ruined by it.

Notare Abel continues to curse and apologize while her husband coddles her to his chest, looking warily at me, just as the human Diego did. He fears for his Sistana in my presence, which does not trouble me, even though it should. It is always better to be feared just the right amount.

Crunching boots betray faces moments later when Diego returns, three human females carrying guns and a slight, unarmed female with him. He shows the unarmed female the first marking on the tree as they approach it and when she nods, he continues, bringing her forward to show her the rest.

"Anything, Candy?" Notare Abel says to the slight, youthful-looking woman standing among the others.

She pinches her eyebrows together and pulls her shoulders in as she sweeps her gaze among the Heztoichen crowded near her. Her gaze seems to hitch and stall on me and as our gazes lock, she begins to tremble.

The right amount of fear. I would be satisfied had her fear not been slowing our progress.

Diego glares and a vision of flogging him returns. Deprived of such an outlet, I feel remiss and long briefly for Sistylea, then return to the present where the world smells of wet leaves and human scents. Diego turns his back to me, blocking me from view from the small red-haired woman with the dark, blank eyes, and asks her to concentrate on the signs and ignore the rest of us. He promises her in low tones that she's safe here and that none of the Others have any intentions towards her. That she'll be bitten only over his dead body.

Very fragile, this human, and utterly unlike Abel. It is a mystery to me as to why she was summoned until her soft as ash voice says, "This is where they're going to try to break in."

The humans and Heztoichen stir and I blink once, twice in quick succession. I am pleased that the others present did not notice.

Notare Abel moves in line with Diego. "How do you know?"

"The marker back on that tree." She points to the tree one hundred or so paces from us. "Diego was right, it was a warning, but not to us. It's a sign to them, warning whoever will break in that there's a shift change at three am."

"You got all that from just three lines and an X?" Notare Abel says.

I shift slightly so the female comes back into view. She nods and presses her fingertips to her lips. They are very pink those lips. Her bright red hair that I suppose is really more orange than red falls all the way to her waist in tangled tresses. The rest of her is pale and clenched.

"Three lines for three am. If it were three pm, they would have drawn the X under the lines, not over them."

"Shit," Notare Abel curses at the same time Notare Kane does. Diego rubs his hand roughly over his head. His hair is short and uneven around the scars that cross over his skin.

The little red-tressed human says, "This tree has the same mark, but the one behind it has a hook with a circle under it. That means there's a breach point somewhere here."

"And the third tree?" I glance to the tree in question and the sign mutilating its natural state. A five-pointed star with two circles connected by two lines just beneath it.

"What is it?"

"The Five Point Gang. The one that Jack was working with. That's the star anyway. Five points for the five lines they wear." The ones I branded them with.

The humans hiss. I struggle to maintain a neutral expression while inside, I feel a strange…guilt.

Hm.

Prior to Notare Abel's arrival, I culled Brianna of the Heztoichen I felt were…unfit to cohabitate with humans. There were many of them. Each one, I marked with a series of scars as a warning to humans. Already, several of these Heztoichen attacked Notare Abel and her contingent of humans and Heztoichen on the road.

One of my soldiers, Laiya, killed two who attempted to murder the human doctor, Sandra. *Perhaps, I should have killed them.* I feel my mouth twitch harder with the desire to frown.

"The one under it, I think is the sign for another human gang — they call themselves the Disciples. They work together sometimes." She shudders at that. "But I'm not totally sure. It might be a warning from the Five Point Gang to the Disciples that they've claimed this territory, or it could be a rallying beacon. I'm not sure," she repeats. "I don't know." She shakes her head, hiding once more beneath her hair. "I'm so sorry I can't do better."

"No — no, of course. You've done great." Abel curses again and continues to curse until she notices that the red-haired female is shivering properly now. I do not see how she could be given that the air is warm and she wears more clothing than anyone else — a grey misshapen turtle neck that stretches all the way up to the underside of her jaw and down past the tips of her fingers, a pair of equally large grey pants that are so large they drag when she walks, and a dirty apron to cover both.

"Shit. Sorry, Candy," Abel concludes. Candy, I think, not for the first time. What a foolish name. Abel reaches out as if to touch the other female, then balls her hand into a fist and brings it back to her side. "Sorry," she says again. "I hate to ask, but would you be willing to hang out here a little while longer and see if there are any more signs you can read?"

The Candy human closes her eyes and though I have never been adept at reading body language — with my gift, I have not had to be — her grief is clear.

I speak. "There is no need. If *Candy*..." I say, tasting her name for the first time and finding it odd. "...would allow me to touch her, I can pull the information I need from her memories and her services beyond the perimeter walls will no longer be required."

Abel grimaces. She hesitates. I wonder absently, what for. I do not like to wonder. She looks to Candy. "Candy, would that be alright with you?"

Candy shakes her head and closes her eyes and tightens so stiffly together, one push would surely crack her down her rigid center.

"It's really not what you think. He just needs to touch your arm or something, then he can like...download the information from you. All you have to do is think about the symbols — try to picture them in your head. It will take a minute max."

"Seconds, at most," I coo.

It takes some more time. Time. It just wastes away. These humans squander it, and I wonder if they do not realize how little time they actually have here. I can already see the dust that their corpses create drifting through the breeze. Their bones will litter these fields.

Eventually, the female extends her arm. Her eyes remain closed and I find myself momentarily offended, then I move past it. She's just a human.

Abel looks to me and nods and I enter the orbit of the human female's heat with every intention of making this unpleasant trip as quick for the both of us as possible.

I straighten and cut off my next inhale so that I am not too distracted by the smell of the dew beading under her arms and along the soft hairs between her mane and her forehead. The scent of her sweat is oddly pleasing. She smells like earth, like clay, and a little like the bright sky of Sistylea after a rain. My nose wrinkles and I frown so slightly I doubt any of these humans would notice it.

"This will pass quickly if you concentrate on the symbols you know and how you know them," I rumble in a voice that attempts to be soothing in order to speed this process along. It does not seem to matter though, because she flinches all the same. Infuriating...

...is what I would think were I base enough a creature to allow emotion to rule me.

But fortunately, I do not.

I brace, steeling myself for the onslaught of what is sure to be a barrage of emotion and memory and visions and hopes and wants. It is inevitable, given that humans have very poor control and, even when directed, often open themselves to me too much.

I take hold of her forearm.

When rheaching through memories and time, it has happened that I run into walls. Only the very strong Heztoichen have the ability to keep me out. Notare Elise was one of them. She was, perhaps, the last of them. And even with her thousand years, she was no match for me. Using Abel as a vessel, I was able to damage her mind and rip out the mental barriers she'd erected without touching her at all. It was, as is the case for most things, merely a question of time as to how long it would take for her mental blocks to crumble like dry sand castles in a monsoon.

Even the virgins of Syth, who are trained in this art form, fail more often than not. For all the luxury given to her, the female selected to mate with me still was not free of desires of her own. She still had wants that made it impossible for me to couple with her, no matter how pure and strong and beautiful she was or not.

And this female is none of the above. She shivers like a leaf in the wind. Her eyes are closed in fear even though sightlessness has never been an effective defense for any creature, no matter their species' planet of origin. Her skin is pale, her color weak. There is pink in her cheeks that makes her skin seem nearly transparent. She *is* transparent. My thoughts tunnel through her body without any barriers at all to stop me. There is nothing there at all.

There is nothing there at all.

I glance down to my fingers and confirm that I am, in fact, at the present moment, *touching* her tattered grey sleeve. However, where there should be sensation and memory and feeling and horror and terror and blind, white hot pain, there is only a cataclysmic void.

Nothing.

I free-fall through empty space and the longer I touch her, the longer I fall, and there is no bottom against which to shatter. My stomach does not lurch up into my throat. My body is not ruined at the bottom of some well. There is only the purest emptiness. But it cannot be mistaken for *loneliness.*

There are no things. There is only the pure perfection of their absence.

Now, I feel a new sensation, one just as foreign as this nothingness. I feel *sweat* building between my shoulder blades and beneath the curtain of hair that shields the back of my neck. I flick my gaze to meet hers, but her eyes remain closed. I focus on the shape of her eyelashes, their gentle curve, on the smooth slope of her nose between her eyes, on the soft brown color of her eyebrows.

I dig my toes into my hard-soled shoes and I push into her mind with my own. I claw, bite, gnash and tear my way through her thin, transparent exterior and I sink into the bleak emptiness of her mind over and over again because here, there is no gate, no fortress, no moat, no castle to plunder. There is no army. She is not my enemy.

There is only a field, a peaceful jungle where I might lose myself if I'm not careful...

Confused and terrified, I attempt to retreat but I find that I have already lost my way. The thoughts and words and emotions of the others that had been so near to me moments before become muted.

I can no longer hear the two hearts beating inside Abel's body. I can't hear blood pounding through Diego's veins. I cannot feel the fear radiating off of the human guards — a fear that they cannot hide in my presence, no matter how tough their Population-hardened exteriors or how hard they attempt to cage it. I can't hear the two humans hiding in their small cove anymore, still so far away. Two humans who do not even know that Abel will attempt their rescue and that they may soon be saved…I can't even hear the voices of those in the compound, or standing two feet from me…

I can only hear her breath. I can only feel her pulse. Her blood moving underneath her thin skin. The pilling fabric of her cotton shirt beneath my fingertips.

In an effort not to alarm the humans present — and to keep calm myself — I allow myself a single inhalation. It is, in retrospect, a mistake. I can taste her scent in my mouth and it tastes like that jungle, a rich fragrance perhaps enhanced by the scent of wet earth smeared all over her apron. She must work in the greenhouses. She smells like earth… She's sweating more than she was, but it smells like bark from the trees around us. It's…it's *confusing* me.

I cut off my breath. Swallowing thickly, I slowly maneuver my swordstick into the scabbard inside my cloak so that I may free my second hand. I marshal my tone before I speak, being very careful with my volume, pitch and treble. *They cannot know.*

Know what? What is this? What's happening?

"I will pull your sleeve down so that I may touch your arm directly," I tell her. I am already in motion, but she jerks back.

I shame myself — I do not let her go — and wrap my long fingers around her thin wrist, my thumb and fingers overlapping by inches around her very much smaller limb. Her eyes fly open. She looks over her shoulder at Diego.

"Diego," she whimpers.

"Hey," he barks. He steps forward. I hold up a hand.

I do not like the sensation that moves through me and I willfully push it back and refuse to identify it by name. "Apologies. I struggle to…decipher her thoughts. Touching her skin directly will help guide me and provide much-needed clarity," I say and it is…*a lie*. Hm. I return my attentions to the female and say, "I will only touch your fingertips and only for a moment. The briefest instant." I'm begging.

First, I lied.

Now, I've begged.

Hmm.

Distaste sours the sensations rippling over my body and I do not want them soured for they are so very precious. In three millennia this has never happened before, neither to me nor to any of my kind. There is no mention of this in our recorded history and I would know, because upon arriving to this planet, I copied each volume that I memorized into books by hand.

Distracted as I am, I miss the words exchanged between this female and Diego.

I return to the present world to see Diego squaring off to face me, his hands on the weapons on his sling — what has he chosen for me? *Hmm… A grenade. Smart man.* Shoved directly into my mouth it is the only weapon he carries that might kill me. He should hope it does, because my feelings towards him are surprisingly…lethal.

"Mm-m-m-mmmmake it qu-qu-qui-ck-ck."

"It would help if she would focus on me." *Another lie.* This one has origins I, again, refuse to acknowledge.

Still, she looks up at him, eyes wide and afraid but trusting *him*. I do not like that. I do not like that at all. I believed that he already had a female. Pia. I watched them together through the memories of others. So, what is he to her?

He stands with his feet spread to hip distance and glares down at her in a way I do not understand, but that seems to calm her. "You-you-you're alright. D-d-don't pull your sleeve down, just let him touch what he c-c-c-can already sssee now, then you nnnnever have to d-d-do this again and we can keep everyone in B-B-Brianna safe. *Y-y-you* can."

As she visibly relaxes into his gaze, my hands harden and I have to extend concentration slightly beyond usual measure so as not to break every bone in her wrist. Human bones are so fragile, temporary, weak. I pull her sleeve down to reveal her fingers. Her nails are short and badly bitten. I frown.

I drop her hand so that it falls against my palm. I brace. And then, when nothing happens, I wait but there is only more *nothing*, that endlessly calm and magical jungle. There is only *her.*

Her fingertips have their own weight, each one. Her bitten nails are crusted with dirt. There are calluses on the small raised parts of her palm just below each digit and fully covering the heels of her hands. They are red and look like they hurt her.

I do not know why it is, in looking at her dirty hand of all things, that I begin to feel the makings of something I have not felt in a long time. So much time that, though I know it has happened before, I cannot remember it…

Arousal.

My otherwise dormant erection begins to shift in my trousers, cock stiffening against the zipper, bulging against it in a way that is entirely undignified and unacceptable. I panic — *I. Panic.* — and release her. This red-haired human with a name that is nonsensical may be the weakest creature on this planet and I am the strongest one. I *cannot* be aroused by her, least of all by her dirty hand that makes me hallucinate madness.

Her. In the jungle. Naked. Reaching for my hand.

Me. Following in a silence that is spellbinding.

Her. Smiling.

Me. Lost.

I drop her hand and put a healthy length of space between us. Leaves crunch beneath my feet, sounding like shattering glass. I swallow and my pulse rushes like a strong wind through my ears. I stare down at her, shocked and horrified to find that the female has finally granted my request and is looking up at me.

My heart beats hard. A hammer against stone. *Which will crack first?*

Thunder washes over me. I urge to maim, to hunt, to kill. An ancient tribe, it is said that our abilities were borne over millennia of hunting the icy plains of our pre-Frost. Being able to touch the few living creatures that roamed the planet allowed us to discover their migratory paths, where they laid their young, where we might find more prey. It came at a price. The *feeling*. The *rheach*, that was the name for it that the oracles gave. Having studied it from the males of my line before me, I always had the most profound respect for the *rheach*. Respect, and even admiration. But in this moment, I fear it. For what I have seen upon touching the female…what I smelled, what I heard…

Nothing.

Her lips move and I am distracted by their color. They flower an obscene red color and I am distracted by the thought that she is a living creature with blood pumping through her body and that, though I cannot rheach her face or her body, perhaps I could rheach her blood if I drank it directly from the source.

I glance at her wrists and then my treacherous gaze drops to her upper thighs and I feel a dagger in my gut twist as my cock decides to swell without provocation at the thought — *no, the premonition* — of tasting the blood running through this female. Savoring it. Sucking her dry through her upper thigh, like a good little blood whore.

She says something, but I am too tangled in the web of my own thoughts that I do not understand her.

She waits and I have no reply.

"Lahve, are you finished with Candy?"

Notare Abel's voice grates, but I do not look at her. I cannot. This female with the ridiculous moniker holds me bound. *Unacceptable.*

"C-C-C-Candy, get aw-aw-away from him."

I look up at the male called Diego and my left foot, the mutinous beast, jolts forward. *Kill him.* No.

Candy gasps and I freeze, holding everything inside of my body together as I watch her swallow several times — *she could take my cock down her throat and swallow and I would not have to endure the pain of her memories at the same time* — and backs up until her shoulder brushes Diego's chest. He steps away from her quickly, making sure to keep space between them. The sight of that space is what causes her to relax for him. *What is she to him?* The thought rushes up on me again moving with the speed of emotion — a human's, not mine — and it has no business here.

Because I do not feel emotion.

"You got what you needed...sir?" She asks me.

"Lahve," I respond, the reply automatic.

Her voice. It is... "Lahve," she repeats, pronouncing it wrong in a way I don't like. It makes me want to offer her something else by which to call me. "Are you finished?"

I would laugh at the question had I an answer for it. I take another step away from her, but my hand twitches, reaches for *her.* It has not done such a thing before. I take another step and my mouth dries. A third and the fresh sweat coating my body instantly cools.

I will my erection to subside, but it takes more energy than I have to force it down completely. This is...a physiological response I am unprepared for and unused to. The female does not notice. She does not look anywhere but at my face, if that at all. But Diego clears his throat and angles his body between mine and the female's. *Candy.*

"Yes. We're d-d-d-done here." He gestures for her to walk and she does and when she does, he follows and I fight not to follow and tear Diego to pieces, rip the skin from his body, what little of it that there is left. Make a necklace of his scars. *He is taking her from me.*

But she is not mine…

I swallow the thought again and again, repeating it with force, though I don't dare say it aloud. There are Heztoichen present and I want none to hear of this, to know of this, to ever be made aware of my interest in someone like her. And not just because she is so beneath me, but because I am the strongest being, impartial, and I do not want. I do not feel.

Abel glances between the retreating Diego and I and crosses her arms, a peculiar look on her face. "You did get what you needed from her, right? Sorry, I didn't hear you answer."

I did not answer. I should have, but instead I allowed Diego to speak to me with flagrant disrespect. His disrespect was not even among my thoughts. There is no space for it in my mind with how hard I was and am concentrating on the sound of her footsteps. One step more. And then another.

"Yes," I say stonily. "I got from her what is required," I lie. But there is no other truth I can allow. That I am ready for.

Chapter Two

This is a problem and it is a new kind of problem for it is one of my own making. I have never had such a problem before.

The red-haired female — Candy — was not incorrect in her reading. There was a weakness in the wall near the clustered tree markings where the corrugated tin had rusted and caved, yet was concealed by shrubbery from view.

The human council gathered and decided on a course of action. High risk, but this is to be expected from these mortals. They elected not to close the gap but to increase patrols within the compound in the hope of catching the gang that would dare breach these walls.

I would, perhaps, have chosen a more conservative route had the territory been my own, but I do not voice this suggestion. It is not my territory. I am the Lahve and I remain above the decisions made by those who hold the light. They are their own. Elise's decision to drain other Heztoichen was her own territory's failing until it became a failing of mine when she drained Heztoichen Notare and their families.

The council's plan was implemented and carried out. However and, as is the case with most of the humans' first attempts, it was done clumsily. This first problem was not my problem at all. I watched them station too many noisy humans behind the compound wall. Watched as, for nine nights, there was no attack. And on the morning of the eleventh day at some time between five and seven, their problem became mine once more.

I took to the woods and returned to the trees and their signs only to find that they had all been scratched out. All except for the one.

The star symbol remained, a new symbol etched above it in the shape of a bolt of lightning, hastily etched.

I alert the Notare at seven twenty-one and their council is roused and the guards who were stationed on the other side of the barrier are detained and questioned as to how such a thing could have happened under their watch — particularly given that three Heztoichen were stationed among them. All problems for the Notare and the ones protecting Brianna…

But my problem lies in the symbol itself…

I do not know it.

And I have no excuse.

Attempts to raze the human female from my thoughts have not been met with success. Attempts to seek her out in the human compound have been less successful than that mostly because I have tried to hunt for her again and again but…I cannot read her mind, I do not know its flavor, so I cannot root it out.

And now it is nine thirty-three and I will have to summon her again, bringing the ghost of her that haunts my thoughts to life. *Finally.* The thought fills me with some small measure of…rage. Hm. Because I want to know where she was these past nine days. I want to accuse her of hiding.

But I am a calm male. Unequivocally. So, I will not.

"This image did not appear in the human's memory," I say and it is not a lie, for nothing did. *But it feels like a lie. One that could get humans and Heztoichen killed. My pride has never misbehaved like this.*

And neither has my cock.

It is half stiff at the mere mention of the female and the nothingness she brings.

Notare Kane sighs deeply, tightening his arms over his chest. Notare Abel does not join us on this morning, for she has a sickness commonly associated with humans' child birthing process and has been locked inside and perhaps, possibly, strapped down to her bed. I do not know if Notare Kane meant this in jest.

"Her thoughts were..." My voice trails off, not entirely certain as to how to conclude.

Notare Kane does so on my behalf. He grits his teeth and his eyes flash with transparent rage before bottoming out to grief that I can feel tangibly. It feels like a wet breeze. A *curious* response, made more curious when he says, "I understand that her thoughts might have been...*difficult* for you. More difficult than most."

"Hmm," I say. It is all that I offer on that account. I cannot risk confirming or denying this until I am able to make a second judgment. Worse, this uncertainty combined with my lie means I may never understand Notare Kane's true meaning. My lips twitch, daring a frown, but don't.

"It may be prudent to have the female join us here to provide her assessment and so that I might make a second attempt to harvest this information. Perhaps, the flow of her thoughts might offer more on a second attempt, one that she is more open to and prepared for."

Notare Kane grits his teeth and grinds out the orders. It is nine forty-nine according to my wrist watch and I stare into the trees with a concentration that I am forced to mask into something less intense. I remind myself to blink upon occasion and to take breaths so as to make the other beings gathered feel more comfortable. But these small corrections are hardly necessary... After all, there is nothing to mask when I feel no emotion. Certainly not curiosity. Not the rare nibbling of a forgotten excitement in my toes, causing me to lean almost imperceptibly forward and shift my weight into them.

The crunching of feet and then the flash of red hair bring her into view. I inhale deeply, wanting to reprimand her for absence in my life these past nine days — a crime she was unaware of, yet guilty of all the same — but not so strong as I want to indulge in the smell of her skin. As she draws nearer, I find that I am not disappointed. The smell is both the same as I remember it and entirely changed.

On Sistylea, I often found myself at large symphonies and noted that, even when listening to the same concerto played a second time, different pieces of it would move me in ways they did not on my first listen.

It is the same way with her smell, that earthy perfume. Sweat and clay, but today the rain is stronger. So strong, I can hear the patter of purple droplets cascading against cities made entirely of glass. I can hear the symphony. I can hear the soft sway of branches in the almost silent jungle.

But there is another scent that taints it.

Lurking like an intruder in the dark, there is a ripe odor that touches her in places. Not everywhere, so I can only smell it when the wind pulls in precise directions, but when I do, it causes my nose to wrinkle and my lips to harden over my fangs. The scent is *male*. She has been with a male *recently*. At least she has been far, far too near a male recently. I loathe that I am unsure of which it is. How close did she come to this male? Does she have a male that claims her for his own? How easy will he be to kill? *Root out the source and drag it from the crypt.*

I do not move because emotions do not drive me — cannot, when they do not exist. I do not look away when she shuffles into the clearing, her shoulders even more hunched this time than they were the last. She does not look at me and I am not disappointed. No, I am not disappointed in the slightest. Why would I be? She is a ragged creature torn from the soil and hellbound to return. I am a creature of the stars who may, as yet, outlive even this galaxy.

The female gives the tree carving a quick glance, but shakes her head. Her entire body is shaking very slightly, like autumn leaves clinging to branches in desperation. "That's the sign for Malmon," she whispers under her breath.

I can hear her, but the others cannot — not even the other Heztoichen. "What was that, Candy?" Notare Kane takes a step towards her.

Candy's reaction is rapid and incomprehensible. She shakes her head quickly and her right knee gives out. She lands on hands and knees in the wet leaves. "One of Jack's friends. He's the leader of the Five Point Gang."

"Hey," Diego barks at her side, but he makes no move to catch her or help her find her footing. He keeps his arms crossed over his chest and a healthy distance between their bodies that I can make little sense of. I had thought these two humans shared more camaraderie than this. *But I hoped they did not. And his is not the scent she wears on her skin.* I frown and I make no move to moderate the expression. Again.

"Sorry," she whispers.

"Nnnothing to be sssorry about."

"Of course not." Notare Kane echoes and he takes the step I expected of Diego and reaches his hand down to help the female to her feet.

She looks up at him with wide eyes. And then she raises her left arm. Just the one. She flinches back. It is the posture one would make were they under attack. As if she has already been struck...*or once was...*

I am between the pair before I even have a chance to fully categorize my emotions. I know that rage is among them, panic, too, perhaps even a little shared fear. Hm.

My body moves me without consideration of my will. I edge into Notare Kane's space, forcing him back the necessary steps it takes for my body to relinquish control of itself to my brain and it is only then that I turn to the girl, grab her outstretched hand, pull her to her feet and return to the place where I had been standing previously.

I do all of these things in a time that does not exist for these humans. It is too small.

But the moment that I touched her hand — just her fingers — felt, to me, like a year. Because in that fleeting moment, I felt it again.

Nothing.

I returned to the jungles and was lost in the labyrinth of her quiet.

And I know then an absolute truth: She is a problem that I cannot ignore.

Chapter Three

"**M**almon. That's the name of the Other who runs the Five Point Gang." Her voice is soft as ash as those of us from the woods and several humans in addition, along with the members of my own guard, crowd Notare Abel's office. A large space, it feels small and cramped now, so many thoughts pressing so dangerously close to me. I am grateful for the distraction of three humans, in particular, who help focus my thoughts away from the rest.

One is a blonde female with a remarkably symmetrical face who stands very close to Diego. Rather than concentrating actively on the problems of this ridiculous Five Point Gang and their attempts to lord over Population, I am more interested in the relationship between Diego, this blonde female and the redhead.

Diego has his hand on the small of the blonde's back. Occasionally, he rubs the visible skin between her short hem and the top of her jeans. Sometimes, he slides his hand into her back pocket and prods her as if they aren't in public view of a dozen sets of eyes or more. But he *also* keeps his body angled toward Candy. He ensures that no others step within the small sphere of space that surrounds her.

Does he claim them both?

I become suddenly very aware of my swordstick in my coat and desire very, very much to free it. How easy it would be to slaughter every soul in this room and just be done with it.

Irritation plagues me.

Hmm…

That is…unusual.

I shift imperceptibly and refocus on Notare Abel and Notare Kane in the center of the room. Shelves covered in books and maps line the walls. Heavy leather seats stud the floor at random. No one, however, is seated. All are straining forward, attempting to hear the words uttered by the small, fragile Candy. Kane hangs back, half seated on the edge of a large cherry oak desk while Abel leans in towards the girl.

"Malmon? Is that his name?"

She nods. "The girl is called Idreline."

"Girl?"

"The woman. The Heztoichen. His sister."

Sister. Hmm. My memory flits over the faces of those I branded. I ensured to brand them each myself so that I might brand their faces in my mind. I've seen their faces through the eyes of those present at the battle of Wall Drug but I do not recall delivering brands to these siblings.

Notare Kane is looking at me. "Lahve, do you know them?"

"No. But if the human is *certain* of the names, then I may know of their father. I believe he may be of the youngest generation of ancient Tretaro, born to the virgins of Syth. That was six hundred years ago. His rheach was…light. It's for this reason that he was able to couple with a Heztoichen. Their offspring were born naturally and without the rheach as well."

It is a…disappointment. Likely, the rumors that another of my own kind gracing this planet pertained to them. But I already knew of their existence here and, without the rheach, they are little different than a Heztoichen, but for the half-Tretaro blood they carry. If mixed correctly with blood from a much more powerful Tretaro — me — then *perhaps* a child could be born with a Tretaro's ability. However...my gaze strays to Candy. The thought of coupling with one of these rebels doesn't hold as much interest to me as the single question: why does Candy stand so close to Diego?

"I am certain," Candy whispers, giving the room a jerky nod.

Abel smiles at the female, though I can sense her concern, *taste* it. "Can you tell us more, Lahve?"

I nod, but my eyes do not stray from the woman. Her head is bowed forward. Her fingers are scratching at the backs of her hands. They are covered in dirt. *Not dirt, clay. Perhaps, she works with the ceramicists then, not the farmers. It would explain why I did not see her at the greenhouses. Not that I searched for her there. No...of course not.* I am made somewhat calmer by this realization.

"Certainly, Notare. But I must first offer my apologies to miss Candy." She stiffens as I say her name, but does not turn to look at me. And, for all my sight, I cannot see past the curtain of her hair. It...irritates me...were I capable of irritation, that is. "It was not my intention to imply that I do not believe you."

I wait for some time, but she does not say more.

I return my attention to Notare Kane, aware of the surprise radiating through the room, mixed in with the earlier confusion and anger. I wave my hand, disrupting them all. "Their father, Mernon, was a respected member of our Lower Council and by our, I refer to we Tretaro who have the rheach.

"Though he could only rheach a little — emotions, not memories and even those, only when strong — I always held his views in high esteem. But his offspring..." I flip through my rolodex of memories, finding little information on them. "I know little about. They were born of a Heztoichen mother. She was young, less than sixty, and not of a Tretaro line. From what I recall, Mernon did not have views of superiority, nor did he have a particular allegiance to Notare Elise that would explain the behavior of his children."

He did not have an allegiance to Notare Elise however… he did once fight to defend Carata when the former Notare of Srentara attempted to annex its easternmost region — these battles were fought on Sistylea, five hundred years ago, yet their memories have not dimmed in my mind. I remember fighting alongside Mernon then. He was an admirable male and good with a blade. He does not know Elise. But he knows Tanen. In the heat of the battle, when all was nearing its brutal end, Tanen saved Mernon's life.

His children may know of this, but what does this have to do with the attacks against Brianna? Mernon fought to protect Carata from a foreign invasion. The Notare of Srentara was killed. Her territories passed then to Notare Morgana who rules Srentara as it exists here on this earth. *And yet…* The thought festers in my mind, roots forming trunks to trees that have no shape. I cannot quite see the clear picture yet, but I feel as if these seeds may have sprouted.

"Lahve?" Notare Abel says.

I snap back to the present and continue on. "Given the loose record keeping and the loose borders that form each region here on this planet, I unfortunately have no documentation pertaining to them specifically since our arrival here. Malmon and Idreline outlived their father and their mother, who died honorably on Sistylea and, since their arrival, they have been unremarkable to now.

"But one's ability to be remarkable is not finite, as we have seen. This new world births many new splendors all to its own."

Notare Kane glances at his Sistana and quietly, she says, "Thank you, Lahve."

I stand a little straighter, surprised. I was not speaking of her. My gaze strays to the female with red hair but I still nod to Notare Abel very slightly and say, "Certainly. It would seem however, that not all new wonders are for the benefit of the whole, but a mere few."

Notare Elise comes to mind. Candy does, too. What is she? A creation made for me alone? For my benefit or for my ruination? I smirk, aware that I have just bestowed onto the slight female far too much power. She is, at the end of the day, just a human, bound to this earth but for a fraction of a moment.

"Perhaps Miss Candy could enlighten us more than I can hope to."

"C-C-C-Candy, d-d-do you know what J-J-J-Jack was trrrrrrrrr-ading them?" Diego says.

She winces dramatically, as if slapped. Weak, this female. Cowardly. I glance around at the other warriors and soldiers present here. It is a wonder she stands among so much strength at all.

"Blood." Her voice is so soft as to be near inaudible.

The humans have to ask her to repeat herself several times. It grates. "I believe Candy said blood was being traded. However, I am inclined to believe that Malmon and Idreline were receiving more than flesh. Flesh, for Heztoichen of their strength, would not have been difficult to come by. They would have been after something more. Something rich, like information."

"But information on what?" Notare Abel is picking her lower lip. She looks up when she feels my gaze on her. "Me? But why?"

Mikael makes a brutish sound. I frown. I despise this male and recognize that I was wrong earlier. Candy is not the most cowardly individual in this room. Mikael will forever own such a title, no matter the room or its occupants. "First human Notare ever? Why wouldn't they be after you?"

"That's not what I meant. I meant why would they trade Jack for information about me? Jack didn't have any."

"Maybe information about Population in general." Mikael shrugs one shoulder. "Diego, y'all traveled pretty far. Maybe Malmo and Idrina needed the lay of the land."

"Malmon and Idreline," I correct, having had enough of this. "And it matters little. Their current motive is clear. Their methods will be revealed upon their capture. I believe it is up to Notare Abel to determine how to proceed. If she would prefer to send teams of warriors out to scour Population for the rebels and attempt to root them out, or if she would rather focus on securing Brianna and reinforcing the perimeter."

"Or expanding it." She winces as she speaks, knowing already that this is of the riskiest options, which is why I did not even mention it. Things are different, knowing that Malmon and his gangs are organized and able to coordinate effectively, even across species. Even some of the Notare aren't able to do that. Their numbers could be dangerous.

She looks from Notare Kane to me around at the rest of her people. "I can't stop thinking about those people the Lahve heard out there. I can't give up on them. We called the humans home and then we abandoned them to the road." She shakes her head, her dark curls flopping forward before all at once, she sweeps them back. "I can't give up. And I can't ask y'all to help set up the outposts..."

The blonde female holds up one hand. "You can. You're the Notare, remember." She winks. Several of the humans laugh. The redhead is not among them. Her words seem to settle it. Tension leaks out of the humans, out of the Heztoichen, too. But not out of Candy.

She remains fixed in the center of the room, her arms clasped tightly around her body, as if she's one wrong breeze from falling into pieces.

"Alright, well let's go to lunch. I'm hungry. We'll make a plan after I eat and can think a little about outposts and reinforcements and gangs and all that miserable stuff." She sighs and light chatter resumes as the room clears.

Candy is first to depart. She disappears so quickly she could pass for one of the Tretaro. "May I?" I approach Notare Abel at her desk as the room clears. Several of my soldiers linger in the doorway, but I tip my head to them, wanting them to leave. I do not wish for any to overhear this conversation. I glance to Notare Kane. I don't want him here for this either.

"Oh, yeah. Of course. Do you have an early proposal for the outpost or something?" She moves behind her desk and begins rifling through her papers. She presses keys on the laptop and illuminates the screen that I cannot see but for in the reflection of her eyes. I focus a little harder and see the pixilated outlines of blocks that roughly come together in the shape of the continent we're on. She spins the screen around. "Kane and I have been trying to figure out where we'd put it. There aren't a lot of options."

"I too, have been studying the maps. There are some smaller towns that I believe may be suitable candidates, though reconnaissance teams will need to investigate. I have a small contingent of three guards willing to travel here." I point at a place on the map roughly one hundred and fifty of their human miles from the edge of Brianna, and then at a second place just closer than that. "And here. The trouble comes here." I point at a larger city beyond it.

"Nashville?"

"And this other one here." Human letters spell out the word *Knoxville*. "According to my sources, there are several large camps here, our Five Point Gang among them. It would seem that they are positioning themselves to cut access to Brianna by creating a perimeter." I draw a half sphere. "By continuing your attempt to retrieve humans from the lands beyond it, you draw them directly into the fire."

"Fuck."

"As we have seen, there are humans within the boundary between Brianna and these camps in Nashville and Knoxville. By moving your perimeter further out, you can save these humans and begin reinforcing your boundary. It will help ensure, at the very least, that these gangs cannot build their walls closer." Unless they bring war to Notare Abel first.

And if I were in their position, that is exactly what I would do. They have the advantage. Because if anything this lawless world has taught me, it is that it is far more difficult to protect than it is to slaughter.

"That's a good idea," she murmurs. She looks up at Notare Kane. "Do you think it's a good idea?"

Notare Kane rubs his chin and rotates the screen to face him. I have no trouble reading it in the gloss of his eyes, so I see when it flickers. He hisses under his breath and turns his attention to the paper maps spread out across the desk in front of him.

"Still having trouble with the satellite imagery?" I ask.

"Yeah. How did you..." Notare Abel looks up at Kane and squints. "Nevermind."

"I will ask Mithra to look at it for you. She is adept at fixing these corrupted technologies."

"Thanks. We've already had Star take a look. She got this hunk of junk up and working, but that's about it."

Silence lingers.

Notare Kane is first to break it and he only does so at the sound of Notare Abel's yawn. "We will think on all you have offered, Lahve. Your input is invaluable."

I incline my head, understanding that I have been dismissed, but...I don't leave.

"I did not come here solely for this." I say.

They both look at me with identical shock. "Oh?"

"I came with a request."

"Alright...shoot."

"The human who assisted us with the signs in the forest, Candy."

Notare Kane's hand stills on the back of Notare Abel's neck. Notare Abel's hand has come to a stop on the curve of her stomach. "What about her?"

"There is nothing about her. She is the request. I want the human."

Chapter Four

Notare Abel stares at me in a way I neither approve of, nor appreciate. "I'm sorry. What?"

Notare Kane places his hand on Notare Abel's shoulder, keeping her from standing where she remains seated behind her desk. "Stay calm. No excitement," he rebukes her. "Remember what Sandra said?"

"Are you for real?" She says to me, ignoring him as she tries to shrug out from beneath her mate's touch.

"Abel." He steps into her space, bends at the waist and kisses her deeply in a way that leaves me unsettled for the very first time. Because this time, unlike any other, I hallucinate an image that I have no right to — a vision of my mouth pressed to that of the female's with the pale skin and the full, pink lips. Not because I find her attractive, *even though I do,* but because I *can* and she will not hurt me. She is the only female in two planets to whom that credit is earned. *But she is weak.* But it doesn't matter. To touch and be touched will be worth it.

"Better?" He asks her.

She nods, dazed, then shakes her head. "I don't understand what he wants."

"Neither do I," he says, speaking to her as if I am not present. Irritation.

Hmm.

He stiffens and Abel's lips part. She rubs them before her eyebrows bunch together, evidence of her concern as she finally returns her gaze to mine. "What do you want with Candy?" Her voice is hard now, unexpected and gruff. And what's worse is that, for once, when she is untoward, her mate offers nothing in the way of consolation or defense.

He turns with his arms crossed stands by her, the two of them against me, in this flagrant display of disrespect. I am disappointed in both of them by it. But I am Lahve, impartial. It is not my duty to question the whims of fickle Notare. They will be gone from this world soon enough and I will remain. I am unchanging. *Except by a slight female with the jungle in her skin, I am changed.* And I do not like it. *I worship it.*

"Candy is of particular interest to me. I would like to seek her out."

"If you're implying what I think you're implying..." she chokes. She's pointing her finger at me. She starts to stand, as if I could not reach through her chest and pull out her heart and her Tare with a flick of the wrist.

But I would never.

Because the Tare rules all things.

Even me.

Notare Kane clears his throat and tries to pull his Sistana back, but she shrugs him off and stands and drops onto the desk on both of her wrists. They crack simultaneously and she shakes them out and curses quietly under her breath. "You want to fuck Candy?"

Unwanted visions flare. I slash and burn them. "Absolutely not."

But...those visions...for that moment they appeared, they were magnificent things.

Abel huffs and allows herself to be corralled back into her seat. Notare Kane steps forward, coming to the other side of the desk and standing tall, as if we were equals. But we are not. Purpose and history are the only things that keep him from kneeling at my feet. Temptation tickles me in ways it never has. *I could rule all of them. Tear the Tare down. Create a new world order* —

No.

No…

Notare Kane clears his throat and begins in a… cumbersome way I am unaccustomed to hearing from him. He may be young, for a Notare, but I have always respected him.

Until this.

"Lahve, you have not come to us with a request of this nature before. Apologies if our concern causes us to behave…out of turn. My Sistana and I have a particular fondness for the female. She is family to us and your interest in her is unexpected. If you could define the nature of your interest in the female, it would go a long way in making this situation more…comfortable for everyone."

"You also can't request a person — you know that right?" Notare Abel grips the leather arms of her seat and leans forward as if she means to take a bite right out of me.

I clench my teeth together with force. I wouldn't have this problem with Notare Elise. She'd have given me the girl to do whatever I wanted with. "I have no intention of harming the woman." It irks me to call her *girl*. It irks me that I do not know how old she is, if she is even…of age. But she must be, I convince myself, to have the experiences she has lived and for the Notare to call on her for expertise in such a way.

"Then, what do you want with her?"

Irritation. It's…more difficult to ignore it in this fresh wave. "As Lahve, there are things which I may choose not to share with Notare."

Abel stiffens, shoulders squaring, jaw setting, eyebrows pulling towards one another. Her gaze meets mine and I see ferocity and defiance and I feel…like crushing her.

I reel from the thought and frown. In three thousand years, never have I *ever* let myself stray to baser whims, fantasies of murder are for the weak who lack the tools to seize their own power and honor themselves through more civilized means.

"Pardon me, Notare?"

I missed what she said. I've never been distracted like this.

"No," she repeats, thumping her fist down on the desk. Notare Kane smooths his hand over hers.

"I understand your concern for the female, but I must insist that Candy…"

"No. The answer is no. You stay away from her."

I stand to tower over her, but she does not quiver beneath my shadow. Rather, her chest beams like a torch and my darkness is rendered powerless against it.

"Lahve, I mean no disrespect, but my Sistana carries my unborn child and I won't have any reason for her upset in this precarious time." He gives me a long look, one that says so much more, that speaks to incalculable violence.

Time. My right hand twitches towards my swordstick. He does not see it. I should leave…I know that leaving from this place would be the correct thing to do. My gaze flicks between the two of them, a united front that, with all my thousands of years, I do not seem to be able to break through.

"Would you be more amenable to my request if I were to approach the female and seek her consent directly?"

Notare Kane's voice grows ever deeper, darker. "We do not condone the selling of sex here. Other humans have engaged in this practice and we have done our best to curb and control it…"

Abel thrusts her arm out at me, cutting off her mate. "You can *have* Candy over my dead body." She makes air quotations around the word. "I don't know what you want her for. You say it's not for sex, but you won't tell us why and I frankly don't give a shit. I don't want to hear any more. I expect it from freaks like Leif and Chamberlain, but I cannot hear it from anyone in my inner circle, least of all the one bad dude who's here to like…fix all this shit."

"I am neither bad nor good, but impartial."

"That's not what I meant," she stammers. "Just…get the fuck out of my office."

Rage. It ripples over my skin in a way I haven't felt in over a decade, when I learned that we did not have enough vessels on Sistylea to accommodate the entire population and that so many lives would be sacrificed, including those of my fellow Tretaro and even then, it was different. I had already moved on to damage control by the time I was even aware of my own anger. This time…rage is allowed to spread unchecked by logical thoughts of a way forward…because I haven't one.

I stammer — stammer — like a human, "An agreement can be reached between the female and I without your involvement…"

"She's under my protection and she isn't for sale. I'm not going to gift her to you like a slab of meat — whatever your reasons for wanting her." Heat rages in her expression, radiates from her pores like the light she bears and it is the only thing that keeps me from launching across the short desk and pressing my thumb to the base of her spine, severing her spinal cord and letting her head dangle from the rest of her like a flail loose on the chain…

Were I one to rise to anger. But alas…I am not.

I press my lips together and straighten the jacket of my coat. I draw deep from the well of my civility to speak in a level, easy brogue. "But if I were to speak to her independent of you, this would be no flagrant offense."

"Candy can't be spoken to without a chaperone."

Confusion.

"May I inquire as to why?"

Notare Abel opens her mouth, but her words, they short out. Her mate places his hand on her arm to calm her and, when I look into his face, I see that his expression becomes even more dangerous.

"Lahve," he says, "It intrigues me, your interest in this female. You, of all beings, should know why Candy cannot be approached without a chaperone. You read her history when you touched her arm, did you not?"

That he remains standing is a credit to his Tare — his Tare and my restraint. He *knows*. Or rather, he suspects. Notare Abel remains blissfully unaware of our exchange…for a moment. And then she catches up. "Wait. Wait wait wait wait wait…you don't mean that he can't…"

My calm holds but only just. I am unaccustomed to feeling this way and I do not enjoy it. "Do not say more." I glance between the two of them. Notare Abel's eyes grow large.

Notare Kane's eyes radiate a strange expression, one I can nearly feel as well as a breeze floating through the air. *Humor.* He is more relaxed when he next speaks. "Ah. I see."

"With respect, you see nothing."

Notare Abel shakes her head. "No…you don't…you're not…this isn't…"

"No, it isn't," I reply, edgy in a way I've never been. Not in my entire long life. I raise a finger to my ear with subtle implication. There are ears all around us. Whatever these two baby Notare think that they may, perhaps suspect, I cannot allow knowledge of it to leave this room.

I make a mental calculation and decide to reveal to these two creatures something I had no intention of revealing to anyone. I pull a pad and pen from my breast pocket and quickly scrawl a note.

I cannot rheach Candy.
Say nothing.
It could mean her life.

It takes Notare Abel much longer to read the note than her counterpart. He crosses his arms over his chest, straining the threadbare tee shirt he wears. I do not understand why he dresses like the humans when there is material enough on this planet to fabricate more dignified wear.

By the time I finish assessing his crude garb, Abel has slumped down in her seat. Her mouth hangs ajar, arms and legs splayed in an unrefined way. "Why did it have to be her?" She says, surprising me.

But I have no answer for her. "Do I have your permission to approach the female? For research purposes only. Not to harass or harm in any way." *Yes, for research only.* It helps assuage the nagging discomfort I feel with all of this. *My interest is merely scientific. My response to her touch merely another physiological reaction, easily explained by the fact that her touch is permissible.*

"Shit." She rubs the space between her eyebrows. She rubs her bulging stomach. "I don't know what to say."

"Then say nothing. I merely wished to inform you of my intentions as a courtesy."

"Diego is going to freak out." Notare Abel shares a troubled glance with Notare Kane.

It's on the tip of my tongue to inquire as to the nature of their relationship but, in the final moment, I'm able to curb the impulse. It doesn't matter who he is. I do not have intentions towards the female beyond my research. *Yes, research...* My hand flexes towards my swordstick.

"This conversation is concluded, then?" I rip the paper from the pad, grab the lighter from my pocket and take both to the fireplace against the right wall. I burn the paper, watch until it crinkles up into nothing, until I'm sure the information cannot be resurrected and used for harm.

I glance between Notare Kane and his Sistana, focusing on her. She is the weak link here. A swollen, oversized heart, likely to bleed this information all over the place. "I trust your silence, Notare?"

She nods.

"I need not describe the suffering that could befall your friend should the information slip, I'm sure."

"What?"

"This has never happened, Notare. Not in all of the annals of Sistylea's lengthy history and not in its annexes. While your people copy the records, the originals themselves live in my mind and their pages, in my war chests. It is clear that she plays a role. It is my role to add her name to those books, if history requires it. But first, additional study is required."

"Shit," she says.

I take my leave of them.

Chapter Five

T he streets of Brianna are cacophony, as usual. I move through them, steeling myself for battle as the pressure of so many living souls flood my senses, overwhelming them.

After the time of the pre-Frost, our gifts were honed over generations…enhanced to extend beyond animals and one another. Having among the strongest abilities to rheach of any of my kind, I can rheach anything *with* blood without physically touching the specimen, or having a link to that blood through the blood of another. However, with the physical distance, comes a distance to the memories as well. With no link, the sensations come as feelings and emotion, rather than living history.

Many of them cause just as much pain, though.

To reduce my own discomfort, I ordinarily close myself off to them but, in this moment, I allow the Tretaro its full reign. It lashes out of me in ropes and waves, pushing through the bedlam of human energy in an attempt to seek out a solitary figure, hoping that perhaps the results of my first rheach into the female and even my second were, in some way, wrong.

A small quivering in my chest rattles and confuses me. I do not attempt to make sense of it, but move stiffly down the asphalt. My heels click-click-click as I walk. My guard, which trails a dozen paces behind me, moves in a solitary unit, always in sync. Far leads them. Laiya was second in my personal guard, until I gave her leave to join the humans attempting to cross Population by land. She has not rejoined my guard since and I believe, may have been swayed by the heart of another human. A female. A doctor called Sandra. With Sandra, Laiya appears as I have not seen her in the five hundred years we have known one another.

She seems so very happy.

Perhaps even happier than Notare Kane without the shackles of rule to bind her and without so many after her mate. Together, Laiya and Sandra are afforded the liberty to just…exist.

How miraculous.

The light is heavy in the air, turning the red world to a sinister shade. I flex my hands as I continue to sort through the bedlam, finding no traces of the female with the clay and earth-scented skin.

I come to a stop at the foot of the marketplace on Starlight. The hill leads down and, from this vantage, I can see everything. A split second's assessment tells me that she isn't here. My swordstick clatters against my thigh when it twitches.

"Far."

"Lahve."

He does not need to approach to hear me or be heard by me. "I seek a human female with pale white skin and red hair."

There is a small conference between the five members of my personal guard. There were six, until Laiya defected for the sake of love. "There are four living within the walls of Brianna."

"The one I seek is shy, painfully so. She wears ill-fitting garments and carries the scent of clay."

Another short conference, but my guards know nothing.

"Her name is Candy."

Another conference, but it would seem that this female has made no impression on my guard and they are the most observant of all Heztoichen living. Perhaps, this female makes no impression on anyone.

"She smells often of clay. I believe it possible she works in the ceramics workshop."

"I know where that is," Teera says.

"Thank you, Teera. Take me there."

Teera steps out in front of me, Nethral at her side. They move as a cohesive pair, guiding me swiftly through the market, much to the awe of the humans gathered over long, canvas-covered tables where they laugh and discuss and trade their wares.

Six blocks away, we stop in front of an enormous single-story home. Teera and Nethral peel back on my order and I rap my knuckles on the back of the heavy red door. I wait an insect's full lifetime for it to open up before me. As I wait, I allow my mind to wander. There is no star on the front of this door, which pleases me for reasons I cannot decipher.

The sound of laughter radiates through the wooden home and the sensation is one of calm. It pleases me, as well. A door somewhere in the bowels of this home opens and closes and then another. The sound of feet on hardwood flooring become louder, looming closer, yet I continue to search, to rheach as best I can.

My mind's eye is almost entirely consumed by that, so I am grateful for my guards in ways I am usually not. In all black, they present a looming and intimidating presence that will draw the passing humans' stares and keeps them from interrupting me.

I see nothing but the sight of my dark hand against her pale arm, my pointed nails raking over her flesh. Her ugly garb and hideous tunics. I'd burn them if I could, leaving her in nothing at all...

The door opens with a breeze and the female behind it starts. "Holy fuck," a human woman says. She has skin nearly as black as my own and coarse hair that frames her face. Her eyes widen. "Sir," she blurts, "what are you..."

"Lahve." A Heztoichen female appears behind her and drops to one knee in the hall. The human, seeing what the Heztoichen has just done, mimics the position.

"Rise," I tell them and they do. "I do not mean to disturb you, but I come to speak with Candy. I believe she is on the premises."

The human woman blinks stupidly, and it is the Heztoichen who speaks. "She's out in the workshop. We're... making plates today." She shows me her hands, which are covered in mud. I inhale deeply and my gut clenches without me ordering it to. The scent is...pleasing, too. "You are welcome to enter, Lahve." She keeps her gaze low and I am lightened to know that there are at least some still in this world that understand concepts of respect, honor and civility otherwise alien here.

"Thank you, *minersha*," I say, calling her by a Heztoichen moniker that translates to 'honorable one,' and the female beams. "I won't be long and my guards will remain outside so as not to disturb you."

I step inside the foyer and follow the two women through a kitchen where six humans work alongside two Heztoichen. They are working industriously to prepare a large quantity of food. "Pardon me," I offer as I pass through the room.

"Holy shit," a human male says followed by a female, "What the hell is he doing here?"

"Shh," a Heztoichen rasps, a female called Luan. "He can hear every word we say. Apologies, Lahve."

I smile as I descend two stairs, pass through what appears to be a human's bedroom, before finally stepping into a breezy corridor that ends in a door. The door hangs open revealing a large four-car garage. The doors are all open wide, allowing in afternoon air and light.

Organized neatly throughout are different stations. One on the right is a series of large, industrial sinks, the one slightly left of it features an enormous kiln, as well as two smaller ones — these are being manned or, perhaps more accurately, womanned — by several humans moving clay plates in varying stages of readiness into and out of the stone interiors.

There is a long table directly in front of me covered in large buckets of what I assume are glazes, given the varying assortment of colors, and then finally, closest to the open garage doors and spilling out onto the large, flat driveway, are women seated at turning wheels, spinning clay.

Candy is seated at a wheel in the thick of it, surprising me. I had expected to see her seated away from the other humans, as isolated and shy as she seemed. Now, she has her hair pulled back into a ponytail at the nape of her neck. She still wears her long, hideous turtleneck, covered in a smock, but...she looks like an entirely different female.

Here, surrounded by other women, she is *smiling*. It isn't a grin, per se, but her rounded cheeks are high and light and filled with color from her exertion as she leans her full weight into her arms and hands and then, finally, into the clay on the metal wheel, which turns quickly beneath her. Electrical cables and cords slither across the floor and I step carefully past them as I approach the females who make the plates and bowls and flatware for this community.

As the human female leads me closer, she looks over her shoulder at me and her expression is...pained. "Would you wait here?" She whispers under her breath and I feel... irritation.

Hm.

I stop walking in the center of the garage and feel eyes canvas my body from every direction. I ignore them, settling into the weight of their stares. I have been Lahve for a very long time and am accustomed to it.

"Sorry, Lahve," Luan says. I turn to look at the female who stands a few steps away from me to my right. She wipes her hands off on her apron and offers me a contrite look. "You know how it is with Candy and our kind."

No. I do not.

I tip my chin as a means of masking my expression. She responds with a worried look and rubs her auburn hair out of her eyes with the back of her wrist, smearing clay across her eyebrow. It is strange. With the pink in her cheeks and the worried look on her face, she looks remarkably human. Her height is the only thing that distinguishes her from the rest at all.

The human female's voice draws my attention forward. Though almost all in the room have stopped working, Candy's concentration is fixed on the wet mass of clay between her hands. "Hey, Candy, you got a second?"

"Sorry Kassie, I'm not quite finished yet." She doesn't look up as she replies, but it doesn't matter. Her soft, feminine voice has the ability to rearrange my insides, especially like this. Without stiffness in her tone, without the barriers, soft as ash, that she erected to keep herself in and everyone else out. Perhaps, the reason for her rigidity was Population. It has an unfortunate effect in putting even the most seasoned of Heztoichen warriors on edge. My guard is often less...at ease beyond Brianna's gates and they are Heztoichen, well-trained and have extensive experience in battle. This female is most certainly not battle hardened. As slight as she is, as fearful, she wouldn't survive the slightest skirmish.

"Um..." Kassie looks back over her shoulder at me and must register an imperative in my expression because she makes a second attempt. "Well, you see...I think it's okay. You can scrap this plate and come back to it."

"But I'm so close…" I watch her concentrate furiously on the moving tray before her and find it…interesting. Her tongue peeks between her lips and she seems to be muttering words softly to herself, but even I cannot make them out.

"Candy…"

"It is…not a problem," I offer. "I can wait." I have all the time in the world.

The sound of my voice unsettles the space. All hushed whispers cease until all that can be heard is the crackling heat deep within the heart of the kilns. Candy, meanwhile, looks up, sees me and her hand slips, slashing directly through the clay in front of her, ruining what appeared to be a rather promising-looking plate.

She does not take her foot off of the pedal and wet mud slings off of the metal tray into that of her neighbor's. Neither female reacts.

Candy's eyes meet mine, but only for one tenth of a second before she looks straight down and then straight back up at Kassie. She rotates around on her short stool and the tension that I thought had been a product of Population comes back full force. *So it's me that is the problem?*

Irritation.

Hmph.

"What does he want?" She whispers so softly she has to repeat herself three times.

Kassie moves her hands rapidly as she speaks. "I don't know."

I clear my throat, for their benefit rather than for mine. I find that the clearing of a throat always helps reorient the focus of a room to where it should have been from the beginning. An odd human function. "I wish to speak with Candy in private."

Candy gives no reply. In fact, her silence is utterly eerie. Most other humans make subtle sounds they themselves are little aware of. The flutter of breath, the twitching of hands, scratching of fingers, rustle of clothing. The only sounds that come from her now, hunched over on her short stool, are the sounds of her toes on the dry, dusty concrete. Her feet move about half an inch, but even as I narrow my focus, I can only perceive the hurried beating of her heart.

"The matter will take only a moment." When she still doesn't reply, I add, "It is in reference to the conversations struck earlier in the Notare's war room." It is...not an untruth. Not a lie, either. But which conversations do I refer to?

"Do I have to?" She asks Kassie.

Kassie's mouth opens. She massages her forehead. Beside me, Luan moves forward. She rounds the group seated clustered at their wheels watching Candy like falcons might watch a mouse. She drops down into a crouch so that she appears at Candy's eyelevel and pivots her body slightly away from the female as she speaks. Like one might approach a wounded or wild animal. *Is that all she is?* My hand flexes at my side, a product of my disappointment.

"He can't touch you. He can't touch anyone. He has a gift that makes it hard for him, so you don't have to worry."

"He touched me earlier when we were in the woods."

The female reels back. She looks at me and my teeth clack together as I fight the desire to offer explanation. It's a fight that I...lose.

"I touched Candy in order to decipher the signs in her mind so that I might better understand the movement of humans beyond our gates." Did I succeed? No. Do they need to know that? Also, no. "I cannot discuss the matter further. My request is simply that Candy escort me for a moment so that I may ask her a question in private. Candy, will you join me now?"

It is not a request, so why is she treating it as such? Frustration gnaws on my bones. The muscles in my forearms are...tense. I have an unexpected urge to move forward, toward the female and wring her neck.

When she continues to play dead, I bark to the rest of the room, "Leave us."

Two females fall from their stools. One knocks over a bucket of glaze and three others step through it. Cursing and mumbling ensues. The room clears out...but it does not empty. Kassie remains, as does Luan. And there is a third female who stands at the kilns and walks slowly over to us, a strange bounce in her step that seems contrary to the occasion.

"I know who you are," the female walking towards Candy says, gaze lingering over my belt, my chest, my ankles...*she searches for weapons. A warrior, assessing.* "My name's Star. I'm not a part of this whole plate-making conference. Just came here to help fix the kiln. Temperature gauge is shot. It's a pleasure to meet you." She doesn't offer me her hand, which...I approve of. Not that I would have wanted to shake her hand regardless. Her hands are covered in black smudges. She gestures at me with a wrench. "I'm a friend of Candy's and, since you're asking her to be alone with you, I'm not so sure *you're* a friend of Candy's. So, if it doesn't bother you, I'll wait right here while you talk to her. That sound okay to you, mister Lahve, sir?"

Her voice is fully insolent, even as she attempts to mask it by blinking at me with bright round eyes, a stunning shade of grey. Her high cheeks are tan and freckled. Her curly hair is short and streaked with blonde. A female that spends much time out in the sun.

I glance around and I have the odd sense that the females present with me in the room now truly have no intention of leaving. Meanwhile, I can hear the others listening at the door, straining to hear through the walls. The humans are asking the few Heztoichen among them what is being said. I do not like this. But I have been left with few options. Short of slaughtering.

And that would displease the Notare in my charge.

I don't reply to this...Star creature. I cross the space purposefully and kneel a pace away from Luan, six feet of distance between myself and Candy. I speak to her directly, blocking the sight of the others out.

"Candy..." I pause, allowing the weight of her name to pass across my tongue, if that's what it even is. It tastes more like a moniker. Just like Lahve. *I wonder what she would think of my true name...*

I clear my throat needlessly. "I did not have the opportunity to properly introduce myself the first time we met. I am the Lahve, delegated council to all Notare and justice dealer across the seven regions."

She stares at her knees, which are soaked through with muddy water from her hands. She makes no move to wipe them.

"Thank you for the assistance you have provided myself and the Notare."

She does not acknowledge my introduction in any way, but merely allows time to pass, as if she has an excess of it as I do.

My lips tilt down. Not to respond to the Lahve when spoken to directly is a flogging offense on Sistylea, as so few are afforded the privilege, but my hand is staid not only by the threats leveled toward me by the Notare, but by curiosity. What genetic makeup sets her apart from everyone else I have come across in my three thousand year existence that spans not one but two separate galaxies?

Her appearance provides no explanation. Though I continue to think of her as being tiny I realize, in this more thorough inspection, that she isn't tiny so much as... insignificant in the way she carries herself. Physically, she is tall for a human woman and too thin. Her skin is lighter than many of the others and clear, all but for three small freckles on the curve of her jaw below her left ear. Her turtleneck and smock cover the rest.

The smock is brown, covered in rather hideous yellow flowers. Her turtleneck is black beneath it and so are her black pants that extend all the way to her heavy black boots. The mane of her vibrant hair is not quite orange, not quite red, but is the color of the sunrise meeting the blue horizon over the jungles of Hom. Yes, the jungles…perhaps this is why I think of them when I see her.

On Sistylea, I once saw a bird in the hanging jungles of Hom. At night, it had glowed just that same color. A violation of evolution, such a color made it easy prey and yet against the very laws of nature it continued to thrive. The bird was called Ipalora, or 'shines at night'. The Ipalora was vulnerable and exotic and capable of holding my interest in all of the same ways this human female does now.

I want to move forward, but that would terrify her even more and she. is. terrified. I can taste her terror in the air, as sour and pungent as sweat. My hand flexes. Her eyes dart to it.

Inhaling sharply, she says in a rush, "I can't help you. I don't know anything."

"I do not seek your help. I merely seek your company. Would you be available to dine with me tonight?"

"Company?" Candy says slowly. She seems…almost…as if she is more relaxed.

Perhaps, she is pleased by me. The thought fills me with pride. Given my status alone, I am always wanted. Being desired here and now by a female is no new sensation. But perhaps it isn't a female…it is being desired by *this* female that fills me with an eagerness unbecoming.

"Yes. For the evening. At my estate." I'll provide her with dinner enough for six, perhaps fatten her up while I attempt to learn her mind's secrets.

"You'll pay?"

I'm confused. "I will certainly pay for the dinner…"

"No, me. You'll pay me?"

My confusion increases. "I…can pay you."

"Candy," Star admonishes. "What are you doing, girl?"

Candy sits up a little straighter and swivels back to face Star. "Nothing. It's okay. He'll pay." She turns back to face me and her hair forms a sort of shield between us. "Right? You'll pay?"

She would like me to pay for her to provide her with dinner. But perhaps...my thoughts flit through the words the Notare uttered earlier. Thoughts of exchanges made over bodies and flesh. My pupils dilate slightly, my breath rakes harder down my throat. "I would pay you to join me for dinner *only*."

She nods rapidly and I wonder if she's heard me when she mutters, "Dinner only," under her breath, surely too low for the other humans to catch.

"Would dinner at my house this evening at approximately nineteen hundred hours be acceptable for you?"

"Sure," she says louder, nodding a little more easily. "One hour. No biting. Okay?"

I have never been so insulted in my entire existence. Three thousand years and I have never been supposed to be so...depraved. That I would take a weak human female to my home for *one hour* to enjoy entering her flesh and then sucking her into mine in exchange for *pay*. Were it possible for me to enjoy a female, I would have done so three thousand years ago and I certainly would *never* have selected such a female as this. Weak, scrawny, struggling to hold my gaze.

Only she isn't struggling. Not anymore. She seems more...confident now that we have struck an accord and I have the nagging suspicion that, were I to voice my concern and the ways she has slandered me so sloppily before all of these beings, she might...not come.

"Agreed," I seethe through clenched teeth. "What is your price?"

The silence this time seems to last lifetimes. In fact, I play particular lifetimes over in my head. Leorth, the Notare of the Diera at the time of my birth. He and Kane share a distant bloodline. I think of Elise. Her blood and Kane's illuminating the Tare in Abel. My belief is that some are born with Tare that is not passed or shared but that it is turned on. But that I do not know for certain. For a time I believed it something otherworldly. Perhaps, it is... Because this slight human without Tare is taking me now to places I cannot return to. The hanging jungles of Hom. In the cool clean air that wafts from her skin and hair, I smell the universe that I lost.

"Ipalora," I whisper. She hears it. I am...surprised. I spoke out of turn.

Hm.

I do not continue, even though she waits for me to do so. She waits a long while. She is...comfortable with the concept of time, this female.

Hm.

"Whiskey."

"Whiskey?"

She nods.

"This is your payment?"

She nods again.

I bristle, understanding more slowly than I am accustomed to. "How many bottles?" It was clearly not a question she expected me to ask for she makes a soft, balking sound that remind me of her lips. The palest pink and appealingly smooth. She holds up three muddy fingers.

"Done." I straighten and move into the driveway, no intention of walking past the prying eyes of the house. "I shall see you this evening."

My hand flexes, but...it does not flex toward my swordstick. No. This time, it flexes towards the female. When I blink, I picture her face and I recognize that the female is quite clever. How had she known that I no longer desire just to touch, even before I had?

Because with the blood flowering beneath her cheeks and sounding like a Sistylean symphony pulsing through her veins, I want to *taste*.

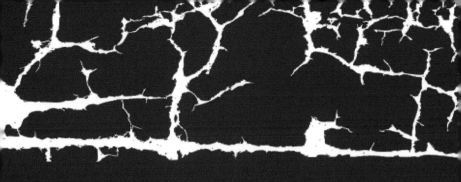

Chapter Six

"Do you have the tableware arranged?" I ask the human who manages my estate.

It is...odd. I have never given much thought to the female who cleans the manor I have claimed for my own here in Brianna. I have estates in each of the seven regions, short of Carata where Tanen rules less with the iron fist of a king and more with the bloodthirsty savagery of a warlord.

Here, in Brianna, the home I was bequeathed is rather small. All of the homes here are somewhat modest. There are only three floors and a basement. The first floor is clearly meant for hosting. In the back is a large kitchen which spans nearly the full width of the house. In the front is a foyer, a formal dining area, as well as a den with a separate cigar lounge.

The second floor is made for...relaxation, I suppose. It is fitted with a large living area that had an enormous screen mounted to one wall which I promptly removed and replaced with a piano. The instrument is similar to one I owned on Sistylea and I find that it plays just as beautifully. Perhaps, not quite just. But beautifully enough.

The third and uppermost floor is where the sleeping occurs, or would were I one to sleep. I do not often sleep. On occasion I find it convenient to rest my mind and so I lie down in the largest of the bedrooms. This is not a frequent event. It is, in fact, as infrequent as my desire to eat, which is why the conversation this human female and I are holding now is the first we have ever held.

"Uhm yes. It's set. Patty and I set out bowls and plates for two."

"Patty?"

"Yes, my twin sister and I." She nods quickly, keeping her gaze lowered to the floor between our feet, an acceptable human reaction in the presence of a superior being. Appropriately afraid without being incapacitated by that fear, so unlike the female I have invited to dine with me.

The first female in hundreds of years. I cannot even count how many. Perhaps… No. It cannot be. She cannot be the *first* female I have wished to dine with privately, not politically, for no other purpose than to speak with her.

I feel the corners of my mouth twitch into a dangerously forming frown. The female must notice, for she jerks back.

"There are…two of you?"

Her mouth quirks and she's able to hold my gaze slightly longer as she struggles to assess her humor against mine. It should be an easy question for her then, for I have none. "Yes. The past few months Patty and I have been working here and at Abel and Kane's estate just to help tidy up, but mostly we help out in the greenhouses. It's how we're able to get you the best fruits and veggies uh…sir."

"And there are two of you?"

"Yeah. We swap duties, except for tonight. I asked for Patty's help with the cooking. You haven't made a request like that of either of us before and she's a stronger cook than I am so I wanted her input. Not to say that I'm a bad cook or anything. I can cook," she stammers.

I consider her for a long, long while. In this time, I wonder if I should feel…concerned that I did not know that two separate human females have been conducting the affairs of my manor without my notice. Then I decide definitively against such concern. Had one of them wanted to bring harm to me, then I would have taken notice. Though what harm can a human cause? They are inferior creatures in both strength and cunning.

Moving on, I say, "Full place settings?"

The female has brown hair and white skin marred by a scar that extends from her right temple to her soft cheek. I had not noticed this scar before now. She tucks her hair behind her ear and nods quickly. "Uh yeah. Here. I can show you."

I move ahead of her into the dining room…only to find it empty.

"Actually, we set you two up in the den. We thought it would be homier and more comfortable in the den."

Irritation.

It plays at the edge of my thoughts as I turn and follow the female across the foyer to the den. Lights are low — no, they're off. Candles have been strategically placed around the edges of the room and the fire has been lit. A much too small table sits in front of it, two plush sitting chairs placed to one side of it facing the fire. A gramophone sits off to the side, waiting to play whatever records these siblings have elected to play, despite the fact that I have not requested it, or any of it.

The setting can only be described in a word — intimate.

"No," I hiss. She shivers, despite the elevated temperature in the room. "Please make up the dining room and do so quickly. My guest will be arriving soon."

I turn on my heels, my restraint…thin. My cloak snaps behind me as I approach the front door and put the female — *females* — working in my home behind me. I refuse to allow myself to haunt their steps, ensuring that they place things where I'd like to see them and I most certainly refuse to allow myself into the kitchens to inspect the feast that they will have prepared for myself and my...guest.

"Teera." The single word suffices as a command and, because this is a female who has known me the better part of half a millenia, she knows what I want and what to tell me, unlike the humans in my manor.

"She is making her way to you from Starlight now." I can hear her voice like the voice of the wind and, because we are not too far now, she can hear mine.

"Is she coming directly from the ceramic workshop?" I murmur under my breath.

"No. She's stopped into one of the homes first."

Irritation.

Only...it isn't irritation this time. It's something stronger that I...cannot put name to.

"Her own?"

"No. Tasha's home."

"Heztoichen Tasha?"

"Yes, Lahve."

Hm.

"She changed her clothes and bathed."

In Tasha's home? My mind is reeling. Tasha is a known designer and seamstress and among Sistylea's elite. What would she be doing consorting with a lowly human female? And what in Sistylea's name would she be doing providing said female with a change of clothing?

"Do the clothes appear to be Tasha's designs?"

"No, Lahve. Or rather, it is difficult to tell. She wears a long cloak over her garments."

"And you're sure she isn't simply wearing her painter's smock beneath?"

"I am confident she is not. Her coat fits her too well for there to be materials bunched beneath."

Then what is beneath?

I wrench away from the thought, hating that it crossed my path. At least, I would have hated it were I a being capable of such fickle, vain emotion…right…of course. But the words are repeated with sullen defeat.

"Thank you, Teera."

"Lahve?"

Curious. Teera rarely speaks without being spoken to. "Yes?"

"The female would appear to be…well-known within the community. There are females who approach her. There are also males."

I take a long, long while formulating a response and battering back the more visceral ideas that sneak past my defenses like warrior spies coming to soften the battlefield before the war begins in earnest. "Is she receptive?"

"She seems…pleased to converse with the females."

"And is she receptive to the males?"

"No."

Why do I care? The answer is that I do not. "Leave the female to her life. Do not interfere."

"Certainly," she says, but do I not detect a slight hesitation there?

I ignore it and stand waiting silently before the door.

She arrives at dusk but she does not immediately knock. Rather, she waits a long, long while.

And thus, we stand, mirror images of one another in posture and inverse mirrors in everything else. I am strength and she is weakness. She is human and I am…more.

She waits long enough for me to entertain the idea that she can sense my presence on the other side of the door. Long enough for my hand to flex — not toward my swordstick — but toward the door handle… Long enough that I lose my very first battle and reach for it.

I open it six inches and then when she does not run as I had half expected her to, another twelve. "Good evening. Please, come in."

I stare at the top of her shiny red hair. It falls in waves and tattered tendrils, looking like curls of fire in the muted red darkness behind her. Her head bobs twice and I notice the female is making soft sounds with her lips, but I cannot make out the words. It irks me.

She looks up at me abruptly and I feel my weight shift slightly into my heels. She flicks her gaze past me and I step aside. She enters with both hands balled into fists at the ties of her coat. It is a trench coat. A *well made* trench coat. My teeth clench, but I force them to part.

"If you would adjourn to the dining room."

I walk past her, ignoring the scent that wafts from her skin and hair now that she is clean. Forgetting the hanging jungles of Hom, I enter the dining room and step to the head of the table. The table has been laid out in an…acceptable fashion, for humans — a large bowl and small plate, two glasses, several pieces of cutlery, cloth napkins. The chandelier overhead casts bright light around the room, rendering the single candle at the center of the table redundant.

She moves to the right of the only other place setting, so that it rests between us. Her gaze strays first to the door at her back, then to the door against the left wall that leads to the kitchen before finally moving to the sideboard made of heavy black wood.

I gesture to it. "Would you like a drink?" She shakes her head and glances to the single bottle of wine laid out on the table. Tension threads her bones and she moves her hands away from the ties at her waist. Jerkily, she angles herself towards the door and takes a large breath. Her eyebrows knit over her nose and, just as I nearly debase myself and ask her what I have done to offend her so gravely, she holds up three fingers.

I look at them without understanding…until I do.

Rage.

Hm.

I grip the back of my seat and squeeze lightly enough that I do not pulverize the wood. I then go to the sideboard, open a cabinet and remove the three bottles of whiskey promised to her. The light catches their smooth surface and casts patterns against the glossy oak beneath.

"Those are for you." She nods and her shoulders slump before steeling all over again. She fumbles with the ties on her waist and I watch her, confused. "Please, be seated."

She nods repeatedly, then gives the ties at her waist one final rough tug. She fusses with her buttons before finally freeing them. She pushes back the shoulders of the coat and it makes a soft swishing sound as it pools on the floor around her feet.

That is, for the coming moment, all I hear.

I know immediately that Tasha has made her this garment and I make immediate plans to gift her all the riches that I have…did she make this for me? And then the thought hits again. *What if she did not make this for me? She would not have gone through the trouble of creating a garment just for one, one-hour dinner with one male.*

I arrive before the female with no awareness of arriving there, my fists clenching and flexing over and over again as my gaze sweeps her body. Instead of shapeless sacks, Candy is wearing black, thin, transparent fabric that reveals *everything*. Through it, I can see her collar bones, her breasts, her wide round nipples, the flat of her stomach, the pale outline of her ribs when she inhales deeply, and then again, like she can't catch her breath.

But what is more worrisome than what I can see, is what I cannot.

She wears a little swatch of black satin to cover her crotch and, disconnected from her panties but just below them are thick black cuffs. Wide enough to cover the top half of her thighs, they conceal the piece of her I'd like to rip into most, followed closely by the thick cuffs she wears at her wrists that cover most of her forearms and finally, the choker that covers the full length of her throat.

No biting, she'd said. My sharpened nails reach for her throat and graze the outside of the fabric, so very gently, not daring to tear it. She'd meant it and seeks to remind me, too.

"Nothing with the neck, wrist, or thighs," she says in that soft as ash voice.

"I can see that."

She twitches beneath my touch, but does not move. Her gaze does not meet mine, but there's a stubborn set to her smooth chin that is so pronounced it seems to speak for her. "Do you consent?"

"Do I consent?" Huh. What an odd choice of words.

"You won't do anything to my wrists, neck or thighs?"

"No."

Her fingers immediately move to the clasp on the front of my pants. I move away from her so quickly she wavers in the light breeze my body creates and blinks several times around the room as if unsure where to find me. I shuffle purposefully so as to help her. Odd, my behavior. But not so appalling as hers.

"Is this the same deal you offer every male who asks you to dinner?"

"Men don't ask me to dinner."

Irritation…flares into disgust. "And males of my kind?"

"They ask me to be dinner," she says softly. "I offer them this instead." She gestures down at her body as if it were a dish towel, a malformed plate she made one day in her pottery studio, something unworthy of anything but perpetual use. Then she has the audacity to shrug. "It's easier."

It's. Easier.

Disgust…flares into fury.

I look down at her body, fully aware that I will need to rearrange my erection, but willing to suffer that consequence. I am *not* attracted to her — I cannot be attracted to a whore — but touching the outside of her collar to the bliss of *nothingness* had felt absolutely mesmerizing. She may disgrace these halls with her words, but...I am not willing to throw her out of them just yet.

"Miss Candy, I understand that you and I have had limited interaction to this point. As such, you are not yet aware of how deeply you have offended me. With this in mind, I too, must reconsider retribution for such an offense knowing that I have culled obedience from the unruly for far, far less severe offenses. I believe, at this impasse, we have no choice but to begin again on what you may consider a stronger, more transparent foundation. Now, look into my eyes, Miss Candy."

She's staring at the floor but after a careful breath, she tilts her chin up and back. She rocks onto her heels, nearly toppling over in her effort, but at the last second, she catches herself. I reach out a finger, lowering it to her thick collar, before stroking a single line up past her three little freckles, around her jaw, to the tip of her chin.

Her skin against mine is warm and soft and I think of jamming my claws into a ripe grapefruit, ripping open the thick white skin and devouring the pink flesh beneath. I withdraw my hand immediately and flex it at my side. She shivers. Does she know how close she is to death at any given time? These humans are terribly thin-skinned and this one is so very weak.

I could reach out and touch her and kill her with the lightest brush of my hand. I imagine that someone of her... fragility would not survive a brush with my kind. An uneasy stirring of my gut alerts me to the violent vision that sweeps me. No, the little Ipalora would not survive a Heztoichen's fangs...which is why she offers them her cunt. It's easier.

"Hear me now when I tell you that I have no desire for you, body or blood," I lie, "and when I tell you something, it is as I have said it. Do not ever attempt to compare me to another living being on this planet. I am not of your species. And I am not a Heztoichen, either. I am Lahve. Impartial, rational and uninterested in the fleeting affairs of humans — or their flesh."

I step behind her chair and drag it out for her with an intentionally loud scrape. She jumps. I glance at the seat. "Now please, if you would be so kind as to join me."

But, rather than obey me, the female steps back. "What do you want, then?" She all but gasps. Her eyes are wide and round and her nipples are hard and stiff. *I should not be looking at her nipples.*

"I seek what is more enduring than pleasures of the flesh, or human existence. Truth. Truth and history."

"What does that have to do with me?"

"We shall see, won't we?" Sensing that this answer is not sufficient to keep her in the room as what little confidence she had disintegrates like ash in water, I add, "You hold truths about Population that I myself do not know. I seek answers. Please, Miss Candy, sit."

She lingers on the threshold of terror and confusion for quite some time. Long enough for me to grow…antsy. Were I capable of something so frivolous, of course.

"You'll really give me all three of those alcohol bottles just to answer some more questions about Population?" She's shivering again.

"You were willing to trade the pleasure of your flesh for those three bottles. I fail to see why it should matter to you what is traded so long as it occupies the allotted time." My words shock me to my core, which freezes over like the tundra. It is…untoward to speak to a female of *any* species with such disgrace. I have…insulted her. And I have no intention of apologizing for it. Worse, she does not seem to expect this of me, either.

She takes the insults, just as she'd have taken my cock — for three bottles of whiskey.

I glance at the three bottles, startled by my…irritation towards them. Not that they are my payment for her presence, but that she values her own flesh at so low a price.

In her eyes, three bottles of whiskey are the value of her time and the swatch of black silk guarding treasures between her thighs.

She sits, her eyes on the empty bowl and plate in front of her. I push in her chair and her cheeks are blazing with color by the time I find my own. It…distracts me. My ears ring with the thrum of blood pumping through her veins. I promptly ignore it.

I ring the bell and the sisters enter and, to my surprise, there are, in fact, two of them. The one with whom I spoke earlier starts at the sight of the female seated at my table. She smiles widely to show all of her teeth. One in the back is missing on the left side. Many of the humans, I have noticed, have missing teeth. I am not sure if Candy has all of her teeth and frown. I don't know because she's never smiled at me. I've given her no cause to.

"Hey Candy. So good to see you. How you been?" She comes to Candy's left and places a bowl of biscuits in front of her.

"Good," Candy says in a small voice before inhaling deeply. Her stomach makes a rumbling sound that surprises me and colors her with embarrassment. "Smells amazing. Thanks Lima."

The female called Lima's twin does not, however, ignore Candy's outfit and stares at her breasts with a severe expression that makes Candy's cheeks flare an even brighter and more alarming shade of red. The twin, who must be Patty, has not fully entered the room and stands there holding a steaming pot wrapped in a towel beneath her arm. She glares.

"Diego and Pia know you're here?"

Candy's coloring moves down her cheeks. She's begun to sweat. "No…"

I slam my fist on the table — not hard enough to shatter it — but hard enough to rattle the settings. "Serve in silence, then leave."

The females obey, Patty with a glare, Lima with efficiency. I plan to speak to the Notare tomorrow about having Patty removed. The soup that has been served smells adequate yet Candy stares down at it with wide eyes.

"Is there a problem with the food?" I knew I should have had a Heztoichen prepare the meal. I had assumed humans would understand their own palate better than my kind would, but humans are relatively useless in…

"No. No, of course not." She's biting her bottom lip so hard the skin around her teeth turns white. She will break that skin soon, spilling her own blood all over her bowl. Her eyes flick up to mine and there is…desperation in them. She looks at the bottles on the sideboard. "What do I have to give you for the soup?"

Rage stabs me like an intruder with a knife. "Miss Candy, I will not repeat myself a third time. The bottles are in *exchange* for your presence here at dinner. I should not have thought it needed to be said, but *to dine* consists of eating food. This here, what your fellow humans have concocted, is edible food." I scoop a bite of the soup absently into my mouth and swallow, surprised to find the taste flavorful and rich. "Do not insult me again in my own home…Miss Candy." My pitch is…unstable.

Hm.

Unfortunate.

Candy stares at me. Simply stares until some of the fire in her face dies off. And then, without ceremony, she leans over her bowl of soup, her bare breasts pressing against the table. She lifts a large spoon and she takes a heaping bite.

She moans. I ignore the sound in its entirety, focusing on the rich taste of spices these humans have added to flavor the stew. I take another bite without looking at Candy's mouth or the sinful way she eats and I proceed with my questions.

"How is it that you come to know more about these symbols than the other humans?"

She scoots her seat forward and speaks between bites. "I spent time with gangs."

She spent time with gangs. I do not...understand. "Out in Population?"

"Yes."

There is clearly a miscommunication between us, undoubtedly the fault on her part. I clear my throat and move on. "How many...*communities* were you a part of?" *There. That sounds better.*

She moans around her next bite of soup, louder this time. I shift uncomfortably in my seat and do not watch her eat, but rather, reach for the wine. I pour myself a glass and pour her one as well. Perhaps intoxication will ease the discomfort that exists between us — hers, not mine. I have no desire to be intoxicated in her presence.

"Miss Candy, how many communities?"

"I don't know." She shrugs.

I grunt and attempt a third time. "In the past five years, how many communities have you been involved with?"

She gives me a peculiar look and shakes her head. "I guess...nine gangs, maybe? I don't know. I stopped counting the last few months."

I continue to...misunderstand. Unless...perhaps, she means what it is that she says in the same way I do — bluntly and directly. I test this theory. "I believe we are barreling towards a misunderstanding. To be clear, I am to understand that you have been a *member* of as many as nine gangs over the past five years and that these gangs are defined as roving bands of human and-or exiled Heztoichen, often male — "

"Always male," she whispers under her breath softly enough that I believe she believes I have not heard her.

"And that these gangs are often violent — "

"Always."

"And exist only by pillaging and raiding other gangs, scavengers or communities they cross?"

She nods, taking smaller bites. She is…uncomfortable. I can see it in the way she shifts in her chair. Her bare thighs press against the cool wood. I should offer her a robe, a blanket, to put back on her coat…but I don't. Did I tell her I did not find her attractive? How misleading. Did I tell her I had no intention of pursuing her as a whore? How tragic.

And then she whispers one foul word to unnerve me. "Yes." Pushing her hair over her shoulder and reaching with her other hand for a biscuit, she nods, as if to punch home the word she speaks so nonchalantly. One of the first words any human infant would learn…and I struggle to define it.

"You participated in these gangs and it is for this reason that you learned the symbols carved into the trees?"

"Participated," she murmurs. Her hand stiffens around the bread and squeezes. Red flowers in her cheeks and she blinks many times. Her other hand moves over her heart and she seems…for want of air. "Yes, I *participated*."

Hm.

"Hm."

She shoves the bread into her mouth, closes her eyes, leans back in her chair. Her physiological response to me, my questions, or to the bread, is…discomfiting. I move on. "How old were you when you first learned of Heztoichen existence?"

She swallows, the sound making my throat hurt. Her eyes flutter. I have to repeat my question another three times.

"Miss Candy?"

"What…" she gasps… "what did you say, Rick?"

"Rick?"

"Sorry. Shit." She bangs on her temple with the heel of her hand in a way that panics me. "Sorry, Drago, I'm so sorry."

"Miss Candy, please have some water." I gesture to her glass and she reaches for it, but she's sweating and her hand has started to shake and the rapid beating of her heart has begun to accelerate.

Her pupils have shrunk and she wipes the back of her hand across her forehead. "Where…where am I?" She glances around and I rise immediately, intending to hail the human doctor my guard has taken up with. "Jack…oh god, not Jack…"

She clutches her throat, reaches for the water, knocks over the glass and then promptly…passes out. She slips off of her chair and I watch her slump in slow motion. Time hangs suspended from the noose of her hair. It slashes across her face like blood from a wound. She will hit the ground soon. Once she does, what will I do with her then? What if she injures herself?

I slip beneath her body, moving faster than time can tell. I have no other options but to catch the back of her head and the chair. I right it and lower her to the ground in the same movement.

The door to the kitchen opens and in come the women. "Oh my god, what did you do to Candy?" Patty accuses.

"Is he eating her?" Lima shrieks.

Patty surges forward, dropping the tray in her hands. It lands on the floor, plates and glasses shattering amidst whatever the second course had consisted of. She grabs the chair Candy just fell from and tries to lift it. With two fingers pressed to the seat, I keep it grounded.

"Leave us," I bark and I use the threaded cords in my throat, cords that other beings, even Heztoichen, do not have. My voice reverberates throughout the room and whatever additional dishes Lima had been holding crash to the ground. I look up at the two not-quite-identical females, my gaze flitting between them. "You would risk my wrath for this female?"

"Or any-any other," the Patty one stammers.

Fools, these fickle humans. I know this…and yet…I feel a certain…*softening*. As a result, I kill neither of them. But…I do not allow this disobedience to go unpunished. I release the chair and Patty goes cascading into the sideboard. The heavy bottles clatter and she releases a scream that is pure agony as she and the wood clash, the wood evidently the victor. Her sister catches her.

"You are dismissed."

"Don't hurt Candy, please," Lima begs.

A muscle in my jaw ticks and my fangs press angrily against the insides of my lips. "Miss Candy fell unconscious when I began questioning her about the gangs she traveled with in Population. In her panic, she collapsed. You fools are wasting both your own, as well as her precious time."

"Fuck." I do not know if Patty curses in response to my statement or the pain shooting through her side.

Lima's face falls. "Oh."

"Now, tell me where she resides so I can return her to her home." I need to get her out of my arms. Holding her feels like holding a barrel of live wires. Electricity surges through me in sharp pulses and magnetic waves.

"She lives with Ashlyn," Lima says.

I stand, bringing Candy up with me and holding her out away from my body as I do. No, I don't. When I look down, I see she's pressed against my chest, her body looking like an offering dressed in the scandalous clothing Tasha covered her in. *I can't take her outside like this.* Her coat is still on the floor. I make rapid work of concealing her in it and take a step towards the door.

"No...no, she lives with Moraine," Patty wheezes. She's taken a seat at the table — my seat — and I wonder fleetingly why she's still alive. These humans are savages, the lot of them. The female in my arms is not — should not be, *cannot* be — any different.

"Which is it then?"

The females exchange rapid words before Lima shakes her head. "We aren't sure. I could have sworn I saw her coming out of Ashlyn's house last week."

"Just yesterday, I overheard Kassie asking her how it was rooming with a Heztoichen. Luan and Tatiana live with Moraine."

"She wouldn't live with one of *them*," the female sneers.

My lips draw back from my teeth and the deep tone of my voice vibrates the air. Glasses clatter on the table, one of them falling. The entire room shakes. "Useless creatures that you are, remove yourselves from my presence."

They do not rebel. Not even Patty. The two females go stumbling off. I run through a short list of available options before leaving the dining room and moving to the stairs. I carry her to the uppermost floor and select the larger of the guest bedrooms. The beds are all made up here and I have the momentary thought that it is rather...wasteful. When resources are so thin, to keep so much available material here when the humans might make better use of it...

I am distracted by what comes next. Placing Candy in the center of the bed, I debate with myself for a moment.

Take the place beside her and feign sleep in order to have the opportunity to feel her warmth for just a little while...or give her the space she so desperately needs and remove myself from the room.

The thought disturbs me. I don't know why. Perhaps, I worry about her safety, even alone. I don't know why. She has no weapons and yet, it seems even her own body is out to kill her. She needs watching. A compromise, I take one of the heavy leather armchairs facing the window and swivel it around to face the bed. Light filters around me through the window at my back. It is an abysmal red that casts sinister shadows over her sleeping form. She looks so...close to death.

I return to the bed and pull the heavy blankets out from underneath her. As I maneuver her body, I *accidentally* stroke my hands down her legs. I ignore how soft they are and I don't examine every freckle, every russet colored hair, the scrapes on her knees from scars long healed. I don't like the sight of those scratches, though mere scratches only they may be. Her bones feel thin through her skin, her muscles, weak and plush. She feels like a pillow my stiff and aching body longs to lie against.

I *want* to sleep beside her.

The thought is as persistent as my heartbeat and as fragile as hers.

I am...unused to desiring anything, least of all from a creature who frustrates me more than anything. She gave me no usable answers and her equivocations only confused me more.

But...I have never slept before beside anyone.

And she claims to be a whore. Or does she? She said, and I think back carefully over the words, that she was in a gang but that she was no gang *member*. I submit everything I was told, everything I have seen, under careful review.

Tucking the blankets around her, I pull her hair out from beneath her shoulder and fan it over the pillows. It glitters, the red against the black beneath her. There is a crease between her eyes. I stroke it, hoping to smooth it away, but it only appears more pronounced after I pull back and some things click into place.

I see now my latest, but perhaps not my first, mistake.

How often I forget the barbaric savagery of this primitive alien species. No, she was no member of a community, not out in Population. Abel and her cohort are perhaps, the only community left. So, if Candy was with a gang and she... participated in the gang...then it stands to reason that she *participated* as a victim, then. But of what? Torture? Rape?

My jaw clenches. I pull my hand back to myself and stand, wondering about the cuffs covering her wrists and throat and thighs. My hand flexes against my thigh over and over again, even as I retake my seat. I do not like the thought of what a slight, fearful female might have endured at the hands of a gang. A violent gang. A violent gang of males who do not...have honor. I clutch the arms of the leather seat beneath me, realizing only too late that my claws have bitten through the leather and into the wood beneath.

And I thought of her as a whore. I frown deeply. I have wronged her, as well, even though it was not my intention to.

She makes a soft sigh in her sleep and follows it up by a snort unbecoming of a female…though what do I know of females? Of anything?

I snort, just as she did, just to make the sound out loud as I see now my most recent mistake. I may have been…*wrong* in my initial assessment of this creature. Perhaps, for her to have survived at all, she is not so weak.

Chapter Seven

I watch her until the lights against her cheeks turn from red to grey to black. I watch as she has a fitful, restless sleep. I apply and then remove the blankets, then apply them again. I turn her words, few that there were, over and over again.

Saying yes is easier than saying no.

Her eyelids flutter, then open. She looks up at the ceiling, her awareness kicking in swiftly. Her breathing becomes shallow. She is afraid.

Carefully, I clear my throat to alert her of my presence in the least threatening way I know how. She gasps and turns to look at me, fingers coiling into the blankets as if to use them to defend herself.

"You are safe," I tell her, trying to keep my tone as even as possible so as not to activate my insiria, the lower vocal cords we Tretaro have that other Heztoichen do not. I know that these frighten the humans. "You and I were having dinner. I began questioning you about your...involvement with various gangs in Population. In an effort to block the memories, I gather, your conscious mind shut off."

I expect a reaction. I receive none. She merely continues to stare at me with round eyes, irises surrounded by oceans of white.

My hand twitches...but towards what? I'm not sure. She glances down at the arms of the leather chair, tufts of whatever interior material is used, peeking out of the folds. "You passed out. I would have returned you to your place of residence, but the females occupying my manor were not certain as to its location."

She still doesn't speak, but muscles in her neck tighten like bow strings.

I continue speaking, feeling rather...foolish. I am not often the one caught blabbering. I am never. "I brought you here. You are on the third floor of my manor, two floors above the dining room where you ate soup earlier. Should you like, I would be happy to escort you home. You are, alternatively, welcome to stay here for as long as you like."

I watch her acutely as her right arm reaches beneath the cover of the blankets and she pats herself down. Her hand fiddles with something...her face screws up. She withdraws her hand and looks at her fingers and I see that they are glistening and there is no mistaking the scent coating them.

I am...aghast. I would be...horrified were I not so aroused. My trousers no longer fit me properly despite having been tailored to my frame by Evyleen, a known seamstress even more prolific than Tasha. Her pod...did not make it through the barrier between our two galaxies.

I clear my throat again and look away as she wipes her fingers off on the sheets. I block my breathing and attempt to think of sullen, sad things. *It has been too long since I have allowed myself to be tempted.* Watching me, she lies back down. Her breathing evens. I am waiting for an answer that she seems reluctant to give and I...do not know how to proceed.

"You didn't touch me."

I know what she means, but wish I did not. I expect anger to rise within me, but I don't feel that either. "Is that a question?"

She nods.

I narrow my gaze and speak from deep within my throat. "No, I did not."

"Because I'm human?"

"Because I would never."

"Why? Is that why you don't want to have sex with me either?"

"If you continue to insult me, I will have to ask you to leave."

Her face screws up again and I am reminded that we did not grow up speaking the same language. It feels as if we still are not speaking the same language here.

Before she can speak — and I can tell that she will continue to insult me if she does — I lean forward and brace my elbows on my knees. I look deep into her eyes. I speak slowly and softly. "I am not a male to take that which is not willingly given."

"I said yes."

"When you were awake, your offer was…made. Nothing had been offered beyond that, nor would I have accepted had it been."

"Because I'm human?"

I snarl, my insiria working, making my pitch roll in low and deep. *Because you were sleeping.*

She quiets. Time stretches and bends. She sits up and glances up at me sheepishly, a burning red in her cheeks that makes me sit back up as well. Her entire demeanor…shifts. It is…remarkably subtle, yet it changes the shape of her entirely.

Whatever confidence she had is…not gone, but *changed*. She keeps her head down, she struggles to meet my gaze, her breathing deepens and she clutches at the blankets against her chest. She bites her bottom lip and peeks up at me between thick eyelashes. Her lips look red and fuller than they did. She looks so, so very much like an offering.

"That's nice of you," she says.

"It most certainly isn't. It is what anyone should do. Now please, rest. I will take my leave of you and escort you to your home in the morning." I leave before she can say more and move down the hall to my bed. I sit upon its edge, but my conscious mind is somewhere else. I watch her through sound alone, taking note of every twist, shuffle and reverberation. It makes me wonder why I bothered leaving her room at all.

I wait for a long while for the sounds of her sleeping. What I hear instead, are the sounds of her awake, moving. She leaves her room and plods down the stairs. I have dismissed the bulk of my guard, except for Teera who will guard the door this night. I normally would dismiss the entirety of my guard on nights I know I will make no attempt to sleep. I do not know why I asked her to remain behind tonight. *I do though, don't I?*

I warn Teera not to intervene should the human slink through the front door and disappear into the night but follow at a distance. However, instead of reaching the bottom of the stairs and turning towards the front of the house, the human female turns towards the back of the house.

Clanging in the kitchen finally causes me to stand. I appear within the doorway two floors below in time to see Candy standing up on a stool, reaching into a pot on the stove, a spoon in her hand. "What are you doing?"

She gasps, turns, slips and falls, but I am in front of her in time to catch her. She jolts when my hands lock around her waist and I carefully lower her to the ground, then step back just as quickly.

"I'm sorry, Lahve." She holds up both hands and I notice she no longer holds her spoon. She must have dropped it in the pot. Her gaze does that tremulous flickering thing again, where it moves rapidly between my face and the floor.

Strange then, that her fear seems so much less than it was before. No longer distracted by it, I can taste more of her on each breath. I can taste Hom and hear the Ipalora perching on the branches of her hair. I can smell the lingering liquid from her pussy on her fingertips. *I want to lick them.*

"What are you doing?" I repeat.

"I was coming for more soup." She bites her bottom lip.

I step up beside her and peer into the deep pot. "Cold?"

"I didn't want to wake you."

"Your logic presumes I was asleep."

"Weren't you?"

"No."

She gives me a curious look as my gaze flits over the controls on this human machine. There are numbers and letters corresponding to settings and temperatures, but I find myself at a rather peculiar loss of how to proceed. "What were you doing?"

"Listening to you." I look at her sideways and lift a brow. "Certain that you would make mischief at some point in the night. I wasn't wrong, it would appear." To convey softness and that she does not need to apologize to me for such a disruption, I clamp my lips shut over my fangs and curve one edge of my mouth up in a...*friendly*, closed-mouth smile.

She looks at me, dumbstruck for a moment and I worry that I have miscalculated until...it happens. With all the magic of a Sistylean sunrise over Hom's vertical jungles. Floating cliffs defying gravity for they are built with their own magnetic cores that work against that of Sistylea's...

The female with terror branded into her heart by countless horrors committed against her by the cowardly, by the desperate and by the weak, tilts her head back and meets my gaze and curls her hands together in a submissive gesture beneath her chin and...she grants me the grace of a small grin that shows just a glimmer of her front teeth. The curves of her cheeks change the shapes of her eyes. Small crescent moons blink up at me and shine bright.

I smile more broadly then and the flash of my teeth makes her tense. It must be the sharpened points…humans do not have these. Hm. I step back, giving her space.

"Sorry," she murmurs, though it seems to be a rather hollow reply.

I nod. "You are forgiven." I turn back to the pot and wave at it in frustration. "I am…unfamiliar with human cooking devices and do not know how to warm the soup for you. You are welcome to it, if you understand this machine."

"A stove?" Her grin splits again and this time, she tries to squash it. She steps forward and her fingers pass dangerously close to mine on the controls…but she doesn't touch me. It is…a pity.

"Yes, a stove."

"You don't know how to use a stove?"

"I do not spend time in human kitchens."

"Did you spend time in Sistylean ones?"

I am…taken aback. The female is *teasing* me. I can see it in the restrained smile she wears and I fight the urge to…to laugh. "No. I don't suppose I know much about kitchens at all."

She turns two dials and presses a button. A clicking sound starts the gas and flames momentarily appear.

The odd desire to explain myself so as not to appear… inadequate before the female presents itself as she steps up onto the stool and begins turning the soup with a larger spoon, this one made of wood. She fishes the smaller metal one out of the pot when it scrapes the sides on her next smooth stroke.

"I do not spend time in kitchens because I do not need to eat."

"You don't?" She is curious.

I am amused. "No. I am an ancient Tretaro. One could say I am a different species altogether from a Heztoichen. My body processes food differently as a result."

"So you don't need blood, either?"

I frown at the hopeful look on her face, knowing I will crush it. "I do." Her face falls. I continue, hoping to restore her confidence in me without even processing how strange it is that this is something I want. "However, blood is…*difficult* for me to imbibe." It hurts me. "I do not…enjoy the experience." I would rather never drink it. "I drink rarely. Perhaps, once every few Earth years. Or after a battle. Blood helps restore me after a wound, but I have not been wounded in over a decade."

"A decade?"

"Yes. Fourteen years, to be precise."

Her hand stills. She looks up at me and I wonder why she is not alarmed as I am alarmed at how close we are standing. I could slip my hand around her lower back and pull her flush against me without pulling her from the top of the stool.

"When you fell from the sky?"

It is my turn to smirk. "Yes. To put it so plainly. When I fell from the sky. I was injured in the fall, as many Heztoichen were." My torso was nearly separated from my lower half in the crash. "It was actually a human family who found me. They offered me the blood of their youngest. A young boy. He must have been younger than ten Earth years. His blood was less tainted by cruel memories and he willingly offered some to me. It was…brave." Exceptionally brave. Also foolish.

"Where is he now?" Candy whispers.

"He lives in Hviya with his family, the region that occupies what was once the southern third of your African continent. I believe they are well-treated and happy." I do not believe it. I know it. I have asked Siandrathil about the boy and his family many times.

"What's it like there?" The soup is forgotten. She hasn't turned her body to face mine fully, preferring to keep her shoulders slightly curved in to her chest, a defensive posture. "In the other regions, I mean?"

Her expression is so…open, her curiosity so guileless. It makes me want to touch her face. She has the face of a female who has never known a lie though I am certain she has heard several. It wounds me to think that she was cut by them every time.

"Moltanithra, Hviya and Hurgada occupy your African continent. They are well managed by the Notare governing them and the humans have accepted their rule, in large part. They are rich in resources. There are pockets, particularly in the East, that resemble Population, but the gangs that patrol the wildlands seem to be fairly well contained. The larger issues concern lack of access to technology, which is being…" Hoarded. Guarded. Destroyed. "looked after by Tanen in Carata. That, one could argue, is the least…" Stable. Survivable. Pleasant. "well-managed region." Only that isn't true. It is well managed…as a barbarian warlord would manage it, one who intends to rid the world of humans.

I frown, thinking about Tanen. He does…contradict some of my opinions of human and Heztoichen kind. How can I consider us the evolved species when spiteful, savage and rage-filled Heztoichen like Tanen exist? I cannot even use his own age to defend him. He is older even than was Notare Elise.

"Even Brianna has had more success than Carata…" I'm about to go into detail about Srentara and Moltanithra when she shakes her head.

"I didn't mean their politics. I meant…what are they *like*?"

"I do not understand the question."

"What color is the sky in…in Hviya?" Her pronunciation is perfect. Hm. So she *can* pronounce Heztoichen words. Did she once mispronounce mine as a small sort of rebellion? The thought makes me alarmingly giddy. And then I recall her question and tip my head to the side.

"The sky?"

"Are there flowers?"

"Flowers."

She lowers her head timidly, then brushes her hair behind her ear — behind both ears — in an odd gesture. "Never mind." She returns to her soup but I...cannot help myself. I reach forward and smooth my hand over hers before taking the spoon from her. *Nothingness. Euphoric jungles where nothing but the sensations of her body exists.*

She bites her lips together and glances up at me and I quickly fetch her a bowl and ladle hot soup into it. I start to lead her back to the dining room but...hesitate. It does not have fond memories for her.

My thoughts flash to the den and the way it had been set up by the twin females. I head there instead and settle her soup on a small table beside a plush arm chair. All of the other chairs have been returned to their disparate parts of the room... I pull out the ottoman and, undignified as I have become, I perch on its edge and watch as she sits before me and takes the soup in hand. She looks at me hesitantly.

I nod. "Eat. Eat while I tell you tales of the seven regions of Earth."

And I do. I tell her of the southern continents. I tell her of the rains in Hivya, which come down thick as pellets, but are still not so heavy as the rains of Carata in what was formerly southern Asia. I tell her of the colors they turn the sky — sometimes orange, sometimes yellow, but always full of light. She asks me if I've ever seen a sky that's blue. I have, I tell her. I've seen skies that are without cloud cover, too, but not for a very long time...

I tell her of the animals that have survived, the pelicans and the parrots, the elephants and the lions. Populations of monkeys have overrun towns in Hivya and Carata. Meanwhile, snow and plains of ice make life difficult for the humans of Srentara. So far north, the change in landscape has made it impossible to harvest. Large greenhouses were built and Morgana, who lived among the ice dunes of Sistylea, smuggled seeds illegally with her when she came through her pod in the sky. She now grows fruits and vegetables of Sistylea there, grains that are as electric blue as a current and taste hearty and divine.

"Do you have any?" She asks me on a yawn. Her soup bowl lies empty before her. I wonder if she even noticed that I got up and refilled her bowl three times. She eats like a maltron for such a little thing.

"I do not. It's been a while since I received a shipment for my own gain. And the humans that have sampled it, haven't been particularly impressed. No, she grows this as a Heztoichen delicacy. Though it serves nicely with soup, I'd imagine."

I grin slowly and look down at her empty bowl. She follows my gaze and a blush creeps over her cheeks. "Good soup."

"It was."

Her fingers curl around her cupped knees and squeeze them. "I didn't eat it all, did I?"

"No," I smirk. "I think it would take three of you to eat all the soup those females made. Or perhaps only two given your…appetite."

She blushes harder. I wonder what I've said this time. But her smile — just a tenuous, little thing trapped between her teeth and her lower lip — still manages to hold. "I'd make you more, but I don't know how."

"That's perfectly alright. As you've seen, I don't either. But you would be welcome to take soup with you. I have no need for it."

"I don't have any way to heat it up."

"Well…if I could entice you to return, I'd be happy to let you use my kitchen."

"Oh no." She shakes her head and there is a tension in my gut that causes it to…to fall. Until she says, "I mean, you don't want me messing around in there." The hopeful look in her eyes, more than her words, causes me to feel a mirrored pleasure.

I rumble deep in my throat and, without opening my mouth, the sound that I produce is very much akin to a lion's purr. Her eyes widen, but I don't feel like answering her questions about this now. It would require a greater explanation, one in which I confess to liking her, for this sound is not common among my people and largely considered a sign of affection.

I have made it only a few times before.

And I have never made it in a situation like this, seated with a female, so very pleased with her.

Hm.

"It would please me greatly to have you *mess around* in my kitchen anytime you like."

She yawns again, but tries to cover it with her hand. She laughs lightly and it sends pins and needles shooting through my thighs. My hand flexes, wanting to capture the sound in my palm and slip it into my pocket. "Did you mean for that to sound so dirty?"

My abdomen clenches. "No."

"I didn't think so." She shakes her head and her smile slowly falls. She searches for me in the dark, gaze never quite settling. She inspects me more boldly than she has before, perhaps emboldened by the darkness. It occurs to humans so rarely that the abilities of other creatures could be more developed than their own. But I find that I...do not mind, her looking. I do not mind it at all.

"I just — " She pauses and coughs lightly into her fist. She reaches for her glass of water, takes a long draught, sets it aside and makes a fluttering, flustered gesture with her hands. I do not understand human hand gestures particularly well, this one even less than most. "I don't have anything to trade if you don't want to fuck."

I do not know if I believed in a soul before this moment, though I've spent many eons pondering it. But I am fully aware of mine as it shrivels and shrinks, becoming a husk of a thing, desiccated and left to rot in a non-existent sun.

I brush off the arms and shoulders of my jacket and its lapels and I bite out careful words, "I think it's quite late enough. You should rest. I will escort you up to your room."

She simply blushes and stands when I do.

"Is that a piano?" She asks, peeking her head into the living room on the second level.

I press my fingertips into her lower back. She does not react at all and I find that I do not like this. It makes me wonder how freely other males touch her. Though I already know the answer to that.

"It is." My voice is clipped, my mood soured.

She hesitates but she doesn't say more and lets me lead her back to the guest room in silence. "Do you want to sleep with me? I mean, in the bed? I know you don't want to have sex with me, but I don't want to steal your bed. You've already given me so much that I can't pay back."

"Soup?" I frown.

She nods.

I sigh in defeat. "No. I do not require sleep. Take your rest."

I linger in the doorway while she looks up at me from the bed. "Lahve?" She yawns again, the word twisted around the sound, making me unsure if she pronounces it correctly this time. Perhaps, I *should* give her something else to call me by...

"Yes?"

"If you aren't going to sleep, what are you going to do?"

Likely sit and listen to you. "I have not...decided yet."

"You could do it in here, if you wanted."

"I would not wish to disturb you."

"You wouldn't. It wouldn't. I sleep deep. I mean, I don't, really, but I know I'd sleep better if you were in the room. Not that you have to stay." She swallows hard and touches the collar on her neck. "I'm sorry." She blinks very quickly and shakes her head, the scent of her fear returning, sharp and ripe.

I stand and unbutton my suit jacket.

"I'm really sorry."

My vest.

"I don't know what's gotten into me."

I remove them, along with my coat and swordstick.

"I don't normally ask for things like this."

I unbutton my shirt.

"Or any things."

My pants.

"I…"

I pull my belt free.

She licks her lips. "I'm sorry."

"I will join you this once."

Her blush has returned in full force and, when I remove my shoes, socks and pants — all of my clothing — I wonder why she stares so hard. "Is my body not to your liking or is there another reason you behave as if you've never seen a male bare before? I know you have."

She blushes so feverishly, I'd find it alarming had I not seen such displays from other humans before. "I…" She shakes her head and does not say more.

"Hm." I slip into a pair of soft cotton pajama pants. They are light blue and striped. Odd that humans would choose to sleep thus, but I don't question it now as it seems to make the female more comfortable.

"I would prefer it if you would slide to the other side of the bed."

"Oh sure. Of course." She quickly scoots and I slide beneath the covers where she once laid, her warmth an imprint on my bare back as I sink into the sheets. "Is that the side you normally sleep on, when you do?"

"No. I would usually sleep on the side where you are now."

She waits and I can feel her struggling to voice her next question. "Then…you wanted me on this side…because…" She merely lets her voice trail off, lacking the confidence to ask me directly what it is she wishes to ask.

"You want to know why?"

I turn to look at her. Her face, so close to mine, is simply magnificent. The smooth, rounded curve of her cheek. So much bright hair tangling with my much darker locs. She nods and pulls the blankets up beneath her chin, but does not break my gaze.

"I wished to be closest to the door, just in case."

She makes a soft sound, a startling sound — it is, not quite a moan, not quite a whimper, not quite a gasp. She seems just as surprised as I do that this sound came out of her and immediately, she rolls fully onto her back and closes her eyes. "Thank you, Lahve." So she *can* pronounce it better than she once did. Almost perfectly…but not quite.

"It is normal."

"No, it really isn't."

I tense at the feeling of her fingers on the outside of my wrist. She jerks them away too quickly and a similarly awkward grunt escapes my mouth. One of pleasure. "You need not fear me. I will not harm you."

"I know."

"You do?" I glance over at her, aware of her in ways I wish I could control because it feels so wild.

"If you wanted to hurt me, you would have already. It would be easy for you," she sighs and settles into the sheets, turning back to face me as her breathing deepens and the creases smooth out above her eyes. She looks frighteningly young with her hands folded in prayer beneath her cheek and, when she sprawls out some time later and flings one arm above her head and shoves the blankets off of her chest, giving me a clear view of her pert breasts, she looks far too tempting.

I close my eyes, but I am awake the entire night regardless.

Chapter Eight

"Lahve?"

Judging by her tone and the weight of the stares of everyone in the room, I am beginning to believe that I have missed something. I trace back the conversation in my mind, but find that I departed from it rather early. Instead, I have spent much of the council meeting replaying the contents of my week. After our first meeting, Candy came to join me three additional nights.

Three nights of sleeping beside her. Three nights of telling her tales of the other regions of the world, and of this one and of Sistylea as it existed before. Three nights of playing the piano for her, to her endless delight. Three nights suppressing base instincts to grab and hold and squeeze. Three nights of her hair tickling my outer arm, her body tucked into a tight ball, forehead and fists wedged beneath her chin, pressed against my side…her silky nightgown riding up, me pulling it down, the backs of my knuckles grazing her pert breast accidentally as I maneuver her…

And then the last two nights…nothing.

She did not come. She gave me no explanation as to why she didn't, either. I haven't seen her and I haven't been willing to…debase myself yet and return to the ceramics shop to find her. The females there did not like me asking the first time for Candy's company, I doubt they'd like it again. *What does it matter what they think?* I'm not sure…but it does matter regardless…

"Yes, Notare."

Notare Abel's face scrunches up. She has bags below her eyes. I wonder if she slept as poorly as I did last night without Candy by my side. "Yes, you think it's a good idea or yes as in yes, you're present here today, but you really have no idea what we're talking about?"

"Lahve, my Sistana is tired. Forgive her outburst," Notare Kane grits, his arms crossed snugly over his tee shirt. I stare at it a moment too long and wonder if perhaps, he dresses himself in such a way because it…*appeals* to his Sistana. Oh my. What a thought…

"She is not wrong." I offer her a conciliatory bow. "It was the latter, unfortunately, Notare. You will need to repeat your proposition should you want my input on the matter. If not, I am happy to defer to your judgement and proceed."

The room falls silent. It does not bother me.

Too much.

Notare Abel starts again from behind her desk, belly proud, hands splayed across the maps in front of her, one in particular. "Have you heard from the scouts you sent out to canvas the suitable cities for the first outpost?"

"Yes. One team has already sent a scout to report back that the small town of…Chattanooga is a viable option for the outpost. The town is small and deserted. My guard reports no gang sightings, though there were several markers suggesting that gangs had at one point been through." I produce a series of sketches from my inside coat pocket and pass them to the Notare who merely stare at the images blankly.

"Do you know what these mean?"

"I do not, though this one looks the same as the star."

"The Five Point Gang, yes," I add. "Though it would appear to have been scratched out."

Notare Abel frowns at the pages. "Diego, can you take a look?" Notare Abel looks up but Diego is absent.

The blonde human steps forward, a look of concern on her face. "Diego walked me over here, then said you wanted him at the perimeter."

"I did?"

"Pregnancy brain?" Mikael drolls affectionately.

The way he covets his brother's Sistana is sickening, particularly after his failure. Were we on Sistylea, I would have insisted by now on taking his head for my collection. Notare Kane smirks, ignoring his brother's outburst as well as his over-friendly stare. Still, he slides his hand beneath Notare Abel's hair and gives her a squeeze that makes her moan audibly, "God that feels good," she mutters.

Mikael looks out of the window as Notare Kane steps forward and kisses her temple. "Abel gave Diego no such order. She's been with me all day."

"Whatever," Abel tuts, "I'll show the sketches to Diego later. What were these signs found on?"

"Miro?" I gesture toward the desk.

A younger member of my guard, not even as old as Notare Kane though older than his brother, steps forward. He has white skin tanned by the sun, dark brown hair, a face full of freckles, narrow eyes and a severe jawline, which contrasts to his otherwise boyish features and gives him a lethal air overall. He has been with me for over a century and is one of the beings I trust most on this world, more than the Notare. Much more.

He gestures toward one symbol — a square with a triangle over it. "This was painted above the doorway of a large brick house in the center of town. The three guards and the two humans I left behind have taken this for their residence. It is relatively well stocked for an abandoned building."

"Wait wait wait wait wait. What two humans?"

"The two that were a few miles away, on their way to Brianna."

"You found them?" Her glee radiates with all the shine of her Tare when Miro says, "Yes, we did, Notare. We brought food enough to last the humans several weeks and offered them the option of either remaining put and fetching them on the return journey or joining us and making it to the new outpost."

I add, "You were slowed by their progress, but my guard determined that the benefit of their knowledge of Population outweighed any delays they'd cause. Is that correct, Miro?"

"Yes, Lahve."

"Amazing! I mean thank you! That's brilliant. What are they like?"

Miro considers, expending the necessary time to do so thoughtfully. Returning his attention to the Notare, he says, "Two males, battle-hardened and reserved. Fearful, but cooperative, they navigated us to a safe path across the river. The town we found is located along it. One of the males has taken a liking to Sebine, I believe."

"Really?" Notare Abel's smile lights up the room. I do not understand it, or my own scout's statement and its relevance to the conversation at hand.

I cut in, meaning to put an end to it. I've experienced too much confusion these last days. Confusion and irritation. *Why did she not come back? Did I…say something to displease her? Perhaps I should have offered to pay her again. I have not paid her since that first union.* And then it hits me — I gave her three bottles. Perhaps, she took one bottle per payment per meeting…*she could have asked for more, though.* My voice comes out more acerbic than intended. I do not like that theory in the slightest.

"They await my command, Notare. Should I advise them to remain put and go about a preliminary canvas of the area, or should I recall them until a time at which we are prepared to return to the potential new outpost in force?"

"No, no. Advise them to stay there. We're coming."

Kane grunts, "*We* are not doing anything. If Diego were here, I'd tell him to get a force together. Either him or Constanzia can lead it."

Shock. It spills out of my throat in the form of words, "You do not wish to have a Heztoichen lead this effort?"

Notare Kane gives me a longer look. His eyes crinkle at the corners. He nods, understanding my surprise and still he says, "We've seen more success from the mixed groups led by humans. They know the terrain better, the gangs, the markings and, more importantly, they know when humans need to rest. If we have a mixed group led by a Heztoichen, they drive our humans into the ground and it creates a more dangerous situation for all of us."

I refuse to allow my displeasure to be known and nod. It is not my place to interfere with the will of a Notare. Were it to me, however, I'd refrain from allowing the humans to do anything but simple labor, given their tendency to make a mess of everything. Good thing, for their sakes, it is not.

"How quickly can you amass a force and supplies? Building materials, trucks to carry them, gasoline to fill your vehicles."

"We can be ready in, I don't know, three days?"

"Try three weeks, if that," Pia says. She steps away from the wall she'd been leaning against. "Supplies are low. We used most of the steel we had for the walls of Brianna which means we'll have to scavenge both wood and-or metal from the houses and buildings we pass on the way to the outpost."

Before discussion can break out in earnest, my lower vocal range strikes silence. I say, "Then it would seem to me that the group would benefit from some small measure of reinforcement. Miro will take another four members of my guard along with supplies enough for them and the humans until your…back up arrives."

"Do you have enough guards to spare?"

"I will send my personal guard, keeping only Teera here."

"Are you sure?"

"I see no need for them here." And they invade my privacy. I do not want them listening in to my conversations with Candy. "Your humans pose me no threat. I can do with a few less guards on hand."

"That would be great, thanks Lahve." Notare Abel smiles at me and I tip my head towards her.

"It is what I am here for." I bow more deeply. "Miro, I will equip with a radio. I will wait for scouts from the other scavenging parties to return and, when they do, they may form Heztoichen members of the party intended for the outpost, should they arrive in time."

It is nerve-wracking, having access to only six functional radios. Unfortunately, the batteries are being embargoed by Carata, who refuses to send any supplies to a human or those who hold allegiance with her. I clench my teeth, *hating* that he uses the term *allegiance* with me. He knows I am bound to the will of the Tare. Tanen will need to be dealt with another time.

Notare Abel agrees and, after equipping Miro and escorting him to Brianna's gates, I finally take more of this… *time* and I indulge in it. I dismiss my guard, for their eyes on me now would lead to questions and I refuse to have any more of that, and I think of the human female. I think of her with a nagging intensity that has me moving down the streets of Starlight to seek her out. I refrain…with difficulty and eventually make it back to my own manor.

Stepping inside, I wonder if it would be too…forward of me to ask the twin humans to make more of that soup and for me to take it to her to her residence. And then I remember that I don't know where she resides. Also, since the twins were…displeased with my treatment of them, only Lima returns and she cannot come every night. She prepares food for the alternating nights she is not able to come, like tonight. It is eerily quiet in my home without anyone in it.

Quiet, but not silent.

Click.

The slightest sound of a weapon being engaged pulls my attention to the right. The blast fires from the tip of the gun but even a bullet I can outmaneuver…and my adversary seems to have known this. The bullets shatter upon release from the tip of the sawed off shotgun and shrapnel tears across my chest, embedding in it in a dozen — a hundred — perhaps a *thousand* — different places.

Irritation.

Severe irritation.

It builds within me and I open my mouth, recalling the years when I fought in the Sistylean wars. Over two thousand years ago, I was green as far as a Tretaro is concerned. Young, I believed myself impenetrable. I did not realize it was possible for a species to be even more formidable than our own. When we were invaded by a neighboring planet, my kind was called on to fight when we so seldom are. I thought myself invincible. I was nearly torn apart. We…we were nearly torn apart.

We lost over eighty percent of our kind in that battle. We struggled afterward to rebuild. The chief elder of the Tretaro back on Sistylea once told me that it would be pride that dooms us. He also said that we were nothing without our pride. Our doom was inevitable.

I feel the sting of that failure ride over me as aggressively as his scent. Singularly focused on the scents of the female curling throughout the house like smoke, I had not even registered him. Weak. *She is a weak thing and she will render me weak just like her.* The thought triggers some small measure of sadness. *She is not weak. She is defenseless. And if I cannot even defend against one human male, then I do not deserve her…*

Embarrassed is how I feel, more than pained. Pain is…a human sensation. I feel nothing of the like. I feel every inch of my rage. I advance on the male with the pale brown skin riddled with scars and ice eyes riddled with determination. Yet…I am caught off guard.

I continue making my way towards him, a battle cry ripping out of my throat loud enough to rattle the painting hanging beside the front door and send it toppling to the floor, but instead of attempting to reload his weapon or run as any human *should* in the face of my rage, he moves towards *me*. He comes at me with his hands outstretched and I shame myself yet a second time.

It has been so long since I have been touched by anyone but the female because things like honor and rank and respect exist on Sistylea where here, they have been replaced by determination and desperation and a certain…wile. He comes at me with his hands outstretched. I bat him off. A quick sweep of my hand sends him crashing into the banister. Beneath his bodyweight, three posts shatter. I believe his head may have sunk into the dry wall. He groans in a pain of his own, but I am not able to focus on it. I drop to one knee, momentarily paralyzed.

I am struck down by what I felt when my bare hand came in contact with his skin. Terror and hopelessness and a terrible, gut-wrenching pain fired at me in one concentrated dose, more lethal than any gun or blade. *He knows my abilities. He has used his own agony against me.*

I look up at the male lying back on the steps as I am choked by sensations, more than visions, of my body being broken again and again, the sickness of hunger, of being burned and cut, the desperation of drinking filthy water, the way it rots from the inside, but more than that I see a male's face — one that looks distinctly like Kane but I know is a human, is the feared Jack, a male who died — and I feel a devotion and a love of this male that leads me to allow him in, allow him to cut me open from the inside like an inventor fiddling with the wires of his creation.

I press *harder* than I should have to in order to cut my conscious mind from the thoughts Diego assaulted me with. No Heztoichen has ever done anything like this. None of them ever *could*.

No Heztoichen has ever lived through what he has.

We are both breathing hard, chests straining as we are locked in battle even though neither of us has moved at all. I look up at him, intent to murder, but he clutches the back of his head and hisses in pain as he spits out words that both damn me and keep him alive. "If you-you-you thhhhhhh-ink that was b-b-b-b-bad, then you shhhhhould see what the ins-inside of C-Candy's mmmmmind looks like."

Chapter Nine

"T his is unacceptable." Notare Kane punches his
hands back through his hair and stands up from
where he'd been seated behind Notare Abel's
desk. "Diego, what the fuck were you thinking?"

He shrugs, the insolent welp.

"I want him exiled. I was attacked in my own home."
Using weapons I could not defend against.

I can see it in his eyes, his irreverence. *He will do it again.*

"No…you can't exile Diego. Please."

My spine stiffens as the door slams open and a soft voice
fills the space. The scent of clay is stronger today than it was
last I saw her. She also smells more strongly of sweat and I
wonder if she has not bathed since I last saw her. I frown.

"What is she doing here?" I glare at the female — Pia —
shutting the door behind her. She's breathing hard, cheeks
flushed, as if she's run here. In defense of her mate. They
both stand in defense of him. The thought grates.

"I thought it only fair that we include Candy in this
conversation since, you know, it's about her," Pia says, just as
irreverent as Diego.

"That was not your call to make." Notare Kane narrows
his eyes.

She gives him a haughty look. "Oh? Because as far as I'm aware we're in Brianna and you are not Notare here. This isn't *your* call to make. But I'd be happy to go and wake Abel up from her nap or…do you not want me to do that?"

Notare Kane has the indecency to clench his jaw. His Tare pulses brighter and he scratches his neck. He looks down, admitting defeat in this, all because of a human female. His Sistana. His mate.

And her nap.

"This is not to be borne," I hiss. "The male assaulted me in my own private residence. This is against every tenet that Notare Abel set forth for the governance of her own territory. Exile is a more acceptable punishment than the alternative."

"What's the alternative?" Candy whispers, her hands clenched around her arms, making her look so small and powerless, so unlike the female who has shown up at my home the past three nights and prodded me for questions about my life. Who *asked me* to play the piano for her. Who dressed up in provocative clothing and attempted to…seduce me — to whore herself to me for alcohol. My hand flexes towards my swordstick.

I reach up and touch my collar and speak slowly. "Death." The realization that I want this scarred male dead comes upon me rapidly and with growing intensity as I stare at Candy and watch her face collapse on itself, watch red come to stain all available parts of her skin…watch her cry. "Death is penance many have paid for lesser infractions on Sistylea."

"We aren't on Sistylea," Pia shouts, "and you'll kill Diego over my dead body."

"That can be arranged," I sneer.

Diego, who'd had a bored look on his face until now, thrusts forward away from the wall. He comes at me and I withdraw my sword. "Touch me again with those filthy hands, I'll take them both, throw you into Population and follow you long enough that I may see you starve."

"Hey!" Pia.

"D-d-don't fuck-fuckin' lllllook at either of 'em ag-ag-again or I *will* ff-f-fffff-ff-fuckin' k-kill you."

Notare Kane attempts to speak, but I speak over him, my own chest blazing with heat and unspent aggression. When was the last time I just…let go? Properly dueled with another adversary? There *was* no time. Because up to now, I have met no equal.

"Do you claim ownership over these females? Is that what this is all about? Have I infringed on your harem? As far as I am aware, a female may say yes to any male she sees fit to say yes to and Candy has said yes to me…"

Diego's face twists into a snarl that manages to appear particularly menacing given the cruel contortions of his facial scars. My toes curl, remembering sensations that do not belong to me — how he got them — and my blade glitters between us as it bobs. His gaze moves lazily over the sharpened point, unconcerned. He looks at Candy standing closer to the door, her face in her hands, shaking while Pia attempts to comfort her.

My heart squeezes terribly but I refuse to back down on a cause of a human's tears. *Especially* if he claims her. Especially if she cries over him.

"You think you're special?" He says this sentence flawlessly and it comes as another shock, one that delays the motion of my hand. "Sh-sh-sh-she sssssssssa-ays yessssssss-yes to ev-ev-every-on-on-one! Wh-wh-when L-Leif told-told the g-guys she had a tight eas-easy pussy, it-it was a fffff-fuckin' frenzy. You th-think you're the f-f-f-first g-guy I've fffffucked up to g-g-g-get off her b-b-back? She's n-n-n-n…" He huffs, his face turning red everywhere but on the scars. Those remain a gleaming, malicious silver. "Sh-she's nnnnnineteen y-years old. Fuck!" He rubs his head, turns in a circle, paces to the wall and kicks it.

I feel…I don't really know how I feel. "She is…not your female?"

"*I'm* his female, or whatever," Pia says. "Candy's like a little sister to Diego. She's family to us." She tries to touch the female on the shoulder, but Candy winces away. She has her palms over her eyes and stumbles forward blindly, landing directly before me, even though Diego and Pia both attempt to stop her.

They don't touch her, though.

No. She does not like to be touched. But she let *me* touch her. Just a brush of my fingers over her wrists, a gentle press of my hand to her lower back, a soft trace of her cheek.

Candy stops directly in front of my feet, her toes pressing up against my toes. She reaches up and places her right hand directly over my heart where I bore the wounds of Diego's attack before they instantly healed over. Now, there is no evidence of his assault against me, even though I am very certain he will wear bruises on his arms and the back of his head for days to come.

"If you let him go, you can drink from me," she says and her voice is a terrible whisper. She sounds like the most tender flower, dragged over jagged embers, like a wound's fresh stitching pulled open.

"Jesus-J-J-Jesus Christ."

"Candy…"

"There won't be any bartering like this, Candy," Notare Kane says severely. "And Lahve, if you even think of accepting such an offer, I will have *you* exiled from this region and from the Diera."

I wish I had the strength to look away from her face, slaughter Notare Kane, rip the heart out of the human female and the throat out of the one with scars…but I do not. My gaze has dropped to the collar of her turtleneck, seeking the thud of her blood and the rich highways it travels through her throat. They call to me. I should not want to drink from her there, a place where I would only drink from a mate, but I do. It is because I long for closeness, not because I long for her…

But, since I've known her in this fleeting thing these humans call time, has she not become synonymous with it? Candy and closeness? They are one in the same because I have never had closeness with anyone else and I…enjoy the closeness we share together. *But she shares that closeness with everyone who will pay for it.*

No biting.

The words replay themselves once, twice, a third time, causing my mind to snag. I cannot seem to push past them as dangerous realizations cloud my desire to murder. Her high turtlenecks, her hideous clothes that cover the skin, even the particularly tailored outfit Tasha created for her…

Hm.

I reach a hand forward. Her tears have dried, but her face is still red and swollen. I brush her hair over her shoulder with one finger and, like the good little submissive that she is, she closes her eyes and tips her head to the side, exposing the soft line of her throat to me.

My finger trails down, down, over her ear, over the three small freckles on the curve of her jaw and the soft baby hairs that grow on her neck. Nineteen Earth years. So few lifetimes. Not even a complete one. She is the youngest being I have *ever* interacted with and I know I should feel shame in touching her and desiring her, but I don't.

Not in the slightest.

Reservations? I have none. None whatsoever.

She was made for me.

The thought comes and passes but as it sweeps me, it settles and sticks. I can touch her. Sistylea is a fickle creature. First, giving Tare to a human and now this?

Now that that's settled, the odd and distant urge to smile revisits me. I repress it, sensing it would be inappropriate here. Equally, I repress the urge to claim her publicly, knowing that it would not follow logic after the speech I gave Diego and yet…oh? What's this?

My finger stops at the collar of her high turtleneck sweater, but I can feel the hard ridge of something else beneath. A shaky breath squeezes out of Candy's throat. Her eyes flutter beneath closed lids. She clenches her fist. She does not stop me.

"You told me once that saying yes is easier," I whisper, my finger finding that hard ridge and pushing down...down until I reveal more of her neck.

My insides hollow and plummet. Explosions go off in my mind. Diego is so easily forgotten, his female, his transgressions, his crimes. The focus of three thousand years zeroes in on the scars slicing up the side of Candy's throat. Thick and jagged, the marks wrap entirely around her neck, touching even the column of her throat, and are in varying degrees of healing but there is no mistaking — they are *healed,* which is the most wretched thing about them. Were they healing or fresh, I could be rid of them. I could free her.

I push the collar of her shirt down until I come to a point where I can gently push it down no further. There, at the curve of her neck, which should be clean and bare and ready for my cut, which would be small and easily healed so as not to hurt her...never to hurt her...is one solid mass of scarred, overlapping flesh. It's hideous. Brown and red, streaked through with silver and pink.

I release her immediately and touch her cheek. "Where is the one who did this to you?"

Her eyes open slowly, too slowly. How can it be that she has so much time for these things when she should be seeking vengeance?

She meets my gaze and fear travels through her. I can see it in her eyes, heedless of my rheach. I understand the reason for it — I am not myself and have lost control over my expression — but I cannot seem to get it in check. She backs away from me and both of my hands flex. She stumbles into the center of the room when I follow, until she bumps against the seat in front of Notare Abel's desk. Gingerly, she perches on it.

"It's too gross to drink out of, isn't it? You can try my wrists." She yanks up on her sleeves and reveals more scars. They look like satin ribbons in red and silver and pink lacing over her pale skin, brutally holding muscle and bone together. "They aren't much better. I'm sorry. My thighs aren't as bad, I promise. Just please don't hurt Diego."

I had never understood the human concept of a heartbreak. A heart can be cut and burned, sliced and stitched together but it cannot be broken. But I understand now. *I understand now...*

My desire is to leave this room, find my guard — Kane's guard, Abel's guard, every Heztoichen in this entire region — and have them come at me at once. I need *release* before the calm and grueling task will begin of opening the full extent of my rheach until I find any male that has touched, looked at, dreamt or thought of her wrong. I will hang them by their insides until the life leaves their eyes or they choke on their own blood. Candy would have the option of carving out their eyes if she would like to keep them. It was a tradition of my people once long before civilization truly began and we still fed off of the energies of the air and our basest instincts. *Candy, my mate would wear the eyes of my kills around her neck as a necklace...*

But for now, I turn over Diego's words, I turn over the sight of her scars, her pain, and the hurt my kind has delivered her and I recognize that she is still in pain and I have caused much of it.

I will do anything to alleviate it. Anything.

And I understand, with this vow, the strange...affections Notare Abel's people and my own have afforded this fractured human with the ribbons on her wrists and the scars in her eyes. She can do whatever she wants. She can have whatever she wants.

I just...want to be the one to give it to her.

Notare Kane and Diego and Pia are utterly still and totally silent.

I approach her jerkily and drop down to one knee at her feet. Carefully — because my hands are flexing and straining all on their own and the rage in my breast needs an outlet and soon — I stroke the back of her hand.

She gasps and shoves her sleeve back down, but I halt her progress. My fingers dance slowly over her palm. Clay makes her hands dry. It burrows in the lines crossing over her palm. Life lines. Because she is alive despite the scars she has borne. I lean into her rich, earth-scented hand and inhale deeply. My tongue slips between my teeth to stroke her, but I taste only clay, salt and heat. No pain. No memories.

I move up her wrist, dragging my lips over her scars, tasting them, seeking…something. I want to know who gave her this mark — just this one — but I read nothing. I kiss her and it is the first time I have ever kissed a female. The Syth virgins did not tempt me in the slightest. I had wanted them to and I did try, but had I known then that I was merely waiting to find the female covered in scars, I would have spared myself the pain and the disappointment.

"I am not disappointed," I whisper. I look up into her eyes, wishing we were alone, but I hold her gaze regardless as I drop another kiss to the inside of her wrist. I wonder if she can even feel it through the scar tissue. It pains me that this is the first kiss I've ever given a female in three thousand years and she might not.

"D-d-don't even f-f-fucking…" Diego says.

My rage holds thin. I hold up a hand to quiet him, but I do not look away from Candy's face. Her brown eyes glitter and glow. Her enflamed lips look soft and pliant. She licks them and my gut clenches and I want to do something for her. Something profound. Something that will help unwind the wounds she wears that I should have, but did not know about til now.

"Blood has always been exchanged by mates on Sistylea, but only out of love and if not that, then at least respect. It is a treasured, cherished gift, not to be used recklessly. Certainly, never like this."

"I know it looks bad…"

"Does it pain you?"

She winces and I have my answer, even when she shakes her head. She pulls her arms away from me and scratches her wrist, the one I did not lavish with attention, though I mean to. "Just itches."

"I will make a cream for you."

"No, please don't." She shakes her head feverishly, red curls sticking to her lips as she does. "I already owe you so much."

Anger…

No.

A heart that is broken.

I clear my throat and retract my hands. I look at my claws for a long moment before looking back up. "Do you remember me telling you about the hanging jungles of Hom?"

She nods, mute.

I offer her a smile and notice that she tenses at the sight of my sharpened teeth and I feel…ruination at the thought of bringing her this discomfort and why she holds onto it. *How many fangs made those scars? How many Heztoichen stole from her what should have been given with trust and taken with honor?*

"Ipalora is a type of bird from my home. Its wings are the color of your hair. To pluck all of its feathers does not damage its ability to fly. Cruel hunters have tried, but the Ipalora merely rises and grows its feathers anew. The second set of feathers is stronger than the first."

Candy's eyes are rimmed in red. It makes my heart bleed when she shakes her head and touches her lips with her long elegant fingers and tears spill down her soft cheeks. "But what about after the third or the fourth or the four hundredth time?" A sob bellows out of her that she manages to catch. She glances to the side and tries to curl her shoulders in on herself. She tries to hide.

I rise without thinking and crush her to me, my hands pressing between her shoulder blades and against her lower back as I bring her against my. chest. "They grow stronger each time. They need their feathers to reach Hom. They could not go home without them."

She shudders against me, but fights against her tears. I can feel all the muscles in her body straining and I squeeze, squeeze her to me, squeeze to let her know that she's safe. I have never…comforted, but I know what it looks like and when, with slow, syrupy movements, Candy untangles her arms from the protection of her chest and wraps them around me, I know I've comforted with some small measure of success.

I look up and Kane is staring at me, mouth ajar. Pia has tears in her eyes. Diego's expression is no less suspicious.

"Leave us," I order quietly.

Pia is first to move. Kane follows, running his hands through his hair over and over again. A heavy breath puffs his cheeks. Diego is last to leave and only when Pia tugs him physically through the doorway. Candy weeps painfully, without truly letting herself go…she holds herself together until it feels like she could burst apart at the seams.

There are no docile platitudes I could give her now that would help, of that I am sure, so I do the only thing I can for her. I rattle low in my throat until the sound resembles a rumbling purr. She jolts at first, and then squeezes my jacket harder. Her knees bend and I quickly sit in the armchair and arrange her on my lap, my fingers digging into her hips to pull her close. She allows me to do so, but her fingers twitch as she retracts them from my jacket.

"You are welcome to touch me," I offer, only to become immediately aware of how obscene that sounds. I correct, "You do not need to fear touching me. You do not need to fear me. And should you like me to release you, you have only to ask."

"I don't want you to let go." She speaks against my neck, her lips brushing over my collar, making me wish I had chosen to wear a human-style tee shirt so that I could feel her better against my skin. Hm. Perhaps there is utility in Kane's clothing... "Is it because I can touch you?"

"What?"

"I heard from...some of the others that I'm not supposed to be able to touch you, but you let me. Are you nice to me because you can touch me?"

Shock. I do not...enjoy it. "You would do best to keep that information to yourself. The only ones who know of your unique abilities are myself, the Notare and I suspect now, Diego and Pia."

"Oh."

"And to answer your question, perhaps once, but not anymore."

"Is it because you pity me?" She pulls back, her chin jutting out stubbornly.

My cheek twitches. "No. I do not pity the Ipalora, nor do I want from it except to bask in its presence. Because without it, the jungles of Hom would cease to be so magnificent."

Tears well again in her eyes and she wipes them away roughly, too roughly for her soft skin. Then again...she is not so soft as I once thought. How *wrong* I have been. How shamefully wrong. *And if I have could have been so wrong about this, in what other ways have I presupposed inaccuracies in this new lawless place?*

I catch her wrist when she goes to wipe her tears again and replace her touch with mine, ensuring it is soft. She cringes away from me — away from me, or my claws? — but only slightly, keeping her gaze trained on my hands. *How many have cut you with claws such as these?* I want to know, but do not ask.

I clear my throat. This time, I actually need to. "Why did you not come these past nights? Is it because I have not paid for the pleasure?"

She winces as if I have struck her and looks down at her lap or perhaps my chest. Very carefully, tentatively, she reaches out and places her palm on my stomach. It is clenched so very firmly beneath her touch while I batter back any and all feelings of lust that attempt to surface.

"No."

"Were you...with another male?"

"No! No, no I wasn't. I was embarrassed."

"Embarrassed?" Confusion is not enough to drown my relief. It pours through me like a raging river through a canyon.

She focuses hard on her fingers which move up and down the buttons of my shirt, threatening to unravel me. "I didn't have a chance to shower."

"Candy," I admonish. I cup her face between my hands and gently coax her into meeting my gaze. "I like your stink."

She barks out a laugh that's wet and wonderful. It leaves me dazed. "That doesn't make me feel better."

I smile in response, fully, and her pupils contract in the warm brown wells of her eyes and I decide something definitely then. I will need to see Tasha immediately. I close my lips over my teeth and she returns her gaze to my bright orange Tretaro eyes. "You may use my shower to bathe anytime you like. You may use my home, my bed, my kitchen, my food..." Me. "Anything I possess anytime you should need it for *free*. I don't want to trade with you anymore."

I wince, not having meant to say that out loud because I don't mean it. I don't *want* to trade with her anymore, but I will if that is the only way she will see me. "I don't want to trade with you anymore, either," she whispers.

I choke, unable to breathe. I stand, quickly pushing her off of my lap and placing some distance between us. "I don't want you to trade with any other males, either. Should you have need of anything, you already know you can come to me." I hold, tense, worried…

She worries her lower lip between her teeth and nods jerkily, her eyes growing slightly distant. "I don't want to trade with any other males, either."

Hm. I don't know why that phrasing seems…odd. I push past it. She has agreed. I do not want her to renege should I push her too hard. "Good." I clear my throat, finding it full of hair and needles. "Yes, very good." Candy barks out another small laugh that burns me, searing me with pleasure. "Shall we recall the others and deliver Diego the news?"

"What news?"

"That he will not die today?"

Candy smiles and sniffles and when she grins and sniffles like this, I am alarmed by how desperately I want to bite her bond her marry her…*wait. What?* "Really?"

Feeling uncharacteristically flushed, I take a step away from her. She closes the distance. I take another step. "I have…reconsidered."

"Is it because of the crying?" She smiles slightly, seductively. I wonder if she even knows what she's doing…or if she knows *exactly* what she's doing. She has had to use sex in the past as a shield and I am a weapon. I will need to be… careful with her.

"No." I take another step back. "It is because of the feathers you've lost." Her eyes glaze and get that terrible sheen that precedes crying. "Don't cry or you'll force me to abandon my plans of homicide and stay here and comfort you."

"Hom…homicide?"

I nod.

"But you said Diego wasn't going to be hurt?"

"And I meant it."

"Then…homicide who?"

"Anyone who has touched you."

She shakes her head and stares at the floor. "Please don't hurt anyone because of me. I'm not any different from any of the girls in Brianna. Or the boys. I'm not an Ipalora. I'm not magnificent…"

"Have you seen an Ipalora?"

She pauses, shakes her head.

I invade her space because her self-depreciating candor makes me want to pull out all my hair and I…rather like my hair. Beneath the speed at which I arrived before her, she staggers half a step back. I catch her upper arm. "Then who are you to judge its magnificence as it compares to yours? Now come. Let us recall the others before Diego interrupts us anyway. I can hear him breathing like a wolf at the door."

I start to turn from her, but she grabs my lapel and pulls. Curiosity spins me back to face her and, when she tilts her face towards mine I fail to understand…everything. The world and how it spins in this strange galaxy. The pain and humiliation of being opened by a Heztoichen for her blood. The scent of the jungles. The only aroma there is comes from her lips, a scent that is so distinctly her own. She rises up onto her tip toes, slips her hand around the back of my head, tangling her fingers in my locs, and presses her mouth to mine.

I free fall into the abyss.

Time and its weary metronome cease to hold any meaning against her warmth. So…so *fucking* soft. I have felt fabrics only whose softness can rival hers sold in distant, exotic markets and yet, they did not contain the fire of her touch as she presses her lips against mine…cups my jaw with her soft palm, tugs gently on the locs of my hair.

The sensation radiating through my scalp is unfathomable bliss. I step forward, losing control in an effort to deepen the sensation. She bumps into the chair, but I push her around it, staggering and stumbling until she can stumble no further, then I push her half onto the desk, maps and papers rustling and crinkling and tearing beneath her as I hunt for the unknown. I open my lips and pant against her mouth. She opens and her tongue peeks out between her teeth and slides over my bottom lip.

A groan bellows out of me. My toes curl into my hard-soled shoes. My hand flexes around the small of her back and yanks her hips against my hips where my erection attempts to squeeze its way past the barrier of my belt. I rub against her and, even though she is so many lifetimes younger than I, I feel like a child.

Her tongue spears my mouth, sweeping it like it is a thing to be owned. If it is, I am more than ready to relinquish the right to it. I attempt to push past her tongue and enter her mouth, wanting to taste, but as I maneuver, I do so clumsily and her tongue scrapes against my teeth. She jerks back and I jerk back simultaneously.

Candy drops back onto her hands and blinks. I stand across the room by the door, ready to invite Diego inside to shoot me again — not with his gun, but with his memories — because reliving that pain might be the only thing to stop me from falling into a cannibalistic rut over the female whose body is splayed far, far too openly for her to be looking at me in such a way.

I don't want *anyone* seeing her like this. A sudden primal rage floods me and when a heavy knock lands on the door, my foot juts out to block it. I count to six, turn my back on Candy once she's climbed down from the desk and turned around to face it. I am pleased to no end by the way she smooths down her rumpled garments and flushes high in her cheeks, looking slightly dazed, just slightly affected by me. But I don't want them to see that either.

I wrench the door open only as wide as my shoulders.

Diego is first to face me. He has the butt of his gun ready to slam into my face. I catch it a split second before Kane catches the gun by the barrel. I allow Kane to take the weapon from us both. "You're fucking *asking* for exile here, man," he grumbles.

I open the door a little wider and step away from it, moving closer to…my girl. Yes. My girl. She kissed me, so she is *mine*. Is that not how this works? I haven't anyone to ask and, even if I did, wouldn't care to hear a contrary answer.

"On the contrary. Diego will be quite useful for me."

"In wh-wh-what?" He sneers, slipping past me into the room. His gaze moves over Candy, as if checking for wounds.

"In finding the Heztoichen who have harmed Candy and torturing them."

Diego blinks, as if surprised. I do not see why he would be. "Sh-sh-she's just a b-b-b-b-lood b-b-bag and a wh-wh-wore to you people. What d-do you c-care?"

I grab him by the throat, wrapping my fist in his tee shirt to dampen the sting of his memories and use every ounce of my gift to lock down and restrain the rest. I lift him off of his feet, let him dangle, surprised when Pia does not come to his defense.

Low enough for him to hear and him alone, I snarl, "Whatever she may be to me, she is *mine*."

I toss him against the far wall only to be shocked when Pia steps directly up to me. She…embraces me, enveloping me in a hug I cannot escape from. Feelings assault me, memories and visions pressing at the barriers of my thoughts, but all of them are warm and filled with the purest love. *She is Diego's opposite. Perhaps, this is how they became mated to one another…*

"I heard what you said." She releases me. I do not know which part.

I straighten my jacket, chest still slightly tender beneath my clean clothes from the shrapnel Diego felt he needed to embed into my skin. I…no longer blame him. I still hate him a little bit, but I don't blame him. And I cannot harm him for looking out in Candy's best interest. I turn my attention back toward Candy a little surprised and unnerved to see her frozen in her position at the desk. Did my kiss overwhelm her so much that she can't move? One could hope and yet, I do not. I am not an expert. But if I'm lucky, perhaps she can teach me.

"Candy?" I say. But she does not answer. Her hands continue to move over a paper on the desk in front of her. Notare Kane moves to round it. Diego steps up to her and peers over her shoulder.

"Candy?" Pia says, moving to Candy's other side.

I advance, following until I can see what she's staring at.

She isn't looking at the maps though, as I expected her to be. Instead, she's staring at the drawings Miro brought me. "Where did you find these?" She says, looking over her shoulder, eyes finding mine.

"My scout brought them back from a town just beyond the river."

"A town? Which town? Why are they there? They're leaving soon right? Tell me they're on their way back…" She glances around at all of us, panic in her eyes.

"No," I say slowly, "On the contrary, I deployed additional reinforcements this morning to supply the guards already there as well as the humans with them…"

"The humans — did they have scars on their wrists?" She yanks up her sleeves to display the patchwork horror that lives there.

"I did not…inquire. Would this be…"

"Can you find out?"

I glance at Kane. He nods and pulls the walkie talkie from one of the locked drawers in the desk. The lock is an illusion, but it functions to keep the humans out. He hands it to me and I press the button to speak.

"Miro," I say simply.

The response comes in seconds. "Lahve."

"I am here with Kane — Notare Kane," I correct quickly, "and several human council members. A female member of the council has inquired as to the nature of the humans that you came across. Did they bear any scars?"

"Allow me a moment to consider." His light breathing comes through the line, letting me know that he is likely moving at speed with the other Heztoichen guards that carry the supplies. They will attempt to reach their destination before the coming daybreak. "Yes, they did have scars. They spoke of torture at the hands of another gang…"

"Did the scars look like this? An X on one arm, an O on the other?" She displays her forearms for us and I can see, beneath the wreckage, the illusion of shapes.

I hold the walkie towards her and ask her to repeat her question. Miro thinks for a moment, then says, "Yes. Now that you mention it, they did bear those exact markings…"

"Oh my god. Oh my god, it's a trap! You have to get your people out of there. Those aren't human scavengers, they're bait. They belong to the Five Point Gang. They have to leave the humans behind — wherever they're being led, it's into a trap."

"Wait wait wait. Candy, please, talk slower. What do you mean?" Pia says.

Candy holds her wrists towards the other woman and speaks to her imploringly. "Blood bags, that's what they call us. As a way to barter messages and as a show of good will, the different gangs trade blood bags back and forth.

"One of the human gangs will give up a blood bag to Malmon. He'll give one of his Others the blood bag to drain, then refill with their own blood, then they trade the blood bag *back* to the gang in exchange for weapons or access to compounds or information. And sometimes, blood bags get rewarded by being — I don't know — taken out of rotation or off the menu completely by acting as decoys or setting traps to lure other humans in. If they can get a blood bag to replace them, then they won't get bitten anymore and they'll get another job. But this…this is a big prize. The blood bags were sent by Malmon to capture your guards and torture them and then try to use them as bait to lure more of you out. You have to stop going for them. Abandon them now or everyone you send will die…"

I snap, disappointed by her rhetoric. "Is this the council you would provide your Notare?"

She nods.

I shake my head quickly. "Is this what you would want her to do for you?"

She stares at me, confused. Perhaps, disappointed, too. "No one has ever come for me."

"I would come for you." Heartbreak. Its sting never lessens. I rub the center of my chest as she stares up at me clutching the wrists of her opposite arms. *No, no one has ever come for her.*

Pia reaches out a hand and lets her fingers brush over Candy's shoulder before falling away again. "We would come for you. All of us."

Her eyes get glossy again. I can't bear it and raise the walkie to my lips. "Miro."

"Lahve, how do you instruct us to proceed? Should we heed the human female's warning? She might be mistaken. These humans were…convincing. They were not in…a healthy state."

"All the more reason not to trust them," Candy whispers. "Terrified people do terrifying things."

I nod. "Exercise extreme caution. Go around the town. Approach from the north, rather than the south. If it is a trap…"

"It is," she whispers.

"…then it is unlikely they will expect you from the north…"

"Apologies Lahve, but the problem is the river. There are few remaining paths across and the humans have directed us to one of the only ones we can verify, directly south of the city."

"Which city?" Candy catches her gasp with her hands. Kane gestures her forward. Diego clears valuable materials off of the table with one broad swipe of his arm. Pia lays down the map. Candy hunches over it and starts when I point at the city.

"Chatt-aah-noo-guh," I say, pronouncing the odd word carefully. I wonder which human language it is, as I have yet to learn it. And I have learned several. Six, to be precise. Mandarin has been the most useful, particularly in dealing with Tanen's regions, followed by Russian and then English.

"Oh...okay yes. Here. There's a functioning bridge here that leads out of Chattanooga to the north. And here. This is the one, way to the east, is the one we took to get to Brianna."

"T-t-too far," Diego says.

I nod, reluctantly agreeing with him. "I...concur. It would be an additional three day's journey for my Heztoichen, which may be too much time to spare if Far, Sebine, Morithan and the other guards are at risk with the humans in their company."

Diego glares at me. I return it, breaking only to give Candy my full attention when she says, "Yes, that's too far, but right here, just a few miles east, there's a spot where a bridge once stood. It fell, but there was a community living there that dammed the river using the fallen bridge. That community's gone now and the dam never really worked, but the chunks of concrete and stuff that they used for the dam make it possible to cross the river without...you know, drowning. My brother and I used it a couple times when we were looking for somewhere safe."

"You...have a brother?" I ask, flagrantly off topic, as if this were my first conversation. I am frustrated with myself.

Hm.

Candy blushes. She shakes her head. "No."

"Rick's still out there, I'm sure," Kane offers softly.

"I don't want to talk about..." She chokes, shakes her head, grows cold.

I glare at Kane. "You know her brother?"

"Candy met Abel and I long ago. Back before Abel received her Tare. Back before she was my Sistana. Though I had wanted her to be, even then." He smirks, as if recalling a fond memory, then shakes his head. "But back then, she had no idea and she wanted nothing to do with me."

Candy smiles a little more certainly this time. "You fought Drago's whole gang for her."

"But without you, we would not have gotten out alive." He smiles and they share the tenderest of moments. I feel… angry…upset…for reasons I cannot determine. *Jealous. I am jealous. He has had more time with her. They all have and Candy is human, with a short life span. There will never be a way for me to recover that time with her and ensure I have the most of it, the most of her. There will always be others with more and I hate that.*

"Lahve?" Miro's voice crackles through the walkie talkie.

I raise it again to my lips. "Yes, Miro. The human scout, Candy, has found an entry point for you." I explain to him how to arrive there and Candy interrupts only to provide much needed nuanced instructions — an abandoned warehouse that may be safe to sleep in, and that may even contain leftover supplies from this old community, as well as which routes to avoid as they are patrolled by the Disciples. Lastly, I deliver the orders to report back as soon as he has eyes on our guards and is able to recover them. "It should be no more than two days from now."

We five stand apart from one another and release a collective sigh as Miro signals his departure. I hear footsteps in the hall and turn to face the door as Abel opens it. She waddles through with a yawn, looking larger and more pregnant by the moment.

She freezes when she steps into the room and glances between us suspiciously. "What did I miss?"

"Nothing." Kane shoots me a glare and, under his breath, whispers loud enough only for my ears, "Do not speak of this until we hear the report from Miro that the guards are safe."

"Understood, Kane."

Louder I give Abel a slight nod, "Nothing, Abel — Notare Abel." I keep…slipping in my manners. These humans are rubbing off on me. "Nothing of concern. I came only to use the radio device to check on Miro. He and his team are making good progress."

She blinks at me, then narrows her gaze. She looks from Candy to Diego to Pia. "If they won't tell me then y'all better…what's going on?"

"N-n-n…"

"Don't nothing me, Diego. I know something's going on."

"How?" Candy quips.

"One — you're here and your face is all red like you've been crying and two…" she flings an accusatory finger at me. "He just called me Abel — not Notare, not Sistana, *Abel*. Something's up and if y'all don't tell me now, I'm going to… to freak out!"

While I ruminate over the fact that I could not lie successfully to a sleepy, pregnant human and cobble together a response, Candy, shy little Candy, lifts a hand, as if asking for permission to speak. Abel gives her a surprised glare that only grows more shocked when Candy pulls down her sleeve to cover her markings. *So many markings.* "I kissed Lahve and Diego got mad at me."

"You did *what?*"

Surprise.

Just like that, the true cause for alarm is easily forgotten.

Abel runs forward and grabs Candy by the shoulders. She shakes the poor female until she lets out a squeal. A laugh. She's pleased. It makes me pleased. I find myself smiling, even as Diego glares at me. Abel shrieks, "Tell me everything!"

And while Candy stammers out a response, I slip the walkie talkie into my pocket. To Kane alone, I whisper, "I will inform you of Miro's whereabouts. Then, we reconvene."

Chapter Ten

Despite the kiss we shared and tenuous promises we exchanged...or perhaps, because of them, Candy does not come to my home that night and I. do. not. like. it. So, the coming day, I abandon all pretenses of work and I do what it is that my soul aches for.

I follow her.

I follow her to the ceramic studio where she sands a few plates and applies glazes to a whole host of bowls before loading them into the kiln. I wait for her to leave and then I approach Kassie and request all of them in exchange for any other things or materials they need.

I expect a request for alcohol. Instead, I received a request for linens...linens and manpower to help physically move one of the kilns outside so that it sits beneath one of the awnings built just along the perimeter of the driveway, but out from beneath the garage. It overheats the room and dries the greenware too quickly, according to Kassie.

I offer Teera to move it that day, but Kassie asks *me* to do it with a salacious little leer. I rebuff her advances, to which she says, "It's not for me — well, it's mostly not for me. I just think Candy would enjoy it."

"You believe *Candy* would enjoy watching me perform menial labor, below my rank."

"Oooh well when you put it that way…" She waggles her eyebrows, confusing me even more. "Yes, Lahve. Yes, Candy will enjoy it."

I stare at her for another long while. "When should I return?"

I return the following day having spent another restless night alone, pacing the long, empty corridors of my home, wondering…wondering and worried. *Why does she do the things she does?* After leaving the ceramics studio the day previous, Candy had avoided certain roads, but I could not determine why, and then she had slept in Ashlyn's home, a home that I know now *not* to be her own by the way Ashlyn invited her in and made a guest bed for her on the floor. She retired early and without dinner. When Ashlyn offered her food, she declined. *Why would she decline?*

Now, standing and staring at her from my position, hidden amongst the trees just beyond the circular drive, I watch Candy seated at a work table where she sands a stack of plates and arranges them into piles according to size. *I want all of them.* She does not notice me at first, so focused on her task until Kassie, who had been clearing a new space for the kiln, looks up, sees me, smiles and ruins everything.

"Thanks for joining us, Lahve!" She calls *loudly.* Confused and concerned chatter lights up the inside of the enormous garage. Heads turn. Eyes turn up towards me. Most turn down, but not all. Candy's doesn't. Candy looks up from the stack of plates before her and meets my gaze. A hesitant smile lifts her left cheek. She raises her fingers and offers me a small wave and I…cannot reply. I am liquified below the knees.

"Uh, you know you should probably come out of the woods. It's a little creepy." Kassie jerks her thumb over her shoulder and dusts her hands off on her smock.

I give her a gentle nod and struggle not to stare directly into Candy's gaze even while speaking to her pottery kiln master, or whatever her title. "Kassie."

"Yeah. Also, you should probably stop staring at Candy like that. People around here are pretty defensive of her and aren't going to want you around if you keep watching her like that."

Defensive of her. Because she is the most wounded creature in this entire camp. And I understand better now that it isn't pity they feel for her, no. She has hurt so...badly. They don't want her to hurt again. I admire that. *Perhaps, these humans aren't totally without honor. They merely show it a little differently...*

I tear my gaze forcibly away from Candy's pale face, growing rapidly red in the cheeks. "Indeed. How may I be of assistance?"

Kassie beams and I notice that her smile is quite... pleasant. I don't suppose I've considered these humans much beyond their ineptitudes, but I'm looking harder now. She escorts me from the edge of the drive into the garage where she clasps her hands and says, "Lahve's going to be joining us for a little while today to help us set up the new kiln."

Situated deeper in the woods, but well within striking distance, I am grateful that Teera is my only guard on hand. Were Far and the rest here to witness this, I would never live down the embarrassment.

"You...you are, Lahve?"

It slipped my mind that Luan, another Heztoichen, worked here. Perhaps, I won't live down the embarrassment after all. "Indeed."

Her narrow eyes round, almost comically. Her mouth falls open. She glances around searching for answers in the faces of the other humans in the room. Her gaze knowingly snags on Candy, but I...don't like the way she looks at her. Why should she be so surprised that I might have an interest in her? She is magnetic, resilient and beautiful *especially when she falls asleep with her hand on my bare chest, her fingertips curling into my skin, wanting to be close, wanting me…*

I clear my throat. "Where would you like me to move the kiln, Kassie?"

"Here. Star's got an electrical hook up already prepared. We just need some muscle to help us move the actual machine."

"He can't move that all by himself. It's huge!" One of the humans shouts.

I give her a stern look and carefully shrug out of my overcoat. I place it gingerly on the far end of the table where Candy is working, and ensure my swordstick remains covered. Several humans mixing glazes separate Candy and I, yet I hold her stare over the tops of their heads for an extended moment. Then, I unfasten my cuff links and drop them into my coat pocket. I roll my sleeves up to the elbows, aware that it will likely make little difference. The weight of the thing is not the difficulty, though it is likely that it weighs half a human ton. The difficulty lies in the shape. I frown, knowing I will get dust all over me and not liking it.

But Kassie thinks Candy will like this.

I don't understand. But I dare to *trust* the dark-hued female with the bright white smile…at least in this. "Is it disconnected from the power source?" I ask as I approach the large red kiln. It's weather beaten and worn, aged, but resilient and recovered. Clearly something that survived the fall of civilization on this planet — a civilization I feel just as far from rebuilding. I always thought it didn't matter. We have so much time. We…

My thoughts pass to Candy, as they are so often apt to, and I recognize that if I had moved with greater purpose, been more involved in the affairs of the Notare, guided them with less…resigned apathy and given them more direction, maybe Population would not be such a threat, now. It could be that Population wouldn't have caused so many humans so much pain. Candy could have made it to Brianna with fewer scars.

Kassie is talking, but I'm not listening as I hoist the kiln up onto my shoulder in one smooth motion and carry it from its position in the garage out to the covered awning in the driveway. My shoulders and thigh muscles flex as I carefully lower it to the ground. Kassie plugs it in and thanks me.

I cross my arms. "I want all of the plates Candy is working on currently." She chuckles, her gaze lingering on my forearms in a way that causes me to lift a brow. "Do you see something you like?"

"Can't help it," she says, shooting me a wink. "I'm a forearm girl." She tosses the rag in her hand over her shoulder and doesn't bother to reign in her gaze as it sweeps my forearms a second and third time. "I can't give you all of them. I can give you four. We have a lot of people living in Brianna and people are clumsy. They break plates. We're also running out of glaze as it is and it's hard to make more."

"Wood ash and sand. Fire them at thirteen *metees*..." I run a quick calculation. "Approximately twenty-four hundred degrees. You won't get the color variation you have here, but the plates will hold."

"Wood ash and sand? I've heard of that...remember something about it from my earliest pottery classes. I think the ancient Japanese used this technique." She mulls it over, coming to the conclusion that I am right. I am always right. "Wow. Okay yeah. The ash will take a lot of work to sift through, but it'll be high in silica. We can test fire a few of the plates Candy is working on now."

"I'll take any deemed imperfect, as well. I want them all."

"Like I said, I can't give you all of them."

I glare down at her.

She holds her position. I grin unexpectedly and her eyes widen and her lips slacken. I use her momentary lag to continue the negotiation. "Six."

"You don't need six."

"I want six."

"I already promised you the bowls she was working on last time. I'll give you, in total, a set of four large plates, four small plates, four bowls and four glasses."

"Glasses?"

"Glasses. She makes these beautiful, hand-carved water glasses. No one else makes them. She has a talent for this stuff."

She has me interested…and then it hits me — this female is attempting to manipulate me. "Are you attempting to manipulate me?"

She grins, shameless as she is, and I stand straighter and flex the muscles in my forearms, dragging her attention down to them. Her jaw drops and her pupils dilate, then she shakes her head and laughs, "Now, look who's trying to manipulate. Are my attempts working?" She steps closer to me and her eyes smolder.

"Yes." I frown, a prickling awareness caressing the back of my neck driving me to turn around and face Candy. Kassie told me to expect a response from her. I want to see it.

"Good." She sidles up even closer and lifts her hand.

She moves like she'll touch my arm and I hiss, awaiting something horrendous. "You are aware of my abilities, are you not, human?"

"I am. Don't worry, I'm not gonna touch you." She licks her lips. "Lean down, I have something I want to tell you in confidence."

"I can hear you from here."

She clicks her tongue against the backs of her teeth in a manner that I've heard before but that has never been directed at me. She's *annoyed* with me. "I know that, but I want it to look like we're being naughty."

I seethe, "Excuse me?"

"No! Don't," she squeaks, a forced smile still plastered across her face. She grabs onto my pants pocket *carefully*. The female is good. She holds onto me but her warmth is all I feel. No pressure of her hand at all. No memories. "Just trust me."

"Why would I when you've just confessed to attempting to manipulate me?"

"Hey, you did the same."

"My manipulation would appear to be much less effective as I am losing this negotiation."

Kassie rolls her eyes. "In case you haven't noticed, oh great one, you aren't the only person left in the world. You also aren't the only one I'm trying to manipulate." She rises up onto her tip toes as if to speak into my ear. Irritated that she would thus approach me, yet too curious to deny her, I lower to her level and tilt my face towards her neck. "Candy likes you. I can tell. And I didn't think it was possible for her to ever like anybody ever again. I'm just trying to give her a kick in the rear. Speed things along a little, you know?"

"I don't know." It pains me to admit it.

She chuckles and releases my pocket, then rocks back onto her heels. "I think you would understand very well, Lahve, if you saw Candy talking to a guy like I'm talking to you." She winks at me — no, not at me, but at my exposed forearms — and turns, leaving me properly speechless perhaps, truly, for the very first time in my life.

"Alright my lovelies, back to work. Reba, Ahn, Tina and Molly, Lahve had a really good idea about a new glazing technique. Gather round and I'll explain what we need. Candy, pack up a full set of your four best, including four of your glasses."

I turn to see that Candy looks a bit...struck. "Oh. Okay." Her gaze moves between me and Kassie over and over. Her cheeks hold color in an alarming display considering that nothing has happened — I haven't kissed her, no one has threatened her, I merely moved a machine from one place to another and spoke with a human who I dare say Candy also respects. Yet she looks...nearly...distressed. I don't like it and feel frustration with the leader of these clay makers.

The four females addressed were the four other females at the table with Candy working with the large tubs of glaze. This leaves Candy and I...not *alone* but without bodies separating us. Dozens of people still mill the room, but I feel tension in the center of my chest blooming outward. *It feels as if we are alone.*

"Is the flatware for you?" She speaks first, surprising me. I did not expect her to speak first. We haven't spoken since we left the study, since she again proved her utility in this new world. She knows things I don't, including her own memories and thoughts. I covet them ruthlessly.

My hand hesitates over my coat. I nod, leaving it, and move towards her.

I follow her gaze, track every move it makes, dropping first to my hand, then moving to my other forearm, then to my collar, but not higher. She swallows and I watch, fascinated, as her throat works. There is something oddly *erotic* about watching her swallow. I picture her swallowing in...other ways.

I should ask her again why she did not come to me last night, but I know that any way I phrase the question would come out an accusation and a demand. I want her in my bed tonight, but I don't know how to force her there. What am I doing so...wrong?

"Are you..." She swallows again, this time, her gaze moving past me. "Can you touch Kassie, too?"

"Pardon me?"

"I saw you touch her and it didn't look like it bothered you. I was just wondering if you could touch her, too?" Her face is so brutally red now and I wonder if she's noticed that she's wrapped five small plates in paper instead of just four. No, she hasn't. Because she's stacking them into a crate for me and is moving onto bowls with shaky determination.

"No."

"No, you..." She does not say more.

Ordinarily, I would feel irritation that I am being forced to explain myself — particularly to a creature that will not meet my gaze. Now, I feel irritation that I don't know what's prompting her awkwardness. She kissed me just yesterday.

"Candy, I thought I made myself clear." Fuck.

She glances down at her hands. "Sorry," she stutters automatically. "About what? Sorry. I don't know about your abilities, for sure. I just heard about them from other people…"

"No, not that. I am happy to explain to you my rheach — my abilities to read blood — in further detail. I'm talking about why you didn't come again last night. I thought you would. I had hoped you would."

"You did?"

And then I think back to what I said, expressly. Fuck. I didn't ask her to dine with me, I merely offered my home for her needs. Why didn't I ask her to dinner? Fool…

"Maybe, I wasn't sure you'd be alone." She packs the next plate into the box with force enough to break something.

My jaw hinges open, then snaps shut. "You what?"

"I'm sorry. Nevermind. It's just…you kissed her neck and she put her hand in your pocket. I didn't know that if I didn't come, you'd find someone else. I'm sorry, I really did try to come. I went to Ashlyn's for dinner and then I went home."

"I…" What is happening? I shake my head and drop one hand onto the table, needing to brace myself to keep myself upright. "You're lying."

Her shoulders tense beneath her ears. "What?"

"You slept at Ashlyn's."

"No, I didn't."

"She made you a guest bed. I heard her say that she would."

"She did, but I only took a little nap before I went back to my house. I was going to come to yours — I *tried* — but I'm glad I didn't. I didn't realize your bed was already full."

She slaps another piece of brown paper down onto the dry, dusty table, but her hands are shaking slightly when she reaches for a glass — a beautiful glass etched in geometric designs that I would love to spend hours examining in greater clarity, but now is not the time. Now, we are speaking past one another, words getting twisted and confused. She is lying to me and I don't know why. And she is angry with me and I don't know why. And I'm angry with her, though I could give a *fuck* about the lying. I just want her in my house, at my dining table, in my bed this night and every other.

"Wait — are you following me?" She blurts very softly. She shakes her head and her curls cascade around her shapeless black garments. As unflattering as they are, at least they aren't patterned. Black and pink are her colors. She'd also look excellent in white and red. I plan to speak with Tasha about this later this evening. We already have an appointment.

My gaze, which had been hovering over her clothing, lifts to her eyes. She is still bright pink, tantalizing and maddening at the same time. "Yes."

She stiffens. "You...you didn't see me leave Ashlyn's house though, did you?"

Wait — what? I had assumed she would be outraged that I have been following her, not outraged at what I might have seen. What *might* I have seen? I take a half step toward her and my insiria respond against my will as I speak, the chime both low and menacing though I don't mean for it to be. "No. Did you do something after you left Ashlyn's house last night?"

"No." But her voice catches.

I balk. "Here I am, in the face of your disdain that I might have touched another female while you meanwhile, spent your evening whoring yourself out to another male."

She slaps me. The action happens so quickly, it almost didn't. Her touch was so light, yet her scorn is so palpable. I reach up and press my fingertips to the warm skin on my cheek. Candy's eyes widen magnificently. Her lower lip trembles. "I…I'm sorry. I didn't mean…"

But I can bear it no longer. I crash down onto her, lips meeting lips, tongue tangling with tongue. I invade her mouth, sweeping it eagerly, wishing I'd just gone ahead and met with Tasha yesterday or the day before so I didn't have to worry so much about catching her on my fangs, cutting her.

I cradle the back of her head and stumble into her body. The entire table jolts beneath us as we crash into it. The wooden box holding her plates jerks, half falling off of it, but I catch it easily with the fingertips of my right hand and press it back to safety while my left hand fumbles for the hem of her shirt and slips under it. Bare palm against her lower back I pull her against me.

"Lahve," she breathes, pronunciation still begging for an alternative name by which to call me. I want to hear her say my name. My true name. I want her to *moan* it. She bites my bottom lip hard and a strangled grunt leaves my throat that I can do nothing about. How dishonorable, such a public display, yet I cannot prevent it, nor stop it from happening twice. By her hunger, I've been made ravenous.

She pecks and pulls at my lips and grabs and tugs at my hair. "Lahve…"

"Candy," I groan. She winces and wrenches back.

She's breathing hard, but her gaze seems to clear faster than mine. She releases me and clears her throat, then gently pushes me back. "I'm sorry," she says meekly, offering a small, mortified wave to the other occupants of the room who I can now hear giggling amongst one another like school children.

Someone releases a lascivious whistle that causes the rest of the room to laugh. I'd have murdered them all — at the very least, brought the roof down on their heads — had it not caused Candy to smile nervously. She tugs down on the bottom of her shirt.

"I wasn't with anyone else last night. I told you I wouldn't be with anyone else." Her voice is tight. She is…offended? "I just didn't think you could touch another woman. I didn't even think to ask you to make the same promise, too."

"Candy, what are you…" I replay Kassie's words in seconds. Picture it, were I to catch Candy with her hand in the pocket of another male, one who is leaning down to whisper into her ear meaningfully, imagine that I could not read her body language, or hear his words, but could only his smile. *Candy does not have the Heztoichen hearing I do. She saw… something else than what happened. Kassie knew. Kassie engineered it. And it made Candy jealous.* A smile threatens to tear through my composure. It's only more dazzling than my hope in that moment.

I clear my throat forcefully and grin with my lips pressed together over my sharpened fangs. I shift my weight awkwardly between my feet and I reach forward to cradle her cheek and she lets me. She lets me and she does not wince in fear.

"I can touch no other female. Kassie was…speaking on your behalf, providing me with encouragement to approach you."

Candy lifts a brow. I smooth my finger over it, careful with my claws, needing to see Tasha urgently. "Really?"

"Really."

"And you won't…uhm…be with other women while we're together? I mean…not saying we're together. I know we're not dating or anything. I know you probably don't even date. I'm not actually sure…I didn't ask you about dating on Sistylea. But here, on Earth, to say we won't sleep with other people means that we're kind of exclusive and I'd like that with you, not that I'm asking you to be my boyfriend or anything…"

My heart is racing. I can feel my pulse firing through each of my fingertips. My mouth has gone dry and I've lost my mind, every ounce of it. "You wish to call me yours?"

Candy shakes her head rapidly, looking absolutely terrified and I wince, ashamed by my insinuation. "Apologies. I am getting ahead of myself. I realize, I merely offered you my home and any equipment and supplies you may need." I recover quickly. "However, I did not expressly ask you to come by. Will you join me for dinner tonight?"

She nods, gaze still distant. She looks...upset. "I'll try."

"You'll try?"

"I mean, I'll be there."

"I await you eagerly." My answer does not smooth the line between her eyebrows. I take a step towards her, coming close enough that her heat crashes against me in a stifling wave. My vocal cords rattle and reverberate, creating an audible sound she responds to with a soft gasp. "Is there something the matter?" I stroke her cheek with the backs of my knuckles, bathing in her silent flame. *Do it.* I bend towards her and I...hesitate. *Do it.*

She lifts up onto her toes and her mouth sears across mine like a spell. I am enrapt, and melt. But the moment is brief and again, she is the first to pull back. She's smiling more honestly now than she was, wavering a little on her feet. She's so fucking cute I can't stand it.

I absorb the smell of the clay on her skin, the powder on her hands comes between her skin and mine when she cautiously strokes my bare forearms. Hm. Perhaps, Kassie was not wrong in many things. "You will come tonight, then."

"Yes."

"And I will not allow another female to touch me in the meantime."

Candy gnaws on her bottom lip. Softly...so softly, even my ears strain to hear her, she says, "Same."

Chapter Eleven

Miro does not answer the walkie talkie when I buzz. I frown, concerned by his absence. I am unused to being concerned about my guard. They have battled the most ferocious of opponents. They are not likely to be overtaken, not even by gangs of Heztoichen. My guards are ancient, seasoned and violent.

No matter. Perhaps, the batteries have died. Tanen crosses my mind once again. He holds the cobalt supply. I growl, irritated. I have other things to deal with than Tanen and the damn guard. I just want to kiss Candy again.

I announce my arrival as I near Tasha's door. She is there, awaiting me when I arrive and, the high-born female that she is, invites me inside with a flourish and a bow. Red hair. Pale skin. No scars. I look her up and down and find myself surprised by the direction of my thoughts. Even if I could touch her, I would not want to. I want to touch someone else.

"Tasha. Thank you for seeing me on such short notice."

"Of course, Lahve. How may I be of assistance?"

"I have two requests, the first, a garment for a female you have designed for in the past. Candy."

"Candy?"

"Yes, Candy." I speak quickly, past the furrow in her brow. "And the second, are…outfit selections for me."

"You…have the finest clothes in all the seven regions. What are you…" She shakes her head and pulls at the long measuring ribbon that hangs around her neck like a scarf. Straightening up in a controlled, methodical way, she says, "Of course, Lahve. What type of garments do you desire?"

"Garments intended to attract a human female."

"Garments intended to attract a human female. Candy," Tasha repeats. She rakes my frame with her gaze, and then she smiles. "You won't like what I have to offer you, Lahve."

I clench my teeth, already fearing the result. "Will it work?"

"Yes," she says, not perhaps, not maybe, not might. But yes. Confident. I like that. It is the same confidence Candy has when she looks over the markings and knows what they all mean.

"Do it."

What feels like a short eternity later, I'm knocking on a few more doors, this time, attempting to cajole and coerce both Lima and Patty into my employ for the night. They agree, but only for Candy, just as I suspected they would.

I compliment them, surprising them both, and ask them to prepare any dish they feel Candy might desire and to set it up as they had set it up originally, in the den. I noticed Candy eyeing the piano upstairs as well. Perhaps, she would like me to play for her…I lift the baby piano and bring it downstairs, arranging it in a pleasing way against the far wall. I do not have to take off my coat to do it. In these new garments Tasha provided, I don't wear an overcoat at all.

I feel like a simpleton dressed in…what is this? Dark blue jeans? A white tee shirt? I frown. I had expected more from Tasha. Perhaps, something like one of the human suits I've seen several of the Notare wear to formal galas. I enjoy human suits. They most closely resemble the traditional garb of our people. But this? This feels like something one would wear to...shovel manure.

"You look great," Lima pipes up. She's standing behind me with her sister, who elbows her promptly in the ribs. "Ow..."

"I don't know. Is this truly how males of your species dress to attract females?"

Lima blocks her sister's next strike and steps forward. "Guys can dress up fancier, like you usually do, sure..."

"Just as I suspected," I grumble heatedly. "Why did Tasha put me in this?"

"But I think..." she hesitates, and tucks a lock of brown hair behind her ear. Her lips quirk. "You actually *care* what I think, right now, don't you?"

My eyes narrow to slits as I watch her face in the mirror over my shoulder. She stands in the hallway, silhouetted in lights. "In this precise moment, yes."

She smiles and, even though she covers her mouth and leans against her sister and whispers very quietly, I can hear every word she says. "See? He's got some human in there, after all."

"Absurd," I mutter. "I am Tretaro, the most ancient of Heztoichen. I am concerned only with your assessment of my...human attire and whether it will attract Candy." Attract Candy. I wince, aware that I have given away far, far too much.

Patty's face is a mask of shock and horror. Brashly, she hisses, "You want to attract Candy? You hired her for sex. Why would you bother?"

I snarl, rounding on the woman, "I *hired* her for dinner. I *want* her willing acceptance. Tasha seemed to think these... rags would help me achieve that. I want only your assessment of the clothes. Should you have any other opinions, I suggest you keep them to yourselves."

Patty starts to speak again, but her sister speaks over her, perhaps sparing her life. "*As I was saying*, most guys would try to dress up to impress a girl. Tasha put you in this because you already dress nice. She dressed you *human*. You look less threatening, especially with your fangs filed down in the front."

My canines she left sharp, at my request. I shame myself with the reason as to why. I envisioned myself sinking those fangs into Candy's mutilated neck, through her scars. I want to unwind time, create new memories in their place, less painful ones, show her what an exchange in blood can feel like when done the right way. I've heard the blood bond can yield *exquisite* pleasures...

And yet... She asked not to be bitten. I dishonor her, even with my thoughts.

"And without the claws." Lima gestures at my hands. My nails are black and look odd, filed down and rounded as they are.

My swordstick is affixed to my belt, at my insistence. My shoes, Tasha replaced with heavy boots. Clunky and odd, I don't understand their purpose. "This is the...human fashion?"

"Except for the cane on your belt, yeah." Lima shrugs.

"Hm."

"When is Candy supposed to be here?"

"Any moment. I worried she might arrive before I did, Tasha took so long."

"She did good work." Lima beams.

Patty grumbles over her shoulder. "Dress up a monster and he's still an asshole."

I snort and turn to meet her gaze directly, "Clever." My tone carries a hint of humor.

Hm.

Even stranger? I have no urge to kill her at this insult whatsoever. I glance at my watch — one of the only articles Tasha allowed me to keep. I pace to the door and open it. The air is dry tonight, a welcome reprieve. The sky is lighter in color than it is other nights as well. I will light candles and the fire to warn away the red. I don't like when the sky's red tint touches Candy.

"Light the candles. Candy will be here any minute." The ladies move on, but Candy does not arrive. Eventually, I leave my place on the stoop, and return inside. "She must be freshening up." In her home...that I cannot locate...

I wait. I pace. I stand on the stoop. I glare at every human and Heztoichen that walks by. The groups are, as of yet, mostly segregated...but not all. I notice that the humans and the Heztoichen who made the trek across Population to arrive in Brianna *together* tend to be those who breach the divide. The rest will come around, I'm sure of it. All it will take...is time...

Hm.

Since when did I start *enjoying* the sight of inter-species pairings? *Since I wanted one...* "Where is she?"

I pace back inside and slam the door. The twins stand, as if guarding the entry to the dining room. Patty wears an apron. The scent wafting from the kitchens behind them is decadent. They cooked some meat. Meat is hard to come by.

"She agreed to come. Why would she lie if she had no intention of joining me?" I seethe. My skin is hot. I am momentarily grateful for the lightweight nature of these human garments. *Perhaps, I should have asked Tasha for more? Only if they attract Candy, which I will not know unless Candy shows up.*

Boom, boom, boom!

The crescendo is not coming from the front of the house, however, but the back...I breeze past the females standing in the dining room and enter the kitchen where the scents are strongest and most magnificent. There is a back door here, one that I have never used. It rattles now beneath the next knock.

Boom, boom!

I rush to the door and fling it open and find Candy standing there dressed in an appalling combination of garments. Her hands cup either side of her neck in an attempt to hide her scars, but I don't give a fuck about her scars. She's *shirtless*.

"Candy…" The word gusts out of me like I've been punched.

She glances over her shoulder wildly, her hair swinging in the breeze. "Can I come in?"

"Of course." I make room for her to pass and instinctively grab her shoulder, wanting to know what happened and why she's arrived like this before me, wearing the ugly black pants I saw her in earlier and no shirt to speak of. Two small lace triangles cover each of her perfect breasts and I would be gleeful at the sight of them if she weren't also breathing so heavily. But, when I touch her, sound, sight, taste, touch, scent — all of these things coalescing inside of me fall to ruin at her touch. To rapture.

Because I felt and I feel nothing. *Nothing but skin as soft as dust.* I don't know if the sensation will ever become normal to me. *But I hope it does.*

Frowning, I pull my shirt off over my head and slip it over hers. She pushes her arms through the sleeves absently and thanks me. Her gaze snags on my bare chest, but I don't care about the way she looks in my clothing or the open appraisal she gives me now.

"Candy, what…are you only wearing one shoe?"

She glances down and wiggles the toes of her exposed foot against the tile. "Yes," she says, as if there could be any other answer.

I balk, "Why?"

"I…I ran here." She's quick to shut the door behind her, carefully checking in either direction as if fearing she's been followed.

"Ran here, or were chased?"

The way she wraps her arms around herself tells me everything I need to know. "Candy…" The growl bellows out of me, my insiria creating an overlapping sound that causes

Candy's pupils to dilate. Interesting, when I intended to drive fear into her, that she would have such a reaction. Interesting, but unhelpful now. "What happened? Who chased you?"

"No one."

"Candy, those boys giving you trouble again?" Lima speaks from the mouth of the kitchen.

I focus hard on Candy's face, watch her expression shutter. She shakes her head feverishly. "No. I mean…it's fine."

"Candy, do not lie to me a fourth time." My voice ripples through the room, fury pricking my dangerously exposed skin. I reach for my swordstick.

Candy steps further into the kitchen, but she's limping slightly. "It's fine. I don't want to talk about it."

"You're hurt." I grab her upper arm and stop her from taking another step.

"Candy, you should tell Lahve about…" Patty starts.

"Shh!" Candy whips to face the twins and her face floods with color. "Don't. Please. I said no. I want to handle it myself. He doesn't need to know." She pauses, then whispers, "I don't want you to know about anyone I was with before. Please. It's humiliating."

The sincerity in her tone does nothing for my rage and everything for my own mirrored humiliation. *She is beneath me, a human whore, and I am Lahve, untouched and awaiting only the purest vessel with whom to bond and share eternity with.* But Candy is not pure and she does not have eternity. All she has is this one fragile lifetime that could be so easily snatched by any foe…and she does not want help from me.

Too stunned and enraged to speak, I scoop her quickly into my arms and make my way into the den where I deposit her in a deep leather armchair. The fire is already going and is the only light by which to see, other than the candles.

"Wow. It's beautiful. Did you do this for me?"

I kneel at her feet and carefully lift the sole of her bare foot to the light. She has a few small cuts, two splinters and a small rock embedded in her heel. "Yes. I'd like to give you a drop of my blood. Just a small amount. It will heal this instantly…"

"No! Please, don't. I don't…I don't like the feeling of Other — Heztoichen — blood in my system."

Frustration warps my tone. It is as deep as the ocean and rougher than its waters. "I understand you do not enjoy reliving your time in Malmon's clutches, but less than a drop of my blood would heal this immediately and cure you of any other ailments you may encounter for the next several years." It may even prolong your life and keep you with me.

"No, I just…"

"It would be giving, asking for nothing in return."

"No, Lahve."

"Candy."

"No," she squeaks. "No, I just like feeling human. And these are little scratches. I didn't even feel them."

"You didn't feel them because your adrenaline was propelling you through the woods. You didn't feel them, because you feared something else. Like your shoe, these were a necessary sacrifice and Candy, I am telling you now that I will not let this go. I will pry it out of the minds of Patty and Lima with ease, but I do not want to. I want you to trust me enough to tell me…"

"It's not that I don't…trust you," she groans, rocking back in her seat as if she's reached the end of her exasperation. I wonder if she's even aware that her hand is trembling slightly. "I just…I don't know how to explain it." She shakes her head again for the thousandth time and huffs, blowing hair off of her face only for it to fall back into place. I reach up and tuck it behind her ear. She focuses too hard on my hand and, I wonder why, until she says, "You cut your nails."

"Candy, stay focused. And yes, I did. For you. Now, I want you to try to explain it to me."

Her gaze remains unfocused. She's still watching my hand as I mold it back to her toes, trying to warm them. She looks up at my abdomen, my chest, inadvertently attempting to excite me to arousal, but this time, I refuse to be moved.

"Candy."

She inhales sharply and speaks so quickly it takes me an additional moment to sift through her words. "I know that you're…too good for me. I know I shouldn't have come back after that first night, but I um…like the way you make me feel, like I'm a little bit more…confident?" She twists her fingers together to the point of pain. It splinters her face. I keep one hand on her toes and the other I stretch up the length of her body to cover her fingers and still them.

"Stronger maybe? I know I'm not strong or confident but I feel like I'm confident in…you? I…you didn't…do anything to me when I passed out and you're nice to me and today you even let me slap you and you didn't get mad. You kissed me."

Her tone mellows, deepens. Her eyes crinkle. "You make me feel like I'm a person and not a punching bag. I'd like to *stay* a person."

The rippling in my chest and the carnivores in my stomach chewing through everything in their path make it impossible for me to calm my insiria when I speak next. "Patty, Lima, can you fetch a human first aid kit?" I call over my shoulder. I know they are at the door, eavesdropping on our conversation. I don't care. I can barely process what it is that she has said.

"Thank you," she whispers. "I don't mean to insult you."

"I…" I clear my throat — I *have* to clear it. "I am not insulted. I…understand your justification as to why you won't accept my blood, but not why you won't give me the names of your attackers."

She swallows hard and bites her lower lip so long, she leaves me no choice but to reach up and free it and rub my thumb over its perfect, indented center. "It's not because I don't trust you…it's because I do. And I…I'm embarrassed about who I am…who I was…when you seem to see me so differently. You don't…know about what I've done, not like the others. And I don't want to see you look at me like I'm disposable. I don't want to go back to who I was before I knew you."

I'm going to break something. Or rather, she is. Just my heart. My stone heart is nothing against her culling words. It is shattered, denuded, reduced to rubble. I sit up into a crouch and grab either arm of her chair. I pull myself up so that I arch over her completely and press just the slightest kiss to the center of her forehead.

"I will press you no further this evening, but I do have one single request."

"Yes?"

"Call for me." I slip my fingers under her chin and force her to meet my gaze. "Next time, call for me."

"But what if…" She trails off and rubs her hands between her legs, balling them in the fabric of my tee shirt. Her hands are dirty. She's unwashed. Why is she so badly cared for? Why won't she give me that honor?

"What if what?"

"What if you don't come?"

I growl, unable to catch the sound before it slips. "You say you trust me, but this question…this is not trust."

"I trust the way you are with me. But I don't trust you'll want to come and help me with…it's stupid." She bunches her hair in her hand and rubs the side of her head. "It's not you, I just…it's embarrassing. I don't want you to see…you're busy! You're the Lahve — *the* Lahve — you have important stuff to do and I'm not…"

"We have the first aid kit," Lima says from the doorway.

I settle back onto my heels, crouching as I lift Candy's injured foot up onto my knee. "Thank you Lima, Patty. You may serve dinner now."

"Sure thing."

They leave the room again and I struggle to determine what to say. I will not be able to convince her of her own worth. This, I know. Only she can do that. Carefully removing her splinters, I focus on the sole of her foot as I say, "Nithril."

"What?"

"*The Lahve* has important matters to attend across the seven regions. He is impartial and does not concern himself often with the matters of humans. But Nithril? He has only one focus, a human close to his heart that matters to him above all other beings." I lift my gaze and she looks down at me, struck as understanding slowly plays out in the slight widening of her eyes. "I mean *you*, my Ipalora. My name is Nithril and I was Nithril long before I was ever made Lahve. You may always call for Nithril."

I go back to bandaging her foot as Patty and Lima return and set two plates on the table between the two arm chairs. They light the candles on it, filling the room with a little more light than there was.

"Nithril," Candy whispers and I don't expect the surge of discomfort that crawls over me, or the greater surge of pleasure that follows.

"It has been...hundreds of years since I have heard this name. It sounds good on your tongue." I attempt a smile.

It startles her. "Your fangs..."

"Filed."

"For me too?"

"Yes."

"You look..." I wait, hopeful, sick with yearning. "You look hot."

That is...not what I expected her to say and choke. "Thank...thank you." I clear my throat on an embarrassed cough. I glance at the steaming plate of food on the table closest to her. "You should eat."

Silence passes. She doesn't eat. But she says, "You know, Candy isn't my name, either. I...a Heztoichen gave it to me.

It's…the only name Abel knew me by, so everyone uses it and I never told them not to. My name is Meredith, but my mom called me Edith."

My heart is fractured and shaky. I understand the gift she has just given me for what it is and lean in and kiss the tip of her dirty toes. "Edith. It is a beautiful name."

"Eeeww, don't do that." She tries to pull her foot back and I am grateful as some of the tension sloughs off of our bodies and slips through the floorboards below.

"I can do what I like, Edith. I am Lahve after all." I wink up at her and she grins broadly enough to change the shape of her face, turning it from a heart to a circle. So, so fucking cute.

"Or you could also call me…"

"Also call you?"

"You can call me Ipalora." She sucks in a breath and I look up and hold her gaze. "I really like it when you call me Ipalora. It makes me think of your jungles."

"The hanging jungles of Hom."

"Yes."

"You make me long for home, Ipalora."

"You miss it?"

"No." I shake my head. "Just to show it to you."

I finish bandaging her foot and rise to stand, resume my place at her side. We share dinner together and then my bed — I have yet to tell her that there is more than one bed in my home. We whisper until late into the night. I ask her questions about her likes, her interests, how she came to know ceramics as she does, her love of music. I do not, however, ask her about her past, about Population, about Rick, about mother and father and her life before we arrived on this planet's unwelcoming soil. I tell her of the attacks against us right when we fell. I explain our response that was pure violence. She understands in a way I know many humans do not, but perhaps she would be more apt to understand. She has been in desperate situations, forced to do desperate things.

I close my eyes with her at my side. Teera has been dismissed for the night. I close my eyes while holding her hand, wondering what it would feel like...

Not her body. No, that has much less allure.

But her trust. I'd like to earn it...

And my prayers are answered as I am forced to earn it far, far too soon.

Chapter Twelve

"Where is she?" I snarl, pacing back and forth through the shin-high leaves. "I should never have let her out of my sight." After she bathed at my home, she dressed in her oversized pants and one of my largest shirts, but it did not cover her neck. I offered her an alternative —

"I asked Tasha to prepare it." I hold open the box and though she looks inside at the long-sleeved pink shirt with the deep-V and the tailored pair of jeans that would fit her snugly around the waist before flaring out as they reach the ground, she does not touch.

"I can't wear that."

"Why not?"

"Everyone would see my scars."

"I know. They are something to be proud of."

"No. They aren't." She takes another step away from me and puts another mile of distance between her heart and my heart. "And it's easy for you to say. Your skin is perfect. You are perfect."

I don't bother trying to contradict her. It would take too many words and she is right that I have no scars. I cannot share the pain of them with her. So, even though it kills me, I offer, "Diego wears his scars with pride."

"Diego is a warrior." Her front teeth clench together. *"I'm not. It's different."*

I tread carefully. "You have nothing to be ashamed of. I find your scars beautiful…"

"Don't patronize me, Nithril." And then she turns and leaves and orders me not to follow under threat that she'll never forgive me if I do or trust me again.

It is childish and petulant and knowing that is not enough to keep me from being wounded by it all the same.

Patty and Lima have been sharing meaningful glances and attempting to communicate without my knowledge, which isn't working. I can all but read the words in their expressions. "Say it."

"Say what?" Patty says, looking nervous in a way that I *despise*.

"Whatever it is you two are trying not to say."

"I think she could be in trouble," Lima blurts.

"I think we shouldn't rush to conclusions. She was late yesterday. She's probably just late again…"

"But *why* was she late yesterday, hm?" I round on Patty and watch terror flit across her deep set eyes.

She rubs the scar running up the side of her face and hisses through the gap between her teeth. "Didn't you also say that you mighta pissed her off, though?"

I reel back and shove my hands into the pockets of my jeans. I look out at the woodlands, waiting…endlessly. Lima makes a move to pass me, but I bark over my shoulder, "Don't." She doesn't. She moves back toward the house and stands on the bottom step of the short stoop leading up to the kitchen door. Whatever it is out here in these woods that was chasing Edith, I want nowhere near these other females, either.

And I let her go. Fuck me for letting her go.

"Do you think she…" I shake my head, completely rattled. "There is a human expression for it, when one fails to show for an appointment set with another."

"Stood up," Patty says.

"She didn't stand you up," Lima adds. "I think you should check on her."

Patty presses, "She wanted to handle this on her own."

"You *know* who's after her. He's not going to let her go easily if she told him no."

"Enough." That answer enrages me. Fury bites at my wrists, making my hands flex towards my swordstick. Though I'm dressed in another pair of jeans given to me by Tasha, I'm…wearing the shirt Edith wore yesterday, the white one. I like the smell of her it carries. "I want to decapitate you both."

Patty nods, distracted as she thinks and utterly unconcerned with my threat. Have I really lost my edge? "Maybe, Lima's right. It probably doesn't hurt to check on her. If she's changing or naked or still at her pottery workshop, she'll be mad, but she'll forgive you. I just…don't trust Leif."

Leif. A name I've heard before, but the male is so insignificant in the scheme of things, that I have no face or attributes with which to ascribe him. Other than the fact that he will soon be dead. "Show me this Leif."

"It isn't just Leif. It's Leif and his idiot friends. They work in the chemical plant and they combine the toxic runoff to create nasty drugs. They've got half of Brianna hooked already. Think they're invincible…"

"And that anyone they've ever done anything for *owes* them," Lima adds. She looks at me with meaning.

"Show me," I repeat.

"What?"

"How?" Patty and Lima say in the same breath.

"His face and the face of those that follow him. I do not know them. I will know them now."

Patty and Lima share a look ripe with determination. "What do you need from us?"

"Picture Leif first, I want to see his face. Only his face. Repress your human emotion. I want only an image. Can you do this?"

They both nod robotically, identical expressions on their identical faces. Patty does not look like she wants to kill me, for once. That alone would worry me, were I not already imploding. I extend my hands. The twins each place their palms in mine simultaneously.

White skin, shaggy brown curls, small eyes positioned too close together, full lips, a smile that one could perhaps view as kind were the image not framed with discomfort shared by both of these women — discomfort. disgust. hate.

The image transforms and I watch as Leif is dragged bloody through the streets by a male that I recognize. Diego. Diego is stopped by Leif's cronies. Both women allow their opinions to shine through as I extend my rheach over them. They seem to think that Diego should have been allowed to continue. To kill.

I want to know more about this experience…but I don't. *Edith did not want me to know.* And I want her to be the woman she *wants* to be when she is with me. I don't want to abuse a half-trust so hard fought. *Why did Diego do this to Leif?* I physically jolt beneath the desire to ask…but don't.

"Now his scent. What does he smell like?"

The vision of Diego being hauled off Leif's bloodied form disperses like sand in a strong wind and, carried on that breeze, comes a scent — unwashed male and chemicals. I nod. "Now, the other males he keeps near to him who may have harmed Edith before. I want their faces."

Memories flash and I see too many things, disparate moments — *Leif laughing in a cluster of other males. Leif being beaten again. Leif in a bar at the end of Starlight where the humans are oft known to congregate, laughing as he pulls an unwilling woman onto his lap. It isn't Edith and she pushes him off, but he leers after her with an unfathomable gracelessness I can't quite grasp.*

I let go. "Thank you, ladies." I leave them panting, unable to catch their breath. Diego displayed no pain at the invasion he pressed upon me, but these females remind me that it is a difficult thing, to feel the power of the rheach, for a human. For anyone.

I walk to the edge of the woods and close my eyes. I inhale deeply. It takes me several tries before I'm able to root out the chemical-laced scent in the air. I cock my ears forward and listen…and two things happen in tandem.

I smell his distinct brand of sweat, but it is too faint to track from here…I need something else…

"Nithril?" It's a question carried by the breeze, not a command, but I am no less commanded by it.

I close my eyes, unable to pinpoint the direction beyond the woods…*she's out in the woods. What the fuck is she doing out in the woods?* "Come on…come on," I murmur.

Silence. She does not say my name again. She's asking for me. There was fear in her voice and I'm not there. I wanted her to call for me, to command me to arrive at her side and yet…I'm not sure she expects anyone to arrive, hence her trepidation. And I know without any shadow of a doubt that she will not call again.

"Come on!" I close my eyes, take a step forward and then another.

"Lahve, are you…" Lima starts until I whip a hand up, demanding silence.

"Candy…" The wind changes direction and I catch both the word, wreathed in laughter, and the scent in the same moment. I fly.

To call it *running* would not adequately describe the way we Tretaro move. It's a skill learned at a young age, one that I mastered in my youth at two hundred and two. To be able to move without being seen, heard or felt by surrounding humans is possible for a Heztoichen. But for a Tretaro, I can move without being seen, heard or felt by anyone. Heztoichen do not see me as I move past them, first back into the streets of Brianna, and then to the woods at the end of Starlight Road.

Sticks and twigs snap beneath my heavy boots as I move deeper into the woods. My swordstick slaps my thigh as I slow, pause, listen again. Laughter to my right. *Why here? Did these men, this Leif abomination, lead her to the perimeter of Brianna? If so, for what purpose?*

Through the sparse trees, I can already spy the metallic gleam of the wall, but just before it, there is a dilapidated wooden shed with a tin roof. Nondescript, I may have passed it a thousand times before. Now, there is an assortment of drunk, drugged males wavering on their feet as they stand before it, surrounding it. *Why would they lead her here? Did she run to it?*

It smells of decaying wood and I can hear the sound of small insects scurrying beneath the tin roof, happily making their homes inside of it. I also hear something else… something much larger than an insect shuffling behind the shack's thin exterior, and then nothing. *She's hiding from them and she's calling for me to help her.*

A balloon in my chest nearly lifts me off of my feet. I wish, for the very first time, that she were Heztoichen so that there might be a way for me to communicate with her and let her know that I'm here, I've come at the sound of her voice and she has no more reason to fear. And then it occurs to me that this is the very first time I have wished for her to be anyone else because I like her for everything that she is. Even before I liked Edith, I never once thought to change Candy…

And I still don't want to change her. I just want her to know that she's safe with me, this moment until forever.

I stand out of line of sight of the males, three of whom are wielding lights. *They struggle to see in the dark.* No matter, they wouldn't notice me anyway, so focused as they are on the door of this shack, which is tin and flimsy and closed. I inhale deeply and I scent Leif's stench, but I also smell *her*.

Leif knocks on the tin door and it rattles. He and his five humans laugh. "Candy, open up."

I crunch loudly through the foliage as I advance, my hands safely laced behind my back lest I do something foolish, like kill them much quicker than they deserve. Branches give and a small, wiry bush protests my invasion as I stomp past it loudly, in a human manner, and grab the males' attention away from her. They swing and swivel and stagger to face me, two of the three holding flashlights pointing the beams directly into my eyes. It doesn't bother me. I can see well enough to murder them in any light.

Red-rimmed eyes and the stench of too much sweat assault me as I step within their midst and I frown in distaste as I recall once a scent lingering on Edith's skin. Had they touched her then? Or simply drawn too near? Do I want to know the answer? I don't. I truly don't…

"Oh shit. This is the Lahve guy," one of the males informs the rest. He points at me. He is an idiot. And it matters not. Stupidity will not save him.

"Edith, I'm here." I pitch my voice loud, aware that she, too, is human. Though I don't understand how. How can she be the same species as these males? It took six of them to intimidate one of her? How powerful do they believe her to be? I hear shuffling inside the shack. The males speak to one another, Leif insults me, but I don't bother with that.

Yet.

"Thank you for calling for me, Edith," I laud, even though I want to punish and kiss her senseless for not having called for me sooner, days before…*years*…And yet, if she had not experienced the horrors she did at the hands of so many males in so many gangs, she'd have had no reason to stumble into my path, or for me to fall across hers. I frown even more severely at the thought that I have profited too well from those horrors. *Never again*…

"Nithril? Is that really you?" Her shaky voice calls.

Leif staggers towards the door and slumps against the threshold. "Sure is, baby. Come out and say hello. Your buddy here can clean up your pussy after you give us what we're owed."

My lips tighten and my hands flex. To use such crass language before a female is a flogging offense. To use such crass language before *my* female means death.

I fight for composure and speak evenly as I say, "Edith, you may open the door. Leif nor his…*friends* can harm you."

"Wouldn't trust this guy, Candy. He can't do shit to us."

"He's just Abel's bitch."

"Even if Abel found out about this, the worst that bitch could do is take away drink tickets…"

"Like we need 'em when we've got access to way stronger shit…"

They laugh and continue to bolster their own confidence. I allow them. Were I to kill one of them now, the rest would scatter and I don't want to do that. I want them here for a while more. I need to see Edith with my own eyes. I need *her* to pass their judgment, help me decide between a host of creative and exciting tortures.

"Are you sure?" Her voice is shaky and small. I'm not even certain the other males can hear her.

I step forward, moving squarely within the circle the males create. I move only as fast as the slowest Heztoichen, but they still take a cautionary step back. All but the one. Leif urges them forward again, his brow drawn. "You want a piece of this ass, you're going to have to wait in line."

I swallow the fire in my throat and allow it to char my stomach, turning the calm, composed male I have become, to ash. My entire body shudders. Leif sees and his eyes widen. He lowers the bottle of alcohol from his lips — the bottle of whiskey.

My voice cuts. "That does not belong to you."

He follows the direction of my gaze to his hand and snickers, "Sure does. This here's rent money. It's either this or she pays on her back."

"Or on her hands and knees," one of the other males croaks. They all laugh and I close my eyes and tilt my head to the left and to the right. It cracks. Unusual.

He laughs and runs his hands back through his hair. Rocking back onto his heels, he stumbles slightly. "You see, she goes and fucks you for booze, then she gives it to me. It's a neat little system we got goin' on here, don't you think?"

The door cracks open with a jerk and Edith looks at me with terror in her eyes. "I'm sorry, Nithril."

I am...angry. It takes me to that moment to realize that I am also angry with her. The situation was needless and it... hurts me knowing I have been, in any way, complicit in it. I should have asked. I should have followed her more diligently. I should never have given her the bottles and yet I fear deeply what would have happened had I not. She didn't trust me, then. She would have told me none of it.

I nod and hold out my arm, voice thick with emotion that I choke through. "Come. You don't need to hide here anymore."

She nods and there is a hope and a relief in her eyes that makes me feel like I just swallowed nails. I was wrong before. *She didn't trust me then, but perhaps now, she trusts me a little.* "Let me just grab my things..." She takes a half step back into the shadows.

"Your things?"

"Yeah." Shuffling. The rearranging of objects.

I walk calmly between the males to the door of this shed and gently, with only the backs of two knuckles, push the door open. It swings inward and my stomach...I...I may be sick. The stench of males is overpowering, nearly enough to rival Edith's sweet scent, and it's concentrated on a flimsy mattress on the corner covered in a threadbare pillow and a thin blanket.

There are clothes stacked in piles on the packed dirt floor. Above them, there are two shelves built into both the left and right walls covered in small trinkets. Lopsided pottery, clearly a demonstration of earlier attempts for nothing she makes is so clumsy nowadays, line one shelf in its entirety…but as for the other items, they don't make sense.

A silver hairbrush, a few scattered bills from countries that once existed but don't anymore, a white ball with red stitching, two gold rings, three paperback books, a small handheld music box, one cookbook, a small six-sided puzzle… Though my rheach does not extend to inanimate objects in the way I can a living flesh and blood being, I can still get a sense of them. And they were all previously owned by men. Males. This one, the cookbook? I can smell the blood of a Heztoichen lingering in its shell.

I am…

I am stunned.

The cage has been ripped off of my rage like skin from a soul. I try to fight against it. I lay on top of it like a body over a bomb, but it just rips through me. The sound that pours from my vocal cords shakes me to the foundations of my boots. I have been wounded. Oh, how I have been wounded. I have lived a million lifetimes. I have seen the end of wars. I have been there when the final blade falls and the war is won. I have been there when the final blade falls and the war is lost.

"Edith," I choke, vocal cords deep and vibrating, making my tone threatening. I have no ability to temper it now. "Do you sleep here?"

She glances at me over her shoulder and it is then that I notice the blood at the corner of her mouth. I shift into the room, arriving before her in under a breath. She jolts and jerks up to standing and I notice that she's holding a change of clothes balled up in her hands. Just one change of clothes. *Because she intends to sleep at my house tonight and then return here.*

My gaze travels down to her bare toes and then moves over the packed dirt floor, to the pile of blankets in the corner. There is a pillow there because she sleeps here. That she has fucked men here does not devastate me in the same way I am ruined at the knowledge that she. sleeps. here. She says that she has not touched another man since we have started to…dine together, and I believe her. She said no to Leif and I can see evidence of that in the slight swelling at one edge of her mouth and the bottle he has half depleted. She traded with him and, when she had naught left to trade but her own skin, she ran and hid and called for me.

It's good. She called for me. She trusts me. I repeat the words over and over. *This isn't a straight line, it is a process. Trust-building does not come easily for her…* I repeat the words until they infest my organs and infect my muscles, until they turn everything rancid and grotesque. *She is trying. She tried… She failed. She fucking failed.*

Because she's been sleeping here since I've known her, out in the woods in a pile of trash.

"Answer me."

She jumps and steps back until her spine meets the wall. It shudders beneath her weight, which is so very little. A strong breeze could take down this shack. Five males could, easily. She swallows and has the gaul to fucking tell me, "Not every night. Sometimes, I sleep at Ashlyn's or Kassie's or… with you…"

"Oh shit! Bro didn't know about the whorehouse," Leif crows and the others laugh uproariously. Liquor sloshes in the bottle that they share between themselves.

"Silence," I bark.

He does not listen. He does not care. He is…unfamiliar with his place in the hierarchy of this world, but he will learn. "Welcome to the whore's house, my friend. It's the whorehouse because you know, Candy's a whore, and it's the whore's house. Get it?"

"Silence," I bark. *Oh yes, he will learn.*

"Fucking make me."

My composure…*shatters* just a little bit. I shift and round on Leif and when I advance on him, it is with my hand outstretched and my mental barriers up. I want to feel *nothing* of his memories as they relate to Edith and I am grateful that he is so fucked up as it creates a better buffer on his memories than even I can. Instead of painted images and visions accompanied by sensation, all I feel are sensations and pleasure. Unrivaled pleasure at the superiority he feels he has over me and the superiority he knows he has over Edith.

I grab him by the neck and carry him outside, away from the shack and slam him down onto his back amidst the leaves. I quake with the desire not to kill him and concentrate hard as I back away from him only as far as his feet. I shatter all of the bones beneath his sneakered shoes and it is even quicker than envisioned in the steel-toed boots Tasha provided me.

Hm. Perhaps, I will need to thank Tasha for these, too.

I repeat the process five more times, treating each male with *care*. It is only as I reach the sixth male that Leif even recognizes his own pain and releases a belting scream. *He will wake the camp and they will come searching. I can't have that.* I re-enter the shake, then depart again, grabbing fistfuls of leaves from the ground and using leaves and dirt and the prickly bushes I find to create gags for each of the men. I bind the materials into place using strips of Leif's shirt, torn and fastened behind their heads.

Then I remove their eyes. All twelve of them. I know that they will survive without their eyes. Their tongues, however, would have been a problem. Eye sockets don't bleed nearly as much as tongues do — the muscle is too thick, you see, so, without a flame and a sharp knife to cauterize the wound, the eyes for now will have to do. I'll return with flame and a sharp knife to remove their tongues later. I lack the control for such an activity now anyways.

I am shaking as I arrive before Edith and drop the eyes at her feet. She gasps and releases a high-pitched squeal as she attempts to stumble away from them, but this shack is too small, she has nowhere to go.

"Come." It's all I can say.

She looks up at me panting, flames in her cheeks, eyes wide with emotions, none of which I can name. I cannot rheach into her thoughts and, in this moment, I do not want to. I don't want to touch her. I feel...too ashamed.

She is a perceptive female and has a high drive for self-preservation. She does not speak, merely nods, and reaches for a small canvas sack into which she shoves her spare set of clothing. She reaches for a book on her shelf of...*collections*, next and I debase myself even further before her by moving to intercept her.

I slam my fist through both shelves in the same motion. "Why?" I roar as her many *gifts* go tumbling to the floor amidst crumbs of wood.

She gasps and covers her mouth with her hands, dropping her sack in the process. Good. I don't want it near me. I don't want any of this fucking shit near me. "Why what?"

"Why have you been sleeping here with the rats?" My chest is tight, my lungs are searing.

"I didn't...I just..." She cups her elbows and cowers, watching me between fluttering eyelashes with eyes rimmed in red. She's going to start crying and I'll lose whatever tattered shreds of sanity I have left.

"Don't you dare cry," I hiss. "Explain this to me. Your shelf of trophies. Your filthy rags." I gesture to the bed.

"You...you have no right to come in here and judge." She sniffles. "Sex work is honest work."

"Candy, do not test me!" I shatter the wall with one sweep of my arm, sending the roof pitching towards the ground.

She drops down to one knee and covers her head with her hands and looks up at me with something like...betrayal. Tears drip down her cheeks.

"What?" I have the awareness to ask. I don't know how when all I can feel is my broken heart shattering to the same nothing I feel when we touch. I am lost in the shadows of the jungle now, and she is nowhere in sight to guide me.

She hesitates, then whispers, "You called me Candy."

I close my eyes and gesture to the door with my hand… it's…*shaking*. "Edith, go outside now."

She glances at the ground. Scattered around her bare feet are the bloodied ends of glossy white eyes, streaked with red and in so many different shades. Brown, grey, blue. I believe she's stepped on two of them. She's kneeling on a third. She covers her mouth with her hands and her back heaves, like she might be sick.

"Or what?" She sniffles, lifting her hands carefully from the floor and rubbing away any vitreous jelly or blood on her shirt. "Are you going to take out my eyes, too?"

My fist crashes through the tin door, wrenching it from its frame. I toss it onto the bodies of the males writhing outside in agony, attempting to crawl some kind of direction, then I return and kick out the left wall, bringing both sides of the shack down on Edith's head.

"Wait!" She cries out, surging up onto her feet. She comes towards me and falls to her knees in the debris. Her shaking fingers close around the music box. She plucks it free of the wreckage and I quickly take it from her and smash it into pieces. "Don't!" She screams, but I could give a fuck what of this she wants to keep. I kick out the final wall and, before she's crushed beneath the flimsy tin, I grab her around the waist and throw her over my shoulder.

I deposit her outside and decimate of the rest of the shack in a clash of thunder. It takes almost no effort at all.

She stumbles back as I work and bumps accidentally into one of the males. She gasps and looks down at him in horror. "Chamberlain?" She calls him. She calls him by *name* as if he deserves so much from her, as if she, mate of the Lahve, were not towers above his pathetic station as the most abominable and hated male in all of Brianna.

Were there any doubt before over whether or not she is my mate, there is no longer an ounce. *Only a mate could drive another to such madness* — I think inadvertently of Diego and

Pia and the bond that they share and the horrors that Diego faced before knowing her — *or bring them back from it…*

Pia loved Diego with all of his flaws and responded to them in only kindness. Kindness is not what I'm showing Edith now. Not in the slightest. Yet…I cannot pull back.

"Candy please…please help me!" The blonde male — Chamberlain — calls. She stretches her hand down to him and, before I can help myself, I advance on the male and rip his arm clean off.

"Don't you *dare* help one of them!" I shove the bloodied end of the arm in her face and slam one foot down on Chamberlain's spine, sinking my boot straight through him. It had…not been my intention. I wanted him alive. *Fuck.* "Go! Get the fuck out of here, Edith. Go straight to my home and don't you dare tell another soul about this."

She looks like she might rebel but, on consideration of the disembodied arm I thrust into her face, she turns on her heel and runs, red hair thrashing behind her. I use the seconds of her departure to level the rest of the shed, ensuring that everything inside of it is pulverized should Edith think to betray me and come back for any of it. I shred the blankets and sheets. I destroy the books, I ensure that the insects will have plenty of mulch to make their new homes in. I level the shed until it never was and, when I'm finished, I scatter the debris.

I spare only six planks of wood, and only the sturdiest beams. I can hear Edith still running through the woods. She is shaken and hesitating, as if she still thinks to come back for them or for me. I am too angry to care which. I just know that I will need to finish with the men before she makes it back to the village. I have half a mind to believe that she might be driven by her soft heart to alert one of the Notare to what I'm doing and I do not want anyone asking questions. I will need to catch her before she has that chance.

I move at speed, breaking the planks of wood into spears. I am careful when I impale the men — I don't want to puncture any vital organs, so I choose the fleshy parts of their thighs and stomachs, one of the skinnier ones I puncture in his broken foot.

Realizing that I have unfortunately already killed Chamberlain, I use the last plank to puncture Leif twice — once in either hand. I nail him to the ground, like the prophet of the cross that hangs around his neck that he has no right to wear.

I cover the men's writhing, screaming forms with the rubble from the shack so that they won't be so easily spotted by the errantly wandering Heztoichen, and then I leave with a vow to return to torture them some more in a few days…and then every day after that.

I make my way after Edith, catching her before she stumbles onto the paved street. I sweep her legs, toss her over my shoulder and, before she can mount her first attempt at rebellion, we are in my home, on the third floor and she is in my bed. I lay her in its center and move immediately to the door.

"I will leave you in privacy in your home."

She glances around, shocked, then looks up at me, vengeful. She stumbles off of the bed, knocking a pillow into the nightstand and sending the lamp on top of it crashing to the floor. I watch it happen without making any move to stop it. I want to break more things.

"You have no right to judge me for that!" Her swollen mouth quivers as she speaks and the red blood staining her lips calls to me tantalizingly. It insults me, making me desire when I know who gave her such a mark. "It's not wrong to want things and to barter for them. When I first got to Brianna, I didn't even understand that you could have a skill as a woman. When I was married to Drago, I would do… stuff for him and he would do stuff for me and that's how I thought it worked," she shrieks.

My mind is spinning. "You…are *married?*"

"Was married...bonded...whatever." She shrugs one shoulder, her rage building. "But you…"

"You are bonded to another Heztoichen?" These bonds are sacred and difficult to break, except through death. Exchanging blood is only done when love is pure and true. To know that she has shared this with another makes me feel suddenly worthless…

Edith throws out her arms, "My brother, Rick, sold me to Drago. Drago made me one of his wives. I would trade sexual favors with him and he would play music for me or whittle me little figurines. It was nice…sometimes."

There is too much in this sentence for me to unpack. My rage makes it impossible, anyway. I storm forward two steps, then jolt to a stop, afraid to touch her, afraid to stay, afraid to leave… "Where is this Drago now?"

She shudders again and crosses her arms. She uses her overlong sleeve to dab at the blood on the corner of her mouth. "I stabbed him, but it was Kane and Abel who killed him." *Yes, I remember Drago. A false Notare exiled to the woods. And he had her.*

A wretched choking sound pours out of me. "Is there no perversion you haven't endured?"

She looks away, cheeks blazing, shoulders curling in. She stumbles over nothing and plops down onto the bed. She shrugs as she picks at the bedding. "Dunno."

She punches the fight right out of me. I hold my forehead in my hand and massage my temples with my thumb and middle finger. "This home, it is a gift to you. Yours to own privately. Patty and Lima will be available to assist you, should you need anything."

"Where will you go?"

"I will be fine," I lie. I am not fine. I am everything but.

"I can't take your house."

"Don't worry, I will find somewhere else to rest. Somewhere with running water and electricity that isn't covered in the scent of different males."

"You're an asshole."

"Is that where Leif fucked you?" The words...are heinous. I can't...believe I said them.

Evidently, Edith cannot either because she's silent for a beat before she screeches and throws a pillow at me. It doesn't reach its mark, but I advance nonetheless. She rises up onto her knees in the center of the bed, like she might try to attack me. I grab her wrists. She thrashes and shakes her head trying to dislodge me. "You're such a dick!"

"Edith," I say, trying to calm her, but she just jerks more and harder, exhausting herself. "Edith, you might hurt yourself. Stop. I'm sorry." I wrestle her down against the sheets and use my legs to still hers. When we stop moving, I realize that we are in a precarious position, my knees spreading hers open wide, one of my hands holding hers above her head, the other pressed beneath her left breast, feeling the rapid, rabid thump of her heart. It strains her skin, worrying me.

"Edith, please. I'm sorry. I shouldn't have said that..."

"I like having sex! I liked having sex with those guys. It's not wrong to get something out of it..." She's panting hard and I have the strange sensation that something large and unyielding between us is about to break.

I should pull back...but her words rattle me in unfamiliar ways. I clench harder and bare down against her, my hips grinding against her hips even though I don't mean for them to, as if to prove to her that I'm just like the rest... "Then why did you cry at dinner the first time I spoke to you? Why do you cower every time you're out in Population? Why do you remember Drago with fear and Rick with regret?"

Her eyes squeeze shut and she shouts, voice hoarse, "I don't! I wasn't scared of them. I was scared of you!"

"Scared that I'd bite you, because you've been bitten before." I drag my hand up her chest and slip my thumb beneath the collar of her shirt. I drag it down, exposing her scars and she tucks her chin, trying to stop it. "And you didn't like it."

"No… Drago…took care of me. He was a good husband."

"He was no such thing. Did he treat you the same as Kane does Abel? Do you think she asks him not to bite her, or do you think she asks him to bond her because she knows the pleasure it brings."

Edith sucks in a breath sharp between her teeth as I bend down…down…lower…and place a featherlight kiss against her scars, cherishing every one.

"Do you fear me so much that you'd yell at me like this? That you'd slap me like you did before?" She shifts underneath me, pushing her hips up into mine. I ignore the spike of pleasure that slams through me and create more distance between us. It isn't easy as the energy rolls and shifts, moving from rage to become another monster entirely. "If you fear me so much and you enjoy Leif so dearly, why didn't you slap him, hm? Why did you prefer, rather to trade him the bottles I gave you?"

She doesn't answer. Instead, her calves brush over the backs of my legs as she tries to fold her legs around me. Her eyes are closed when I pull back. She licks her lips. I stare at her scars, memorizing their every inch, before sliding her turtleneck back into place. "Is that why you didn't come to me those nine nights?"

"Nine?" Her eyebrows pull together. She blinks. "It was only four."

"It felt like forty."

She searches my gaze for something. I allow her to look and brush a hand through her hair. Cold. It shouldn't be so cold when her face is so hot. "He and the guys found out I was coming over here and they wanted me to steal from you. I said no, so they tried to block me. They would block the routes but they get drunk so early, I could sneak around them most nights."

"And the night you showed up without a shirt?"

"They were chasing me through the woods and Greg grabbed my shirt. I slipped out of it and got away."

I exhale, bereaved and say, "Why didn't you tell me? Why did you expressly ask me not to intervene?"

She shrugs as best she can in her prone position, immobilized beneath me, and tears well on her lower lashes. "I'm embarrassed. I didn't...I didn't know the other women weren't trading sex for things. When Abel told me I wasn't allowed to bring a guy back to Ashlyn's to trade sex with, I found the shed and took them there. I didn't understand that she meant I wasn't allowed to bring a guy back to trade sex with *period*. And by the time I did realize that other women didn't do stuff like that or that even most men didn't want stuff like that from me, I was too embarrassed to tell Abel about the shed or ask Ashlyn and the other girls in her house to move back in. I lied to everybody and told them I was living other places and I..."

She sniffles deep and exhales, just as defeated as I feel. "I was too embarrassed to tell the guys that still did want from me no, too. I don't know. They would give me little things and I...felt like I owed them."

I hang my head and slowly, slowly roll off of her. I lie on my side, my bare arm pressed against the outside of her long sleeved shirt.

"Please don't tell anyone about the shed," she whispers, "especially Abel and Kane and Diego and Pia. Please."

I shake my head and stare up at the ceiling. There's a fan there. I've never used it. I wonder if Edith would like to. I haven't asked her. "I won't."

"I'm sorry."

"You should be."

"I know you're some big shot on your planet and probably used to having sex with pretty virgins or queens or something. And I know I shouldn't have been having sex with those guys for stuff and that I should have just told Abel in the beginning. So, I'm sorry."

"No. This is not what you should be sorry for."

She hesitates. "What do you mean?"

"You were abused and have been abused and I approached you just like one of your other abusers. You had no reason to think me any different..."

"But I *do* think you're different. You...you've given me more than any other guy ever has but I still don't feel like I owe you. I've been trying to figure out why, but I can't."

I close my eyes. My heart...my poor, fragile heart. It has been so battered today that I don't think it will ever recover... in fact, I know it will not. "It is respect."

"Hm?"

"I respect you. I am glad that it shows."

"I don't think that's it," she whispers. She moves and, when I tilt my head to face her, I see that she's rolled onto her side to face me. Her hands, she's slid beneath her cheek in prayer, making her look too tender. As tender as the bruises that grace her cheek. "I think you make me respect *me,* however you do it."

She blushes. My heart...my poor heart. "Thank you, Edith."

"Thank you, Nithril."

"I am sorry for not having been more clear in my initial approach, or perhaps, for not having attempted to seduce you with more finesse. It was desperation to talk to you that had me asking you to dine with me in the first place. I was powerless against my curiosity and your allure."

A smile flickers across her lips before dying. "I wouldn't have believed you."

I nod. "Perhaps not."

"I'm sorry."

"Your apology is not owed for this either. You did not know my intentions and were acting only with the prejudices you harbor against all of the other males you have known."

Her face scrunches. "Then what do you want me to apologize for?"

"I want to be the knife in your hand when you go to battle and, when you're backed into a corner, I want to be your shield. The moment you realized that you no longer wanted to have relationships with Leif or the others, you did not call for me. You hid, you allowed them to chase, you ran, you allowed them to humiliate you. Why? I told you I would come. Why did you not call for me?"

I roll onto my side to face her and prop myself up on one elbow. With rage beating through my breast, I lean forward and I carefully — *oh so carefully* — press the flat pad of my thumb to the blood on the corner of her mouth. I smear it away and even though it's the most painful thing I've ever done, I do not taste. I wipe it on the sheets and watch her eyes widen, then shutter. She glances at my mouth, at my chest, lower…and then closes eyes altogether.

"You…you make me feel like I'm not helpless. When I slapped you, you didn't…" She shrugs, a defensive response I do not like but that I understand, just like so many others. "You didn't hit me back. I thought that if I could slap *you*, I couldn't…shouldn't be scared of Leif. He's just a drunk and a bully."

"You slapped me because I allowed you to slap me. Because I would never hurt you and you *know* that. The same is not true for other males like Leif."

"I…didn't think of that." Edith licks the bloody spot at the edge of her mouth, sending painfully acute sensation straight to my groin. I ignore it, touch her chin very softly and tilt her face up to see mine. I want there to be no mistaking my words as I offer her a true Tretaro vow.

"It is not a weakness to ask for help. Many would find it even more difficult than coming to someone else's aid. There is…something about asking for help that makes us feel vulnerable, frightened, afraid of rejection, perhaps, or of failure. But asking for help is a sign of strength and of confidence, not just in yourself, but in the one you choose to ask.

"Believe in me, Edith. Please. I beg this of you. I will come every time. If you need wood ash for your glaze. If you have a splinter. If you need warmth in the night, I will come. If you are cornered by six attackers looking to hurt and violate you, I will come and I will *slaughter* and I will not ever think less of you for having asked. It..." My voice chokes without me meaning for it to. A funny thing, it is...not something that has happened to me before her.

"I want your trust more than I want your body or your blood and, until very recently I believed your body and your blood to be the things I wanted most in this world. When you allow yourself to be harmed when you *know* that I could have helped you and *have* offered to help you in the past, it makes me feel like you do not trust me...like you don't even like me. And I like you..." I lick my lips, feeling every bit as vulnerable as an opened wound. "I like you very, very much."

She blinks, her jaw hinges open. She swallows hard and then says, "I like you, too."

I shake my head, ribbons of my thick hair draping over her hands as I lean forward, kiss her tenderly in the center of the forehead and then pull back. "We shall see. For now, I take my leave of you."

Edith sniffles and nods and I wonder if she understands how shaken I am, or if she is merely shaken herself. This was all too much for her on this day. An assault followed by my... *small* meltdown. I need a chance to calm down before I speak with her again. I need...I need a fucking drink.

Sitting at the edge of the bed, I grab my knees and force myself to stand. "You have lived through Population's horrors, but this is not Population. You are not there anymore. And even if you do, for some terrible reason, find yourself there again, you would not be there because you can bring Brianna with you. You can bring *me* with you. All you have to do is ask. Call out to me for help. You remembered to do so today and for that I'm grateful, but you have forgotten too many times in these past days. Do not forget again or you will break my heart into pieces that cannot be repaired."

I move to the bedroom door and start to close it when I hear her whisper, "Leif really won't come back?"

"Only a God could bring them back, and gods forsook your planet long ago." I nod, intending to leave, but again, her voice arrests me.

"You'll really come?" She says as I step towards the door, her voice needy and vulnerable, begging me to stay in tone alone.

My hand tightens on the brass doorknob, leaving it warped like melted gold, as I fight that urge. I pry my hand off of it just as the radio on my belt crackles. No sound comes through. My nostrils flare as I try to find center, but in the span of an evening, the world has shifted and turned.

"Neither death nor time could stop me." I shudder on the exhale, my bones feeling swollen in the casing of my skin, so much harder than hers, so much more lethal.

"Thank you, Nithril," she says.

I nod. "Patty and Lima will be up with food and I will send Sandra, the human healer, to check on you."

"Thank you."

"You don't need to thank me. As you've already assessed, everything that is mine is already yours. You owe me nothing." *Nothing but your heart.* It seems only a fair trade to replace the one I've lost to her.

"Thank you all the same."

I am out of the house, halfway down the street when I finally hear her say it, so quietly, like it's a secret she does not believe any others can hear. I *shouldn't* be listening. I vowed her space — a foolish promise. Because in the same instant, I know that I would fall on a thousand swords at her command, without hesitation.

"I like him *too* much," she whispers to herself and I can tell there is a smile on her tongue. "Nithril…"

I fight back a ragged grin of my own, startling the group of drunk couples walking towards me and causing them to give me a wide berth and I am still grinning, even as I hear it said...

"*Nithril.*"

I freeze, my next step not yet fallen to the pavement as I hear a voice call to me, but not the same one. It isn't Edith. Instead, the crackling of the machine at my hip draws my hand to it. I lift it from where it had been clipped to my belt and hold, waiting, tense.

"*I forget, you do not respond to such a name anymore,*" comes the deep brogue. He coos, the sound using a range of vocal cords he should not possess. He is not Tretaro. He should not have this second set. "*Lahve. I believe it is time that you and I properly met.*"

Chapter Thirteen

"Ｗhat did he say?" Notare Abel pierces me with a look that might have appeared stern under any other circumstances. Because in any other circumstance, I would have had a better hold over my own rage.

Stern. Stern? Stern has nothing on the raw emotion I display.

And I do not feel the smallest, most tattered shred of embarrassment. Rather, I allow centuries of repressed emotion to roll over me, unrestrained. *I will need to go visit Leif later today,* I think with a grim smile that causes most of the Heztoichen and all of the humans looking in my direction to look elsewhere. *That will make me feel better.*

"Malmon wants to meet with me." I close my eyes and hold them closed. I flex my ears forward and listen to the sounds of sixteen different hearts beating. I stand in the damn council chambers with both Notare and the damn council of Brianna, but there are feet on the stairs and a voice saying my name. Teera's. She is close. She should not be... She should be at my home, guarding Edith.

"Lahve?" Abel says.

I ignore her, the disgrace that I have become. And I don't give a fuck. Instead, I stiffen as the front door to this house opens and shuts. The sound of two different footsteps drags my attention to the door and ice and heat roll down my frame in alternating strokes. I am...not prepared. Abel is speaking, but I don't hear her. All I hear is the sound of Edith's soft voice echoing through the walls. *"Are you joining the council meeting, too?"*

"Not quite," Teera answers. "But I'll go in with you."

"Oh," Edith says, not quite understanding.

I can hear the smile on Teera's voice as she replies, "I'm not here for the council meeting. I'm here for you."

"Really?"

"Indeed."

Abel is still speaking, but I'm not listening. I have more important things to listen to. The sound of the doorknob turning. The human heart beating in the thin chest of the female I intend to make mine through every declaration, vow, form of worship or bond that exists between our two planets, and all the rest we don't yet know. The door opens and Edith steps inside, making space for Teera to follow her.

Teera. It pains me to see her. After all, the rest of my guard is most likely slaughtered, making her the last of them.

The two females hover near the door as attention in the room turns to them. My lips pinch together as I take in Edith's face. The blood is gone, but the bruising on the right corner of her mouth is more pronounced today. Purple strokes her jaw. Her lower lip is still slightly swollen. *Yes, I will go visit Leif today. That will be nice.*

Against the wall opposite from where I stand, Pia sucks in a small breath and Diego starts forward.

"C-C-Candy," he barks. He stares across the room at me before looking back at her and I understand the implication. He thinks *I* did this to her. Were he not *something* to Edith, I would have no problem decapitating him. Cleanly. With just one single swipe of my sword. No need to stake him in the forest. It's the smallest mercy I can afford.

She looks up at him, wide eyed, and shakes her head quickly.

"Y-y-you lllllyin'? D-D-D-on't need to be sc-sc-scared."

Perhaps…not so cleanly, then. Perhaps, with a dull axe.

"N-no, Diego. No, Pia." She tucks her hair behind her ear and takes a fortifying breath that…surprises me. It also saves Diego's life. Because when she looks up next, her shoulders shrug down her back and she looks almost…not fully, but quite nearly…confident. No, not confident. Brave. She's trying and I have never seen her try before to anyone else. *To me, she tries all the time.* It fills me with pride. My feet edge towards her. I want to go to her and wrap her in my cloak and tell her that all will be okay.

"It wasn't Nithril…Lahve."

Diego's eyebrows arch up high on his forehead, the scar bisecting the left eyebrow exaggerating what would have otherwise been a subtle expression.

"It wasn't," she insists, turning red in the face as she seems to notice, for the first time, how many gazes are on her. "I promise."

Fuck this.

I move rapidly to her side and, arriving there, shove my hands into the pockets of my coat. It is my normal coat however, I am wearing another of Tasha's tee shirts beneath it. Edith focuses on my tee shirt, black today, before looking up at me, cheeks exploding in even sharper color. I am… regretting having moved across the room — I did not want to make her uncomfortable — but, now that I am here, I am bound.

"No, Nithril didn't do this," she says to him, to me, to the room.

"D-D-Don't f-ffffffucking t-tell me it was Leif."

"It was not." I clear my throat and wrench my gaze away from Edith's. The shape of her eyes is lovely. Round and big, eyes slightly too far apart on her face. Mouth, slightly too big. I look up around the room, speak to them all casually, easily, with flourish. "It was not this…Leif, individual of whom you speak. In fact, I believe I heard talk that Leif and several of his…*associates* had enough of your rule, Notare, and wished to take their leave. They may have left already, as I have not been able to rheach them within the walls of Brianna for days."

Silence.

Abel smacks her lips. "Are you lying to your Notare?"

"I would remind you that, as Lahve, my duties extend only to communicating information relevant to each Notare. Nothing more."

"What the hell is that supposed to mean?"

It means yes, I am lying to you. "It means that it would not behoove you to ask any further questions."

Pia's gentle voice cuts in. "Leif did that to you, sweetheart?"

"No. I fell." *My Ipalora. My sweet, bloodthirsty Ipalora. I never did tell Edith that the Ipalora are carnivores…*

I touch her lower back with the palm of my hand, pressing it flat against her. She tenses up, but does not pull away and, after another moment more, settles into my touch. She leans against me. I am…overcome. That I manage to restrain myself from backing her against the wall ransacking her mouth with my tongue is truly a testament to my strength.

"You two are assholes." She means the words in jest, but I feel as the muscles in Edith's lower back bunch beneath my fingertips. I recall the words I said to her last night and regret all of them.

"No," I blurt, feeling deranged. "*I* am an asshole. You owe Edith an apology."

"What?" Abel drops down onto her hands and stares at me. I do not say more, but wait for the apology to come. Edith is attempting to make excuses for my behavior, but Abel's gaze and mine are locked, as are our wills. Finally she balks and looks over her shoulder at her mate, "Is he for real?"

Kane leans against the wall beside the window and he's hiding his mouth with one hand. It does nothing to cage the amusement however, radiating out of his eyes, crinkling their corners. "I believe so."

"Invasion of the body snatchers?"

Kane tilts his head. "No idea what that is, but based on theory, I'd say no."

"Then he's lost his mind. Is that it?"

"Most certainly."

"Augh," Abel huffs. "Well, *Edith*," she says, trying the name out and smiling slightly as she says it, "Short for Meredith?"

Edith nods.

"I thought I heard Rick call you that once. Anyway, I am very sorry. You are not an asshole. He is an asshole. And let's just move past this before I send for a doctor to take a look at the both of you. I'm not convinced there isn't some sort of face swap or personality disorder going on right now." She levels me with a glare and, when I do not relent in the slightest, she shakes her head and grumbles beneath her breath about what a bunch of sorry liars we are, and how she hopes Leif gets his comeuppance, wherever he is.

I smile as she repeats her previous question. "Malmon. What do you think he wants?"

"Malmon wants to draw me outside of these walls. Now that he has taken my guard, he believes me to be more vulnerable. I suspect that he believes that by killing me, the two of you stand little chance against whatever forces he has amassed. I believe it within his...confidence to take both of your territories."

"He thinks you're that big a deterrent?" A female seated in the window box says. She has dark hair and skin just a shade or two darker than Abel's, a round face and high cheeks. Her intelligent eyes are filled with humor, as if the idea of war is a joke. "I mean, he thinks that you alone determine whether or not he can take over not one but *two* different regions? One of them controlled by a three hundred year old dude?"

I don't like her tone or her insinuation, particularly in front of Edith to whom I have already pledged vows of protection and plan to pledge many more. Were we standing now at the time of the pre-Frost, I would have knelt before her and let her scar my chest with a sign all her own, to confirm my pledge of devotion. Perhaps I should. *Would she like that?*

I shrug it off. *She can scar me later.* I lean forward onto the balls of my feet and level the female with a penetrating glare. I drop my tone, insiria straining as the words come out of my mouth in overlapping tones. *"While I stand within these walls, there is not a Heztoichen army nor a thousand, that will breach them. Any who try to conquer will be slit from neck to naval, their heads impaled on pikes mounted on the perimeter as a warning to any who dare to think or dream or even wonder what it might be like to enter a territory to which they have no right and hurt* anyone *who resides within it."*

Silence.

A soft pressure around my wrist makes me wince wildly. I am so unused to being touched, I don't…understand it. I wrench away from it only to look down at Edith's outstretched hand and quickly, I grab it, not wanting to discourage her from touching me freely. The sensation of her fingers on my skin is exquisite.

"Pardon. I did not mean to," I whisper directly into her ear, so close to her, I can feel the tickle of her hair against my nose. "I am unused to being touched. But *you* are welcome to touch me whenever you like."

She tips her head to face me and I am surprised when I find us nose-to-nose. "What about wherever?"

What.

She grins devilishly and I start to sweat. Meanwhile, the other female is speaking again. "Well, that's uhh…clear enough for me."

Kane speaks after her. "I thought it was the policy of the Lahve to remain neutral?"

I look back up into his gaze, but pitch my voice loud enough for all to hear. This is…important. "As I am the *last* left of my kind and there are no Tretaro elders from whom I may seek council, it is left up to me to determine the scope of the duties and the reign of the Lahve." I speak clearly and articulately, though it's difficult when I feel the lightest fluttering of fingertips against the back of my sleeve. I react, though I try desperately not to as her fingers slide down. "I have, as such, determined that my reign of neutrality has ended." Down. "In the advent of my guard being killed, likely tortured." Down. "And a direct threat to my…" She touches the inside of my wrist, skims her fingers so tentatively over my palm I almost can't even feel her touch… and then she laces those soft, clay-encrusted fingers through mine. "To her," I finish.

"Her?" The female in the window ledge says. I recognize the female standing beside her as Star. She looked after Edith in the ceramic studio. Perhaps, these females may be afforded a rudimentary amount of trust.

"Brianna," I fumble. "It is a female name for you humans, is it not?"

The female snorts. "You believe that, Star?"

"Not sure I do, Constanzia. Think he could be talking about something else."

"*Someone*, maybe?"

"*Ohhhh*, you might be onto something."

Abel starts to laugh. Kane covers the back of her neck with his hand, and covers his mouth with his other.

"You *dare*," I hiss at the females, rattling a soft battle cry — a warning. "I am…"

"They're teasing you," Edith whispers at my side. "They tease everybody. They're harmless. Well, not *harmless*. But harmless in this."

"Teasing?"

More laughter echoes throughout the room. The one called Constanzia says loudly, "Oh my, I think our Lahve might be blushing."

"I do not blush. My skin is far too dark for it to show color." More laughter, louder now. I groan, "Humans..."

Edith gives my hand two soft squeezes. I don't know what they mean, but I like them. It feels...like a soft reassurance. I'm so caught in the act that I don't immediately notice the mood of the room grow somber until it's silent.

"Lahve," Abel says. I meet her stare. Her dark, flinty blue eyes are a fascinating contrast to the color of her skin and the darkness of her hair. She manages to somehow be both naive and cunning at the same time, triumphant in everything, but insecure. A contradiction. And her mate worships her for all of it. "I can't say I'm not happy to have you on team let's-not-genocide-all-the-humans. Now that you've chosen, what do you suggest? We should fortify the walls, obviously. I mean, right? Should we try to send in a team to free your guard? How did they even get captured? Aren't they the best? And I guess we should find a new location for our next outpost. Maybe Candy — Edith, sorry — could help with that. We should maybe think..."

"No." My voice carries through the room, reverberating with madness. I clutch Edith's hand tighter, worrying about the pressure, but she doesn't complain or pull away from me. "The time for running is over. You will not be corralled and duped as you were with Jack. We will not lose more fighters to torture by walking into their traps. We will not cede anymore ground. *Not. another. yard.*

"We will divide our forces, keeping some behind to hold Brianna should we be outmaneuvered, but the bulk of our war party will move on Malmon. We will take back the outpost. He has asked for me and I will not disappoint him. But he will not expect me to align with the humans — with you. He will not expect your full force at my heels. We will take the ground they believe they have stolen and rip it from beneath their feet.

"We will establish Brianna's first outpost and we will create safe passage all across Population until it ceases to exist. And I will tear Malmon apart myself."

Silence.

Cocky Constanzia is first to break it. "More heads on pikes?" *Teasing. She's teasing.*

So I make my first attempt...to tease back. "Of course. What do you think will line the safe passage routes?"

Constanzia's eyes bulge. She glances at Star as if to ensure she's heard me correctly. Both women burst into laughter simultaneously. "You're a crazy fucker," Constanzia says. "I like you."

Edith stiffens next to me, holding my hand tighter and I can't help but wonder if this is another jealous display. I don't care either way, I just know I like it.

Abel picks at her bottom lip until Kane pulls her hand away. "You really think we should go out there and meet them? Wouldn't it be safer to stay..."

"No." I shake my head, words as clear as their meaning. "No, it would not, Abel. If you wait for Malmon to amass all of the horrors of Population together, they will come and when they come, they will tear apart everything you have worked so hard to build. You need to meet him. Match his violence with a greater violence. Spare *none.* I made the mistake before of allowing the honorless to live. I will now rectify it."

I swallow and tip my head forward. I...struggle to meet her eyeline. "I told you a lie earlier, one of several. I told you that my neutrality ends now, but I have since realized that this is not the case. It...has been ended for quite some time. Every moment that I favored a Heztoichen life over that of a human's. Sistylea and her Tare were trying to tell me all along that this is a new planet and that I am Lahve of *all* of its creatures. I should have known this. I should have fucking known this. I should have dealt justice accordingly. But it took me a human with a glowing golden chest to see it. And another human with scars for me to believe it." Edith tenses. Everyone is tense. There is nodding all around, tight and clipped. All eyes are on Abel.

"I don't want to kill everyone. I don't…know if I even *can* meet Malmon with greater violence…"

"You cannot. But I can. With Diego, we will lead your forces. We know plenty about violence. You and Kane will remain here, Brianna's first defense. I will take Constanzia and Star, Pia and Roderick, Teera and Laiya, Romalin and the two other Heztoichen scouts that returned as my generals." My gaze flashes to Mikael. I can feel his tension. "Mikael will remain general of your army here alongside you both," I conclude. He meets my gaze purposefully, in a way I do not expect him to. "There are five thousand and twenty-two humans here, six hundred and six of which — of *whom* — are capable of wielding arms." It is a scant few. "We will take three hundred and sixty-six of them to meet Malmon head on…"

"Three hundred and sixty-seven," Edith whispers.

Heat licks the tips of my locs and sets my scalp aflame. "No." She squints up at me and when I turn to face her, pulls her hand from mine. "No," I say again, not sure to which this time. I want to grab her hand again. I want to kiss her senseless. I feel like an idiot.

"We can't walk into any more traps," she says looking between both Diego and I, and then finally to Abel. "And I'm the only one who can read their maps."

I snarl, "We will keep a radio…"

"Just like the one Malmon stole from your guard?" Her voice is so small.

"She is right. We won't be able to use the radios," Kane grumbles. There aren't enough frequencies available. Malmon will know our every move.

"I will not allow it."

Kane speaks so casually, as if we weren't discussing her life, as he says, "You may have made your choice, Lahve, would you deny her the same right?"

Yes. It's on the tip of my tongue, but I bite it. "I will not join, if she goes." I level the threat. A hiss goes up in the room.

"I w-w-wwwon't either."

"Oh for heaven's sake. Fine. Constanzia, Laiya, Teera and I will lead the damn army and Edith will guide us. Women do it better anyway." Pia steps forward, giving Diego a swat on the back of his head as she steps away from him.

He grabs her by the belt loop and wrenches her body back against his own. Against her ear, he seethes, "Don't fffffffuck with m-me, Pia."

She elbows him in the gut, hard enough to bring a small *oomph* from his lips. "I'm not." She struts into the center of the room, swinging her long blonde ponytail over her shoulder as she turns to face me. "Kane backed Abel when she went to kill Memnoch, even though it was hard, and look how that turned out."

"With her tortured and nearly killed!" I thrust forward, debasing myself as I tower over the female.

She does not back down. These human women…are wily. They're also very annoying. "And Diego saved her. And in return, Abel saved him. She saved Kane. They saved Edith. And Edith's already saved our lives at least twice by interpreting the signs written on our own walls. The Five Point Gang was *here*. Malmon is sending scouts to our doorstep. He's planning an assault, just like we're planning ours, only he's miles ahead. We need to move fast and Edith's a weapon, whether you want to use her as one or not.

"And if you don't give her the chance to make her own choices, to stand up and protect not only the people in this community, but herself, do you think *you* really deserve to stand beside her in the same way Kane stands besides Abel? Or in the way Diego stands beside me? *I'm* the one who killed Jack. I couldn't have done it without Diego. But he also couldn't have done it without me."

Too furious to speak, I spin on my heel, leave the room and slam the door behind me so hard it splinters into three enormous pieces.

A quick order to Teera to watch after Edith, I listen to the deliberations from afar, I listen *in horror* as Edith agrees to whatever plans set upon her. After returning to spend some time with Leif and his friends, removing fingernails, toes... and then more skin than I intended, I make my way to Tasha's residence. I wait there, not sure that I'm ready to go and face Edith in her home, while Tasha prepares the things I'll need for war.

Respectful, she would have made a high prize to the most elite Heztoichen on Sistylea. Obedient, yet stern. Perhaps, she would have made a Sistana. A great one. There was always speculation that she and Kane would have been a suitable match, even I had been curious as to why he never courted her and why she never pursued him as so many other Notare sycophants did. *They are friends.* And evidently Kane's tastes lie in the more...lethal. And Tasha would never dare go into battle. I frown. But to protect him? Or her Sistana? Yes, she would. She would battle for any of them.

"Nithril?" The voice on the breeze is quietly calling. I rise from the bed and bid Tasha farewell.

Before I go, she hands me a duffel bag and says, "So. Did she like the clothes?"

I nod, but don't otherwise dignify her with a response.

I find Edith sitting in the same position I left her in yesterday — in the center of the bed, only...today, she is wearing one of her silky outfits with the thick cuffs at the neck and wrists and thighs. She isn't wearing the second of the three outfits I asked Tasha to provide her and I am both aroused and disappointed by the sight of it.

"You called for me?" My gaze sweeps the space, searching for danger. Finding only an empty room, I slouch against the door.

She doesn't enlighten me, however, but sits stiffly and stares.

"Is everything alright?" I say after a pause.

"Oh yeah, I just..." She licks her lips and shifts her weight on the bed. She touches the collar at her neck and I notice that there are no lights on in the room, only the bathroom light is on and the door is cracked. Why is she sitting here in the dark? And why is she so stiff? Perhaps, she expects my ire.

"I'm not mad," I tell her with a resigned sigh.

She starts, as if surprised by my admission. "Mad?"

"About you defying me in the council meeting like that." I glare.

She returns it, then just as abruptly breaks out into a laugh. "I thought I wasn't your property. I thought I was allowed to make my own decisions, too?"

"Yes, you are. I just wish you'd made a different one."

"To sit on the sidelines and let everyone I know get murdered?"

"You did not seem so averse in the past when you suggested we abandon my guard to the humans' trap."

I wince when she does, recognizing the insult, and take another step into the room. It smells...so fucking good. Like her. And like me, too. She wears my scent and stains my sheets with hers. She smells freshly bathed, I can tell in the dampness of her hair as she drags it over her shoulder and combs her fingers through the curls.

"Edith, I..."

"No, you're right. I just...the way you looked at me when I said that. You've never looked disgusted by me when we've talked about my past or any of the things I've done…but you looked disgusted by me when I said that. I couldn't say it again. I don't want to see that look on your face ever again."

"Don't fucking tell me that I'm the reason you're going back out into Population to wage war on an adversary who's hurt you in the past and is responsible for many of your scars…"

She bites her lips, and then blurts all at once. "You make me want to be brave." She glances around, as if to ensure we're alone. "That's why I called you over."

"What?"

"Is Teera listening?"

"No. She's resting tonight."

"So, we're alone?"

My mouth is suddenly dry and my pants feel far, far too tight. It must be the fault of the jeans. I clear my throat. "Yes."

"Good."

She gets up from the bed and she takes several slow steps towards me. Her bare feet are pale against the dark wood. She has long, elegant fingers, but short, stubby little toes. I find them charming. I find everything about her charming. I want to taste her, touch her, lick her every inch. And I don't like the look she's giving me now, because it suggests she might be amenable to all of it.

I exhale slowly. "Ipalora…"

She comes to a stop far, far too close to me. I back a step up…and crash into the wall. A picture falls somewhere and the glass casing shatters. I don't search to see what it was. Edith's face is brilliant with heat and the blood rushing through her skin does nothing to help me. I want to feast.

"Edith, I…"

"Let me be brave…with you." She cups her hands over the center of my chest and uses them to brace herself as she leans against me. She reaches for my lips with her mouth, but I have to stop her in the only way I can think to.

I grab her hair in my fist and hold, hoping I'm not pulling too hard as I struggle to pull any way but hard. "Edith. I do not want to make a trade…"

"It's not a trade…"

"And I will not harass you a day after you were wounded by another male…"

"But that's exactly why I want to be with you — it…" She stammers and gently extracts herself from my grip by placing the lightest touches on my neck with her fingertips. "It has to be today. We don't have much time left and I don't know what will happen out there in Population and I'm not going to miss my chance to be with somebody that I actually like for the very first time. If I'm going to my death…"

"You are not going to fucking die…"

"If I'm going to my death," she says again, grabbing the front of my tee shirt and pulling until our bodies collide. She speaks up against my chin. I stare down into her eyes. "I want there to be a good time. Just one. I just…I don't have the healthiest relationship to sex." Her mouth quirks in an embarrassed smile.

I feel my face form a mirrored expression. "I don't have any relationship to sex."

"Wh-what?"

"It hurts to touch, to be touched and I am no masochist. I have no desire to torture myself."

"Oh my god." She pushes me away this time and I let her go even though it's damn near impossible. My senses are all focused acutely on *her,* but my mind has started to conjure other hallucinations, *fantasies,* that I want to enact. Want is too light a term. No…that *call* to me. With or without them coming to fruition, I will not leave this room the same male I was when I walked into it. That is the only certainty.

She paces to the bed and presses her hand to her lips. "You can only touch *me*…so I'm the *only* woman you can be with. *That's* why…"

"No." I do not rise to anger. I do not fall to grief. I merely tell her the truth of it. "No, Edith. Do not scar what this is between us, you who have felt the power of scars. I won't allow it. I care far deeper for you than any touch, even if touch is what started it. That is not where it ends for us."

She still does not appear convinced. I can't help but smile at that. How insignificant, a thing like lust, when I have had all the time of eternity with which to ponder it. "I told you I liked you already, before I had any expectation of sex with you."

She bites back a sudden grin and lifts a brow. "Unlike now where you *do* have expectations?"

"Expectations is the wrong word. Imaginations is more accurate." I advance a step towards her — a dangerous step — and drop my pitch. "I like you because you make me *feel.*"

"Feel?" She says when I do not.

I shrug — such a human gesture — it makes me smile, though it is a slight thing. "Feel *everything.* I have spent centuries never rising to the levels of lust, anger, interest, desire, curiosity, confusion or pleasure you have culled from me in days. You have made me feel what I have no right to feel — *human.* It is...a first for me and something worth holding onto, for all the time that we have."

She is nodding and yet...it does not reach her eyes. "I just...Look at me..." She scratches her head and looks up at me on a wince. "I can't be your first time."

"You are already my first in so many things."

"You know that's not what I mean. I mean..." She gestures at my groin crudely.

I smirk. "I want no other so, if not you, then there won't be a first and that is alright. I will not ever know what I have lost."

"No pressure." She rolls her eyes.

I grin more broadly. "None at all."

Her lips quirk and she blinks quickly. So much time drones on between us and it frightens me, how she wastes it.

Like she believes she has so much more. Each minute of her lifetime is a year of my own. Seconds become minutes. Blinks take eons. "You make me feel what I've never felt before, too," she finally whispers.

"And what is that?"

"Safe." While my sternum cracks open and my heart bleeds itself dry, she continues, the sadist that she is. She shows me no quarter. "That's why — and I know I have no right to ask you this — but if you would please reconsider coming with us. I know that you don't want me to go and I... think it's really nice. No one has ever tried to protect me from anything before. But I don't want to risk Brianna or the good people living here because you and I..."

"Edith, please." I gesture to the damn bag that I dropped at the door. "What the fuck do you think that is?"

"Your...overnight bag?"

"That is my *overnights* bag," I smirk. "I am already packed for our journey."

She smiles and I can't help but advance. She takes a step back, but I know what she's doing, the little minx. She's not being chased, I'm being led.

"Nothing will happen to you out there. We will have plenty of time if you still feel the same way about me when we return." I glance, with meaning, at the bed.

She waits another small lifetime to answer. "No. I don't want to wait."

"Thank your cruel gods," I mutter, but when she comes towards me, intent in her expression, I say a damning word. "Wait."

"What?" She pouts and my gaze drops to her outfit.

"I want something from you first."

She tilts her head. "What?"

"Your garment."

"You..want my teddy?"

"Yes. I want it off."

She stares at me, deer in the headlights, looking more afraid of my request than she ever has before. "No."

"*Yes.*"

She's afraid, watching me with a worry in her gaze that I want to take from her and stab to death. "Tasha…she makes me these so I can feel sexy but don't have to show anyone my scars…"

"I am aware and I would like to see you as no one has seen you before. Free of them."

She hesitates, rolling her ankles and twisting her fingers together. "You don't like it." She gestures to her body, a vision in black and my gaze strays…before it snaps back.

"You can't distract me." *She can.* "I have waited three thousand years. I can wait another few months." *I cannot.*

My hand flexes. I am lucky she does not notice, standing agog as she is, shoulders slouched, posture not at all what it was. I might find it…almost comical, were I not so tense. Were my cock not about to explode along with my balls. In a move too bold to fathom, I pull my shirt off over my head and her gaze drops. I am pleased, never more so than when her voice comes out as a squeak.

"Months? You want to wait *months*?"

"Why? Is that not long enough? I can be convinced to wait years." I reach for my belt and tug it free.

She opens her mouth to speak, but makes a slight strangling sound that sends heat straight to my groin. It's a wonder I'm still standing upright as I toss my belt aside and free the button. Zipper goes next.

"You're telling me that you are fully prepared to put your clothes back on now?"

"Of course." *Not.* "I'm simply meeting you where I'd like to be met. I cannot ask you to take off all of your clothes without first removing mine." I shuck my jeans down my legs and my cock springs free instantly.

Edith has the gall to jump — physically jump — six inches in the air at the sight of it. I belt out a laugh. It is the loudest I have *ever* laughed. Certainly one for the history books. "Seeing me naked cannot be so frightening."

She wets her lips and that small act alone is enough to cause my insiria distress. They rattle in a low growl — *not a purr, the sound I make before battle.* "What's that sound?" She says.

"My insiria. They are an additional vocal range all of my kind are born with. I...apologize. In your presence it is difficult to stop..."

"No, don't stop. I...I like it." Her gaze flicks to mine. "It makes me wet."

"Ipalora..." I am halfway to her and lacking the awareness of how I arrived there. My hand is reaching for her. I let it curl... "Edith, you tempt me..."

She smiles, but it's...shaky...and then she turns away. "I can't take off my teddy."

"Edith..."

"You're *perfect* and if I take off my Teddy, you won't want me after." I don't flinch from the pain in her gaze when she looks over her shoulder, even though I want to. It is a weapon she wields well. At least, against me.

"We shall see." My voice is even, neutral, flat. I reach down and grip my cock. Fluid glistens along the slit that I hope she does not see. I know everything...but I don't know this planet, this female and I don't know *this* either. I am completely out of my element.

"You can't unsee it, Nithril."

"I wouldn't be asking to see, if I wanted to unsee."

She's weighing her options, looking into my eyes, waiting for my capitulation, perhaps? Or waiting for me to give her an out? I won't. Her gaze drops to my cock. "Fuck it," she breathes. My lips quirk. I have never heard her say this word before and I strangely find that I like it, as uncouth as it is. It makes her sound older, less like a fledgling shield-maiden and more like a Valkyrie.

Her hands are shaking as she reaches up to the clasp on the back of her neck. She unzips the neck brace, but holds it against her skin as she whispers shakily, "Nithril."

"Ipalora."

"Can't you just look away for a minute? I'll get under the blankets."

I move to the light switch and flick them on. "No."

She turns to face me fully. Her lips are shaking as they attempt a smile and fall eons short. "You're such an asshole."

"Yes, so I've been told."

She inhales deeply...and she drops the cuff. The front of her outfit slumps down her chest and, when she peels off her wrist cuffs, it falls away entirely. With efficient movements, she unzips the cuffs from around her legs and pulls down her panties until she stands before me, bathing in light, wearing absolutely nothing.

I focus first on her eyes and only there. My right hand grips my cock as if attempting to chain a feral beast and I force every muscle and breath in my body to still. My gaze drops to her chin, then to her neck. Brilliant silver and red strips of flesh ribbon over her skin. The marks of many fangs can be seen amidst the carnage. Her wrists are much the same, wounded almost entirely from elbow to wrist. A particularly brutal mark cuts across her left arm — the X she spoke of earlier. The O is less distinct, as its marks are composed of mostly teeth.

Her thighs have been torn apart like all the rest, a trimmed patch of bright red hair glimmering between them. They are not scarred quite so jaggedly as her wrists and throat but...*No.* I refuse to think of how badly it must have hurt her, to have such sensitive skin torn apart. I will not retrace memories here that she wants me to help her get rid of.

I swallow hard and look into her eyes, feeling...*emotion* threaten mine. Profound emotion, there has never been a valley so deep.

"It's not that bad, is it?" Her eyes are red and she's biting her cheeks and her lips and her fingernails. "You...are you gonna cry? I made you cry...I told you, I..."

"No! No, Ipalora, no..." I move towards her slowly, as a human might, and drop to one knee at her feet. The carpet is soft on my smooth knees and I try to focus on its texture, rather than the sight of her and what it does to me. "No..."

She reaches down and palms either side of my face, forcing me to look up. "Your eyes are all glossy..." She sucks in a wet breath, her chest heaving.

"It's..." I have no words, but the few that I find, bellow out, "You honor me." She waits while I collect myself. I can barely meet her gaze. "You honor me by asking *me* into your bed to be the one to help you paint new memories over these other lifetimes you have led." I slide my hands up the outside of her smooth, perfect legs and lean in until my nose is pressed to the bend of her thigh and her hip. My lips part and I exhale breath all across her scars as I trickle kisses over every inch of them. "I have never known so great an honor. I just hope..." My voice cracks.

"You hope?" Her fingers comb through my hair and I love the scrape of her nails across my scalp. I hiss and close my eyes as they roll back.

I rattle and moan and inhale my own wet breath as I look up into her eyes, such perfect eyes, *such a perfect mate.* "That I am worthy."

She whimpers, "You are such an asshole." And then she attacks me. She throws her body against mine and we are suddenly wrapped around one another on the floor. Her lips are everywhere and, for all my speed, I struggle to keep up... for the first few breaths, and then lust takes over.

A soft groan I have no control over slips out of my mouth as she yanks on my hair. I flip our bodies over, but every time she wants to resume the top position and pushes on my chest, I let her. She straddles my hips and tosses her hair back, wrenching her lips from mine. I don't like that and charge up after her, but she combs her fingers through her curls and holds me back with a terrible look. *It's too fragile.*

"You *aren't* disgusted?"

My hand moves, no longer listening to my mind. I grab the back of her neck too roughly and wrench her against me until our chests are flushed. "Do I look disgusted?" I retake her mouth and roll our bodies over until she's beneath me on the floor. In a brief moment of lucidity, I worry she is not... enjoying things as much as I am and quickly aim to rectify it.

My tongue spears her heat and swirls around hers before dropping lower, to her jaw, to her neck... She tenses when I reach the part of her skin where the texture changes. I wish it didn't pull me out of the moment as it clearly does her, but I can't say that it does not. It makes me think of the other Heztoichen who have bled her, claimed her, who she once called husband and who once called her wife. It infuriates me. Infuckingfuriates me. And I know that I have Kane and Abel to thank for their part in ending Drago's bond to her along with his life. I have yet another reason to spend the rest of my lifetime repaying them...or, at least, the rest of theirs.

"Please..." She begs, I don't know what for, but I don't stop.

I kiss my way across each thorny branch of scar tissue, licking the rough and textured surface down, down, until I reach softer skin. My teeth scrape across her breasts and I'm grateful to Tasha for filing them and so very careful with my fangs as I lave and lavish and worship my way down further still. My cock has lost its mind, my hips thrusting into the floor like a savage, wanting her heat with a desperation I've never known. I need to calm the fuck down. Take back fucking control. I take a moment and merely press my face into the soft of her stomach, needing time. Needing more of it. All of it. Against her little belly button, I growl.

She lifts up and strokes her fingers through my hair. She's trying to coax me back up her body, but I won't let her. "What are you..." Her thighs tremble beneath my touch as I carefully spread them. She resists and pushes up onto her elbows.

"I want to taste."

"No!" She all but shouts and I realize what I've said and shake my head quickly.

"Not your blood. I meant your cunt." I press my nose to the rough curls and spread my tongue over anything and everything in its path. I lave her clit and flick my gaze up over her body, her pert and marvelous breasts, in time to see her head fall back on her neck.

"Fuck," she whispers. "That feels…No one has done that to me in years."

I growl dangerously, hating whoever he was and then I renew my efforts against her soft clitoris, hoping to banish him from her memories. "Tell me what you like."

"I like…like everything." She drops onto her back and pushes her hands through her hair. *Yes.* Giving herself up fully to the sensation, she closes her eyes. *Perfect.*

"Then tell me what you want."

"Press your tongue flatter against me…lick…lick…yes there…fuck…right there…"

I cannot contain my grin. It rips out of me and I find that my body shakes uncontrollably under the pressure of my restraint, but I fight it back. I hook my hands underneath her thighs and I wrench them as far apart as her joints will allow to make space for my shoulders to muscle between them. I suckle her clit and the soft pink lips that flower beneath it while the torn skin of her thighs presses against my cheeks.

I devour her in the way she's requested of me, laving the full length of my tongue up and down from her tight ass hole to her red curls. I spear inside of her body with my tongue, wanting to taste more of her musky arousal. My lips burrow within her folds until I lose myself in them. I am careful with the fangs Tasha allowed me to keep. So careful. I don't want to so much as nick her anywhere. I just want to taste her heat.

"Oh…oh…oh my god… Nithril!" She reaches down and latches onto my hair and uses it to steer my head wherever she wants me to go, my relentless conductor. And me, her willing orchestra. And then I hear it…*the symphony.*

Liquid and moans gush out of her in melodies I don't expect. I devour all of it gluttonously, not wanting to waste a single droplet of her orgasm to the carpets below. It's *mine*. All of it. Heart, body, soul.

I bury my face between her legs and lick her inside out. Her back arches. Her thighs slam against my shoulders. She pulls so hard on my hair it would hurt were I any other creation, but I'm not.

"I…I'm…again…"

"Yes, Ipalora. Again."

"I don't think I can."

"You can."

"It'll take…too long…"

"There is no such thing."

I bring her to three orgasms more and, by the time I'm through, she is a puddle on the floor and I am absolutely crazed with lust. I prowl up her body, certain that even though I bear no Tare, she can see my eyes glow. She meets my gaze with lazy lids and touches her mouth. She grins.

"You're so fucking hot."

I growl thunderously, liking her praise far, far too much. "You are."

"Come fuck me."

Her chest is flushed. Her breasts are small and perfect and, when I twist her nipples between my fingers she undulates in a beautiful wave, rolling her hips up to meet mine as if she wants my cock more than anything. "I will fuck you all night if you'll let me."

"Why only all night? We have tomorrow." She grins and I move back in, kissing my way down her mouth, tilting her chin up with my hand. Her pupils are fully dilated, she looks only half coherent. Seeing her like this, delirious with pleasure, is not an image I will ever forget. Her scars cease to exist. I bury my face in her neck and suck, bite and kiss them murderously, hoping to kill the last of her fear as I roll onto her body.

She spreads her thighs beneath me and hooks her ankles around my back. She's shaking badly…no…fuck. *I'm* shaking badly. "It's alright," she says. She can feel it and I've never been so embarrassed.

"I…apologies," I bark as I line my erection up with her sloppy wet cunt.

"Are you scared?" She teases.

"Petrified."

"What are you scared of?"

That you have come to mean more to me in the span of days than Heztoichen from my home world that I have known for decades, centuries. You have changed my purpose forever. You have reminded me of right and wrong. You have given me back a sense of touch never known to my people. You are my guide, not just to Population, but through the silence of your skin that I find so frightening, so mesmerizing. I know you not half so well as I should, Edith, but I adore you and I care for you dearly and it is utterly beyond reason.

My voice chokes. I shake my head. She smiles up at me and traces the line of my face with her fingers, dragging them across my forehead, over my cheeks and jaw, to my lips, then up my nose. She smooths her fingers over my eyebrows and speaks so very softly. "Me, too."

And then she picks her hips up and the head of my straining erection spears her riveting heat. She urges me forward and I fall…fall completely.

I sheathe myself in her body and am overcome by sensation. "It's…too much," I groan, unable to move. Edith pushes on my shoulder and guides me onto my back without removing me from her heat. She swings one leg over my hips and mounts me while I lay practically fucking catatonic beneath her. "Dear...fucking...suns..." I roar, insiria tangled in disbelief as she starts to slide up and down my length.

I glance between us, the product of her many orgasms glistening on my cock. It looks fucking huge sliding in and out of her pink lips. "Is it...hurting you?" I manage to say, somehow finding a shred of coherency along the way.

She shakes her head, red hair curling around her right nipple like a fucking target. I surge up and latch on with my mouth, suckling while my hands find her hips. I lift her up and slam her down. She screams and I wrench back, check her face, see her blinking wildly.

She grins recklessly. "Holy shit. Do that again."

I repeat the motion again and again, moving faster than a human ever could. Edith grabs ahold of my shoulders and uses them to anchor herself as I devolve into rut and mount her like a beast. My resistance is shot. My eyes roll back into my head. Her hands on my neck remind me to kiss her as she arches up against my chest.

"Nithril...thank you," she gasps, "thank you so much. I haven't...it hasn't ever felt...nothing like this..."

"You are in trouble, my Ipalora, because you make me never want to stop." I grab her body off of the ground and pull us both into a standing position. I stagger to the bed, but don't quite make it. I'm removed from her tight pussy and I can't have that for more than the split second the motion cost me.

"Hands on the bed." I'm seeing red. I'm hearing nothing but the whoosh of blood in her veins.

She does what I ask and I pick up her hips and slam into her from behind. The smooth skin of her back glistens with a faint sheen of sweat and burns from the carpet. I kiss them, wishing I could bite her so badly — too badly — it's consuming my thoughts. *Ask her. Bite her. Just do it!* No.

I stand up away from her and fuck her relentlessly, moving rougher and faster than intended, even with my strength in check. Yet, Edith does not complain, not once even as I slow down and make her look at me so I can check on her expression.

"Don't stop!" Her eyes roll back and I reach around her body while her legs coil mine to better anchor us in this position. Her arms are shaking as I touch her clit and stroke it with a speed a human could not ever hope to make. A high-pitched scream tumbles out of her and her arms give out. I throw her onto the bed, careful to keep myself fully seated inside of her as I feel the effects of her orgasm while sheathed. Her entire body seizes and she shivers out a scream and the *pressure*. By the gods of this great universe, I cannot breathe.

"Fuck…" the word roars out of me in overlapping waves and I…cannot…hold… "I'm going to break…"

"Fill me, Nithril. I want your cum in me…"

Her words are too much to take. Any hope I'd had of lasting longer than this is torn in two. My head kicks back, my locs slapping my spine like thick lashes of rope, my gut tenses, my thighs turn to stone and I grab her hips and slam one, two, a third and final time into her.

"Ipa…" I don't finish the word. My mind slips out of my skull and my hips lose any semblance of rhythm. I come. I come forever. I come until time cannot keep up and begins an ungainly descent into madness. I empty inside of her body, without restraint — without thinking of foreign things like consequence. There are none in this. This is a perfect thing.

I come deep inside of her as her walls ripple around me and a tight ring of muscle near her entrance squeezes in time to a beat I can't keep, and I keep coming as her body goes slack and loose in my grasp until I'm the only thing keeping her from sliding onto the floor in a heap.

My mind goes dark and when I resurface, I'm thrusting into her again, this time more slowly as sensitivity shoots up and down my cock, begging for more — or perhaps reprieve? I cannot tell. But I'm not fucking leaving.

"More?" She croaks.

"I'm not fucking leaving." I pound into her more deeply and Edith moans. Her arms are shaking as she tries to push herself up and leverage herself against the bed. It isn't working. I remove myself from her body only long enough to toss her into the center of the bed. She looks flushed and windswept and her gaze on mine is glossy. It...gives me pause as I climb over her, not sinking inside as I touch her cheek.

"Did I hurt you?" The words are strangled. I have begun to sweat.

Fear climbs up from my toes...until Edith says, "No." She shakes her head and palms my cheeks and pulls me down against her and hugs me...she hugs me. "I can't believe you want to lose your virginity to me. Thank you...thank you, Nithril. I'm honored."

I chuckle and pry her arms from around my neck and slam them down into the bed on either side of her face. I attack her mouth, kissing her until she melts until she opens, until she thrashes with desire and spreads her legs wide for me.

"*You* honor *me*." I press my lips to the center of her forehead and simply absorb the feel of her glistening up and down my cock as I move inside of her body. I slide home and re-enter the rutting madness.

She kisses me madly, scores her nails down my back, scratches and bites and tears. I bracket her head with my arms, slam our hips together, pull her onto all fours and lose my fucking mind when she reaches between her own legs and cradles my balls. I come. I...don't mean to, but I do anyway, emptying inside of her and blacking out as I do for longer than I had the first time.

When I come to, she is kneeling before me with a small smile on her face. "You liked that?"

I don't answer. I can't speak. My hips are making micro-pulses upward, seeking more heat while semen pours down my cock, wetting the bed beneath me.

"Then you're going to love this."

I'm still caught in a dream when Edith leans forward and licks a line up my cock, cleaning it free of her orgasm and my own. "Higora nivieyesh!" I roar, cursing in my own native tongue as pleasure explodes through me. I reach for her to stop this madness, but she catches my wrists in her hands and pins them to my sides. Then she damn near unhinges her jaw and takes the head of my erection into her mouth.

"Mmm," she moans around my girth before sucking my cock up to the tip and releasing me with a loud *pop*. "We taste good together." She winks and when she takes me into her mouth this next time, I start to murmur prayers in my own tongue until I can no longer take it. The pleasure is so extreme it borders on pain.

I lift her up and toss her down and reenter her in one stroke. She squeals as I maneuver her body beneath mine. I grab her chin and tilt it up, forcing her to look into my eyes. "Are you alright?"

She smiles at me sweetly and her eyes grow glossy once more. I frown. She nods. "No."

"No?" I grab my cock before it does something reckless, but she reaches out and bats my hand aside with very little resistance on my part. She starts to stroke and I collapse forward onto my hands. "Edith…"

"No, I'm not alright. I'm spectacular."

I hear her words and sense her teasing me, but right now, the grip of her hands is too much. "I'm going to embarrass myself…" I choke.

"How?"

"I'm going to come all over your body."

"Then come."

Hunched over her, her legs spread wide around mine, I come into her hands, cum spurting out across her chin, neck and chest. I…do not know if this is something that is done between mates…but I am filled with arousal at the sight of it and I want more. I fist her hands around my cock and squeeze, encouraging more milky white to explode from the head of my dick, lashing out across her stomach and groin and pubic hair.

I see red. I fall into a haze. I drop down between her legs and I lick her cum and my cum away until her clit shines clean and she orgasms beneath me. "You're right," I groan as she squirts against my chin and I lap at the moisture. "We do taste good together."

The *thing* beneath my sternum has ballooned to a dangerous size, one wrong thrust and it might burst against my ribs and decimate my insides. I settle my weight more fully against her and return to thrusting, this time, a little harder.

She gasps.

I thrust again.

She tosses her head back and her hair sprays like rain over my pillows. Like fire. "You are an Ipalora, Edith. You have taken me home." I meant to say, that she has taken me to *Hom*. But in either case, both are true, neither are wrong.

I can feel the sunshine on my face, I can hear the birds in the trees trilling their high-pitched mating call. I fuck her twice more though I mean to fuck her twenty more times. Thirty. Fifty thousand. She might have even let me…but after my ninth orgasm, I…embarrass myself once more. I pass out, this time, collapsing completely.

I come to a moment later, lying on my back, Edith draped over me. I start tracing soft patterns over the back of her right wrist, splayed across my chest. She lifts her head at the contact.

"I thought your kind didn't sleep?" She smiles tauntingly and I notice a slight gap between her two front teeth. How have I only just noticed this? It's so adorable. I lean up and kiss her deeply and, when I attempt to roll back onto and into her body, my limbs lock.

I chuckle. "I said we didn't *need* sleep, not that we cannot. And besides, that was not sleep, that was something else."

"What?"

"You've broken me."

She grins. "You come harder than anyone I've ever seen."

"Is that a bad thing?" I lift an eyebrow.

"No, but it's a messy thing." She glances down at my body and hers and I see half-dried stains smeared everywhere. *Everywhere*. "I think the sheets and perhaps the carpets are goners."

"If you let me come on you and in you again, then I'll make you replacement carpets and sheets myself."

"Oh?" She laughs. "And you know how to make carpets?"

"Of course. I worked the loom in my village some... twelve hundred years ago." I can't think. "I can't remember." It doesn't matter. "It's not important." Whatever happened before this moment in time can be forgotten. The history books already have my memories. I have no more need of them when I could be using all of my faculties to concentrate on the smell of her orgasm and the weight of her curls and the way a small notch appears in her right cheek when she smiles, but not the left one.

She shakes her head and I notice cum on her chin that makes my gut tense. *Fuck, I love you.* Wait...what? "Did you hear me?"

I clear my throat roughly. "What?"

"I said, will you teach me?"

I smile and wriggle my arm beneath her body so that I can coil it around her and hold her close, closer, closer still. I mash her against me, waiting until she begs for release, but she doesn't. She clutches me back with all the force of her thin arms and I am undone by her. *I love you.*

I clear my throat, but my voice is still barely understandable as I fight the strange urge to profess my undying love for her, beg her to fuck me again and weep. *I don't want to lose her.* "Was I out long?"

"Maybe thirty seconds," she laughs lightly.

"I take it most males do not pass out after sex?"

She laughs a little harder. "Not usually like that."

"Like what?"

"Like they were hit over the head with something."

I snort. Snort. Have I ever snorted before? Perhaps once, and only in her presence. "I *feel* like I was hit over the head with something. That was...indescribable, Edith. Thank you."

"Thank *you*."

"You thank me for nothing." I kiss her forehead, her nose, her chin, her cheek and she giggles when I work my way down her jaw and does not stop me when I get to her neck. Against her scars, I whisper, "I want to fuck you again."

"I wouldn't mind."

"You're going to have bruises if I fuck you too hard and I'm pretty sure that's the only way I know how to fuck you."

When she doesn't respond immediately I grunt and look up, forcing myself to move so that I can look her over.

"I'm okay, Nithril, really." She pulls me back down onto my side and I grunt.

"I didn't see anything, but bruises will take time to appear."

"Really, I'm fine." She closes her eyes. I shove a pillow under her head and grab a blanket from the end of the bed and pull it over us, praying that it's clean. "Thank you."

Seeing her sleepy makes me shockingly sleepy, in a way I haven't felt since after that battle with Tanen and Mernon on the Regrethal Fields. It also makes me nervous. I feel like I could fall into a dream and never return to this. I feel like someone could storm the gates of my castle and take her from me while I'm unaware and unprepared.

"Teera," I chime quietly under my breath, recalling her to this house where I ask her to station herself for the time being. It is a selfish request, but I am not myself...I don't know if I ever will be again.

And I am perfectly fine with that.

Except...for now. Awkwardness arrests me as I stroke a finger down Edith's nose. "Edith?"

She grabs my hand and clutches it to her chest. The balloon in my chest just fucking explodes. "Yes, Nithril?"

"We should speak of what happens if our...coupling should result in the formation of new life."

Her eyebrows crinkle for a moment, and then she barks out a laugh. "Are you trying to say that we need to talk about what happens if you got me pregnant?"

"Correct. Yes."

"You could have just said that."

"I did," I grunt.

She rolls her eyes. "I um...well, I hope...you're not mad, but I actually am wearing a diaphragm."

"A what?"

"It's this cup thing that blocks the sperm. It's what most women and couples use these days since there aren't any condoms left and we don't have the facilities to make hormonal birth control. Either that, or the ladies that do get their periods just track their cycles. And we...most humans are *clean* because of the Heztoichen blood that gets around. It keeps us from getting sick and, even though I don't...do that anymore, the effects of what I've been given before...helps."

I don't...fully understand all of this. The health aspects are clear however, contraceptives in Sistylea were administered to males and, on this planet, we are decidedly absent of them or any way to produce them. I simply nod, not wanting to confess to my ignorance on the subject. I slide my knuckles down the center of her body and rest my palm over her abdomen.

"Should we ever decide to produce heirs, would you be able to remove this device?"

Her eyes bulge. "What?"

"The device. Can it be removed?"

"You...want to have *kids*?"

"Should you wish to, and once Brianna's borders are secure with the development of at least a dozen outposts, then yes."

"Ohmigod, you mean you want to have sex with — I mean, kids with *me*?"

"Yes, I would like to have sex with and kids with you. You are my mate."

"I'm your..." She just gawks at me and then glances between our bodies. She does not seem to realize she's still holding my hand until that moment, but when she does and looks down at it, she grins. "You're...crazy."

"Perhaps. But I am certain about this. You are my mate."

A distance appears between us that is everything but physical as we lie close. She struggles to meet my gaze but does, eventually, without prompting. "Like what Kane and Abel have? Like a wife?"

"Yes." Her cheeks flare with color and I click my tongue against the backs of my teeth though I don't mean to, "If you would like...of course," I grit.

The divot appears in her cheek again as she smiles at me. "But...we haven't exchanged blood or vows or anything."

"That doesn't matter to me. All that matters is that you accept me and claim me."

She shakes her head, but I am not discouraged in the slightest. "I'm not rejecting you, but I need time. I've never considered having a...a partner and I definitely haven't ever thought about having kids. I'm not ready for any of that. I'm barely twenty."

I frown. "Twenty?"

She nods. "I...it was my birthday last week. I mean...I think it was."

"It was your birthday? Why didn't you tell me?"

She smiles and I don't know what she's thinking, but I wish I did. Desperately. "No one celebrates birthdays anymore."

"I would like to celebrate."

She leans in, stretches up, and kisses me tenderly. "I think this was celebration enough. I've never known a greater pleasure."

"I am relieved. It should go without saying that I haven't either."

She laughs at this and grabs a pillow from over her shoulder and tosses it at me. I snatch it from the air and smother her with it before lifting it up and smothering us both. I kiss her beneath it, senselessly, and we keep kissing until we both tire and begin to slow…

I idle on the edges of sleep — *true sleep* — for the first time in my life. The sound of Edith's voice rouses me just to the realm of the living and I am more grateful now than ever for Teera in the house below. If Malmon truly wants my life, he has only to come for me after Edith has softened the battlefield. It is truly beautiful, this thing called sex, but with Edith? It is a thing worth writing ballads about and building moments for that last the ages. It is magic. More powerful than I imagine, even true Tare…

"Would it be…okay to wait to talk about mating and kids and all that?"

"Of course." *No.* "Take all the time you need." *But just not too long, I'm impatient.* "Decades if you must." *Hmph.* "I'll be waiting." *Yes, I will always wait for her.*

"Thank you."

"You thank me for nothing. Do not make me say it again."

She breathes out a laugh that fans my neck. "I didn't think it was possible."

"What?"

"To care…in Population."

"It is always possible."

She hesitates. "You haven't been out there."

I lift her hand from my ribs and kiss each of her sweat and sex-stained fingertips. "You will be my guide in Population…and in this." I palm her ass with my other hand, giving it a generous squeeze which causes her to swallow a small moan, and huff out soft laughter. "And I will be your guide in this." I lay her hand back over my heart.

Time passes. Not enough of it. I want this moment to last a year. My eyes close and I see only darkness as she whispers, "You don't have to teach me how to care again." She turns into my chest and presses a kiss against my nipple. "I do already."

Chapter Fourteen

My mouth is pressed into a brutal line as I look back at the bus charging down the road behind me. Edith is in it, and I don't like it. Yet, I was given a choice between that and having her beside me in the back of this open pickup truck and that was the less preferable option. Here, beside me, she'd be far too exposed. Not that the other humans beside me share that same concern.

"So." Constanzia is seated on the left side of the truck, Diego on the right. Pia rides passenger while Star drives. She is…a wild driver. I find myself occasionally gripping the edges of the truck for support.

"Yes?" I say when the human female doesn't say more. She just grins at me from beneath her helmet and visor. It…is not a military helmet. It looks more like the helmet one would wear while riding a motorcycle. An odd choice yet I suppose it's better than nothing.

"Abel was hearing complaints about screaming coming from the woods at the end of Starlight."

I wait. "And this concerns me how?"

She shrugs. "I thought you mighta heard something, seeing as you got godlike hearing and all."

"There is nothing godlike about my hearing. It is simply better than yours."

"Still." She grins. "Did you hear anything?"

Yes, I did hear the screaming, which is why I returned to the woods with a blade and fire and seared their tongues clean off. "I had more important matters to concern me."

She has an apple in her hand. It's from the greenhouse and smells of the fertilizers they use on it. It also smells of damp soil and a forgotten sunshine. Crisp, it clacks as Constanzia sinks her large two front teeth into it and rips apart the flesh. I wonder absently if she would make an attractive female to another male. Yes, I suspect she might. At least, for any male who wasn't wholly intimidated by her. She stares me straight in the eyes as if she isn't afraid of me... no...it's as if...she isn't afraid of *death*. This is a female who will die in violence and she will die laughing.

"Whatever. I just thought you'd like to know that Kane went out to take a look last night."

My lips purse. I do not fear discovery. Oh no. But I *am* concerned that my hard work to keep the remaining five alive might have gone to waste. I already almost lost one who'd had the clever idea to gnaw his own tongue off before I so graciously saved him. I even provided them bottles of water and straws from which to sip. I don't know how long I'll be gone on this journey, but I fully intend to keep them in comfort until my return.

"Don't worry. Kane didn't find anything. At least, he didn't find anything worth mentioning to Abel. I got a little curious myself and I went out there and I looked *real* hard, but I didn't see anything, either. Diego also took a look. Did you see anything out in the woods Diego?" She calls across to him, raising her voice loud to be heard over the wind.

His gaze lingers momentarily over the shattered city horizon as we cross over a bridge. From our position, the corpse of Atlanta's downtown looms like a mirage, a reminder of the civilization that once thrived here. *We will rebuild.*

We.

Hm.

The thought came and went quite naturally.

Hmmmm.

"Nope," he says, without stuttering. His gaze swivels to meet my stare. "J-j-just t-t-took a p-piss out there and wwwent home."

My lips twitch. "Good."

I stare at him for a long time. Long enough for the truck to maneuver around the wreckage of two abandoned cars. We cleared most of the highways leading in to Brianna, but we've reached the point now where our efforts have flagged in favor of speed. Still so close to Brianna, yet already in dangerous territory. Anywhere beyond the walls is Population. Anywhere in Population is violence. *How did I let it get to this?*

I roll forward, landing on one knee. His boot jerks away from my leg and his hands reach instinctively for one of the dozens of weapons strapped to his person, as if it is reflex. As if it is his only reflex.

Clearly and loudly enough to be heard by a human over the raging wind, I tell him, "Edith is mine."

The frame of his eyes widens then narrows. "Th-th-that so?"

I nod once, jerkily, finding the words surprisingly difficult to articulate. "I understand that you and Pia are like... surrogate parents to her or perhaps that, by virtue of your shared terror at the hands of the one called Jack, you are the closest she has left to a brother. At least, to a brother she claims."

He shifts, clearly uncomfortable. I would have found it laughable were I not so uncomfortable myself. "Y-Yeah. A-And?"

"And I would..." I don't continue. I feel suddenly...hot.

Diego glances over at Constanzia, but I don't pull my gaze from him, even as he tenses to the point of being unbearably stiff. "Y-Yeah?"

I clear my throat and try once, but nothing comes out. Hm. Unusual. I try again. "I would like to have…" My throat dries up yet once again. Very, very odd.

"Sp-sp-spit it out."

"I would like to…have your…approval," I stumble and, when the truck pops over a bump, I fall off of my haunches and onto my ass.

Constanzia chokes on laughter.

Diego just stares shocked.

I hack into my fist and it is *rough*. Even my insiria work at this. Finally, I spit out, "I do not *fully* understand the nature of your relationship with Edith, nor do I particularly like it. I know that you are mated to Pia and I know that your and Pia's relationship to Edith is entirely platonic. I cannot say that I am *pleased* to have to share her affections in any capacity with anyone," I huff.

My hand flexes towards my swordstick. Diego firms his grip on the machine gun he wears. "*However*, it is clear that you have…cared for her. I rheached through Patty and Lima and saw what you did to the ones who'd previously harmed her. I approve of your actions and I believe that it would… please Edith were we to become…*friends*." The word doesn't even sound right. I cannot even be sure that I am using it correctly.

"F-f-ffffriends?"

I nod. "I intend to curry favor with you and Pia. Would you be amenable to becoming…friends?"

Diego rolls his eyes. "Ch-Ch-Christ." His gaze flicks between my eyes and I feel…nervous. "You fffffucked her, d-d-didn't you?"

"You *dare*." The heat in my cheeks swells to blistering proportions.

His upper lip pulls back from his teeth and he curses beneath his breath. He rubs his face roughly and sits up straighter, but at least he releases his weapon. We ride for a while in silence and I wait a short eternity for him to glare at me again. "Sh-sh-she t-t-tell you what happened t-to her?"

"Enough."

"Y-You wanna see?" He holds out his arm.

I shake my head. "No. She has shared what she is willing to offer. I will take no more."

"Th-th-th-these m-m-mmmemories are mmmine. C-Can have 'em."

Tempting... My hand flexes. "I appreciate your concern, but Edith has shared with me enough."

He grunts, folding his arms back over his knees. "D-Don't like the way you look at her. Don't lllllll-l-like the way sh-she looks at y-y-you eith-either."

My heart flutters. I tilt my head. *She looks at me?* I grin and Diego rubs his face, but I can see that I have him. He is fighting a smile. "F-f-fuck. I sssssound like L-L-Luke."

"Who is Luke?"

"P-P-Pia's dad. He'da c-c-c-come if he hadn't fffffallen for a wo-woman b-b-back in B-B-Brianna who want-wanted him to st-st-st-stay."

I smirk, "I guess it goes around then."

"G-G-Guess so. Sh-Sh-She's even one of y-y'all."

"A Heztoichen?"

He nods.

I grin more broadly. "Are they bonded?"

He bites his front teeth together. "Are-are y-y-you?"

"No." *Unfortunately not.* "As I've said already, I will not take from her what is not offered, no matter how much it would honor me to b...*bond*..." Bond. My voice trails off. The word hits in a recurring loop as my mind sifts through pieces of information and cobbles them together in new patterns.

Diego is speaking to me but I speak louder. "Edith was bonded to Drago until his death..."

"Wh-what?"

"...but it would also stand to reason that, when she was used as a..." *blood bag. No I cannot say the words aloud.* "...when she was *used* by Malmon or Jack or the Dixie brothers, some of the Heztoichen blood that was given, was also taken."

"You-you sssssaying you th-th-think she mmmmmight have b-b-bonded with one of the mmmmembers of M-Malmon's g-g-gang?"

"Yes."

"You th-th-think she might st-still-*still* be b-bonded?"

"Yes. I think it's even possible that..." I curse. "I don't know why I didn't think of this before..."

"What?"

"Would he have fed her his own blood?" I muse out loud, not expecting Diego to have an answer.

His eyebrows furrow and his gaze goes distant. He surprises me when he nods. "Jack com-complained a c-couple times that Hez-Heztoich-ch-ch-ch..." He licks his lips. "That Oth-Other blood was-wasn't strong enough. Mmmmight be a condition that he asked f-f-f-f-fffffor stronger st-st-st-stuff."

I blink at him, concern unraveling to reveal a tight, bright white ball of clarity. I stand and bang on the roof of the cab. "Stop the truck."

Chapter Fifteen

I feel…like shit.

Edith's sitting on the back of the pickup truck with her shoulders curled inward, her feet dangling in the air. She's not wearing the outfits Tasha packed in my bag for her, but another shapeless ensemble that covers every inch of her except for her hands and her face. I don't know why, but the fact that she won't wear the other clothes…offends me. I shake it off, aware that I'm not going to fuck the trauma out of her, as much as I might wish that I could. Two nights with me doesn't change the fact that she's still embarrassed of her war wounds.

"Nithril, is everything okay?" My mouth ticks up. I cannot help it. She starts to grin in reply and I watch as magic unravels itself over her. Her shoulders roll back just a little and she sits up just a little bit straighter and the frightened gleam flits from her gaze. "What?"

"Nothing. I just love the way you say my name."

She passes her tongue over her lower lip and I can't help it. I approach her and place my hands on either side of her on the truck bed. She kisses my neck and I growl.

"Don't get me excited," she whispers so low she thinks I'm the only one who can hear her. I guarantee all of the Heztoichen surrounding us heard her as well. Teera, standing off to the right facing out, I can see in profile. She's smiling.

And I don't give a shit.

I reply against her lovely mouth, "You don't know what you do to me. Had we the time, I'd make everyone wait, take you into that school bus and…"

"Shh!" She covers my mouth with her hand, then leans in and kisses the back of her own palm to torture me.

I rip her hand free and kiss her deeply, cupping the back of her neck and pulling her to the edge of the truck so that I can press the full length of her torso against my body. I pull back only when I feel my erection swell to the point of discomfort. "I…" *love you.*

I blink.

Hm.

The thought. It's coming to me with increasing frequency even though I tell myself again and again that we have not known each other long enough. Yet, it doesn't seem to matter.

"What's going on, Nithril? Why'd we stop? Not for…you know…the truck, is it?" I'm about to answer her with something lascivious when a throat clears behind me. I look over my shoulder into Diego's glare. His arms are crossed fiercely and Pia is rolling her eyes and elbowing his ribs, but even she is unable to move him.

"Diego and I were speaking just now and it occurred to us that you may have Malmon's blood in your system."

She withers, looking between us with notes of betrayal in her eyes. "What does that matter?"

"When we took down Elise, we used her bond with Abel to locate her. Abel had been given Elise's blood to save her life. Elise had been drinking from Kane against his will. Though it was not intended, the blood bond between Abel and Elise was thus forged and when Elise went to ground, I could not find her through normal methods. I was able to locate her through blood alone — Abel's blood..." My explanation is oversimple and I worry she doesn't understand, but she's already shaking her head. "No?"

"It won't work."

"We could try..."

"No, it won't work," she insists stubbornly, looking frustrated enough for me to believe her — and to believe that she would help if she could.

"Why not?"

"Because Malmon never drank from me." Her eyes grow distant and a crease forms between them as she thinks. What I *hate* is that she robotically scratches her neck at the mention of his name and then both of her wrists as if she's reliving her torture now, here, with me.

I cover her wrists with my hands and force her to refocus.

She does, gulping compulsively, and says, "No, Malmon never drank from me. He only drank from his *special* supply."

"Supply?"

"Yeah." Her eyes flash. Her fist clenches on her knee. "My brother."

"Rick?" Pia's soft voice says behind me.

"Yeah."

I palm the side of her face and try to mask the depth of my concern. "Malmon has your kin?"

"*Don't* call him that."

Surprised, I frown. "Why not?"

She pulls away from my touch and my hand flexes once, twice, a third time, suffering from the loss. "He's not my kin. He made his choice a long time ago. He sold me to whoever wanted me for whatever they wanted me for as many chances as he got. I don't want to talk about it. Just know that Malmon only drinks from him. He has special blood. Elise does things to it — at least, she used to before...you know the rest."

"Elise?" Frustration that she won't let me touch her is rivaled by my frustration with Kane. When he ended Elise's life, she took all of her secrets with her to the grave in one last act of defiance. And she was a clever female — a sadistic one. She had her guards working in a rotations system and the only ones that ever got close enough to knowing all of her secrets were killed. Of those who survived her, I interrogated as many as I could, but their information was sparse and did not come together.

Now, I fear that Edith may know more than I do. It stands to reason she would. Elise did not worry about humans, she found them disposable, barely more than animals. She knew I felt the same, and would not have cared to rheach through a human. She knew me. She knew this... weakness. And now, I am at a disadvantage and am forced to ask questions and reveal memories that I wish I did not have to.

"Can you explain, Edith? Why did Malmon only drink from your brother? Do you know what she was doing with him?"

"Experiments. He...when Rick and I got taken by the Five Point Gang, they put us aside. They treated us...kinda okay? We got more food than the other humans and we got blankets. We didn't have to sleep out in the cold. I never knew why until one day, Malmon came and asked us who wanted to volunteer for a special assignment."

She makes this...disgusted sound in the back of her throat. Her eyes are unfocused. "Rick said I'd do it. He didn't even offer. He never did. He just said I'd do it and they took me to some...lab? It looked like a hospital, but there were test tubes everywhere and Heztoichen all in black were drawing blood from other humans but also Heztoichen, too? It was weird. Malmon even went into a room once and, when he came out, he had these patches over his eyes. His eyes were black before but, when I saw him a few weeks later, they were purple."

"Weeks, Edith?"

She nods. "They tried running tests on me for a really long time, but I guess...whatever they wanted didn't work. Malmon took me back to the Five Point Gang and gave me to Jack..." She shakes her head and closes her eyes and I touch her shoulder but she flinches back. "They used me as a blood bag and I never got a chance to talk to Rick again after that. I only saw him once and he was standing right next to Malmon. I heard from others that Malmon was drinking from him and only him."

"Extraordinary." The word bursts out of me without care and I immediately regret it. "No, that isn't what I meant. I'm sorry, Edith. I understand this is painful for you and what happened to you is not to be forgiven." But it is to be revenged. "I merely am...in awe of your insight. You know much more than I believed possible. Much more about this world than I do. Perhaps, in this world, *you* would be better suited as Lahve."

Pink rises in her cheeks and she bites her lips together. "That's silly."

I smirk, "It isn't. I had no idea that Elise was using humans in her experiments. It would not have even occurred to me as a human would have had no impact or ability to impact the bringing of Tare — at least, that is what both Elise and I believed. But it sounds like she was running experiments on *behalf* of other Heztoichen as well." To what end? Elise never did anything out of the goodness of her heart. She never did anything without payment. "And the eyes — could you tell me more about this?"

She nods and blinks at me rather vacantly while she thinks and speaks in tandem, telling me of the violet eyes that are a common color among us, Tretaro. Mine, being orange, are an outlier, a bit more unique. However, I have known Malmon and his sister, Idreline, on Sistylea. They did not have violet eyes. Only their father did.

I tell this to Edith as well and she nods and together, we speculate over the implications of violet-eyed experiments and what her brother could have had to do with them. Wind ruffles her hair and the humans, mostly, whisper between each other behind me. Some are speculating...others are merely distracted by thoughts of lunch. Before Edith and I can continue our rumination, I turn and speak to Pia and Diego.

"Perhaps, since we are already stopped, it's a good time for the humans to partake in their midday meal." Humans, it would seem, are so inefficiently built that I get the impression that they are constantly eating.

Pia nods and begins giving orders to the organization of this superfluous *lunch* but Diego, however, comes towards us. "So, n-n-no chance of finding Mal-Malmon th-th-through Ed-Edith?"

I shake my head. "It would appear not."

"Come Edith, this is enough for now. Why don't you eat?"

"Wait." Edith grabs my sleeve. I can see her thinking and, even as Diego edges forward into her space, she does not look away from me. This pleases me greatly and I hear my insiria work, cooing to her softly in approval.

The sound makes Diego jump. "Th-the fuck is th-th-thhhhat?"

"It is not for you," I hiss.

Edith blinks again, as if processing the compliment and taking far, far too long to process it — as if she's still unsure of my affections, or that I *could* have them towards her. I don't like that. "Yes, Ipalora?" I whisper. Her blush intensifies and I coo louder.

"Fucking ffffffreaks me out. Quit-quit it."

"No..."

"Does it have to be Malmon?"

"What?" Diego and I say in unison. We share an annoyed look before returning our focus to Edith.

She glances around at the humans behind us, forming their lunch groups at Pia's instruction, then she leans in.

Diego leans in. I lean in. How useless. As if I couldn't hear her from a mile away... "Idreline."

"Wh-what?"

"Malmon only drank from Rick, but Idreline...she drank from me. And Malmon had her give blood to Jack through me." She scratches her wrists again.

Part of my mind works to create scenarios...such magical scenarios...of me clearing a nice plot beside Leif and his minions for Idreline and Malmon out in those not-so-silent woods. The other part of my mind remains focused on the task at hand. "Did she only drink and give blood to you, or did she drink and give blood to other humans, as well?"

"Oh, she drank from everyone. She...she tore people apart. She's worse than he is." Edith's eyes grow sad. She sniffles and looks down at her baggy jeans-covered lap. She picks at a loose thread and I cover her hands with my own. "She goes *crazy*, loses it. Tears people..." She hugs her arms over her chest and shakes her head.

"Edith," I bite out. I slip my fingers beneath the high collar of her shirt and rub my thumb up and down the torn column of her throat, feeling her muscles work beneath my touch as she swallows...feeling the scars moving unnaturally over her flesh. With Heztoichen blood in her system — blood of a Tretaro hybrid, no less — she would have had to be torn apart many times for her to scar like this.

"Edith...you did remarkably well to survive. And your knowledge may just be her downfall."

She tilts her head and I watch as the pain and suffering clears from her memories through her gaze. I don't need to be able to rheach her at all. I can see her. Touch her. *Taste...* I wince, knowing what will need to be done and what I will have to ask of her next. But I...can't get the words out.

But Edith surprises me, as I suspect she always will. "Should we try to track Idreline? Wherever she is, Malmon probably won't be far, right?"

I nod jerkily. "Diego, would you agree?"

He's frowning, a furious and fixed expression on his face, making him look rather monstrous himself. It pleases me greatly. I would like to watch what he has in store for Idreline and her brother were I not so intent to be the one to pull her apart myself. He grunts and I take this for a *yes*.

"What do you need from me?"

I don't answer.

"You'll need blood from me, won't you?"

I inhale in a rush and attempt a certain *professionalism*. I just want her to be comfortable with me. "Yes. But only a single drop from your fingertip…" I stumble, unsure of how to proceed. I stare down at her hand. It looks very small in mine.

"It's okay," she says in a clipped manner. She pulls her hair to the side and pulls her turtleneck down to expose the side of her throat. It is…a shameless offer.

"D-D-D-Don…"

I don't want to hear it. Not from him. I raise my hand with speed enough to ruffle the wind. "Don't insult me. Step away, Diego."

"Nnnn-nnn-not a chance."

I growl, this time, as I would before battle, but before I can have it out with him once and for all, I feel the press of soft fingers against my cheek. Edith holds her wrist out to me. "Sorry. I didn't mean to insult you. I forgot that the… honorable Heztoichen only bite the neck of their mates. I didn't want to imply or…I know we never finished our talk…"

I swoop in and press my lips to hers, shutting her up. "I will hear no more of this," I heave, breaking the kiss in a way I'd like to break bone in that moment. Idreline's. All of them. I push back into her hair, nuzzling against the side of her throat. I exhale warm breath through her turtleneck and she shivers, hands grabbing the shoulders of my coat. "You are the one who wanted to wait. If you've changed your mind, then I am ready, but not here and not like this. I want to marry you in the human tradition before I ever entreat to bond with you in my own."

"You don't have to do that."

"Am I not worthy?"

"What? No...no, it's...no one even does that anymore." She's grasping for excuses that don't exist.

I plant one slow, lingering kiss to cover the three small freckles at the edge of her jaw, then another behind her ear. The skin is so soft here, unscarred, yet no more lovely than any other perfect inch of her. "Would you like to?"

She doesn't answer me. I wish I knew what she was thinking. She seems...less perturbed by my suggestions of marriage. Perhaps, merely less surprised. I frown. I want her *eager*.

I pull up and lift the middle finger of her left hand to my lips, brushing my mouth with her finger again and again until her pupils dilate a little and she bites her lower lip. I lift an eyebrow and she reddens, understanding that I'm teasing her.

"Just get on with it, you jerk."

I grin broadly. "*For now*, I will attempt to trace her through a single drop. It may not work. I cannot read your skin, it is likely that I won't be able to find her blood in yours, if there are even any traces left."

"Alright."

"Are you ready?"

"Do I need to do anything?"

"It may help for you to think of her, Idreline. Picture her face, where you last saw her."

Edith winces when I say that. "Oh...okay."

I squeeze her finger and spear it on my fang without any further prelude. Blood flowers in a beautiful red bead on the pale curve of her longest digit. It starts to drip...my tongue moves quickly to catch it. I slide her entire finger in my mouth and suckle it momentarily, but it is...too much. I drop her hand and let it fall and immediately take ten steps back. My thoughts swirl, all of them lethal. *I want to rip her open, bathe in the sweet, spiritual taste of her. She is pure sin. Pure effervescence. A glory to her kind. Nature's cruelest gift. I can't...I can't do this...*

I stagger and I hear Diego move forward as if to catch me. I jerk away from him. *"Don't touch me."*

"Sh-shit. S-s-sssorry. You okay, man?"

"Nithril?"

"Don't...just...I need a moment." I hold up a hand, as if to ward them back. It takes...minutes — not seconds, but *minutes* — for me to recalibrate my mind and return to the Lahve that I once was. Or perhaps, he is gone entirely. I cannot even recall what it was like to be him as I look up.

Edith sits on the edge of the truck, looking worried — worried for me. It hurts my heart and humbles me deeply. "My apologies," I hack out. "You honor me. I...I disgrace myself, but I can't..." Can't fucking think. "I cannot seem to push...I can't...your taste..."

"Is it bad? Do you think that's why Malmon and Elise didn't pick me for their experiments."

"No and yes." I shake my head rabidly, hair cascading around my shoulders. I pinch the bridge of my nose and squeeze my eyes shut tight. "Whatever is in your blood is intoxicating. But it neutralizes all of my rheach at once. If what I suspect is true, then they would have had no use for it. They would not have even understood the gift of it."

"I...what do you suspect?"

Edith starts to move, like she'll come down from the open bed of the truck. I hold up my hand. "Don't...come closer. Please, Edith. Stay where you are."

She freezes. Her face floods with blood, which does absolutely nothing to help me in my current state. My cock has elected to behave without the instruction of my mind. Its length presses firmly along the inside of my left thigh and I close my eyes, though the vision remains and does nothing at all to relieve the pressure.

"I believe that Malmon and Elise may have found kindred spirits in one another. Elise wanted a Tare she felt she was owed, but that was abandoning her. Malmon and Idreline perhaps, wanted a Tretaro's gifts that they never had by virtue of their breeding."

"You-You think they're t-t-t-trying to be-become llllike you?"

I nod, then shake my head, still struggling through the pressure in my body and the blood beating its way through my senses like a sledgehammer through glass walls. "They would have known what a folly this is. Elise never succeeded in truly reclaiming her Tare. She was merely able to…extend its slow death. I cannot fathom how they would have thought to recreate their ancestors' ability to rheach. It…has never been attempted." Yet…I would not put it past Elise…

"Are you okay?" Her voice is a breath and I open my eyes to see that she's disregarded my warning and is kneeling in the soft earth in front of me. The humans pulled off onto the side of the road. I find it oddly amusing. As if, even after all this time, they believe they might cause…traffic. That after all this time, it could still be force of habit.

"Ipalora…" I breathe, shaking my head. "No. I want you now more desperately than ever."

She reaches out, as if to touch me. "No!" The word comes with force, my insiria ringing with the sound. I start to laugh at the hilarity of this situation I have found myself in, a situation unlike any that have come before. "Please. My concentration and restraint are being held together by a hair. Don't touch me, Edith." She lowers her hand and I rock back onto my ass, falling onto the dirt, the lowly Lahve that I am. I continue to chuckle. Diego stares at me as if I'm deranged. Edith looks at me like I'm a wounded dove.

"You're sure you're okay? If you need my blood…"

"*No.* No, Edith… Let's just call this a failed experiment and move on."

"You couldn't rheach me?"

I laugh louder and shake my head, feeling a *little* more like myself, but only a very little. "No. I couldn't rheach *me*."

She's not really listening to me though, caught in another one of her thinking spells. She's rubbing the offending finger across her lower lip, as if she's not culling restraint out of me, bit by bit, like digging soil from a grave. Or perhaps, showering me with it as I lie six feet under.

"Let-let's gg-gg-ggo eat Ed-Edith…"

"What about Ken?" She says abruptly, ignoring him.

"Ken?" I ask.

"Ken." She nods, ticking her chin up towards the gathering of humans. As if he heard her say his name, one stands slightly apart from the rest, chewing on a bit of sandwich. He tilts it towards me, as if in a wave.

Diego, seated on the truck bed now, welcomes Pia as she approaches him with sandwiches enough for all four of us. He takes one from her and palms her hip, pulling her flush to him before he grunts, "Fuck-fuck Ken."

"Hey. Be nice to Kenny. Wait — why are we talking about Ken, anyway?"

"You need Kenny?" Constanzia and Star approach from behind me before vaulting easily up onto the truck. Pia hands a sandwich to Edith and tosses one at me. I catch it, then toss it back.

"Not hungry?" She says.

"I eat for pleasure, not sustenance, and this, I guarantee, would bring me no pleasure."

"Hey, bite me, asshole," Star crows. "I made the damn sandwiches."

I roll my eyes and look at the sandwich in Edith's hand in distaste. "If you're looking for an apology from me, you won't get it. Especially, when you've interrupted. Edith," I say, attempting to return focus to her without launching myself at her and taking her here on the ground before everyone. "What about Ken?"

"Ken traded blood with Idreline once."

"He did?" Constanzia swallows what looks like painfully and shoves off her hat. Long black hair spills over her shoulders as she turns. "He doesn't have any scars." She gestures crudely to her wrists, cutting an invisible X across them that makes Edith fidget. Constanzia notices, but doesn't seem to care. I'd punish her...were we in Sistylea. And for a brief, shattering moment, I realize that I am...*grateful* I am not.

If I were on Sistylea, I would not be here.

Edith nods. "I think they might have...had sex."

Constanzia spits her water all over Star, who curses and proceeds to bash Constanzia with the rag hanging off of her neck. "Kenny! Get the fuck over here. You fucked this bitch we're going to kill?"

Smirk smug, the tall male with the short crop of dark hair swaggers forward. As he approaches, several others follow — the male called Roderick, with his toothpick in his mouth and a billed hat pulled low to shade his eyes, Laiya and Sandra, two males called Mo and Matt, Romalin and Teera...

Realizing he has an audience does not deter him. He merely smiles a little wider up at Constanzia, tone practically a leer. "Why? You jealous?" Most *definitely* a leer.

"Get outta here." She laughs, but I do not like the way this...Ken human looks up at her, if he is human at all. There is something wholly carnivorous about his gaze. It reminds me of the way some of Elise's former guard watched the humans they tortured in those cells. He looks at her like she is something *owed*.

"Answer the question, Ken," I say. I do not miss the furious way Diego watches this male either, nor do I miss the way he has his arm draped possessively across the back of Pia's neck.

Ken shrugs. "Yeah. I fucked that crazy bitch."

"She coupled with you willingly?"

"Don't look so surprised."

"I am surprised. I was under the impression that she hated humans. She spent her time...torturing many of them."

Ken actually manages a thoughtful expression then and nods down at Edith, his face somewhat solemn. "Yeah, I saw what she did to some. I'd have tried to help, too, if I weren't so wrapped up in that shit with the Dixie brothers. I'm sorry, Edith."

She chews on her bottom lip and nods, but does not meet his gaze. She is...inching towards me. I stiffen, then roll forward, coming directly beside her and taking a seat. I am... honored that she would look to me in the face of uncertainty and feel another little piece of my heart shell swell and burst. "Thanks, Ken."

"I could see how you'd think she hates humans, too, but I don't think her issue is not liking us enough. I think she likes us way, way too much. She's all composed until the blood hits the air. Then she gets overwhelmed. I don't think she even meant to fuck me. I mean, not like I minded, she's fucking crazy in bed. But halfway through things got...uh...less fun. She tore a chunk outta my neck. I thought I was a goner until I felt her wrist in my mouth. She gave me her blood and she gave me *a lot*. I healed right quick. It was my only time with her. Didn't volunteer for that again." He speaks to Constanzia alone.

She takes another drink. "Got lucky then."

"Luck had nothin' to do with it, sweetheart. It was all charm."

Diego grumbles insults beneath his breath while I roll my eyes and stand up. "You are bonded with her, then."

"Yeah, guess so."

"It wasn't a question."

"What's that supposed to mean?"

I advance on him while he glances around, looking unsure. He puffs his chest and reaches for his weapon with a confidence I will rip from him in a moment. "It means that you will do just fine." I give him no warning, but lift a hand

and press the tip of my finger to the center of his forehead. I barrel into his thoughts, like a canon blast, and shred through everything. He has no defenses.

Idreline is already on his mind, though images of her are spliced dangerously with thoughts of Constanzia — fantasies not yet realized. I shove her aside and hold onto the images of Idreline's face. Her pale brown skin, dotted with freckles. Her unusual mismatched eyes. *Eyes given, not inherited, but only the one. I wonder why...*

I sift through blood bond, rheaching past past memories and into the present. I close my eyes and tunnel across the terrain, her blood in this male seeking its master. I follow the trail of longing it makes.

I find her easily — Ken was right, she gave him *a lot* of blood — but I make no effort to call her forth. I do not want her to know that I am here. With Notare Elise, there was no chance of that. She was aware of her connection with Sistana Abel from the moment it was forged. Aware of Abel's presence. On the hunt for her. But Idreline? Foolish, cocky female. She made blood bonds with what sounds like dozens of humans. What was she thinking? Or perhaps, Ken continues to be right. Perhaps, she's not.

I press harder through the blood ties that bind them and Ken falls back against the truck amid many cries of concern, but it does not matter, I follow, keeping my finger pressed to the center of his forehead, bending him over backwards. "Fuck, man, let go!"

He tries to beat at my arms, but I grab his neck with my other hand and hold him still with little effort. "Idreline..." I whisper to myself as I spear through his thoughts, spilling out of them, finding a route across the road, through the trees, through the woods... "There."

I release him and pull back, refusing to allow my discomfort to reveal itself in my expression. His thoughts were...troubling. I glance to Constanzia, worrying for the female. However...were there any female capable of handling this cretin, I imagine it would be her. The guns strapped to her chest and back scream loudly.

A set of soft fingers lace through mine and immediately, the pressure of rheaching through Ken's mind fades. I glance down at her and smile.

She smiles back, though she looks rather worried. Worried for me or for Ken? I will kill him if it's the latter. The former however, pleases me very much. "Did you find her?"

"Yes. And she is not with Malmon."

"No?" Pia says.

"No. Malmon and Idreline have divided their forces. Idreline is only six miles from here. She's headed straight towards us."

"Lahve, could it be possible that they're moving already to take Brianna?" Laiya says, her arm slung around Sandra's waist.

Cursing and worried whispering picks up across the gathered crowd as word spreads to the trucks that glimmer with human and Heztoichen alike down the highway. So many gathered in defense of this region. Their home. *My home. My Hom.* I squeeze Edith's palm twice in quick succession and she squeezes it back just the same and I feel more relaxed than I have all day, despite talk of war looming so close to our horizons.

"Yes, I believe so."

"They must know we're on the move," Roderick adds.

"I do not know how they could be aware of our presence, but I suspect that Malmon sent Idreline ahead to soften the battlefield before he sends the full weight of his forces. It was his first mistake. Idreline's thoughts are more scattered than any...I've ever seen." *Than any Heztoichen's* is what I intended to say, but on reflection, I'm not certain these days that there is much of a difference.

"Sss-s-ssso we mmmmove on Idreline b-b-before we take M-Malmon?"

I nod.

Diego considers. "Th-that's a lot fffffor us to manage, holdin' captives wh-wh-while we over-over-overtake the outp-post."

"There will be no captives."

"You want to kill everyone? Even your own kind?" Pia asks, her head tilted thoughtfully to the side, yet voice utterly devoid of concern. She is perhaps, a little more bloodthirsty than she appears.

"That I spared them before was a failing on my part. I will not make the same mistake a second time."

"Not how Abel likes to d-d-d-do things." Diego rubs his chin, thoughtful. I know already he has accepted my position. He merely acts as if he has not for the show of it.

I am...reluctant to admit that I quite like this Diego. Perhaps, we will be friends after all.

"The Notare are not here and I am no longer Lahve. I am a general of this army alongside you, Diego. I say we move on their camp and take it by nightfall. What's say you?"

A grin is his only response.

Chapter Sixteen

Bullet fire zings and fire chars the night sky. Thick clouds of smoke rise up from the gas station where they've taken shelter. It is…a dangerous location. Smart, on their part. When they heard us coming, they abandoned their trucks positioned just less than a mile south of us now and Idreline and her forces made their way here. The scent of spilled gasoline fills the air.

Fire is more harmful to the humans among us than the Heztoichen.

So are bullets.

She believes us weak, given the quantity of humans in our party — I do not need my rheach to know this, for it is how I once thought — and I am perfectly happy to let her continue to think it up until the moment I rip her muscles apart. My only concerns now are for the small contingent holding the abandoned trucks as well as our own — more specifically, Edith among them — and the fact that Idreline appears to be well-armed. *Too* well-armed.

Their guns are...high tech. I do not understand where they could have gotten them. Well, I understand where they appear to be from, but I do not like the lines my mind is intent on drawing across borders and oceans they have no right to cross. Like lines in the sand. *Tanen is behind this.* At the very least, Tanen is funding it. Without Elise in the picture, there could be no other explanation. There is a Notare involved. *What if there are more than one?* I hiss, hating all of this.

"Lahve!" Pia shouts. She is hunkered behind an overturned car while I stand behind a tree. We both take fire. Lots of it. I've not yet been hit, but I think I may be one of the few. They keep the bullets coming with such *fervor,* I cannot get through.

"Yes?"

"Can't you do something?" She shouts. She has blood on her arm. It isn't hers. She was engaged in combat. Diego slit their throats and bathed her in the blood of his foe. Then he kissed her after. I was nearly hit as I clung to that moment, finding it...oddly...romantic.

Bullet spray sends bits of tree flying into my vision. The blackness of the night is corrupted by the fire's light. The tree line where we crouch is a disco of oranges and yellows. Shouts of pain illuminate the fact that we will not all make it out of this alive.

"They are well-armed," I answer her. "And I may be immortal, but that does not mean I will not die if a bullet chooses to hit me at the right angle."

Pia's eyes widen, like she's actually *seeing* me, perhaps for the very first time. Then the moment is ruined by explosions. The tree disintegrates around me and I pity the loss. Against the undercarriage of the overturned car, Diego spins to cover Pia entirely with his body, bracing his hands on the car's blackened underbelly as he kneels on the ground before her. Bullets spray against the other side. I...worry for the vehicle.

I just need one single lull in the cannon fire…but Idreline is smarter than I gave her credit for. She is relentless.

"Lahve." The word comes to me at a distance in Teera's voice. Teera is, as ever, back at the trucks, guarding my heart.

"Teera," I reply, having to speak louder than I am accustomed to in order to be heard over the chaos.

"Your Edith believes she may have found another marking. It marks a weapons cache just west of us. I have conferred with Laiya, Sandra and Edith and we believe the best course of action is to go to the weapons depot in case Idreline plans to replenish her supply — or attempt to send troops around us, or to surround us."

Fuck. I understand what she is asking me…and I hate it. "I will join you."

"You cannot abandon your position, Lahve." She pauses. Bullets spray. *"I will protect Edith with my life."*

It isn't good enough. It isn't *enough*. Because it isn't my life. Yet…what are my other options? "Fuck!" I roar. "Shield her with everything you are."

"It is done," she whispers back and, like a radio assuming silence, I do not hear back from her.

I glance up at the tops of the trees above me and I…have an unusual thought. I think of gods and devils, I think of fates and stars. I wonder what plan Sistylea has for this planet, if she attempts to refashion it in her own image, or if she has abandoned us.

No. I do not believe we have been abandoned. If that were so, then Abel would have never found her Tare and Edith would never have made it this far. To me. She is a sign, the beacon I needed to choose sides, to choose right from wrong, to choose life over extinction…We will live. All of us. I vow it to you, Sistylea.

I look up, the moment gone. "Diego!" I roar. He looks at me. "I need only one moment. Only one lull in the onslaught."

"I can give it to you!" Comes a shout from my other side. I look up. Constanzia is hidden behind a tree, like I am.

Humans and Heztoichen are scattered in the forest behind her. All look to me for guidance. "Star!"

The female called Star drops to one knee and opens an enormous case. In it...is a weapon whose purpose I can clearly guess at. "Where did you come across this?"

"That matters now?" She rolls her eyes. "Just need to know if I should use it!"

Yes...but then I consider an alternate plan, one based on the words I heard from the illustrious *Ken*. Psh. "We need Idreline alive. If I am allowed close enough to her forces, she will run. I may not find her until she returns to Malmon. I need a reason to keep her here."

Wedged between two sapling trees just behind Constanzia, I catch the face of a male with a toothpick in his mouth. He is not Ken, but he will do just fine. I snort as I shout, "Roderick, come to me."

He does as ordered and he's hit in the shoulder as he runs. *Perfect*. He grunts, but absorbs the blow with a dignity I do not expect from him. "What'dyouneed, boss?" He speaks around the toothpick so that all the words bleed together.

"I need you to bleed." I reach for his sleeve, rip it off, and then drag my nails down the full length of his arm.

He cries out, but shock makes him slow to recoil from me. When he reacts, his jaw sets and he lifts his automatic weapon and slams the butt towards my face. I catch it easily and lower it to the side, impressed...the toothpick does not once teeter, let alone fall, from his lips.

I lean in close, confident in the roar of the fire and the sound of the bullets to drown out my words, if Idreline is listening. She would be foolish not to try. He flinches from me, but I lean in close enough to smell his sweat. No, humans do not all smell the same. He does not smell like Edith. He smells like himself and now, like himself, but bleeding. I whisper to him what I want and he takes off at a sprint, careful to stick to the trees and the overturned cars as he moves further and further away from the rest of us.

Diego gives me a look, but I shake my head, not willing to give anything up.

"Anyone I allow past me, destroy."

He nods, jaw setting. Pia chambers the next round of her weapon. I refuse to be distracted by thoughts of Edith. "Constanzia, now!" I roar.

She starts to sing a song at the top of her lungs... *"Fiiiiiirewooooork!"* I have never heard it before but — as Star mounts the tripod and Constanzia helps her brace and, together, with the help of two other humans, they pull the trigger and a high-pitched whistle sounds before a small explosion lights from the end of the three-foot firing rod and a rocket launches into space — it seems appropriate.

I wait the second it takes for the rocket to meet its mark, decimating the entire left shack of the three-building gas station, which itself explodes as gas cannisters within catch fire. Screams light. Three Heztoichen who'd been hiding inside, die. Our humans are, luckily, far enough back not to be caught in the flames.

I take off, moving at the same speed of the rocket, though moments behind. I watch in slow motion as two bodies, cloaked in flame, emerge from the garage on the left and take to the trees, only to be dismantled by the Heztoichen there waiting for them. Swords slash, heads spiral into the air. I don't bother waiting to watch them fall as I advance on the main building.

A barricade has been set up before the gas station, Heztoichen sit upon it in rows thirty-deep. It is...a structured formation, well thought out. It annoys me profoundly. The concrete moats have kept our bullets from penetrating. It helps that they are reinforced by huge bags of sand. This is a common outpost for them, one we have not taken notice of — because no one ever thought to bring *Candy* out here to read the signs. No one wanted to hurt Edith.

And now she is the key to everything.

I think of her with pride as seconds pass like lifetimes. The commotion to the left has caused all Heztoichen here to abandon their guard — only for seconds. And those precious seconds that pass like lifetimes cost them theirs. My hand flexes towards the sword in my belt with pleasure and I remove it with intent. My shirt rips up the side as I bring the sword high over my head. I am running at my maximum speed, so fast that the first Heztoichen has not even returned his gaze to his gun by the time his head is spiraling through the air.

I decapitate forty Heztoichen in the blink of an eye, but not quickly enough. Idreline has realized that I am upon her. Gunfire rains, dozens of bullets — hundreds — hit me in the chest as I push through the doorway. It *hurts*, but it does not kill me. Only a bullet to the brain would and perhaps, not even that. Complete decapitation is the only sure fire way to destroy one of my kind. The bullets are intended to wound and to slow me down.

I move as quickly as I'm able with blood oozing from my chest. I launch myself against the wall, crashing through it, and then dive through another barrier that's been erected of sandbags against what used to be aisles of food. The clatter rings in my ears and, as I come up, four Heztoichen fighters are on me.

They abandon their guns, opting for swords. I would say it is a poor choice, but it does not truly matter. The way I move makes any weapon in their hand look like a toy. Yet... their distraction is successful.

It takes me seconds to fight them, exactly twenty-two. In that time, Idreline might have been halfway back to Malmon to report our upset...had my distraction also not been met with equal success.

I hear the sound of Roderick cry out. I make quick work of the four Heztoichen here and then the eight Heztoichen loitering outside, unsure of how to proceed now that Idreline has been successfully distracted.

It was…Ken, unfortunately, who gave me the idea. I can see him now, in the trees, fighting with a member of the Five Point Gang — a Heztoichen who thought to flee. *Hm. So… not all are loyal…* Constanzia arrives at his back and engages the creature, giving Ken the opportunity to stab the guard in the throat. *That particular guard was one of Elise's. He should not have been so easy to dispose of for two humans. Yet…he was. These humans are…resourceful.*

"La-Lahve!" Comes Roderick's garbled plea. He has already stabbed Idreline in the shoulder blade, but she is impervious to the pain as she sinks her teeth into Roderick's neck, tearing chunks out of it. He may not live through this and it will be my fault.

I roar, my sword meeting that of a Heztoichen's for a quick moment before I draw my blade down and cut them in half, cleaving clear through flesh and intestines and spinal cords. They collapse in pieces at my feet and I sheathe my blade, charge forward and grab Idreline by her hair and by the leather jacket on her back.

I haul her off of Roderick and toss her toward the trees. She does not run in the direction she should. Instead, she attempts to run *back* to Roderick to continue to feast. Her gaze is engorged with lust that looks like love in its most twisted rendition. She gazes at Roderick with hopelessness, with sadness. A junkie, she is no better than the Crestor, who died by my hand, utterly honorless.

She attacks and…Roderick surprises me. "Fuck this bitch," he growls under his breath. He advances past me with his gun up. He swings it towards the crown of her head. The resulting crack is hard to endure. It sounds *painful,* even for a Heztoichen. Idreline releases a terrible scream and stumbles to the side while the gun splinters all the way up the hilt, wounding Roderick's hands.

"Fuck!" He drops the gun and shakes out his palms. The wounds are deep, but not so alarming as the missing pieces of his throat.

"Roderick, you need…" Heztoichen blood. I intended to offer my own as we have time for little else.

Yet, humans are resourceful as fuck. He has realized the same thing I have and advances on Idreline and swipes two fingers through the blood pouring down the side of her head. He spits out his toothpick, brings his fingers to his lips and sucks them clean.

The sound draws Idreline's attention and she jerks towards him, her gaze vacant, her lips slack and open. She has no control over herself around the scent of human blood, around the threat of its pleasure. Were I not so recently… threatened myself, I would think her weak. I do not think her weak. I debase myself by momentarily feeling…bad for her. *I understand. I will still kill you, but I do understand.*

She staggers upright, but Roderick has already lifted a fallen gun from the ground belonging to one of the Heztoichen I just killed. He stabs the blunt end of his useless weapon into her gut, knocking the wind from her and forcing her to her knees.

"Fuck you, fangs," he calls her. He spits blood onto her kneeling form, leans in and swipes another line of blood from her temple. He groans, rolling back his shoulders as her blood works its way through him.

Does he even realize what he has done? He has just bonded himself to Idreline. I shrug and decide that it… doesn't matter. Idreline has dozens of bonds, my own female's among them. And it is because of that, that I order, "Don't bring harm to Idreline."

"You fucking kidding me?" Roderick freezes. The toothpick in his hand — where does he keep getting these damn things? — never makes it to his lips. He flicks it onto Idreline's heaving form as she struggles to catch her breath.

"Yes."

"Why?"

"Shared blood between our kind and yours forms a near unbreakable bond. Through it, pain can be felt if the holder of the bond does not know how to repress the sensations."

"Maybe, I like hurting her more than I mind the pain." He steps on her shin and pain splinters through her expression.

"Enough." My insiria strain as I pull back on the reins on my rage. "You would do well to remember that you are not the only one she has bonded with."

The confused rage slowly dissolves from his expression. His full lips fall open and he pulls at his thick beard. "Shit. Edith?"

"Edith is, from what I can tell, impervious to the effects of the bonds. But there are others like Edith who are still enslaved."

Roderick nods, concern making his brows draw together as he stares down at Idreline. "How quick will she regain her senses?"

"Quickly. We need to restrain her..." Bullets in the distance have me turning from Idreline and abandoning all that Roderick and I have worked to achieve. I do not care if Idreline flees. I have somewhere else I need to be.

I tear through the forest and follow the sound of shouting. A narrow dirt and gravel road leads to a concrete shed. Unlike the exposed gas station, someone spent much time fortifying this place, because the walls are reinforced concrete and the locks on the steel door dangle open and number near a dozen. Blood spatter is flung wantonly across the threshold, the white walls, the floor. All of it Heztoichen. *Thank fuck.* Six well-armed corpses spill out onto the forest floor, the only evidence that there was a battle here. I don't see any other signs of life. My stomach squeezes. My heart squeezes. My skull squeezes until my brain feels like it's on fire.

"Lahve, we're here." I whirl around and spy Laiya moving out of the woods, Sandra close at her back. She swings her gun around and turns on the flashlight mounted to the end of it.

Sandra, who'd been holding onto the back of Laiya's bulletproof vest, tsks against the backs of her teeth as she takes in the gory sight. "Oh my. You really made a mess of things, didn't you?"

"Oh, you wanted me to introduce myself before I gunned them down, did you?"

Sandra tuts. "I should have figured your battle would be a mess. You're such a messy eater."

Laiya turns to face her human. They are nose-to-nose. Laiya shoves a hand back into Sandra's hair and gives it a sharp yank before dragging her teeth — *her fangs* — up the long column of Sandra's throat. "Unless I'm mistaken, you like how *messy* I eat."

Sandra gasps, her breath coming faster. I look away from them, aware that I'm intruding. "Maybe…"

"Nithril? Is that you?"

I am standing before her before I've fully identified her shadowed form in the woods. She's alone. She's covered in blood. The bottom of my stomach drops through the bloodied ground at my feet. *"Edith!"* The word bellows out of me. "Are you…where…where is your wound. Here, drink from me…"

"What? I…no. No, I'm okay. The blood isn't mine. Really, Nithril. I'm okay."

A deep inhale proves her words. I cannot smell her own blood, except in the flavor of her skin. Right now, it's all tainted by the wretched sensations of Heztoichen blood. I would be inundated by their memories, were there any to be had. But the owners of this blood have all passed on, returned to Sistylea.

I touch her cheeks, speckled in dark blood. I rub it off, but it hardly works as bloody as I am myself. "Are you okay? How are things with the others?" Her fingers reach out to fumble over my chest, blind as she is in the dark.

"Fine. The battle is over. Idreline has been captured…"

"Oh my god, holy shit! You're shot! Are these bullet holes! Sandra, can you bring that light over here?"

Sandra comes running and together the two females gasp over the sight of my body. I roll my eyes. "I'm fine. I wasn't decapitated."

"You were shot like ten million times," Edith shrieks, sounding very close to tears.

It fills me with delight. "Are you worried?"

Her eyes glisten. "Of course I'm worried."

"Fuck, I love you, Ipalora."

"What?"

But it's too late, I haul her against me, lift her feet from the ground and crush her mouth with mine. I…stumble, moving backwards…backwards…until my hands find the trunk of a tree and I brace her against it, using it as leverage as I slip a knee between her thighs and keep her pinned.

"I need to be inside of you," I moan against her throat.

"Wait — did you say…"

"It's not the time for questions."

I drag my teeth down her neck, feeling feverish, feeling undone. The bloodlust and, perhaps more pressingly, the blood*loss* has made me woozy. I start to stumble to the side.

"I think I might love…"

But before she can finish, I have my first accident…in three thousand years. As I stumble, I apply too much pressure against her. As I stumble, my blood fever takes control. As I stumble, my fangs…sink straight through her scars in the place where she's been taken against her will so many times before.

The taste of her explodes into my mouth, liquifying my insides and turning them to soup. I suck in a full draught of her unique, mesmerizing silence before my ears even hear the sound and my brain interprets it.

She gasps.

I drop my knee from between her thighs and her feet hit the forested floor and sink into the damp leaves. She reaches up to cup her neck while fire blazes across my chest and my eyes dilate. I cannot see. I am...horrified. I am elated. I want to rip her open and devolve to the madness that has already claimed Idreline. *I am no better.* No. I am much worse. I have two and a half thousand years on Idreline. She is barely older than Kane. Her lack of control might be explained. As for me? There is no explanation.

"Edith, I..."

She is frozen stiff, eyes dazed.

"Edith, I'm so sorry. Allow me to heal you. You will only need a single drop of my blood. It's potent. More than that could be dangerous." I reach up to my lips and puncture the skin of my thumb. I bring it to her mouth, but she slaps my hand away and places several more feet of space between us.

She looks...shocked.

"Edith, say something please..."

She shivers. "I...it's okay."

"It's anything but okay. I violated my promise. I didn't mean to, I swear. I was...careless."

"Careless," she repeats.

I take another step towards her. "Drink from me. I don't wish to add to your scars." The words just...spill out of me as thoughtless as a human...and Edith winces. "I didn't mean that, Edith..."

"I thought they were something to be proud of for having survived, like Diego." Her tone is cruel. Each arrow loosed hits center.

"Edith..."

"Lahve! Teera is injured!" Laiya's voice sounds muffled and, when I look up, I deduce that she's inside the small shack.

I curse. "Edith, please." I don't know what I'm begging from her, but she's already moving towards the shack, moving to help as I should be. I surge forward, grab her chin, kiss the tip of her nose too quickly for her to stop me. Then I let go, even if it hurts to do so. "This isn't over between us."

Silence. She doesn't say more. She just gathers the torn fabric of her hideous turtleneck and bundles it against the twin wounds dotting her neck. They are not particularly large or deep but, left to heal like this, they will add to the melee of scar tissue that already decorates her beautiful, mutilated flesh and I will be just another abuser among many. *No, I will be worse. I will be one who had her trust and then disposed of it.*

She walks beside me as we approach the building and hovers dutifully in the doorway, making space for me to pass her.

"Teera." I duck inside a darkness that is no trouble for my eyes. Sandra holds a flashlight in her mouth anyways as she and Laiya attempt to staunch the wound in Teera's left leg. Knowing that she was wearing a vest, it appears that her attacker was smart and aimed for her shins. Both are broken. She will not be able to walk on them without help.

"She needs blood," I hiss.

"She can have mine," Sandra offers without hesitation.

Laiya places her fists over Sandra's and shakes her head. "Mine's stronger."

"And yet, mine will be the only blood strong enough to ensure that she can walk out of this building." I move to her side as I make an offer that I have *never* made. It is not appropriate for a Lahve to share his blood with anyone. But fuck being Lahve.

The silence is maddening and broken up only when Teera balks, "Lahve, you cannot be serious. You are…Lahve!" She stammers, "It's forbidden." She groans as Sandra attempts to splint her leg using a belt and two pieces of a metal cabinet.

I pinch my thumb against my fang until a single droplet of blood wells on the tip. In the darkness, I meet her gaze and she looks stunned, more than hurt. "I have not been Lahve for some time." Since Edith. "But when I slaughtered fifty Heztoichen in a gas station, I suppose I *formally* renounced my title." I smirk.

She smiles then licks her lips, eyeing the blood with curiosity and apprehension. "I would be honored, my lord. Yet, I do not think I can. Duty is…hard to reject."

I sigh, sensing that my battle is lost. I lick my own blood off of the tip of my finger and huff, "Are all females built so stubbornly?"

Her teeth flash, so do her eyes as she looks over my shoulder. I can sense Edith's presence in the dark, standing where I left her just inside the doorway, cupping her throat. And then Teera's smile falls. "You're hurt, Edith."

"It's okay."

"You're bleeding. I can smell it. Lahve, she's bleeding…"

"I bit her." Stunned silence looms like a cloud of wasps. I am stung by it over and over. "I…did not intend to. It would appear that I have little more control than Idreline."

"Idreline. Is she caught?" Laiya says after a weighty pause.

I nod. "She is caught. Roderick was instrumental in her capture."

"Good. We can use help emptying this cache. There are hundreds of weapons."

Teera nods her agreement.

Sandra says, "But where'd they get them?"

I clench my teeth together and quickly help Sandra construct a rudimentary stretcher on which to move Teera. We use a ripped up canvas sack strung between two posts from one of the metal shelving units against the walls.

Yes, they are very well stocked. Dozens of guns hang on the walls across from ten times as many boxes of bullets. I grunt, "I have a theory. One I do not like, for it suggests that Malmon has made contact with the other regions and they are forming a mutiny against us."

"Tanen?" Teera grimaces as Sandra binds her legs so that, when she does heal, she does so in a way that won't force us to have to rebreak her legs. Clever healer, this human is.

"Tanen," I agree. "Perhaps others."

"Others?"

"I am the wall between Heztoichen who hate humans and the humans they hate. I have known Tanen for generations. He wouldn't cross me. He wouldn't be so stupid and it would appear that he isn't. He's using rebels to root me out. If they can dispose of me, then Tanen has nothing to stop him from killing every last human in his region and this one. He may even have help. The Notare are divided. They unite because they fear me, because they know that they have to. Because they know the truth of the matter."

"What truth is that?" Edith's voice is small, frightened as we approach her, me, carrying the back of Teera's stretcher while Laiya carries the legs.

I hesitate, knowing that she fears me already. Perhaps, she should. Let there be no mistake about what I am, or who. I swallow audibly and…she does not move away or make space for me as I move beside her, so my outer arm strokes a path across the top of her chest, collar bone to collar bone. The sensation is wonderful, but I don't linger. I want to give her space.

"I could kill any of them if I wanted. I could kill them all. The only security they carry with them is in thinking that I will not choose sides — that I cannot. But I have," I say to Edith, pausing, even though it's awkward as hell to stand here, carrying another female as I speak to the one I care for more than all the rest. "I have chosen."

Her lips purse in a way I can't figure out. She's still cupping her neck, but her eyes are warmer than they were and more focused. *Am I forgiven?* It would be too much to hope for that.

"I choose you. Whichever side you choose to stand on."

I do not await a reply. I merely carry on, aware of her every breath, every beat of her heart as she follows.

Chapter Seventeen

"It is...annoying," I growl around at the humans seated far, far too near to me. Rather than fight on and decimate Malmon this very night, they have elected rather to make *camp* and *sleep* this night, so that they may regroup and re-arm themselves and fight on in the morning.

"You allow Malmon the same opportunity to make plans and discover ours," I hiss across the fire's blazing light. Humans and their fires. It is disgusting, the way they flirt so boldly with death. It is worse because my human's life is among them. She is with Laiya now and Sandra, Pia and a dozen other females. They are cleaning themselves and preparing to sleep. I would be more concerned to have her out of my sight for the moment were I not also keenly attuned to the world surrounding us, reading the leaves in every tree, and conscious of the fact that we are alone.

Malmon has not yet discovered us. Or, if he has, he has not yet made his presence known. I do not know which theory disturbs me more. It was...clever of him, not to share his blood. It was...rather cruel of him to allow his own kin to do so wantonly. She was a lamb to the slaughter. He allowed her to carry on, unchecked and unhinged.

I glance at the school bus where Roderick watches her. She is not lucid enough to rheach as of yet. Her…state is perhaps the only reason I do not press Diego into moving tonight. I want her thoughts. I want to rip them from her like stitches from a fresh wound.

But first…

"F-f-f-f-fuck. I c-c-c-can't sssssleep with that f-fucking smell."

If Diego can smell it, then I am certain her bonds are near to breaking. Matt and Mo lie down together, already tucked one against the other in their attempts to get comfortable. Mo points to the bandana wrapped around the lower half of his face. "Why do you think I'm wearing this?"

I snort. *Snort*. Sistylea, what has become of me? Diego is giving me a look across the fire that suggests he's thinking the exact same thing. "Her bonds will be broken soon," I assure them.

Matt licks his lips and props himself up on one elbow behind Mo. Both fought well. Well, they were far enough from the battle that they did not have to fight much, but for not fighting much, they fought well, the two of them. They move gracefully together, a couple that has known each other for some years. "Will she even survive not having any blood in her system?"

"She will have some blood." Drops. Enough to weaken her until she is little more than a husk clinging to brittle bones. "A little…enough."

"Remind me never to piss you off." Mo's voice is muffled behind his mask and sounds more nasal than usual.

"It-it wwwwill be enough to break all of her b-b-b-b-b-bonds?"

"It will be enough to break all of her bonds, yes."

"B-b-but you'll st-still be able to rrrrrrrrheach her?"

"So long as her heart still beats, she still has access to the memories imprinted on her soul. The greater concern will be that she does not know anything of particular use. It's clear her brother did not favor her."

"I guess we have something in common." Edith's soft voice rouses me from where I'd been leaning against my pack. I sit up straight and then, when I see her, I quickly stand. She stiffens, but takes another step, making me wonder where *we* stand.

"What are you doing?" Constanzia's voice ruins a tenuous moment. "Oh shit. Are you standing in the presence of a lady?" She adopts an accent I cannot place. It is pure ridiculousness. And then the blasted woman starts to sing. "Oh oh oh, she's a lady...and that lady is mine..." The words she makes up in between do not seem to fit to the song, though what do I know? I've inspected nothing of the music of this place. But...Constanzia's song, for as terrible as it is, has still brought a smile to Edith's face.

"Well, since I'm clearly not wanted here, I'll go relieve Roderick then. Make sure he's not getting frisky with the prisoner."

"Y-y-you joking?"

"She's joking." Pia steps up to the fire and holds her hands up to it to warm them. "Roderick isn't feeling too charitable after that bitch tore a chunk out of him." Surprise. It echoes around the circle and I feel it, too. And because I feel something else that they all feel, it makes me suddenly and acutely aware that I am...a *part* of this group. Pia shrugs one shoulder, the faint tint of blood still staining her outer sleeve. "What? She's not exactly a nice lady."

Constanzia cracks with laughter, toppling into Ken who appears suddenly behind her and loops a meaty arm around her waist. He whispers something to her in a language not so commonly spoken here. It is however, spoken on Tanen's continent. Hm.

Are you a nice lady? He asks her.

Constanzia doesn't reply, but glibly shrugs him off and takes Star's hand. The two females bounce together as they make their way toward the bus, giggling while their weapons clatter against their backs, like they aren't in the midst of a war. Perhaps, they know no different. The thought troubles me and I return my gaze to Ken who stands far, far too close to Edith.

"Where did you learn this tongue?" I ask him in the language he shared with Constanzia, a language I learned from my short time in Carata.

He hisses, as if burned. My hand flexes towards Edith and I know she sees it because, when I look at her face, she's looking down at my hand, reaching for her, slightly outstretched. "You speak Mandarin?" He asks me in English.

"A bit."

She comes to me. She's looking at my hand and she comes to my side. She comes to me even though I don't deserve it, because she does not understand that I have wronged her. Or worse…that she understands I have wronged her and she doesn't care. Or maybe she comes to me for another reason entirely. *Insufferable woman and her exquisite silence…*

"You learned Mandarin?" Edith asks me when I don't answer Ken. I nod and find Ken difficult to remember now at all. "Why?"

"On Sistylea, we do not have so many tongues. When we arrived this was the first thing I found beautiful. The first *human* thing I found beautiful."

Edith looks up at me without a smile, without a frown. "What were the others?"

Yes, Ken is easily forgotten. "Careful with the females," I warn him in Mandarin as Edith pulls me down into a seat at her side. "I will not tolerate any misbehavior."

"What? You'll gut me like you did your own kind?" His eyes are steel and mean.

I would have respect for his stare, were Edith not currently in its path. "Gladly." I tick my chin, an order for him to leave.

"Wh-wh-what did he s-s-sssay?" Diego asks me.

"Nothing worth repeating."

"Fffffffucking hate-hate that g-g-guy."

"Be nice." Pia gives Diego a kiss on the cheek and lies down, placing her head in his lap. "Ken's a nice guy. We like him."

"Ssssssay sh-sh-shit like th-that to me ag-again and I'll lllloook th-th-the other way when Lahve goes to gut him."

"Shush. Lie down. We need our beauty sleep."

He snorts at that, but I'm distracted by the way he nestles down at her side when Edith turns to me. "What else do you think is beautiful?"

"Your eyes."

"What?" She makes a face that ends in a smile. "They're just brown."

They're just brown...and yet I am strapped to the tips of all of her eyelashes. I want to count them, one at a time, over the course of time, not all at once. Her face is a thing I want to savor.

"No. They are a thousand different colors, but I was more referring to their shape. You look like you are caught in a constant state of enchantment."

Her beautiful eyes roll. "I look like a deer in the headlights, you mean?"

"No," I say, smiling when I realize how she understood my meaning. "I did not mean that you are caught in enchantments, but the one casting them. At least, you've cast one over me."

"F-f-ffor fffffffuck's sssssake," Diego grumbles.

"Shush now, he's being sweet. And I'm pretty sure you've said a lot worse in front of Luke."

"You n-n-n-need to quit standing up-up for him." Diego grabs Pia by the waist and rolls the both of them over while she laughs loudly.

Edith is smiling at them when I look back at her face. "I don't want to talk about this planet or its beauty. I want to hear more about you." I reach to carefully stroke a lock of hair behind her ear, then ball my hand into a fist as I remember that I haven't earned that right. *No, I had that right, and then I lost it.*

"What do you want to know?" Edith asks, guarded.

"What do you find beautiful?"

"Your hair."

"What?" She gives the answer so quickly, I can't help but laugh. "My hair?" She nods. "What about it?"

"Most humans who have locs...they have to make them. But, and don't make fun of me, but I've wanted to ask for months — does your hair grow out of your head like that?"

I laugh and nod and feel so humbled...forgiven, I feel that too, and I want to accept it even though I shouldn't. "Yes. It grows into coils that mat together all on their own."

"It's amazing. Does your whole family have hair like that?"

I nod. "My mother did. My father did, too. They say we looked quite similar to one another."

"Are your parents still alive?" She seems to realize her mistake immediately and blushes. "I mean, would they be alive if they had come in the pods?"

"My mother, perhaps, but my father, no. He chose to take the long sleep some eight hundred years ago. He was just over two thousand years old and came to the decision that he'd led a good, long life."

"So what...you killed him?"

I smile at the look of horror in her eyes. "No. I most certainly did not kill my own father. That would have been too much for him to ask of me. There are Heztoichen trained in this task."

"This happens often?"

"Oh yes. Most Tretaro do not meet out a natural end. In fact, there have been only two recorded cases. Geviria, a female who lived during the time of the pre-Frost, lived to be twelve thousand and eighty two. Another male, some five thousand years prior, perished of natural causes at the age of nine thousand, seven hundred and thirty four. At least, that is what our history books say."

Edith gawks and then shivers, inching towards the fire, the coat she wears not enough for her. I would give her mine were I wearing one but, as I'm not wearing any shirt at all, preferring to air out my wounds as the bullets push themselves out of my skin slowly — it will take all evening — I reach into my pack and withdraw a long sleeve thermal. I pull it over her head before she has a chance to protest. I help her slip her arms through the sleeves.

"So, basically what you're telling me is that you're like a teenager?"

I laugh unexpectedly, the sound nowhere near attractive and yet, it makes her laugh, too. "No," I finally answer, laughter fettering out, "I suppose I'm nearing middle age."

"Nah. I say you're barely older than I am."

"That is absolutely how it feels."

We smile at one another for some time more, her fingers tangling with the twigs beneath us.

"Would you…like to lie down on my sleeping mat? I have only the one, but you already know it's yours should you need it."

She glances at the flames, pink taking up residence in her cheeks for just a little while longer. "We could share it."

"You…want to sleep with me?"

She nods.

"Edith, I would be honored." I start to move, but she reaches out and takes my hand. She brings it to her neck, where I bit her earlier. Now, beneath her turtleneck, I feel a bandage. My stomach hollows. "I am so…"

"It felt good."

Confused, I swallow thickly. "What?"

"It…upset me, earlier…"

"As well it should have. Edith, I'm so sorry. I didn't want to do that without your express permission."

"That's not what I was going to say. Would you let me finish?" She says with an annoyed huff.

How is this possible? Me? Lahve? *Annoying?* And not for the first time, either. I think of Kassie and struggle not to smile. "Go on."

"I didn't feel it at first, when you bit me. But, when I did, I was…" She gnaws on her bottom lip. "It felt *really* good. I didn't expect that and I've never felt anything like that before. It scared me…not the bite, but liking it."

I remain still, unsure of what to say.

"Is that why…" She inches towards me and glances to the side, as if worried we're overheard. "Is that why some Heztoichen couples exchange blood during sex? Because it actually makes everything feel *better?*"

I don't want to ask about her previous experiences being bonded — if she'd enjoyed her bonds, she would not be asking me this now. Instead, I exhale the rage I feel and nod once. "Yes. Mates often bond one another during sex. It is said to heighten the experience."

Her eyes flare with undisguised interest. That, and lust. "Oh."

"Oh." I raise an eyebrow.

"Well…"

"Well?"

"I…might be open to…trying sometime with you."

I damn near stroke. I cannot speak. I cannot do anything but batter back my lust and stare.

"I mean…" She blushes. "If that's something you'd like…"

"Edith, I don't…deserve to hear this from you now. I took from you without your permission."

She nods and her reply is quiet and thoughtful as she answers. "It always…hurt before. Everything. But with you, nothing hurts and everything feels…" She sighs dreamily. "Amazing. I should have thought about it before but, if you can make me forget about sex sucking, then it stands to reason you could do the same for the biting, too. I wish you hadn't've done it the way you did, but I'm…happy with the outcome all the same."

I launch myself at her, grabbing her around the waist and rolling her over away from the flames just as Diego did to Pia. Edith laughs much in the same way. "I'd bond you here and now if I didn't already have plans to mate with you first."

"You know what humans say about plans." She palms my cheek as hers rests against the inside of my arm. Her fingers move down and trace the small mounds where bullets attempt to push themselves out. If they are unsuccessful, I'll have to cut them out, but I don't want to worry her with that now. "They oft go awry or astray."

"Don't tempt me, siren."

She smiles up at me and then very softly, sighs, "I forgive you."

"You should at least pretend to be angry with me for a few more days."

She laughs and shakes her head. "I don't want to waste any time with you."

My insiria coo. "I feel the same way."

"I used to think Idreline bonded because of how good it felt. Do you think that's why she forms all those bonds?"

Her question is so unexpected it halts the motion of my lips to hers. "What?"

"Do you think she bonds them because it feels good?"

"Why else? Where did this come from?"

"I was thinking about my experiences and how it only hurt before. I never thought about it hurting for anyone else, but I think, maybe…it's just a theory…" She shakes her head.

"I'd like to hear it, *Lahve*."

She wrinkles her nose up at me. "Don't call me that."

"Ipalora, your wisdom has been invaluable so far. The greatest strength we have. Don't be shy now in voicing your next theories."

She rolls her lower lip between her teeth as she looks up at me, as if trying to decide whether I'm lying or not. And then she props herself up on one elbow. "I think...I got the idea that...sometimes watching them...that Malmon thinks of Idreline more like a...like a *weapon* that he can unleash. Whenever she would lose control and kill one, he would always laugh after and give her a kiss on the forehead. But I..."

She shakes her head again and I sense that she will stop talking. Needing this information from her now, I press, "But you?"

Her eyebrows draw together in concern as she thinks and whispers, "I don't think Idreline ever *meant* to hurt anyone. I think she would stop, if she could. I think she bonds everyone she bites not because it feels good, but because it *hurts* her."

Stunned, I cannot believe this. How had this not occurred to me?

Edith continues. "What if she makes the bonds as a way to keep the humans *alive?*"

"She would be creating the bonds as a sort of pressure gauge — she would feel every time a human was in too much pain and it would be a cue for her as to when to stop."

"Exactly," Edith says, eyes bright as she meets my gaze. "When she would drink from me it hurt like hell, but she would stop right before I passed out. I always thought it was to torture me, but what if it's because she was trying to keep herself from killing me and going completely crazy?"

The cogs of my mind are spinning. I sit up and, when I sit up, I see that half the circle of people around the fire are sitting up as well. "Are you eavesdropping?" I hiss, aghast.

"Edith's onto something." Romalin, my scout says, speaking directly to me from beyond the fire. He's standing now.

Mo yanks down his bandana. "She's the smartest person here. Ain't a surprise. God, the scent of that bitch's blood reeks…"

"It's like we're back at that hot spring — remember the one?" Matt prods Mo in the shoulder.

"Yosemite?"

"No, not that one…"

I cut Matt off before they launch into one of their spats. "You are correct, Mohammad, in everything. You all wait here. Edith, stay warm at the fire. Thank you again for your insight."

"Where are you going?" She says as I turn my back on her.

"I think it's time that Idreline and I had a chat."

Chapter Eighteen

I step up into the bus and see Constanzia, Star and Roderick arguing between several short brown seats, clearly built for children. Idreline hangs suspended from the ceiling by her ankles, her throat slit and leaking blood into a large plastic bucket beneath her. She is not dead, but she will be soon if she's not righted and allowed to heal. Roderick's bloody blade shows he has been the one to re-slit her throat each time it heals. He must have done so a dozen times by now.

"It is time," I tell the three.

"We should bleed her out more. I can still feel the bond between us." His hand moves to his throat, which he massages. His eyes are bloodshot and I am certain that he can feel her pain each time he cuts her open. That he is still standing and not yet passed out is a testament to his endurance. I am…impressed.

"Good. Edith has had an idea that leads me to believe that your bond with Idreline will continue to be useful." I drag the bucket of blood out from beneath her and hand it to Star and Constanzia. "Dispose of this in the woods unless your healer would like to make use of it."

"What are you going to do?" Star asks, an eyebrow lifted. Constanzia's wrinkling her nose at the blood and muttering curses — no, muttering song lyrics, the infernal female.

"I need to speak with Roderick."

"Yeah?" Roderick yanks the backwards baseball cap off of his head and runs his fingers through his earlobe-length hair, causing it to stick out from the side of his head. He scratches his cheek, pulls the toothpick from between his teeth and breaks it. "Fuck, this hurts," he says once Constanzia and Star have vacated the bus, nearly spilling blood all over themselves in the process. "Can we get her… up?" He swallows hard.

I nod and go to the half-dead female, yank the ties at her ankles and, as she falls, make no effort to catch her.

"Fuck," Roderick curses again behind me. "That hurt, too. I thought the bond was supposed to break when all the blood is gone."

"Unfortunately, all the blood is not gone and your bond is very new."

"I shouldn'ta swiped her blood. Fuck me. What was I thinking?" He stares at the female sprawled across the ground with murder in his gaze.

"Rage makes us do funny things."

He snorts and pulls another toothpick out of his military vest breast pocket and shoves it in his mouth, twirling it over his tongue. "Doesn't it, though…"

"A few weeks ago, I had no concept of this notion. I have since *changed my tune*, as you humans would say."

"As Constanzia would say," he jokes.

I smile. "Yes, I imagine she would."

"So, what's your plan with her? I thought you wanted the bonds broken."

"I did. But Edith raised a very interesting point about Malmon, Idreline and control. It would seem that Malmon was born with all of the control that Idreline lacks. It would also appear that he has been working with several Notare for quite some time. I'm not sure which and I have awfully concerning thoughts as to why. Put simply — kill all the humans and fake a Tretaro blood line."

"Ooookay," he says slowly. "What's this got to do with me?"

"I will explain in a moment, but first, you may want to take a seat."

He does without waiting for my explanation. He must understand what I mean to do as I hover over Idreline and prepare to grab her by the throat. "Fuck," he whispers.

"Brace yourself. This is likely to hurt."

"Fuck."

I latch onto Idreline's throat and tunnel easily through her memories. And I see...my oh my, the things that I see.

I see Elise. I see families of the former Notare. I see Crestor's sister. I see laboratories. And then I see an orange-haired human, weak, near dead, and Malmon's lips latched onto his throat, drinking deeply. His eyes burning more brightly, becoming an electric violet... And then I see the boy left alive, but barely, lingering in a cell decorated...oddly. I back out of dark tunnels, back out of a dark building, back out until I see signs for a building that was once a tourist destination. An aquarium...

The river is just beyond it, but I don't cross it. I remain here, exploring Chattanooga, the city, the surrounding area. I spot my guard, surprised to find that they are tortured but alive, at least they were the last time Idreline saw them. I see that they are in the building marked by a star, so many of them. I can see Idreline's hand delivering the marking in blood. Her hand shakes as she touches it. She drinks the rest of the bucket. Her brother catches her, reprimands her. He forces her to leave, sends her ahead with a war party to Brianna...the image blurs...fire crackles...

I hear gunfire. I see Roderick's face. I smell his blood. It is... inundating. The sensation is so overwhelming, I feel my own body shake with the force of it.

Edith is right. She's been right about everything.

The blood effects Idreline in a way only Edith's affects me and, even then, my reaction to Edith's blood is *nothing* compared to the scent of Roderick's to Idreline. It is pure *ecstasy*, a relentless euphoria. A conjurer that will not retract his spell. It slaughters and, for just one moment, I hallucinate joining with Idreline and Malmon, only so that I may enslave Roderick and keep his perfection all to myself.

I pull back *hard* and fall on the floor of the bus. I stare up at the ceiling, struggling to catch my breath. Alternating flashes of Roderick's scent and Edith's crash over me. I can feel blood running down my throat, unsure who is crushed in my grip, or if no one is and I'm still caught in the dream. I want to fuck Edith again. I want to fuck her while bathing in a river of her scent.

No.

I want to marry her. I want her to tell me her thoughts and ideas without prompting, because she knows that I will believe her no matter what. I want her to know that I think her the most intelligent creature in the universe, because she is. I want her to know that I find her beautiful not, in spite of her scars, but because of them. I want her to fuck me senseless with her mouth again and I want to taste the river she makes every time she comes.

I suck in a breath that tastes like the horrible sulphuric blood of a Heztoichen — a scent that has no draw for me. It helps clear my thoughts. I sit up and spy the body lying prone before me, chest rising and falling incredibly slowly, before Roderick fists his knees and yanks himself into a seated position. His jaw is clenched. A broken toothpick dangles from his bottom lip.

"Fuuuuuuck," he growls, holding onto his abdomen and neck and skull…anywhere he can reach.

I nod, understanding.

"Is that what it feels like? Her addiction?"

Addiction. A good word for it. "Yes."

"Fuck. It feels so fucking good. I can see why she wants to kill me. I want to kill me and I'm...me. Fuck, that was confusing."

"Me, too."

He grunts and looks up at me from where he clutches his gut. "Don't get any ideas."

I snort and roll my eyes for good measure. I struggle to stand and, when I do, don't make it far. I collapse into one of the children's chairs and conk the back of my head on the smudged window when I lean back. "You're wrong, though. She does not want to kill you. At least, not intentionally. Your bond with her will save your life. It hurts her, too, when she feeds too savagely."

Roderick whistles low and shakes his head. He stands stiffly and paces down the bus away from me, and then back again. "You read that in there?"

"No. Edith told me."

He nods, as if there were no more obvious truth than this one. It makes my admiration for him grow. Her scars have no meaning to him, either. If anything, they only prove that she knows everything that she knows.

"Shit." He stops pacing. "We have to warn the others."

"We will. But first, you must do one thing."

"What?"

"Drink from me. Only a drop should be enough. More than that might kill you."

"The fuck?" He steps back. "Why would I drink from you?"

I roll up to standing, even though it hurts. "Because you will need it. There may come a moment when we are within the walls of their camp that I need to wound her."

"Alright, so? Wound her. I can take it."

"No. You do not understand. She feels your bond more acutely than anything else. That is *why* she bonds. It is not to save you. It is to control herself."

He stares at me blankly and I feel irritation. Edith would have understood already where I am going with this. But he is no Edith. I start again. "Your pain hurts her more than her own simply because of her addiction, the madness it inspires and the fact that she does not want to want it. She *wants* to keep you alive. She wants to not feel pain herself. She wants to not feel your pain. However, there may come a time when we are within their walls that using her addiction — her chaos — will serve us."

I press my thumb to the tip of my fang, just as I did for Edith earlier. "Malmon seeks to use her as a weapon, but I believe we can use her as a weapon *against* him. To do that, I will need to hurt her. To do that, I will need to wound you and, when I wound you, you will need my blood to survive it. It can't be a small cut. It will need to hurt for Idreline to lose control and react to stop her own pain. She will turn on her own kind to save you. I just want to ensure she's actually able to."

"Won't that bond you to her?"

"A one-way bond, and a necessary sacrifice to keep you breathing."

"Gee, thanks," he offers, tone snarky at best.

"I do not do it for you. How do you think my relationship with Edith would proceed if she knew a drop of my blood killed you? Tsk. I know you're human, but I'm sure you can imagine."

He grunts and eyes the drop of my blood clinging to the edge of my finger, a promise of pain and yet, a way to stave away the afterlife. His shoulders slump and he rubs a hand down his face. He staggers forward and swipes the blood off of my finger with one of his, then brings it to his tongue.

His whole body jolts and he collapses down into one of the children's seats. His head makes a loud clank when it hits the window just as mine did but, eventually, his breathing returns to normal. He survived it. *Thank Sistylea.*

"Feeling better?" I ask him when he removes another toothpick and shoves it between his teeth.

He looks up at me from below the bill of his hat and makes no effort to move. "Jesus Christ."

"Not exactly."

"Fuck you."

"I'm with Edith."

He snickers, "You're an asshole."

"On that point, I agree with you completely."

Chapter Nineteen

The pickup truck bounces down the highway and Idreline yanks against her restraints. They are steel and rip against the bolts binding her to either side of the truck. "Sit the fuck down," Roderick snarls at her.

He is seated opposite me. Edith is to my right, in the farthest position from Idreline the truck bed allows. Tucked underneath my arm, she leans against my chest, burrowing there as if for safety, as if she's cold. It doesn't matter the reason. It makes my heart pound faster and harder than any other time I've gone into battle. It makes me regret this choice. I should have left her behind. But I couldn't. That would require me parting from the feeling of her skin against my own.

"Are you alright?" I breathe into her ear.

She nods, seeming somehow certain of her answer. "I'm fine. Are you alright? How are the bullets?" She palms my chest.

I rumble, distracted. "I am immortal, Edith. I'm *fine*. It's you I'm worried about. You remember the rules, correct?"

"Yes, I remember."

"Tell me."

But instead she tips her head to the side and surprises me with a question. "What's it like to live forever?"

"What?"

"You said you're immortal. What's it like?"

I can't help but smile at her even though I mean not to. This is serious business. But I do have an answer for her. "If you had asked me when I was on Sistylea, I'd have told you that immortality is uninteresting."

Wind batters her fiercely and I help her hold her hair. She waits for me to say more, but it's a frightening truth. "And now?"

"Terrifying."

She looks up and I kiss her forehead without asking her permission. I hope it's alright. The way she releases a soft sigh gives me hope that it is. "Why terrifying?"

Against her temple, I murmur, "Because, I am accustomed to saying goodbye. Now, I no longer want to."

I pull back just enough to be able to focus on her face. Her eyes are closed. Her heartbeat is loud and quick. She licks her lips and I jerk, wanting to kiss her but finding restraint. *No, I don't.* I kiss her anyway. "Thank you," she says when I pull back.

"For what?"

"It makes me feel a little better hearing that someone like you could be scared of anything."

"Ha. Someone like me? My precious Ipalora, you must know that there is no one like me."

She sticks out her tongue and gives my stomach a poke with her rounded nail, smoother than it was…she's biting them less. "Cocky, aren't you?"

"I used to be, but that was back before I lost my virginity to a female so knowledgeable and observant that she deserves of my title more than I do."

Edith laughs and my gaze is caught on her teeth. It… occurs to me… "Why do you still have all your teeth?"

"What?" She squawks, then covers her mouth again. "That's so random."

"As if your question wasn't?"

"Touché."

"I only mean to ask because I notice that many of the other humans are missing a tooth or several."

"Some of it is bad hygiene," she shouts over the wind. It's hilarious. *She thinks I'm a human.* I don't correct her. "Sometimes it's fights. And some humans pull theirs as a sign they don't have any Heztoichen blood in them."

"Why would they do that?"

"It's sort of a status thing. Like they're the last real humans left. I don't actually have all my teeth. At least, I didn't. I lost a lot to gangs, but I always had Heztoichen blood in me. They grew back. A lot of gang members will pull a tooth to prove they aren't a blood bag."

I brush my fingers over her lips and then press my pointer finger into her mouth. I feel my way along the line of her teeth, noting how remarkably blunt they are. And then... the little temptress...she bites down. *And sucks.*

"Edith," I hiss, pulling my finger back. "You're distracting me from the battle. We might lose a war because of your perfect teeth." She laughs while I continue to tease. "Did you not hear what I said about being a virgin? I have very little restraint when it comes to you." I touch her neck. "Too little." I shake my head. "You make me want to burn the world and spread the ashes at your feet."

"That seems excessive."

"Perhaps, Malmon's head on a pike, then? As a sign of my affection?"

She grins. "I think that's the most romantic thing anyone's ever said to me."

"I hardly think that qualifies as romantic."

"What do you know? After all, before me, you were a virgin." She sticks out her tongue and I gawk.

"Did you just insult me?"

She laughs and the sound is captured by the wind and dispersed among the trucks barreling down the road behind us. "I would never, *Lahve*."

As she teases me and I look down into her perfect expression that is utterly inappropriate for war, renewed panic and terror fill me. "I want you by my side today, no matter what."

"I know the rules. You said them thirty million times already."

"And I'll say them another thirty million more. If I tell you to run, you run. If I tell you to hide, you hide. If I tell you to abandon me or anyone in trouble and save yourself, you *must*."

She swallows thickly and laces her fingers in mine. "I'll try."

"If I tell you to trust me, trust me."

"I do," she says, but I'm not sure I trust this.

"If you cannot manage this then, at the very least, trust your instincts. You know more than the rest of us combined. Use it. Do not let anything slow or stop you. Not even me or this incessant thing called love that I have for you."

"You…" Her throat jerks and she's forced to swallow repeatedly. "Do you really mean that?"

"I've said it twice, haven't I?" And I want to hear it from her. Time is a cruel thing because I don't want to wait. I want it from her *now*. "Do you need to hear it a third?"

She nods, greedy as she is.

I smile down into her eyes. "I love you, Ipalora and whatever happens next, there is only one certainty. The world may in fact burn to ash, but the flames will not touch you. You will live."

Her fingers tense around mine. Her gaze gets so fucking glossy. I hold onto hope…could it be? Will she say it? "Nithril, I…"

"Maghma mamewlakd hmah!" Words slice between us, uttered by Idreline.

"What did I say?" Roderick roars. "Shut the fuck up! They were having a moment."

I groan, "Humans."

"I think that was Idreline's fault," Edith says. She turns to face the woman and cringes. I can tell that she doesn't like the sight of Idreline as…ravaged as she's been. She is gagged, her hair still thickly matted with her own blood. She reeks of it and I would worry that her scent would carry on the wind and alert Malmon and his scouts were our trucks not so loud as to precede it. They will have had plenty of time to prepare for us…

But they will perhaps have less time to prepare for them. A pickup truck barrels past us driven by Constanzia and Star, and another by Ken and a human male whose name I don't know but who follows Ken around like a sycophant. Two dozen humans lay spread across both, all armed with the knowledge that I cleaved from Idreline's memories of the town and the stronghold within it and, more importantly, the bridge that Edith once used to cross the river with her community that Malmon *perhaps* hasn't recognized yet. And, even if he has, it is too far for him to go there now, should he wish to cross. *Unless he's already fled.* The thought comes and passes. No. He hasn't fled. He's too confident — confident enough to draw out his own Lahve. He would not have called for me if he did not intend to meet me on the battlefield.

Idreline has her ears bandaged and her eyes covered in an attempt to dull her senses so that she does not know that we are using Malmon's own tactics against him. Separating our forces, Diego will lead the charge around to advance across the main bridge and close in on them — or, stop their retreat. Whichever comes first.

I know that Idreline will still have some idea of what we have done the moment she sees that there are four trucks less than there were when we left camp, but by then it is my hope that it will be too late.

The sign demarcating the city's boundary has come and gone. The city has begun to rise up around us, dispersed homes becoming small strips of storefronts, most missing their windows, until eventually buildings begin to clump more densely together and eventually, lift into the air in the form of high rises. Most have been leveled, but some still stab towards the sky.

"There." Edith points to a field studded with graves. A large stone archway stands near the entrance. A five-pointed star is scrawled across it in red.

I see the sign with increasing frequency as we roll forward. I can also hear the sound of bodies moving, retreating as they prepare their reinforcements, thereby leading us to a central point. It is interesting that they have not sent waves of battalions out to meet us head on, and it makes me smile. He has wasted his manpower on sending battalions to overtake Brianna. Militants that were so easily cut off. Now, he is on the defensive.

"Oh Malmon…You made the wrong choice," I whisper aloud. I am certain he hears me, though he does not reply. "Stop here," I order Matt and Mo driving the truck beneath us and a human called Reba, behind us, who drives the school bus.

Both vehicles pull off onto the side of the road. Ahead of us, a short brick building with triangular spires jutting up into the air like shards of broken glass, comes into view. Before it stands Malmon. He makes no move to conceal himself.

"I've been here before," Edith whispers. "The aquarium. He uses all the old fish tanks in the basement as cages for the blood bags, or anyone else they want to punish."

I nod, having seen the cages before in Idreline's memories, smeared with the blood of the bonded she couldn't save, if that had ever been her intent. "Come."

I help her down from the back of the truck and don't ignore that she grips my palm tighter as we move down the street. Broad street. The sign hangs askew. Dead vines drip from it, just as they drip from the window sills in the brick buildings lining the road, as thick as curtains. The world crawls in grey vines, making the entire scene look like the traditional graves of our pre-Frost tribes, back when we would bury our dead in large mounds containing all of the tools they would need to fight the devils in the afterlife.

Broken sticks and dead vines crunch beneath my shoes. Edith presses herself tighter to me as we make our way down the road. "Are you sure it's safe to walk like this?" She gestures around at the buildings. A large parking garage holds many levels from which gunmen could pick us off. Yet, I point to the shell of my ear and shake my head, hoping that she understands that we are not being watched. I lean down and press my lips to the top of her head. Though it is a *dangerous* display, it doesn't really matter. Malmon is no fool. He will know Edith's value to me without this.

"After all your posturing, after all this time, you have chosen a side." His voice hits me the moment I right myself.

My lips curve up, but I cannot call it a smile as I meet Malmon's gaze. He stands at the top of a short, decorative bridge studding the center of a small square at the end of this block. I come to a stop, half the length of the block separating us. The jagged, vine-draped building that Edith knows to be the aquarium silhouettes him and the large force under his command.

"Yes." I smile more broadly, more grimly.

"So many traitors…Traitors! All of you! Traitors to your own kind." He shifts where he stands, uncomfortable or at least disturbed as he assesses our numbers and the quantity of Heztoichen behind me. They do not number so many as his, but he is surprised by their numbers nonetheless. He would not have expected so many to align with us.

"You are the only traitor here. You betray Sistylea."

"Sistylea is gone."

"No. Her Tare remains. And you betray it."

"A human cannot hold the Tare…" He scans the crowd, searching for her.

"I lead in her absence," I tell him. "It is my role as…"

"Do not dare call yourself Lahve. You disgrace your title — a title given to you by Tretaro far wiser and more honorable than you ever will be and ever were."

"Yes, you are right. But I was not going to say Lahve. I was going to say that it is my role as one of them. You have chosen sides, Malmon, to align yourself with Elise, with Tanen." At the mention of his name, Malmon's left eye twitches. I have my answer. "Your desire to be something and to take power not given to you by Sistylea will be your downfall."

"It won't."

"Before the night is through, your head will be lit as the beacon calling all humans home to Brianna. I will personally see to it." I smile.

His teeth flash in the light and he snaps his fingers. Beneath the bridge, the human gang — perhaps, what is left of Jack's, perhaps some other — are shoved aside by several other Heztoichen. *Heztoichen with violet eyes.* No…

"How many experiments were run? How many have you attempted to turn to Tretaro?"

His eye twitches again and he does not answer and I am pulled from my musings by the sight of shuffling beneath the bridge. When the humans are pushed aside, it exposes the bodies hanging by their necks from the railing above — the railing that Malmon grips in claw-tipped hands. *His nails are the same black mine are.* They shouldn't be. They should be pale colored like all the rest…

My insiria rattle a war cry as I meet Far's gaze. His face is blood red, veins bulging across his forehead. He has been blooded. They all have — Far, Sebine, Morithan, Edriggo, Miro, Nethral…a human even hangs among them, though I don't know his face or his affiliation with our group. Either way, they've been tortured, judging by the fact that their feet are all bare and bear the vestiges of burns. I do not allow it to move me any further than it has.

Instead, I whistle between my front teeth and hang back, keeping Edith with me and stepping to the side to make space for Laiya and Roderick to drag Idreline forward. Malmon, atop the bridge, reveals nothing as he looks down at his sister.

We come within range of his archers and — I grin, forgetting that in this world, we no longer use archers. It is a pity. I always enjoyed the words exchanged between kings in the center of the battlefield, the knowledge that, at any moment, an arrow could skewer one or the other, but wouldn't. Because battles have a certain order to them, a certain decorum. And Malmon...he understands and follows this decorum in a way I appreciate. I suppose we might have been *friends* in another life had he not chosen his side and had I not chosen the female who stands to my left.

Edith attempts to slide behind me and I make no move to stop her. I prefer her here against me, using me for her shield.

"Notare Elise made you bold promises, Malmon," I say.

He nods. "She upheld all of them."

"In exchange for helping her kidnap the families of the Notare, she promised you magic she had no right to make. That she has no knowledge of how to make."

"You assume she failed."

I tilt my head. "You were born of a good male and a strong female. You could have adapted well to this world."

"I was born to a Tretaro so weak, even Notare Elise held more power."

"She was a Notare."

"And what is a Notare against a Tretaro? You are the greatest among us and yet, you have fallen. You could have so easily stopped the madness — stopped a human from receiving Tare and yet, you chose to help them. Despicable. You could come. *Join us.* Join us and rid the world of these feral animals. We can remake Sistylea in our own image, a world where Tretaro entreat to no one, no matter what Tare they carry."

The wind moves through my hair, caressing my scalp and I shake my head softly as a soft shudder sweeps me. "I have seen jungles even more beautiful than those of Hom. I have felt the wings of an Ipalora on my face here. Sistylea did not forsake us. Notare Elise misled you. And now you have abandoned your only kin to blood madness, assisted in manipulating the Tare, and gone against the Notare that we Tretaro are sworn to protect."

Malmon's fist, even from where I stand over fifty yards away, tightens so perceptibly, I am embarrassed on his behalf. A youth, guided by impulse and desire for power, he is transparent. "You are no Lahve," he hisses.

"You know my name, Malmon. I am Nithril and I come to protect Sistylea. I am here to guard all of her creatures."

"You come because you've lost your mind to a human cunt."

I…wish that did not hit a nerve, but it does. It reminds me of the horrors he inflicted upon her and threatens my composure more than any other insult. "Would it please you to know that we were able to root you out because of that female? She knew exactly how to find you, how to read all your carefully crafted signs, and took us straight to Idreline. It was so *easy*. You have been bested by a human." I laugh. "A human you once thought worthless and treated as such. She will wear your eyes tonight, like the Tretaro of old — Tretaro who would laugh at the imbecile you've become."

He stiffens and manages to hold his composure when he says, "Then, it is done. I do not relish having to kill you, Lahve. For what it is worth, your blood will ensure that the rest of us true Tretaro live on. The same, unfortunately, cannot be said for the blood bag you are sworn to protect."

I do not react except to smile. Insults are always a part of this. And, for as long as I keep him focused on me, he will not notice Constanzia leading the force closing in from across the bridge. I want there to be no chance of Malmon escaping this.

"Then, shall we begin?"

A moment of tension. A moment of silence. And then Malmon whistles and the first bullet is fired. Chaos reigns.

Shields up, my Heztoichen move forward to cover the front line while humans fall in line behind them and release rounds over the Heztoichens' shoulders. Malmon is…quicker than he has a right to be. I wonder what blood Elise mixed to attempt to create a stronger, more powerful Tretaro. I don't like not knowing just how many paths she's woven across this continent…and beyond it.

Malmon leaps over the railing and drops from the edge of the bridge. He leads the charge forward. Dozens of humans pour out from behind the bridge and then dozens more throw open the doors of the aquarium behind him and charge. *Hundreds.* They are led by a blonde man with a beard braided into three large sections and a head shaved on the sides and covered with tattoos. He wields a machine gun in one hand and, in his other, an axe.

"Forward!" I roar and I allow my soldiers to move past me, a little smile touching the edge of my mouth as I see humans fighting alongside Heztoichen, and even Teera limping into the mix.

I hold back, refraining from joining in until the last soldier has passed. Here, with only Edith, Laiya and Roderick, I turn to Edith and kiss her tenderly on the forehead. "Find cover," I tell them, nodding my chin toward the brick building to the left.

Roderick and Laiya drag a weak, yet thrashing Idreline through the drape of one curtain of vines. In the building, out from underneath the path of direct fire, I watch Edith take shelter. She offers me a worried look. I offer her a small smile. A stray bullet nicks my shoulder. I roll my eyes and then I am off.

I dart forward, moving too quickly for *almost* all eyes to catch. Those with the violet eyes watch me and, as we move between the battling humans and Heztoichen, we fight a battle all onto our own, one where everything moves so slowly around us and time hangs suspended.

There are six with violet eyes, six with reflexes that go beyond the scope of their born heritage. I imagine, as the first two descend on me and I rip out their throats with very little effort, that it might have bothered me, before — killing them. *Before Edith. That is the only before that exists to me now.* But now, I care only for the suffering they've caused to claim those instincts.

I move quickly onto the next two while our forces continue to batter back the rest. They meet me in a clash of violence, firing for my legs. It is…a poor strategy. I stagger once and that is only to withdraw my swordstick and slash it across the stomach of the male who charges me. His violet eyes dim as he slumps over the blade. I rise to take on the next attacker and find myself bombarded by the blonde male with the axe. He moves quickly for a human and, when I swing my sword up and rip open his stomach, I can smell the Heztoichen blood he has imbibed.

I look up, nearly at the bridge now, and fling my sword. It spirals through the air and slices through the hangman's rope cinching Far's throat. He drops to the ground and rolls slowly onto his feet. From there, he looks up through his lashes and releases a roar that is pure rage. He frees Miro hanging there next to him first before launching himself toward a set of Heztoichen deep in the fray, moving toward them as if he has real reason to despise them. I do not doubt that he does and I have no wish to know why.

And then I feel a brush of awareness along the back of my neck…a second too late. Fingertips press against the nape of my neck and, were I any other creature, I would worry about his ability to snap my spine…Were I any other creature, I would perhaps, be more prepared for what is to come next.

Because no other creature on this planet has ever attempted against *me* what I do, every day, against them.

Malmon rheaches into me. He yanks into my thoughts, pushing past weak defenses — defenses erected to thwart an accidental brush against a human or Heztoichen, *not* defenses fortified against an attack. Much differently than Diego's assault, which was purely *him*, Malmon yanks and jerks his way into *me*. The first thing he finds is the only thing I do not want him to see.

Edith. Her head tossed back in pure ecstasy. The sounds she makes as she comes…

I fight back, the battle between our minds easily won, but it…was…*enough*. Enough for Malmon to understand the depth of feeling I have for her. With her at his side, the war would be over easily. I would do…whatever he asked.

"Find the red-haired girl in the building there! Bring her to me!"

He has taken from me something personal, something private, something I had no wish to share ever with anyone. Something I will cull from his mind by force.

I rise in a whirl, ripping away from his grip and, as he attempts to jolt away from me, I latch onto his hand. *"You dare rheach me? Have you lost your mind? I am Lahve. I am Nithril."* I thrash into his thoughts — not with a drill, but with a nail bomb. Not at all intent to extract, I *obliterate*. *"You dare touch her again!"*

I crush, scramble, unravel. Malmon screams as I find the lock he keeps on his sanity, pry it open and release havoc onto everything. I press against his wrist and he falls to his knees, his head thrown back on a scream. And then I hear it — a scream, one that sounds an awful lot like…

"Nithril, I need you!"

I drop Malmon immediately and show him my back as Edith calls my name. I feel a dagger thunk into my shoulder as I retreat. I don't care. I leave it there. Three violet-eyed Heztoichen are dragging Edith from the building — *how many more of them are there?* They hold her by either arm and I would have killed them already…if one of them hadn't had a knife pressed to Edith's neck.

Laiya and Roderick attempt to pursue them, but cannot hold onto Idreline at the same time. Laiya lets go and fires into the stomach of the violet-eyed male on Edith's left wrist. He doubles over, but the distraction gives Idreline the opportunity she needs to break free. Staggering, blood-let and blood drunk at the same time, her eyes are unfocused and she moans, sounding like an animal.

With surprising speed, given her state, she dodges Laiya and the Heztoichen engaged in hand-to-hand combat, swerving to arrive behind Edith and the one holding onto her hair. She shoves that Heztoichen out of the way, pushing them towards Laiya and I tense as she takes the blade.

"Brother, run!"

I hear Malmon order his troops to retreat — but only in the Heztoichen language. The humans he leaves for the slaughter. Fury radiates up my arms, but Idreline knows that I will not move, not even to hunt down the one I plan to butcher. She meets my gaze, her violet eye and her grey one piercing me with famine, with regret.

I know what she will do, even before Malmon calls out to her, "Slaughter the female! Do it now!"

She hesitates for an ephemeral instant, right before slicing that dagger across Edith's scarred neck, and I have never been more grateful. That instant is just enough for me to do two things in the exact same moment.

I pull my sword free and launch it at Roderick. It sinks into his stomach and he roars. Idreline screams as her blade cuts Edith deep enough for her to choke on her own blood, but I am not worried. Because at the same time, I rip the dagger out of my shoulder and I throw it at Edith.

It hits her in the left shoulder and, the moment it penetrates her flesh, pain unlike anything I have ever experienced washes over me. I collapse onto one knee.

Bullets stab me in the back up until the moment I hear Constanzia release a belting screech, *"Ohhhhhhhh I wanna dance with somebody!"* Her comrade in arms and in lyrics picks up where she left off and I can hear the sound of retreating feet. I am grateful as I drag my way forward.

My feet slip over the bloody pavement as I make my way to Edith's side. There is one Heztoichen still standing over her, glancing rapidly between Idreline and Roderick and Edith and I. He pulls a handgun off of his belt and aims it at me. He is too late. A spray of bullets pierces his chest, sending him cantering back. As he struggles to regain his footing, I jump onto him and rip open his throat with my teeth.

I suck down his pain and anger and his rage and regret until there is nothing left but a husk of a Heztoichen, a shell of skin. I rip his head off for good measure and toss it aside while the pain of his memories settle inside of me. Only the pain in my throat is stronger and is strong enough to help me bear it.

"Edith..." I pull the blade out of her shoulder — a blade wet with my blood — and watch her chest shudder. She sucks in a breath and then rolls onto her side, spitting up a lungful of blood that smells of copper...and of sulfur. My blood is strong and I gave her so many droplets through the blade. I worry about her inundation and glance up, worried, too, about how Roderick has fared.

"Holy fuck," he gasps as Idreline feasts on his throat. She moans and his heels kick uselessly against the blood-spattered asphalt. Vines and tree branches crackle like fireworks beneath him and his hand...his hand moves to his belt. I think for a fleeting second that he might be reaching for a weapon but he's...reaching for the unmistakable outline of his erection pressing against his black military pants.

He snatches up a wad of her hair and drags her up, off of him, and then he flips their positions so that he straddles her...and then he lunges down and sinks his blunt human teeth into the side of her neck. Idreline screams and grabs the sides of his shirt. She pulls until the material tears and then pushes on his shoulder, flipping them again. She grinds her pelvis against his pelvis and then goes again for his neck. This time, he seems to…encourage her.

His moan is shattered when Constanzia steps up to Idreline and slams the butt of her weapon against the back of Idreline's head. Idreline flips her hair up and hisses from deep within her throat, accessing her artificial insiria. Constanzia aims for her forehead and this time, strikes true. Idreline slumps back down over Roderick who shouts obscenities and clutches his temples as he orders Constanzia to stop.

"Please, for fuck's sake, stop it, you crazy bitch…"

"Excuse me for helping…"

"Nithril?"

I look down. Edith blinks up at me and smiles shakily. I smooth her hair away from her forehead, hating the dots of blood marring her perfect skin. "Are we…alive?"

I snort, "This is quite noisy for it to be the afterlife, don't you think?"

She releases a clack of laughter that eases every pain in my body, and every pain in my soul. Her trembling fingers reach up and flutter over her neck. I press her hand against the wound that once was. It is only skin now, marred by scars but no wounds. "You're alive."

She nods. Tears well in her eyes. "I called for you."

"Yes. As you should…every time." I lean in and brush my lips across hers, tasting her own blood on them. I suck a little harder on her bottom lip and she huffs against my mouth and pulls back. I would think her averse to my kiss were her pupils not fully dilated. *She can feel my need.* I would be concerned that that is *all* she can feel, but I know better. Because in my own blood, I can feel *her* need thundering madly between her thighs, affecting the state of my cock in this moment that is entirely inopportune.

"I called for you and you…and you *stabbed* me."

"Hm, it would seem that I did." I grin.

"You…bonded us."

I frown. "I am sorry that there was no other way. I intended only to have to stab Roderick, but she got to you too quickly, so I made do."

"You stabbed Roderick, too?" She tries to sit up, but I hold her down, still…worried. "Is he alright?"

"Oh, I think he is more than alright."

"I heard that," comes a grumble from a few feet away. I glance over my shoulder and see Roderick frowning around at everything. Idreline lies prone at his feet. He keeps his gun trained on her, but his hand is not even on the trigger. He is not prepared to use it.

"Are you well enough to stand?" I ask Edith.

She nods. "More than well enough. I think I have your blood to thank for that." She blushes and I help her rise, wanting to apologize profusely but aware now that the gunfire has retreated to behind the aquarium and that we will need to give chase.

"Move on the others," I order Laiya and Roderick and any that can hear me. "Ensure that they make it to the bridge and do not attempt to escape by any other route!"

As I pass beneath the bridge I find two of my guard. Edriggo is clutching his chest while Far kneels over him. "Are you alright?" I can see the bloodlust in Far's eyes. He drags a body onto Edriggo's lap — the body of a human male I killed, the one who once wielded the axe.

"Fine, Lahve."

"Call me Nithril."

His expression clears of bloodlust long enough to echo surprise. His gaze passes to Edith, standing at my side, hand in mine. Understanding falls upon him slowly. "Nithril. I am Far. It is a pleasure to serve you, my queen."

Edith jolts at my side but takes Far's bloody hand when he offers it. The sight makes a certain warmth slide through me. Far rises to his feet, his gaze as haunting as the kill itself. "What are your orders, Nithril?"

"Kill everyone."

"Gladly." He takes off and I follow.

The human mercenaries have had sense enough to retreat, so we don't cross many as we round the aquarium and tear to the right, to the bridge that crosses the river. It is clear that there were several others and, as we pass them, I find it fascinating and oddly…poetic that the last bridge that stands is the only one whose planks are not made of concrete, but of metal and wood.

Malmon's forces move across the bridge but are boxed in by Diego, Pia, Ken and the remainder of our reinforcements. Among the dense crowd gathered, several humans throw up their hands and throw down their weapons in surrender. My hand holds Edith's and I keep her entirely tucked into my side, unwilling to allow even an inch of space to separate us. She doesn't seem to mind. Not even her anger at sharing a bond with a Heztoichen seems to be affecting her. I expect it to, but right now, anger is nowhere to be found. There is panic there, yes, fear, too, but also…hope. She feels hopeful. I wonder if she can sense that the battle is all but won, as I do.

Except… "Where is Malmon?" My gaze flits over the crowd of unwashed human mercenaries, whose scent is as ripe as rot, and I notice very few Heztoichen among them.

Diego speaks to Pia and she shouts across the divide. "Only the humans came this way. Did the others escape?"

The soft creaking sound of feet on these wooden panels almost disguises the sound of something *crawling* beneath. "Everyone, hold onto the support beams!" I shout, but I do not even follow my own advice and I should have, because Malmon was only waiting for me.

The floorboards explode from beneath my feet as fists punch through them, grab my ankles and pull. I try to push Edith away from me, to spare her, but the floorboards are all gone. The clever bastards who crawled beneath the bridge proceed to grab our forces wherever they can. Idreline remained behind with Laiya, Teera and Sandra, but Roderick crashes through the wooden beams at my side.

We fall and the fall is long and frightening. I worry about holding Edith to my breast, but worry more about allowing her release where Malmon could go after her. So I cling to her tightly and we hit the water together. We crash through the surface, me on my back, her above. I can feel her lungs jerk as she takes in water and quickly propel us to the surface.

The water is warm and quick. We move down the river at too rapid a pace. I feel panic tug at me as I worry for the dozen other humans who dot the river around us. I start to swim as hard as I can toward the bank, grabbing Roderick by the collar of his shirt as I propel the three of us toward the grassy bank on the far side.

Something grabs my ankle. I release the humans as I go down and a heavy blade slashes my chest. I kick out with my heel, connecting with bone. It crunches beneath the heavy boot Tasha supplied me with and I draw my sword. I stab towards Malmon who swims below me by several feet, his eyes shining up at me like twin torches.

We spin around one another, locked in a deadly dance. Humans are fighting other Heztoichen in the water beside me and I intervene between one human and another violet-eyed menace. I grab her ankle, jerk her leg out straight and cut it off at the knee. The female screams and releases pursuit of the human in favor of trying to find her leg before it moves too quickly down the river away from her.

In water, the humans put up a weaker stand than they do on land and I frown as two dead bodies float past me. I do not recognize the faces and am ashamed that I could be so grateful. A bullet slashes across my short sleeve, tearing it along with my flesh. Malmon, the psycho, swims towards me and latches onto my arm. He opens his mouth wide and sucks in water, drinking the droplets carried to him through the water. Stunned, I am slow to whip my sword between us. I slice his throat, deep and to the bone. He jerks back, eyes rolling into his skull until they are purely white. I know that this won't kill him, but he won't recover quickly enough to continue this battle.

And thus, I am left with choices… Too many of them for me to decide as fast as I would need to. I could go after Malmon and leave the humans above me to a potential death. *No. Because Edith is among them.* I could lick the blood from my sword and bond Malmon to me so that I can always track him, but then I would be bonding him to Edith, too. *No.* So, as I watch him drift away into the darkness of the river ahead, I realize that I am left with one final promise…I will not be able to deliver Edith his's head *today.* I will have to let him go.

Decision made, I don't look back on it. I turn away from the sight of a retreating Malmon and divert my attention to the Heztoichen who has a male I don't know by the leg. I yank him down and cut off his head. I dispose of three others before the two dozen remaining Heztoichen attackers realize that their leader is nowhere to be found. The living speed off and, by then, my arms are laden with thrashing humans who dare me to question whether any in this species were taught to swim.

I drag three…four…six with me as I move toward the bank. Ahead of me, Edith swims towards the shore, Roderick at her side carrying two humans himself. I arrive at the same time they do.

"Nithril," Edith says, coughing as she plants one fist into the muddy bank. I toss the humans recklessly onto the shore while I spend more care in grabbing Edith by the back of her shirt. I haul her out of the water and glance around quickly, ensuring that there are no other attackers before I leave her.

"You're alright?"

She nods. "Go help the others."

I hesitate, wanting to shove more of my blood down her throat just in case, but she smiles at me and it is soothing enough that I feel safe in abandoning her for the other human lives…briefly. Very briefly.

It takes me minutes — unsightly *minutes* — for me to round up the other humans. The other Heztoichen are gone, fled, lost to the river's rough current. Roderick does manage to confront one final attacker on the beach and slaughter him. I am...impressed. And reminded also that he is bonded with a very powerful Heztoichen. Her blood likely has helped him. Well...I remember what I saw...perhaps it is not so *helpful* as it is powerful. There is no denying the power of a blood bond.

Last of the humans gathered and saved, I move towards Edith. She shivers in the grass as she watches me rise out of the water and stalk toward her.

I remove the vestiges of my shirt and unlatch the buckle of my belt. I toss my sword to the side and am on her in an instant. I scoop her up into my arms, spreading her legs around my hips as I rise to standing. She latches onto my neck with her hands, tugging hard on my hair with a squeal.

"Roderick, do you have the beach?" I groan as I pull her against my body, using her heat to soothe my cock through my jeans. I can feel her arousal pounding now. I'm not going to last.

Roderick glances around and snickers under his breath. "Beach?" He wipes the blood on his hunting blade off on his pant leg and cocks his head to the tree-studded grass at the top of the hill. "Yeah, I got the beach. Just try to stay outta earshot."

I grin back at him wickedly and run. I cover a quarter mile in seconds — until I reach the edge of the park and find a copse of trees. Vines hang from the half-dead boughs and drape to the ground in a sort of layered canopy. It is almost beautiful, were it not so hard and scratchy when I lay her down amongst the debris.

I hesitate, worried about my restraint now that we are bonded. "Edith, I..." I shake my head, trying to clear it...but I cannot clear it. My body swirls with her blood now and it is so very potent. I can feel the lingering pain in her neck and I can feel the power in her bones that says that she is unbroken. She licks her lips and looks up at me and heat simmers between us, pulling the tension taut. I suck in a sharp breath and hold it.

"I'm sorry. I'll carry you back… This is no place for…"

She surges up onto her knees and grabs the top of my pants. She yanks the button free and wrenches my pants down my hips to my knees. A rough grunt escapes me as she takes my cock in both of her hands. "Fuuuuck."

I push the wet strands of her hair off of her face with my pointer finger and lower on top of her, pulling her roughly beneath me. Her back scrapes the vines and I *feel* it. I feel everything…but her memory. I belt out a half laugh and shake my head.

"What is it?"

"I cannot…believe the wonders of this world. You are…"

"No. *You* are…" Her hands come around my back and she tries to kiss me everywhere, but I hold her down.

"I am sorry I did not bring you his head on a pike."

She shakes her head before I've even finished speaking. "I don't care. You know I don't care. I want…please, Nithril…"

I press my hips against her hips. Feeling her legs spread beneath me is a powerful thing.. "I bonded you against your will."

"You saved my life." She bites her bottom lip. "You *stabbed* me." She grins. I don't know why this seems to bring her such pleasure, but I can feel it in her chest and mine, and I can see it in the glittering rays of her eyes. "She had me and I know I should have felt afraid, but all I could think about was that you were here and I knew it would all be okay. Even…even if I died. You…you make me happy in ways I'm not…familiar with. You make me feel strong. Like I could live forever."

"With my blood in your system, you just might."

She sucks in a shiver and bites her bottom lip. She leans towards me and glances at my neck. "It also felt *different.*"

"Different how?"

"I've bonded before with other Heztoichen, like Idreline, but I never felt pleasure from the bond. Now, that's all I feel. And I think it might be because..." She trails off. Her gaze glazes over and then she stiffens. She looks down and reaches for my erection bobbing between us. I block her hand with mine.

"Because?" The tension in my groin is not so hot as the blaze in my chest — this one, all mine. I am hopeful... because I think she might just offer me something far greater than her sex, far greater than the sight of her scars...I think she might just...

"I love you, Nithril."

"Edith..." I surge against her, wrapping her fully in my arms and tearing through the crotch of her pants. I kick off my own wet pants in frustration, hear them rip, don't give a fuck. I rip through the front of her hideous turtle neck and undress her down to her scars. Then I slam into her.

"Yes..."

I lift up onto my knees, dragging her with me, leaving her chin tucked and her feet dangling to either side as I grab her by the thighs and slam into her. I pound *hard.* Her eyes roll back and my core tightens...it...cannot be...

"Oh my god, Nithril...it's...I can feel *everything.*"

Her eyes blaze just like my heart. I can feel hers beating in my breast like a second pulse. I pump into her in deep, even strokes, the slapping sounds of our skin the only sounds to be heard, that I care about. I cup one of her breasts and she moans. When I use that same hand to flick her nipple hard with my thumb, she screams.

"Bite me, Nithril," she demands. "I feel your need. Can you feel mine?"

"Yes, Edith. I feel all of you. All of time. All of us." She scratches my chest and I sense that she wants to kiss me. I oblige, reposition us in a tangle of limbs and awkward curses. Grunting, she pulls me onto her body and I hastily try to yank the uncomfortable vines out from beneath her.

I take my fangs to the side of her neck and I carefully puncture a wound. "I will drink from you. But you must drink from me, too." I cut a hole for her in my shoulder, somewhere she can reach while I suck. I want to feel what it is to be bonded while I bond another. While I bond the one I love.

She hesitates, but only for a second, before latching onto my shoulder with her lips. She takes a long draught from me, the first she ever takes of her own will. Of her own want. I devolve and slam my fangs into the side of her throat. She does not scream or react except to suck harder…and then she moans and comes undone around me.

She comes and I…*holy Sistylea*…I come instantly. I moan around the pleasure of her skin as I empty inside of her. Her inner walls clench and spasm and I…I come again.

I fuck her until I lose myself in her scent, her heat, her taste. And then when I start to slow, so do my movements and we make love for another half an eternity. Biting, sucking, licking, sharing. We are covered in our own blood, mine hers, it's interchangeable in all but scent. Hers, copper, mine, sulfuric and pungent. If the strong scent of my blood bothers her, she shows no sign of it and licks my blood off of her palm.

My hips rock against hers slowly like the tide. I can feel pain in my neck through our bond — not because of the bite, which has long since healed, but because she's thirsty, and her throat is hoarse from all the screaming. Her thighs burn and her pubic bone aches. She has bruising around her sensitive, swollen labia, but she still wants. She *hungers* and I am a male poor of restraint.

One hand presses down on her abdomen and the other circles her softest skin. She lasts seconds, far, far too few of them and when she unravels, I unravel. Explosions sail through my skin and I ascend to the stars and then back. I can feel her orgasm as if I have grown my own clitoris in the seconds it takes for me to wrench an orgasm out of her. I'm coming before I realize that I've released and the moment I do, she shatters.

"Nithril!" She shouts to the sky.

I breathe against her ear. "Edith…"

"I'm sorry," I tell her as I come down from the clouds of my next release. She is covered in my blood and my seed — *again*. I can hear the sloppy sounds I make as I glide through it again and again.

"I love you," she replies.

I kiss the center of her sternum, my eyes welling with a tear I've never shed. "When did you know?"

"I suspected before…but when you stabbed me, I knew for sure."

I look up, resting my chin on her sternum and shake my head slightly. For a moment, I merely bask in her heat. She glows. Her chest is splotchy with color. Her breasts fit into my hands so perfectly. I cup them and flick her nipples, just to watch them peak. "What is it about nearly gutting you that has moved you so deeply, Ipalora? I need to know if it's worth it to try again."

She grins down at me and pushes the hair from my face. "You had a plan."

"Yes?"

"You had a plan for what you'd do if I was in danger. You…thought of me."

I'm still not getting it. "I think of you all the time. You are *all* that I think about."

"No, I mean, as part of your battle strategy. You had a plan for if I got into trouble. You didn't just think of plans for how to use me. You…you didn't need to use me." She shakes her head and struggles to speak. Her throat pains her, but I don't have the decency to tell her to spare her voice. I want to hear this.

"When the knife sailed through the air, glimmering in the light and I hallucinated my whole life, I knew…looking at you, that I was important. I know it…it doesn't make sense. But I…even when Idreline had her hand around my neck, I didn't feel like running away. I felt like, even if I died in that next moment, I belonged. Like I was finally part of all of this." She waves her hand around the air in a flourish.

I can't say that I understand, but I plant a kiss in the center of her chest nonetheless. "I am honored."

She strokes my hair behind my ear, drags her fingernails across my scalp. She tugs me up and I oblige, moving until I can reach her lips with mine. I press my mouth against hers, sealing our love in silence. I inhale deeply, choking a little as I rise up. She cups my jaw in both of her hands and I am wrecked by the mirrored tears I see in her eyes.

"I know you wanted to marry me before you bonded me, but you didn't have to. You don't have to. You made me feel important. You make me important. I've…never had that. And it's enough. It's more than enough. Thank you."

I snarl and deepen the kiss, slanting my mouth across hers and invading it. I tangle my tongue with hers and suck on her gasps until she's primed and ready for me once again. I sink into her deeply and, as I roll my hips against hers, I utter ravenous prayers against her skin in a language she cannot speak, and then in English I finish, "You make me feel human, Ipalora, as if my life has begun again."

She looks up into my eyes and grins. "You make me feel immortal, like my life will never end."

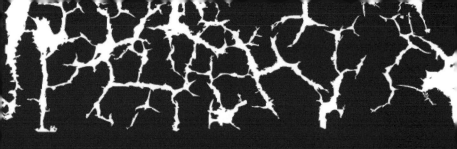

Chapter Twenty

We worship each other until we eventually hear our names shouted on the wind. Far calls to us, his voice grumbled and respectful as he intrudes. *"We are ready to return to Brianna, Lahve."*

"Nithril."

"Nithril."

I carry her back to the others because Edith's legs are sore, despite my blood in her system, and I like her close. They grin and slow clap as we return and Edith buries her face in my chest as she repeatedly insists that, after all of the day's events, she will in fact die, but only of embarrassment.

"Remember what I told you before we began? There is no chance of your dying, of embarrassment or any other ailment."

"Edith?" Sandra approaches us just as we step onto the school bus. It reeks of human stench, blood and medical concoctions. Her hands are covered in blood. Most of it coppery and metallic but some of it Heztoichen, too.

"Yeah?"

"Is the bus for medical purposes only?" I ask, interrupting.

"Yeah, it is."

"Apologies, we won't disturb you..."

"No wait. There is a human we found in the dungeons. I believe that you might…know him?"

"Rick? He's here?" Edith's body betrays no tension. No strain. Meanwhile, I tense around her, wanting to shield her from whatever horror she might see or that his life might bring.

Sandra nods and wipes her hands off on her stained apron while Laiya fiddles with the dials on the bus behind her. "Many of the humans surrendered. We gained about three dozen fighters. But there were over two dozen more in the dungeons. Based on the marks on their wrists and their scarring, I guess they were used as blood…*couriers* between the gangs. I'm sure Nithril can confirm. One of them was in a particularly…bad state, but he claimed to know you. I have him on the bus now."

"How did he know I was here?"

"Uh…there was um…gossip about what you two were up to." Sandra grins and I see that one of her teeth in the back is missing. She must have lost it long before she met Laiya. Now, her blood smells almost as sulfuric as Laiya's does human. "He overheard your name mentioned."

"He wouldn't know me by Edith. He calls me Meredith."

Sandra's eyes widen. "It's…interesting. He seems to know quite a bit. Maybe you should talk to him, Nithril. Maybe, Edith, you should stay behind. He's in…pretty bad shape."

"No. I want to see what happened to the man who sold me."

Sandra's mouth slackens. Over her shoulder, Laiya's brow furrows and her hands, on the controls, still. "He sold you?"

Edith nods.

"How did he claim such a right?"

Edith ambles from my grip, but I still move in front of her as we ascend the short flight of stairs and step up into the bus in our tattered blood-soaked clothing. "He was my brother, once."

The bus has been transformed into a sort of rolling infirmary. The chairs in the back half of the bus have been removed to make more space for bodies. The bench seats in the front are entirely full with humans, most of whom I recognize only from the battle. All look wary and weary. Many seem to be nursing broken souls, rather than visible wounds.

In the back of the bus, a few bodies lie prone. Heztoichen bodies missing limbs that did not and will not regrow. Humans who have accepted no Heztoichen blood or are too far gone for it to repair them, of which there are quite a few. And then, leaning against the back door of the bus, there sits a scrawny male with the same shock of red hair as the female bound to me.

Beyond that, the two siblings are unrecognizable and it is not because of their face shape...it is because I do not even know what shape this boy's face once was. He is *grotesque*. He has been stitched in a dozen different places, and that is on his face alone. He has...bones missing, bones added...human ones or Heztoichen? He has violet eyes, but they are dim and partially clouded. His mouth is purple and swollen and his chest...Sistylea, his chest...it looks like raw flesh without the skin to cover it and, nestled near to his heart, I can see flecks of gold — some sort of metal that refracts light back to us...

"Edith, I...don't think you should see him." I partially block her path, but I'm too late.

"Meredith?" The boy says.

The waves of his voice reach me and are alarming. He has Tretaro insiria. I think of Idreline. *She has the same ones.* I shudder, my mind drawing links that my sanity cannot grab ahold of. Before modifying themselves, they were experimenting on him first or maybe, using him in order to push the modifications through. I don't know how it works. But I am filled either way with disgust.

Edith attempts to look past me for the source of the voice, but I shift so she can't see him. "You think I can't handle it?"

I shake my head. "I don't want you to have to."

She considers my words, considers retreat. And then when the broken bastard croaks her name once again, she reaches out and places her palm in the center of my abdomen. "Will you stay with me?"

"Forever."

She exhales up at me, shaken and nervous. I smile just as shakily down at her, and then she moves past me to face her brother, Rick.

She steels herself and looks down at the boy. She cups her hands over her lips. "What happened to you?" She says down to the broken thing.

He croaks, hand sure as he sips water from the bottle in his hand. He doesn't seem...decrepit, so much as cobbled together crudely. He is...functional, but only in the ways they've so brutally stitched him together. It was with purpose. "Your blood didn't work for the experiments. Mine did. Guess I shoulda taken your place." He tries to smile, but his lips are purple and swollen.

I frown down at him, hating him with a brutality mirrored in his looks. "You would wish that you could have traded places with your sister so that she could have suffered what you did?"

He looks me up and down and bunches his eyebrows. "Are you the one they're trying to replicate?"

Replicate. It is an...interesting choice word. "How do you know their intentions? Why would they have shared them with you?"

"They didn't. I can...they did something to me." His head swivels on his neck. He seems to *see* me just fine, though his eyes don't appear to have any use. "I can like...see people's thoughts now."

I hiss and step back, away from him, pulling Edith back, too. "They succeeded?"

"Succeeded?" Edith says.

"To create more Tretaro — or to give Heztoichen my gifts. It would seem that your brother was the canvas for their experimentation."

"And it worked?"

"In some things, it would seem. Idreline speaks with my voice. Malmon moves faster than he should. Malmon...he too has the ability to rheach. But it is a weak thing. Your brother here...he is of little use to us. As someone who hurt you, I could easily have him staked in the forest. along with the rest."

He tenses, reacting as if slapped. He is a fearful thing, this Frankenstein's creation. "You...can't kill me. I have a bond! A bond with Malmon! I can help you track him..."

"That only makes you a liability."

"There were others like me. I can help you find them, too. I know stuff about what they were doing. I can help..."

I feel...*sorry*, as I stare down at the boy. I wish I did not. I have seen wounded things before clawing and clinging to life. Edith drops down to her haunches before him and reaches out until she can touch his swollen foot shoved into a sneaker too small for him.

"Someone once told me that Abel saves us for a reason. She saved you, too, back with Drago. She's saved me a few more times since. I don't think you deserve to die. But I also don't think you deserve to be my brother." She rises to stand and edges back until her spine meets my chest. "Let's go," she says.

I nod and guide her away from him. He calls her name after her, the one she had before. She hesitates. "I...hope you find happiness after everything you've been through, like I have with my mate."

"Mate?" Rick and I chime together in four different sets of vocal cords.

Edith's eyes widen as she looks up at me. She blushes bright pink all the way up to her forehead. "If…you accept, I mean?"

"Edith." I beam. I cannot control the muscles in my face. They flex to the point of damage. Edith smiles a little warily at me and I laugh so gruffly it shakes the whole damn school bus. "Yes. I swear you're going to be the death of me. I cannot bear this happiness."

"I hope not." She giggles and wraps her arms around my neck as I urge her off of the bus and under the dim red light of the world around us. The red looks much less sinister now, somehow rather reminding me of a beating heart. Hers. Mine. Our shared pulse.

"You did bravely in there."

She makes a face. "I don't know what happened to him, but it's sad that he hasn't changed. Only looking out for himself…even after everything. Still, it hurts me to see him like this. Does that make me weak?"

"Absolutely not."

"Alright everyone," Sandra calls as she ambles past us, returning to the bus. "We're all ready to go."

"L-L-Load up! Let's rrrrrrrrroll!" Diego shouts, vaulting up onto the back of a pickup truck — the one housing Idreline and Roderick, Far and Morithan.

Far smiles at me when our eyes meet and he looks so fondly at my female it makes my chest constrict. "What is it?" Edith must sense the pressure in my chest, for she rubs her own.

Her shirt is torn and I can see her scars clearly through the rips around her neck. I touch them with my finger, unable to find the scars that I made and obscenely grateful for it. "You are the most beautiful female in all of creation, and I am undeserving of you. And I also don't give a fuck. I love you, Edith."

"I love you, Nithril."

"I hope you are well rested," I tell her as I pull her up onto the back of another pickup truck, this one crammed with the rest of my wounded guard, driven by Ken and Constanzia. Sebine sits among them beside the human male who'd been strung up beside her. They both look rather worse for the wear and yet, I can tell that they are bonded and seem to be...pleased with one another by the way she holds him, and he her. I shake her hand first, and then I offer him my hand, too.

I shake the forearms of my guard as well, embracing them each in the Heztoichen way, feeling so deeply relieved that they are all, for the most part, unharmed. Not all have survived so many battles fought before, but so many survived this.

It is a gift.

Especially when one has only one lifetime to live.

"I am definitely not well rested," Edith grumbles. "I'll sleep a year when we get back."

"Hm, that is not going to work for me."

She elbows me in the ribs. "And why is that?"

I kiss the three freckles on her jaw and grin against her cheek. "Because I have lifetimes to make up for and I have no intention of wasting another second of this time I have with you."

Chapter Twenty-One

The gates of Brianna hang open when we roll back through them and I am wracked with worry. There are human and Heztoichen out now attempting to conduct repairs. Star leaves her truck and joins them, as do Laiya and Sandra, a dozen others still able to stand as well.

"What happened?" I bark at Mikael as we roll past. He has his shirt off and gives Idreline a wide, shocked gaze as she lunges at him, only to be restrained by Roderick yanking at the chain around her throat.

"Attack. Don't worry, it wasn't huge, but they had explosives."

"Fuck." I glare at the back of Idreline's head, and then into her eyes when she looks up at me. "You hid it from me," I seethe, surprised by her ingenuity. "Or your brother kept you in the dark."

She hisses out a curse in Heztoichen, which I do not respond to. It could be that I have hit a nerve. But I am not sure about her or Malmon or Rick or Elise who, even dead, is still causing me so many problems.

"How many were there?" I ask.

"They were about thirty, but don't worry. We dispatched twenty of them or so and are holding the last twelve. It was just...uh...we hit a snag. It all worked out though."

"What does that mean?" Edith asks.

His cheek twitches. He exhales heavily then runs a hand back through his hair, then smiles almost begrudgingly. "You'll see at the house." He means Abel's house, though that is not where we head first.

First, I must assist in securing the wounded and the rebellious. Roderick seems rather...reticent to be relieved of his duty watching Idreline, but it is determined that, for now, she stay in one of the basement cages in one of the starred houses where Elise allowed Heztoichen residents of Brianna to keep blood slaves. I imagine that many of the Heztoichen I dispatched today once lived in many of the starred homes just like this one, and kept humans in the cages below. *I should have killed the offenders then.*

I grimace as Idreline is led inside, finding a sort of righteousness in the action.

It takes too long for things to be settled and for us to make our way down Starlight, covered in blood. Members of the community come out of their homes and walk with us. Excitement in the air is palpable. And that's when I begin to hear them...the rumors whispered...I move faster, feet carrying me so quickly, Edith struggles to keep up. Finally, I swing her up into my arms and carry her so that we arrive on Abel and Kane's front yard before the rest of them.

Kane cracks the door, grin enormous for a male whose keep was just ransacked, the doors of his fortress blown wide open. And then I smell it...an unfamiliar scent...a lingering scent of blood...and I see it as Kane turns around to face us.

He carries Abel and her face is drawn, eyes dark circles, smile bright. She licks her lips and holds up a bundle of blankets in her arms and I see a small face wreathed in golden light — a light of its own making.

"Our baby girl carries Tare!" Kane shouts.

Abel caresses his cheek and rolls her eyes as the bundle begins to squirm. "Alright, that's enough! I'm tired and all this screaming isn't helping Becks sleep."

"What's her name?" Someone shouts in the crowd. And then Ashlyn appears, her hands covered in pink. *She delivered the baby. The small healer delivered a healthy Heztoichen-human baby, the child of two Notare.*

"Her name is Rebecca. After my mom."

"And Ashlyn fought like hell to deliver her. Becks would be so fucking proud." Abel starts to cry and Kane ravages her mouth and face with kisses. He does the same to Ashlyn, who giggles and shoves him off, and then to the infant bundle and immediately, the small thing begins shrieking.

"Alright, that's it for now," Kane shouts, "Fix up Brianna. We'll be inside until we feel like coming out. Don't care who you have to kill, Lahve, but make sure nothing bothers us. Somebody, bring my Sistana and her warrior healer something to eat. Make it taste good!"

"We're on it!" Voices — Patty and Lima's — yell collectively.

I nod, but Kane has no interest in an answer. He and Ashlyn and Abel and the kit, Rebecca, have already reentered their home while the humans and Heztoichen surrounding me continue to whoop and cheer wildly.

Meanwhile, I have no thoughts. Not one. Not even *how*, because I know this world already to be one of ceaseless wonder. It will never stop surprising me, of this I am absolutely certain.

My mouth hangs open dumbly and I look down at Edith at my side. She has tears in her eyes and tears on her cheeks and is squealing with delight. She hugs me and I hug her back, still agog and utterly stupefied. I am no more knowledgeable about how or why this could be a thing that creation has allowed. Sistylea, help me. I truly do feel human now.

And I plan to put a baby in this one.

At least, as I grab Edith by the waist and sprint down the street, I plan to practice as many times as her love will allow.

Chapter Twenty-Two

I frown down at Edith, wondering what sort of trickery she is up to now.

"I promise it's not a trick," she says, yet her nervous laughter would suggest otherwise. "Don't you trust me?"

"It is not a matter of trusting you. I just don't like surprises," I lie. I love surprises. But, as she has never given me a surprise before in these past four months that we've lived and loved together, I am far too curious to do anything but indulge her.

She wants to blindfold me. And worse, she wants me to wear headphones that are blasting some sort of terrible music from a little music box that she borrowed from Constanzia whose music choices are…loud, and little else.

"And why do you feel compelled to rob me of my hard-honed senses, might I ask?"

She rolls her eyes and huffs, "Because otherwise, you won't be surprised. You'll be able to sense it a mile away."

"Why should any part of your surprise be a mile away?"

"Augh. It's just an expression. Now, come on. We don't want to be late."

"Late?" Now, I'm even more confused. Still, I take a seat on the footboard below our bed and allow her to fix a rather industrial-strength blindfold around the top half of my head. From there, she proceeds to slap large headphones over my ears and take me by both hands. But first, she leans against my chest and slants a firm, confident kiss against my mouth.

My chest rumbles. "This, I like," I murmur against her lips. "Is this the surprise? I quite like the idea of being blindfolded."

"I'll take that under advisement." She laughs and starts to drag me away, through the doorway, down the stairs, out into the light. I can feel its rays more acutely without access to two of my senses, the sunshine fighting the good fight to press through the clouds, some errant rays snaking out and staining the world, even if it is red.

Edith was first to notice that the clouds surrounding the outpost are less colored than these further south. They are more yellow and give a greater illusion of sunlight. It is for this reason that we will relocate there in the fall, as soon as the first walls are up and securely mounted.

There have been no attacks on Brianna or the new outpost, which has oddly kept its name — Chattanooga. Though, I suppose it is not so odd. It is a *human* outpost, after all, rather than Heztoichen-run.

Plans to expand the outposts are underway. Plans to approach Tanen are equally so. Abel has a plan for him I do not like or approve of, but it is done. The assassin has been sent for him.

And she is human.

With an absolutely terrible taste in music.

It was gracious of her to abandon her music box to us. Then again, I do not believe she thinks she will return from this. I do not believe she will, either. And yet...there is a small part of me that recognizes Abel's preternatural luck. It goes beyond the scope of this world or the one I have come from.

It makes me think that the odds of this chance for success have gone from zero percent to two. Maybe, three.

Whatever horrible melody blasts through my ears at the moment rattles my mood. I frown as I clomp down the street. "Have we not arrived at the surprise yet?"

Her laughter echoes through the headphones. She lifts one of them away from my head and I catch the sound of humans laughing and shushing one another. They are located where I know the market to be. Yet…there is something off about the way they are speaking, as if they don't want to be overheard.

"Just wait for one second. Kane's going to take you the rest of the way."

"Kane? What does he have to do with this? Edith, my Ipalora, I don't like this. I will remove the blindfold…"

"No! No, don't." She laughs and thunks the headphone back over my ear. She reaches up and kisses me once more, a distraction. It is an annoying distraction for I can identify it for what it is yet I am still helpless to stop her cruel methods from succeeding.

She flits away from me while I am still stuck, stunned stupid by the rushing of her blood through her veins and the pressure of her heat against my chest, and my hands are too…slow to catch her before she's too far to grasp.

"You look like you're loving this." Kane's voice reaches me and…startles me.

Annoying.

I frown in his direction and toss my hands into the air before allowing them to land on my hips. I'm wearing jeans, boots and a plain grey tee shirt. My swordstick slaps against my thigh as Kane touches the back of my elbow and guides me forward.

"I don't like any part of this, Notare."

Kane laughs. "Oh the things we do for love. It is nice though, isn't it? To have the love of a human woman? They have a certain way of keeping you on your toes, in my experience."

I release a begrudging grin as the sounds of people milling about get louder and louder, their hushed whispers not in any way effective in disguising their numbers. It is… strange. It would seem to me from where I stand that nearly the entire community is out, clustered near to me. *What* is *this?* Edith should know better than to assume any surprise I would want would involve anyone but her. *Perhaps she does not know me so well.* I frown, suddenly put off by the notion.

Stranger still are the unusual scents on the air. Flowers. Very many of them. They remind me of the hiliria blossoms of my home planet yet, here I would know them by another name. White flowers, lovely when they bloom. Flowers don't grow very often here and, when they do, are treasured. Strange that there would be any concentration of them. Perhaps, it is merely some sort of perfume created by one of the humans working in the distilleries. Hm…

"Are you ready?" Kane says and there is a certain hush that falls over the gathered humans. I hear wood creaking and the sound of a single infant gurgling somewhere not too far from me.

"Abel is also here?"

"No questions until you answer mine."

"Yes, I am ready to be done with this infernal music. Where is Edith?"

The headphones are removed and I feel Kane's large fingers unfastening the blindfold. Then he pulls it off.

Shock.

Confusion.

And then…elation.

"Is this…" I don't dare ask. My mouth is dry, my lips are slack as I take it all in. What looks like the entirety of Brianna's occupants — short of those in cells, like Idreline — appear to be gathered here, humans and Heztoichen alike. They sit in seats of all kinds — long benches, heavy, leather armchairs, folding stools, most of all. The rest that aren't seated spread off down the road, too many to count. And all the creatures gathered wear their best clothing. The females have their hair twirled and twisted in delightful patterns. Many males wear jackets, even, and several even wear ties. Kane is among them. He smiles at me so broadly, he looks a hundred years younger. I blink at him, struck by the magnitude of this moment.

"This…is a…"

"It's a wedding. Yours." He sweeps his arm forward and I take in the flowers. So many flowers. They hang from long lines overhead. Candles stud the walkway, which has been covered with dried leaves. The forest is the backdrop, the one where Edith's nightmares now sleep their long sleep. She asked me to end their suffering and it only took the once for me to oblige. There's no room for monsters in Brianna anymore. No, this is a place of life.

An aisle carries me forward and I walk it, Kane at my side as we reach a sort of pulpit. A wooden archway stands covered in small blooms and Kane instructs me to stand to the left while he takes up his position directly beneath it. I stand there agog as a piano begins to play — *my* piano — and I look up and see Kassie seated behind it, her fingers dancing elegantly over the keys.

She winks up at me. I cannot return the expression because I have looked up now toward the end of the aisle from where I just walked and now see Edith striding toward me, flanked by Diego and Pia. She wears one of the outfits I had Tasha make for her. Not a particularly elaborate outfit, the sight of it on her moves me to tears.

She wears a silk tank top with thin straps. The deep V reveals her entire chest, collar bone to collar bone. Her long, luscious neck. She wears makeup. I've never seen her in face makeup before and find that she looks absolutely beautiful. In her hands, she holds a small bouquet of white flowers. On her face, she wears a grin so bright it hurts my cheeks.

Behind me, Kane exhales deeply. "Doesn't get any easier, does it?" He whispers. "Seeing her? It's like watching your own heart walking around outside of your chest. It's almost wrong. Like anything could happen." And then he stiffens and sucks in a sharp breath. His gaze is pinned to the female he calls his seated in the first row beside Ashlyn who holds their kit.

His expression clears and he looks at me with gloss in his own eyes that makes me feel the pinch of his words so painfully. "But then we have to remember that they can take of themselves just fine and have the scars to prove it." He winks and I turn back to Edith, to Candy, to my Ipalora, who wears her scars with pride.

I realize I have yet to smile or show her any outward signs of encouragement when her steps falter slightly halfway up the aisle. Everyone that was once seated on either side of the aisle is standing, though I had not heard them rise.

I clear my throat, but it does not clear. It is too thick with emotion to clear it now. I just nod repeatedly, rather foolishly, but it seems to please Edith, for she continues towards me with a smile. Diego and Pia arrive with her, their arms linked. Abel bursts into a sob that causes members of the congregation to laugh. I don't…know that any of them have ever heard her cry before. I certainly haven't.

"I'm not crying," she sobs, "it's the baby, I swear!" The infant snores safely and happily nestled in Ashlyn's arms. Ashlyn meets my gaze brilliantly, beaming in a way that I will never forget, no matter how many lifetimes I lead.

The trio comes to a stop and I cannot look away from Edith's smiling face. She looks nervous and excited and overwhelmed and overjoyed all in one. Or perhaps, those are only my emotions. I can feel nothing but radiant joy echoing through everyone and everything.

Pia leans in and kisses Edith on the cheek before taking her seat beside Abel. Diego passes me Edith's hand. As he does, his lips twitch. "Y-Y-Yeah."

"Pardon?" I tilt my head as his gaze bores into mine. He smiles a little more broadly and I feel only warmth from him. He's pushing against my rheach, trying to impart something to me.

And then he says, "Yeah, wwww-we can be f-friends."

I grin and take Edith's hand from him. He gives her shoulder a gentle squeeze that she does not cower from before taking his seat. Edith comes to stand directly in front of me. She holds both of my hands.

"I believe I have been looking at this all wrong," I say and the crowd goes quiet, humans straining to hear me and asking their Heztoichen friends for help.

"What?" Edith's long tan linen skirt flutters in the wind. It is slit up the side high enough that I could so easily slip inside…or merely push the material away and feel the scars running up and down the insides of her thighs, scars that means she's still alive.

I cup her cheek and stare down into her eyes, so deeply moved, I am not even the same male I had been. "I have been looking at this all wrong. It's not about living out the duration of my existence, but merely living a lifetime. One lifetime. And I choose to live yours."

She blinks and tears well on her lower lid as she grasps my meaning. Reaching forward, she grips my wrist and then places her free hand over my heart. "You know I'd never let you do that."

"Unfortunately for you, you will have no choice but to accept me on the golden shores when I follow you. Because make no mistake, I will, whether you call for me or not."

She swallows thickly and balances on the balls of her feet as she leans into my grip. I'm not even sure the movement is intentional, or noticed on her part. "So you do like your surprise, husband?" She beams.

My voice is thick and my chest is pounding as I lean in and press my forehead to hers while Kane admonishes me that this is not the proper order of the ceremony. I don't fucking care. My hand slides down and grips her exposed wrist, fingers running over her scars before gripping them firmly.

I kiss her deeply and as I pull back, I speak against her decadence. "Wife, I have known no greater wonder."

Book Four
Constanzia and Tanen

Preview

Chapter One

It's almost my turn. Ugh. What a drag.

I know I'm injured, but I don't know where. Don't matter. "Livin' on a prayer," I mumble under my breath, the song lyrics one of my favorites for a time like this.

"Move, human," the alien dickhead to my right sneers. He bares his teeth at me in a snarl when I turn to look up at him and grin. I can feel the blood seep between my teeth and I watch his expression morph into one of disgust. I chuck a loogie at him and a bloody wad of spit hits him in the chest.

"Ogh! Disgusting!" He curses again in his own language and lunges for me, but another alien catches his arm and braces his shoulder against the first's.

"They must fight. They don't deserve a quick death."

"They don't deserve a quick death," I murmur in a nasal tone, teasing.

The first alien curses again in his alien speak and surges forward. He punches me in the stomach. Pain radiates through my bottom ribs. Hope to shit they're not broken. I laugh as I stagger back until I nearly fall out of line, but don't. I'm shoved back into it by an alien standing on my other side.

The energy zinging through my bones keeps me upright and my concentration on the cold ground permeating the soles of my boots keeps me from feeling the heat in my stomach as the alien lunges at me again. His friend catches him and throws him back, but I wish he hadn't. My hands flex. I feel like a fight. Except, all I've got between my fingers is empty air. They twitch at the absence of a gun.

I had my gun with me when the city fell, but it's gone now. I wonder where I lost it. In between these two Others probably. I emptied my clip, but it hadn't slowed them down. They'd been the ones to tackle me to the ground and toss me into this lineup. I frown, disappointed in our showing. There are a few hundred human captives alongside me, but that's it. And the city, from the looks of it, had once been thriving. It's gone now. We stand in the center of this wide, open square while the world burns on all sides of us, caught in a crucible.

Abel was right. He needs to be stopped. I just...couldn't get close enough. I couldn't even find him in the chaos and I'm...pissed. She could have chosen any hunter Brianna has, but she picked me. And she's my queen. The baddest of all of us. I wanted to do right by her and by my best friend who I left behind and even the other humans in that ragtag community I've started to sorta like, but instead, I'm standing in a line of soon-to-be corpses while the one I'm supposed to kill sits up above us, perched on the lip of some huge statue.

There are men and women carved into the face of it, one woman kneeling in prayer as if begging to a forgotten god. But I don't know what god she's praying to either. I know only that this carved woman is mounted onto an edifice to a history I don't know and that will exist only in the memories of a handful of men and women after this night — a body falls — now one less.

It's not the first, but it is the first that I can see clearly now that I'm shoved to the front of the line. I don't recognize the human who fell and I'm grateful for it. The man he fought — the one who's still standing — is one I saw somewhere out there in the chaos, but there's no recognition in his gaze when he looks at me. There's just a glassy void. A certain nothingness sustained only by his desire to live as he turns and squares off to face his next opponent.

He needs to kill three more and then me and then Kenny behind me. That's Tanen's rule. If you can kill ten, you go free.

It isn't out of mercy, oh no. I learned from a few of the other humans here — a woman warrior called Mika who's still alive in line somewhere behind me — that he lets them go free so they can flee to the next town. He likes that they can alert the town to his presence. He likes the fight, the sick fuck. He also likes the fear. Because the ones that survive their fights can drive fear into the ones they come across. They can tell tall tales of his savagery. He isn't really so savage though. He hasn't been to Population. I plan to show him just what we Population lifers are made of.

But I need to actually fucking see him first.

I'm shoved forward again by the alien who wants to rip out my fucking throat as the next battle picks up. Isn't much of a battle though. I hear the swing of a sword and a moment later, the thud of a body drop. The alien standing next to me snickers and I chuckle with him, just to annoy the piss out of him.

He's wearing green and black Kevlar, as if the guns this ragtag bunch of humans had were anything more than a joke against the fact that they're armed like nothing I've ever seen — like Malmon was — and their numbers are overwhelming. I wonder just how many they are. Seems like a lot more than Lahve — Nithril — said, but maybe they just seem like a lot right now, all pressed up against me.

"Ever heard of personal space, numnuts?" He backhands me instead of answering and I slip in the blood that stains the cobblestones. I catch myself on my hands and am slow to rise. But I do, and I do with a fucking smile. "You hit like a human."

He swings for me again, but I duck with a speed he doesn't expect. I've got Other blood in me. Of course I got Other blood in me. No way I'da made it this far without it. I clutch my fingers to my palm and brush my thumb over the tops of my knuckles before I squeeze everything together and lunge. My fist flies forward and I clock him across the cheek. My other hand comes up to meet the first and I jab low, below the bottom of his Kevlar…lower. I punch him in the cock.

He groans and canters back and a couple humans in line behind me start to laugh. Kenny, who's two spots back, bursts out laughing and gets a good punch to the gut for his amusement. Meanwhile, another alien shoves numnuts — no nuts — out of the way. He hits the ground and Kenny kicks him in the face. An alien grabs me by the throat and another grabs Kenny by the collar and they tow us out of line.

"You're a crazy bitch," Kenny grumbles as he's shoved forward beside me. "Might just pay off." He winks as he rights himself and staggers forward until we're stumbling side by side. Dragged forward together, I look up at Kenny's face, and am grateful. And that makes me surprised.

I didn't want to come this far with baggage — I knew this wasn't a return trip and I didn't want to feel obligated to try to keep someone else alive. If Population's taught me anything, it's that it's harder to keep others alive than it is to kill your enemies. But Kenny and Star refused to stay behind and right now, I'm so fucking grateful that Star managed to escape and I'm just as grateful that Ken Ken's here beside me.

Unlike Star, who I'm sure is gonna plan an escape attempt — if we even make it that far — Kenny and I haven't known each other that long, even though it feels like it. Abel introduced us when I joined her little outfit and Kenny and I started going on raids together right away. We got along because we both speak Mandarin — he's half-Chinese, half-Vietnamese and I'm three-quarter-Chinese, a quarter black, both raised in the USoffreakingA.

He learned and spoke with his parents. One of the SEALs who trained me growing up was Chinese, too and taught the language to anyone who would listen. She said that once language dies, culture goes with it and that culture is the only thing worth saving.

History.

Art.

Rituals.

Ideas.

Beliefs.

She said that when the bodies rot, the statues crumble and the papers burn, language will be the only thing we have left, so we must protect it. Because of her, I tried to learn every language I could. That I can.

Kenny never cared much about the languages, even though he and I have our own. Beneath my breath, I whisper to him in Manadarin, "You got a plan, partner?"

"Following your lead, partner." He winks at me and I laugh as we're finally shoved forward, through the edge of the crowd and into the arena. It's there that I get my first ever look at the numnuts they call Tanen.

And oh my. He's not a bad lookin' dude. If he weren't trying to wipe out humanity, I might even consider him fuckable but, alas, my tastes lie in the less genocidal arena and more in the regular kind of murderer realm.

He's got deep tan skin, a darker shade of brown than mine, or maybe just the same. Hm. Kinda funny. He's got dark hair, like mine, though mine's straighter than his. He has a beard and is combing his fingers through it as his gaze passes listlessly over me and Kenny, landing on the Heztoichen aliens holding onto us.

"They're causing a disturbance. If it please you, my Lord, can we dispose of them?"

Seated beneath the carved tower on a short flight of steps, Tanen looks bored to be here. He removes a handgun from behind his ass and holds it loosely in a bored and blood covered fist. I grin at the sight of it. "That's mine!" I'm not sure it is — in fact, the odds are against me on this one — but I repeat myself with more confidence. "That's my gun."

Tanen's eyes flash, then settle. He points the gun at my stomach and I lift both hands as the Heztoichen squeezes the back of my neck and pushes me forward, like he's worried the bullet will somehow pass straight through me and his heavy armor and pierce his skin.

"Hey, I mean, you can have it. Just sayin', I didn't take you for a thief."

Tanen sits forward and rests his elbow on his knee. The gun boings lazily in his meaty fingers. They're all dripping in blood. Every one. He focuses on me for just another second, right before his wrist twitches and he fires. I don't jump. I don't even flinch as the guy who'd been fighting for his life in the center of the square jerks suddenly and falls down. His sword clatters to the ground. A useful tool.

I grin up at Tanen even though my insides squeeze and pulse, just like they do every time someone dies in front of me. I told myself a long time ago that it doesn't affect me. I do a good job of pretendin' it doesn't. I even thought it didn't until recently…when I saw so many of my friends fall.

Zala.

Avery.

Marine.

I remember them, picture their faces. Not the way they looked after death, but the way they looked in life. I remember that it was Tanen's allies who struck them down and I feel settled, more resolved, and more capable of looking past the fallen man who killed five humans of his own in order to make it this far. I've killed more humans than that, can't forget it. Population leaves no human survivors, only monsters and savages. And it looks like the shores of Population aren't limited to one continent. Tanen's brought all of its savagery here. I'm guessing, looking up at the fucker now, that he brings it wherever he goes.

He gestures at Kenny and me and says, "Let them fight." His voice is a deep growl. "The female can take the sword. Give the male a knife."

"Aww," I coo, bouncing forward on the balls of my feet and clapping my hands together. "He likes me. I think he really likes me." I spin a pretty circle and sweep the sword from beside the large dead guy who fought bravely, for whatever it's worth.

Kenny's smiling at me as he steps up across the dead guy from me, a knife in hand. "You think so?"

"I mean look at how he dotes." I show the piss poor excuse for a sword at Kenny and he grins.

"I can't have that, now can I?"

An unspoken signal, a word whispered in a glance. We both move at the exact same moment. Kenny spins and throws the dagger in his hand at Tanen, who makes no move to stop it from lodging in his chest. It hits with a dull thunk, but I don't stop to admire how well he took a hit. I'm already running straight at him, Kenny on my left.

We zig and zag past one another, fully expecting Tanen to shoot us down. He doesn't and I remember that he likes the sport, so I stop zigging and just charge straight forward. Ken Ken takes my lead. The pounding of our feet on the glossy red stone echoes louder than the cries of the humans and Heztoichen forming a wall around us. The whoosh of the wind in my ears is fucking exhilarating. My sweat clings to my back like a baby monkey to its mother, causing my tee to melt onto me like a sticker. The flap of my utility jacket like a bird's wings makes me feel like I am one as I soar up to the base of the stairs.

Kenny, the ass hole, beats me there by a hair. His black hair brushes the tops of his ears and his hard expression reminds me that Kenny was always more about the killing. I liked thinking about what I did as saving. What I do. Not that it matters. — the outcome is all the same.

Several of Tanen's soldiers start forward, but he holds one hand raised. It's a clear enough sign and confirms my suspicions that he's got every intention of rippin' us apart himself. Just for the sport of it. Maybe, he and Kenny have something in common, I think as Kenny produces a second blade from the inside of his vest. He sweeps it across Tanen's outstretched wrist, severing it — or not severing it. Because Tanen catches the blade by its sharp steel tip. He rips the dagger to the side, flinging Kenny with it. He switches his gaze to me. His chest is exposed. He's got on no armor and I know this sword is a piece of shit, but Tanen doesn't know what I have in my pocket.

In all of my pockets.

I reach into my right pocket and withdraw a fistful of white powder. I swipe the edge of the blade through it and like a fucking idiot, I underestimate the blade and press too hard, ripping my palm open in the process. Whatever. Don't matter now. Nothing matters but the narrowing of his dark eyes as he glances at my hands, wondering what the fuck I'm doing.

But that doesn't matter either. Because I'm at the base of the stairs and he's going to let me stab him right where the other dagger already is because he likes the competition and he thinks humans are fucking worthless and he's underestimated us one too many times and I...

Trip.

I freaking trip.

Jesus H Christ.

My feet slip-n-slide through deep pools of red blood and, on the fourth of five steps needed to meet him on his throne, I lose my balance and instinct compels me to want to catch myself, so I stab down instead of straight. The blade intended for his chest sinks into his thigh. I careen forward and grab hold of the dagger, catching myself on his chest and using both blades to keep my shaky legs from collapsing inward.

I'm looking right at him, just shy of face-level. I grin awkwardly as he roars out a curse, because he knows what I put on the end of my blade now. Salt. The only substance in the world that slows the Heztoichens' healing — at least, the only one we know about. The wound won't close right away and, if I'd managed to strike him in the heart or the head, I could have had a shot at getting out of here alive.

Now, face-to-face, eye-to-eye, as we are I don't think it's likely. "I'm in heaven," I start to sing under my breath. Face-to-face, eye-to-eye, cheek-to-cheek. I always liked that song. One of the oldies we uncovered on a CD player that ran for a few years. I give him my best and most theatrical nervous laugh as I get my feet underneath me. Standing finally, I dust off my hands and hold his gaze as he yanks the dagger out of his chest and tosses it onto the cobblestones behind me. He does the same with the sword, admiring the blade covered in his blood.

"So. No hard feelings?"

He moves so fast it's hard to track, and I've got practice. It wouldn't be my first time fighting an alien, but I still don't move out of the way in time. His boot slams into my gut, taking me off of the edge of the platform and throwing me across the stones. Pain splinters the back of my head and runs down my spine and I black out momentarily, but don't let it keep me down.

"Oh fuck!" The boot is back.

Alright, maybe I will stay down this time. He slams his shoe down onto my sternum hard enough to crack it. I know I've got broken ribs enough for two, but he's merciless. I smile. I expected nothin' less.

His black hair, inky with sweat and the blood of the fallen, hangs around his shoulders, reaching towards me like rain. His skin is a darker brown than mine, but not by much, and where my face is flat, features broad, he is entirely composed of angles.

The wells of his eyes are deep enough to cast shadows over his face. His cheekbones are high, jaw hard and square, cheeks hollow in between. His neck is meaty and thick and I watch the veins in it bulge and pop as he looks at me…and keeps looking at me.

"Constanzia!" The voice crackles into life like radio static and I suck in a breath, fast and deep.

"Kenny, whatchu got for me?" I groan.

Above me, Tanen twitches. He rips his gaze free from mine and looks to the right — my right — at Kenny closing in on him. Kenny musta found the dagger, because it's already covered in dark Other blood that smells like a fish got beat to death by a bag of dirty diapers and makes my gut churn and my throat work.

Kenny attacks, managing to cut Tanen but only once, and not enough to do anything since he hasn't dipped his blade in salt, like I told him to. Tanen kicks out at Kenny's leg and Kenny's too slow to avoid the ruination. He drops his dagger and it hits me in the face. "Ooph!" Other blood speckles my cheeks and I gag, trying not to get any in my mouth.

Kenny lurches up, trying to attack Tanen even though he's lost the use of his right leg. It's brave and I admire him all the more for it, especially when it works. Because I don't need him to beat Tanen for me. I just need a distraction. And when Tanen leans over to crack his hand against the side of Kenny's face as he hits him once and then again, his bones crunching painfully in a way that I hope to high hell the Other blood in Kenny's system will heal, I've got it.

His boot lifts from my chest just enough for me to be able to curl up and stab. I aim for Tanen's femoral artery, only half expecting to hit it. I do though, and Tanen's whole body lurches as a look of pure agony sweeps his face, but it just as quickly passes. He looks back down at me and reaches for the top of my head. I retract my blade brutally and blood…oh sweetness. Hot sticky Other blood explodes out of Tanen's leg in a way I did not expect despite having slashed femoral arteris before — at least three of them.

Sulfuric scented heat slaps me in the face and I open my mouth on reflex, which is the opposite command my mind gave, urging me to keep it closed. There's a reason I should keep my mouth closed, isn't there? What is it…Hm…I can't remember and soon, I no longer care as a beautiful heat begins to build in the pit of my stomach. I moan, pleased, but Tanen doesn't seem to like that. He grabs me by the arm hard enough to break it. I don't cry out — but he does. Almost like he's the one getting grabbed. Like he can feel it.

And then I feel it…the tugging in my chest alerting me to something…and the knowledge that I should have remembered before. I stabbed Tanen with a salted blade that was wet with my blood and now, I've just drunk his.

I grin when he grabs me by the hair on the back of my head and hauls me up onto my feet. I stagger. The pain making me feel drunk as it clashes with the healing warmth that soothes me. His healing warmth. Because I bonded myself to the savage of Carata and I'm pretty sure he has no desire to be bonded to me.

He roars in my face, shaking my body hard enough I'm worried he'll break my neck. "What have you done!"

When he finally stops, I smile at him and say, "We're married. Is it everything you envisioned when you were a little boy?"

His face transforms into a mask of horror but I don't close my eyes. I'm willing to see this whole life and death thing through to the bitter end. He sweeps the treacherous dagger that I used to bond us from the bloody stones below and lifts it up to my chest. He plunges the tip towards my heart but he…hesitates.

For just one second, he hesitates, and I'm given no chance to ask him when a familiar voice calls out from far away, up above us. From a sniper's position in one of the remaining building windows… "Livin' on a prayer!" She shouts, belting out the first line while I fling my body out of his grip and dive towards the ground. Not a second too late, either, because the wave of bullets follows.

Star unloads whatever fuckin' machine gun she managed to steal onto the bastard standing above me, her aim as true as ever, and there's no mistaking his inhuman roar. Screams light up the night. I can feel chaos around me, but all I can concentrate on is the pain that radiates through my own chest like a distant murmur of a pain I felt once before, long ago. Or maybe just a pain that belongs to someone else.

"Bring her down!" Tanen's voice is a horrible screech shakes the foundations of the entire red square. Meanwhile, the statue presiding above it, watches on without a care. I start to scramble as panic picks up and Others charge here and there and humans try to break free in the scramble. I hear a tussle going on close by. I start to crawl towards it, hoping to get lost in the chaos.

A heavy hand latches onto my ankle and I turn back but, when I look down the length of my body, the sight that greets me burns itself into my corneas. There's no forgetting it.

On the ground now, Tanen starts to claw his way up my pant leg, or rather, pull me down to him. "We might be married hun." I wrench my freer leg out from underneath his still-naked chest and kick him in the face. "But I'm not interested!"

His nose goes sideways and another roar lights up the night. Fire from somewhere sends the scent of smoke wafting towards me. I kick him again without hesitation. His grip on my leg loosens enough for me to drag myself forward, out from under him entirely. I scramble up, feeling energized now and ready for battle.

The bullets have stopped firing and I look back at Kenny, but he's already gone. I run, aiming for the rendezvous point by the water. "Uff." Bullets are firing from the Heztoichen guards and I'm hit. That's my voice and the pain ripping through my side is mine, but another pained roar proceeds it.

"Do not fire at the female! Bring her to me!" I clutch my middle with my mangled right arm and keep hobbling along, totally broken as the blood does its best to fix everything broken within me.

Bodies are moving in front of me, pushing me forward and back. Everyone has a weapon, but I don't know who is a friendly. Why did I take this mission again?

"Fuck!" I scream. Somebody's got hold of my jacket, but I push through it. A ripping sound follows me as I find a gap between two running humans and disappear through it. I keep running across the bloody square, the sound of feet getting louder behind me.

Burning buildings threaten to box me in and, even though the fire only starts two stories up, smoke billows from windows on the bottom level. I can't go inside, but the debris in the roads isn't dense enough to keep me from passing through.

I burn myself a dozen times jumping over metal beams and chunks of burning concrete that have fallen from higher floors. And after I clear them, I keep running. I dodge the cars that are just mangled shapes, all bent and broken. I leapfrog bodies that lay where they died. I sprint past a park where bodies dangle from ropes like Christmas tree lights. I run until the world gets so quiet all I can hear are the sound of my heavy breaths and fires crackling in the city behind me.

And the footsteps.

"Star?" I lurch to a stop at the sudden patter of footsteps to my right. Underneath the awning of what might have once been a storefront, three women, two men and five children sit huddled. The men start to move out towards me in defense of their families, but I'm the least of their goddamn concerns tonight.

"Get your asses outta here!" I hiss in English first and then Mandarin, though I know it won't help. I don't speak

Turkish and, according to the signs, this place once used to be Istanbul. "Run! Go there and don't come out for another forty-eight hours!" I have no idea how long he's going to linger in this city, but I know that the madness that I left behind will last at least the night.

I point to the huge mosque looming across the street. A sign hangs askew on a post just a few feet from me. Entrance, Giriş, and Arabic lettering. The men move back to their families, gathering them up. They run as a unit and I don't move until I see them disappear inside the safety of the mosque.

The footsteps at my back are audible now, and punctuated by curses. "Which way, my lord?"

Jesus. Hubby's come to collect his runaway bride himself. I grin, so touched by the romantic gesture. And then I take off in the opposite direction, moving past the mosque, past the clock tower on the other side of the street, heading straight between them for the water that glistens underneath an amber sky, looking like an ocean of blood itself. We found a boat there earlier and brought enough gasoline with us to fuel a car or a boat for a short ride. We haven't had to use it yet, but now seems like as good a time as any. But where the fuck are Star and Kenny?

My gaze swings left and right and I ignore the wheezing sound of my own breath as well as the fact that I'm noticeably slowing down. The blood is working in my system, but it's not a magic potion and I'm hurt pretty badly. My lungs sear. My bones ache. My breath comes shorter and tighter and I can still hear Others on my trail, giving chase.

"Kenny!" I shout, running right up to the concrete edge of the boardwalk. On the other side is a sheer drop.

Motion up ahead has me moving faster. I can see the boat parked underneath a small overhang, nestled in between the other fishing boats. I think I can see someone there, but I can't be sure and they're not calling out to me and…

Something slams into my side. Something hard and heavy and distinctly inhuman. I go flying right off of the edge of the cliff and straight into the ocean. I hit the water hard and the temperature isn't something I'm prepared for. The cold is refreshing but I shoulda probably mentioned to the Other here, that I don't know how to swim. Wonderful.

I try to move my arms, but my left one is still shaky and there's a monster grabbing my hair and jerking me around like a damn fish on a line. I stare into the eyes of the one who has ahold of me, uncaring that the salty water is burning them out of the sockets. He has blonde hair and black eyes and if I squint just right, looks just like Mikey. Never thought I'd say this, but I'd kill for Mikey right now. Mikey's got jokes. This guy's got a good grip. I need air. I really need air.

I try to claw him off, but I don't have the right breath holding techniques for this underwater adventure, so I end up breathing in lungfuls of that cold refreshing un-oxygenated liquid. Not idea. My lungs sear. The burning buildings I left behind are nothing compared to it. My throat starts to jerk. My eyes would be watering if they weren't already wet. My legs are kicking but I'm going down instead of up — clearly, this whole swimming thing is a learned skill, not an instinctual one. At least not to me. I hope to fuck Star and Kenny make it to the boat and get the fuck out of here…

Something heavy smashes into the water above and as pain recedes and a light that shouldn't exist down here in the depths starts to encroach on my vision, I feel humungous hands grabbing me under the armpits and hauling me up. Kenny?

Nah. Kenny's not got hands quite this big or an anger quite so visible or visceral. By the time we break the surface of the water, I know it's Tanen who has me. I search for air with my lips and teeth and tongue, but there's too much water in the way. Tanen is making pained sounds at my side and slams a hand against my back. He tilts my head forward, holding me out of the water enough for me to choke up lungfuls of water and finally gasp.

The first gasp hurts the worst. Damn. Hurts worse than getting shot. I'd tell him to leave me for dead, because I'm not so interested in being tortured, but I can't stop shaking. Why the fuck am I shaking? It's not that cold. Or is it? I can't tell. My vision is fading in and out.

I blink. There's a face looming over mine and a hard surface at my back... Tanen looms above me and he's breathing so hard, it's like he's dying. Like he's drowning worse than I am.

"Breathe!" He roars at me. He slaps me in the face. Hard. My whole body lurches. I feel a balloon expanding in my chest, and then my throat, and then I start to cough and choke and it hurts worse than when I was underwater.

I blink. I see shoes. I'm on my side. They're pacing. "Did I give the order to have her drowned?" He's shouting like he's commanding an army about to lay seige to a city. Oh wait, he already did that.

"You said…"

"What did I say? What did I say!"

"But she stabbed you, my lord." A loud cracking sound, then a dull thump and I'm left staring into vacant, empty eyes belonging to a head that's entirely disconnected from the rest of it. The Mikey guy doesn't look like he's coming back from this.

Another voice. A new one. "My lord, should I gather the human?"

"The sistana," he whispers, voice cracking as he chokes on what is distinctly rage.

The Other must have heard him because he says, "Sistana, my lord?" His voice is incredulous.

"The vile, treacherous, putrid, human struck her palm before she stabbed me, drawing her own blood onto the blade, then she took in droplets of my own blood when she…attacked me." More silence. Tanen continues, "You will tell no one about this. If you do, I'll remove your skin from your body and use it to patch up our sails."

"I understand, my lord," comes the even reply. He doesn't seem phased in the slightest. "Shall I gather the...human for you?"

"Until I can determine how to kill her without causing pain or injury to myself, I don't want her touched or harmed by anyone but me." A slight shuffle, then a hard step. "And do not return to camp. Find us a ship capable of weathering this sea. Gather the Heztoichen and the humans she called by name, the ones intent on destroying me. Bring the human helpers, but destroy the fighters. The humans need a culling."

Eventually footsteps recede until we're alone. It's not a nice feeling, being alone with him. I feel his presence loom just as large as the cold that's wrapped its sticky fingers around me, and just as cutting as the lightning spearing my chest.

But I still force a smile and, on trembling lungs, say, "Killing me won't come easy, hubby." Tanen's lips curl. Then, he punches me square in the face.

———

Sign up to my newsletter and be the first to know about the release of Constanzia and Tanen's story at <u>*www.booksbyelizabeth.com*</u>

———

Looking for another post-apocalyptic romance to read today? Continue for a preview of Taken by the Pikosa Warlord, *the standalone 7th book in the* Xiveri Mates *series.*

TAKEN BY
THE PIKOSA
WARLORD

Chapter One

A ripping sound. No. It isn't a sound, it's just ripping. Ripping the world. Ripping me. Crrrrrack. Right down the middle.

The pain of it shocks my whole body, like I've been punched in the chest and that fist tastes like metal and blood and is screaming my name. It must be my name because even through the warped pronunciation that my ears reject, I recognize that name. I know it on a deep, fundamental level. Just like I know that I have a soul and that soul is pulled together by skin and this combination of soul-wrapped skin is what makes me human.

I'm human and my name is Halima.

"Halima!"

Her pronunciation is all wrong. It's a deep haa — not a short ha — followed by a laam, yaa, meem and rounded off with a ta'marbouta. But the woman screaming can't help her pronunciation because she's speaking English and my name is Arabic.

English. Arabic. Huh. Strange that, so instinctively, I know the differences between them.

"Halima, can you hear me?"

Yes, I can hear you, but my name is not ha — with a flat a — limb-uh, my name is hhhaah-leem-a, as my mother once spoke it.

Mother.

I can place the word's meaning, but can't seem to conjure the memory of the mother who first told me my own name. The mother who was once mine. When I reach for her, all I see is a hand drawing a ha so elegantly — that flattened roof over the generous curve below — but it's only drawn in this way when the letter exists in isolation…

ح

The hand rustles the paper beneath it as it draws the ha again, but this time with a pointed roof that slopes down before reaching back up to form the laam that is the second letter of my name. Yaa, meem, and ta'marbouta follow. It's light brown, this hand. The same light brown as mine. Halima, she writes for me.

حليمة

I reach again through the fog of my memory, past the chasm of so many vocabularies competing for voice — Cantonese, English, Wolof, Farsi, Turkish, Hindi, Korean, French, Spanish, and my mother tongue, Egyptian Arabic — but when I reach, reach, reach to grab it, that hand changes, becoming larger and callused and menacing and a darker brown than it was.

It stretches towards me from up above, grabs onto the front of my shirt, heaves me upright and then pulls harder. I fly. I lurch. I gag. I choke. I can't breathe. My eyes roll back and my stomach pitches as I'm dragged out of some kind of bed or maybe a bath — a glass case full of liquid that's an unnatural, neon blue.

"Halima, can you hear me?" The voice screeches over the sound of screeching.

I clear my throat, draw on my knowledge of English, and answer. No, I don't. I choke.

My lungs sear and my torso revolts. I feel like I was reborn in a blue goo that sticks like sap instead of in the womb of a mother that I no longer know.

I squeeze my eyes shut again and reach, reach, reach for the image of that hand drawing an elegant ha and I know that if I can just get there, everything will be alright, but...

"Haddock!" The woman roars and her dark hand is met with a second one, this one lighter and larger and rougher.

"Will she survive if you remove the breathing tube?"

The woman's face comes into view on my next blink. Dark brown skin, head just as bald as the man standing beside her. Her eyes are bright white and so are her teeth, but when she looks at me, I can see a pupil that's fully blown, subsuming the brown iris that guards it.

The man beside her has white skin and is equally, terrifyingly hairless. It makes me wonder what I look like. Am I just as bare and exposed as all the others? Do I, too, lack the visual markings needed to identify me?

His green eyes roam over my face. His mouth is pursed into a murderous line, lips thin in contrast to the woman's at his side. An alarm sounds somewhere behind him — another alarm. Something crashes, metal tears, voices scream in so many clashing intonations.

My gaze swivels listlessly to the corner of the room, following the man called Haddock's stare to a cluster of bald people standing in the corner. Where are we?

The room around us is big and full of shattered tanks that are either empty or full of blue goo swirled with a darker, more terrifying color. Blood. It's blood.

I cough, though there's something in my mouth choking me that I can't speak around, and the sound brings Haddock's attention back to me. He blinks several times and shakes his head quickly.

"We don't have a choice, Kenya," he says to the woman.

I'm on my side, on some kind of table. It's hard and I can hear it bending beneath me. Behind me, hands work at something in my butt and then free it. My butt cheeks clench together. My pants are drawn back up over my hips.

"She matters," Kenya says sternly, tone one of reprimand.

Haddock bites his front teeth together and spits, "We all matter. That's why we were chosen. But right now, we need to get the fuck out of here before they breach."

"I have orders from the general, doctor. Just do it!"

"They've breached!" Comes a new voice, another woman this time.

She has no hair and skin that seems unnaturally pale. Based on her accent alone, I'd have guessed she was Korean. Without hair or even eyelashes, it's hard to discern anything about any of these beings. We're all the same bald, wet things, covered in sticky blue on top of grey uniforms that have words stitched into the lapel.

Kenya Pettis. And then beneath that. First Lieutenant.

I glance at Haddock's shirt. Haddock Schwarzmann. Doctor. Surgeon.

And then I glance down at my own shirt. Upside down, it takes me a few seconds to put the letters together. They're written in the Roman alphabet, having been transliterated from Arabic.

Halima Magdy. That's my name. But perhaps, more important, is what's written below it. Etymologist. Interpreter.

I am Halima Magdy.

I am the interpreter.

And I can't breathe.

I start to shake as I become aware of the reason for my restricted breathing. There's something in my mouth. The man curses, but his hands are strong and sure as he maneuvers my head and then... Pain. That ripping returns. Ahlan wa sahlan, I think, welcoming it back.

Haddock pulls and the object comes out from between my teeth, feeling very much like it excoriates my insides as he rips it free.

My back and chest heave when the tip of the thing finally clunks off of my bottom lip. I writhe and buck on the table, trying to grab ahold of that elusive next breath.

My eyes roll back. There are hands on my chest, pressing. I black out. And then I'm awake and there's a man's mouth on my mouth. He's breathing and I'm gasping and he wrenches back at the same time that the woman grabs my hands and pulls me off of the table. I land on my knees.

"Halima, listen to me." My head spins. I fight the urge to vomit. "You are one of three hundred and forty-four people selected to survive the climate apocalypse and subsequent water wars that destroyed the earth.

"We've been asleep for the past four thousand years. It should have been eleven, but we were woken up by a species of humans who survived the wars and what came after." She shakes her head. Her upper lip is sweating. Her entire face is sweating. I'm sweating. "They've evolved."

Fear. Her tone is pure fear. I can feel it screech in the breath that scrapes its bloody nails down my nostrils and throat before settling in my lungs and squeezing.

"They shouldn't be here. They weren't supposed to survive. No one was. But they have and now they're going to take us. They've killed most of our soldiers and, from what I've seen, every male commander that we had. Leanna was the colonel, but she's the highest ranking officer left. She's our general now. She sent me to get you."

She glances over her shoulder, shaking mine as she moves. "Your orders are important. The most important I'll deliver today, so listen to me, Halima. I know that you don't know who you are.

"Memories were wiped when you went into the Sucere Chamber — that's where we are now. The only selective memories left behind for any unranked Sucere member are those pertaining to your skill. Do you know what you are?"

I nod, mute, and glance down at my shirt. With a shaking finger, I point to my left breast.

"Yes. Good. You're the interpreter."

The interpreter because on the Sucere Chamber, there is only one.

Not mutarjima but al-mutarjima. Meem-taa-raa-jeem-meem-ta'marbouta. Jeem has always been my favorite letter. Just like a haa, but with the dot up above it. A sacred letter. Someone said that to me once, but I don't know who. My memories no longer carry the sound of their voices.

"Your orders are to stay silent. Do not attempt to communicate with them. Just listen. Learn. We need to know their weaknesses so we can exploit them when the time is right. It's our only chance to kill them and escape and we need you for that. Halima, when you…"

"Kenya," the male barks, tapping one foot on the ground again and again. He's barefoot. We all are. "We're running out of time."

"They're here!" The woman in the corner's barely finished speaking before the doors explode open and they come in.

Bronze skin. Inky black hair. Thick belts, dripping with weapons, lace around their waists. Shoes lace up their ankles.

They come like a storm, holding swords and spears and whips. The whips, they sing. People — my species of people — scream as the frayed leather ends of their whips find our sensitive flesh. Kenya forces me down, throwing her body over mine. I'm in shock for a fountain of reasons, this only one among them.

Then, less than a heartbeat later, she's ripped away from me and I'm dragged up onto my feet.

Pain shoots through my shoulder and continues to tear apart my lungs as I'm dragged by a man — by a male creature

I can't see — down tunnel after tunnel. There are bodies everywhere, pressed against me on all sides. Most are the bald humans in the grey uniforms. The rest are the monsters hurting us.

I try to catch the different names, different professions, different trades, trying to build a tower of reason in my mind, but the tower is made of splinters. Reason is too hard to find.

There's an architect and an urban planner, a biologist and a geologist, a paleontologist and an anthropologist, an electrical engineer and an aerospace engineer. There's even a woman with enormous blue eyes whose shirt says artist. I wonder distractedly what kind.

The rocks under the sensitive soles of my feet are cold and craggy. I stub my big toe while shoved from behind. Eventually, the lights around us change. The air changes. The heat that was so oppressive dissipates, comes back with a vengeance and then dissipates again. We aren't in the Sucere Chamber anymore. Maybe we haven't been for a while. Somewhere along the way, we descended.

We're in caves. The tunnels are narrow and frightening. Some of the violent warriors carry live flames — torches — but they aren't needed by the time the hallways widen since the walls here are recessed with fire pits high above my head, but not so high above theirs. Them. They're tall.

The woman I recognize from the previous room stands beside me and rattles like stone in a cage. I glance at her shirt.

Jia Kim. Botanist.

She's crying without making any sound and when I reach down and clutch her hand, she holds me back firmly, desperately, without question. She doesn't know me and I don't know her, but we're together now. Each one a little less alone.

As we descend further into the ground, I'm forced to think of Hell.

In ancient Mesopotamia, the Sumerians believed all souls went to Kur, a large hole in the ground just like this. Maybe this is Kur, I start to think, but when we're finally forced through an opening into an enormous cavern, I'm no longer certain. Kur is described as a dark, miserable place. But here? This cave? It's simply beautiful. Zay al foll. As beautiful as jasmine.

Light punches into the cave through a single opening in the ceiling in strokes of pure gold. I can see sand and dust particles dancing through the light that illuminates the full expanse of the cave in brilliant shades of brown and blue topaz.

A river splits the center of the space and on its other side, flat, smooth stone leads up to a single massive rock and the towering throne mounted on top of it — and the creature occupying it.

But even Hades was beautiful in some depictions... Maybe, it's even the beauty of this place that makes it that much more horrible.

I'm not sure where I am — I'm barely certain of who I am — but I'm afraid. Perhaps fear is my only truth.

I'm shoved further into the cave, as big as any cathedral, and as I sweep my gaze around, I can see that the space is full.

People — creatures — are everywhere. Everywhere. Men and women with bronze skin, black hair and whips in their hands stand around the perimeter of the massive chamber. They watch us as we enter and I think fleetingly of Kur and Hell and Dante's nine circles.

Hell is heat and fire and Kur is dreary and miserable, filled with demons and dust. Hearts are weighed on Anubis's scales in Ancient Egypt and in Tibet, one must serve in Narakas deep in the earth until one's Karma has achieved its full result.

How heavy are our hearts?

How much karma did we waste?

What did we do in our last lives that was so wrong?

Jostling bodies part in front of me and through their curtain I finally get a clearer picture of the man on the throne, and any lingering uncertainty I had about whether or not this was the final Judgement, is erased.

Here we are. This is it. Purgatory has reached its conclusion. Because even though I can't remember the face of Allah, I know the word and its definition. And I know it's counter in the underworld. Hades. The Devil. Baal the Prince. Azazel.

He sits in the center of this new world on top of his throne watching us as we're brought in to face him, waiting impassively to deliver his verdict. Anubis, the devourer.

I catch a second glimpse of the creature when I'm shoved forward, closer to the river's edge. It's the jangling sound that pulls my attention up. He's holding a chain in his right hand and when he jerks it, the woman caught on its other end flies off of the rock beneath his throne and lands hard on the smooth landing below it.

Cupping her cheek, she rears up with fire in her gaze that makes me think that, in one past life, she might have been a Valkyrie even though in this one she's wearing the same grey uniform as the rest of us.

Her pale head is bald, but her cheeks are flushed bright pink. It stands out against the grey and drags my attention down…down…to the red that covers the rest of her.

"Is that blood?" Jia, at my side, whispers. "Oh god, what did he do to her?" She's shaking as we reach the river's edge — or I am, but I don't let go of Jia's palm.

I don't know her, but I don't let go.

"Gedabegulibetihi pondari tenirodiki!" Comes the shout from behind me. I can't interpret it, at least not fast enough to avoid the surge of pain that slashes across my back.

I'm too shocked to scream. Too shocked to do anything but absorb the pain of what feels like a thousand knives slicing me from my right shoulder blade to my left hip. I nearly fall off of the stone bridge that crosses the river —

would have, had Jia not caught me and pulled me to the safety of the stone on the other side.

I black out, but when I come to a moment later, I'm wavering on my feet, grey-uniformed people spread out to my left and right. As we're forced into a shaky line, Jia crushes my fingers in her grip. She's sobbing forcefully now, enough for the emotion to shake her chest. She tries to clap a hand over her mouth to stop the sound and stop drawing attention to us, but it doesn't help.

She screams when the flash of the whip comes for her and drops onto her knees. I fall beside her, refusing to let go of her hand as her grip goes slack in mine.

"It's alright, Jia," I whisper hoarsely, but it's a lie. It's not alright. Anubis devours the souls of those who aren't worthy to pass on into their next life.

The sound of laughter and rattling chains echoes across the cavern. The chain in Baal's hand isn't the only one present. There are other beings in here besides us grey-uniformed victims and the whip-wielding demons intent on torturing us.

As my gaze flits around, I notice that there are other species present — at least two, from the looks of it.

Slighter beings with charcoal-colored skin almost blend into the walls and stand in complete contrast to the creatures with blue-hued skin and white hair that falls in ratty knots to their waists.

They aren't like us — the fact that they aren't bald or wearing uniforms all but confirms it. And they definitely aren't like the demons. They look so different from us, from them, from each other, I wonder...I'm lost in wonder...I don't know what to think.

I close my eyes and think of those hands, tracing that letter called jeem. Tracing my name. Spelling it for me for what might have been the very first time. How many times have I drawn it for myself since? And in how many languages?

I am Egyptian, but I am the interpreter. It's my job to find the weaknesses of the monsters containing us and liberate the captives. All the captives, I decide then, regardless of their species, creed or color. They won't die here because I am Halima the interpreter and I will not die here and I will bring them with me.

I will not die here. This is not Hell. Anubis can be defeated.

The thoughts settle the pain in my back, reducing it to a dull throb. Opening my eyes, I inhale in two jerks that rip at my lungs, that tear up my heart.

But Jia's hand is still in mine and I focus on it with everything I have as Baal finally descends from his throne. He makes his way down the line of people and, at every person, he nods to one of the four opposite corners of the chamber.

On his command, that person is taken away and locked into chains that attach them to the other people crowded there.

There are a few exceptions.

Four women are pulled from the crowd and taken somewhere else. The first has a full, round figure and a rich brown skin tone. The second is very tall and thin. The third has my skin tone, but doesn't look Egyptian or Middle Eastern — she could be South American, but I'm not sure.

The fourth is petite, but I don't see her face or her name tag until she's dragged too far enough away for me to identify anything about her. All I know is that all four women didn't look bad, even bald and dripping wet and all I can hope is that they were not taken by the Devil for their beauty.

Even though I don't know how beauty is defined in this new world, I have other words in my vocabulary that are far more frightening. Words like power. Words like rape.

Jia gasps and, when I follow her gaze, I lock up, too. Baal has reached Kenya in the line and regards her now with greater consideration than even the four women he removed. Too much consideration.

Kenya meets his gaze with a ferocity that terrifies me because it's threatening and she's our captain. She gave me my orders. Haddock had been prepared to leave me. For as long or short as it lasts, I owe her my life.

And then the Devil does something truly horrible. He smiles. He smiles and his teeth flash white against his face. His smile is beautiful and I'm sucked beyond the River Styx straight into Hades by the man who holds the moniker himself.

"Memo lithan togo na. Memak haren higo no." His voice is a rich rumble that makes my abdomen squeeze.

Jia says something next to me, but I can't hear her. I'm concentrating, gears in my mind slowly coming to life as I recognize some of the words. Not all of them — not even half — but just two.

Lithan. Haren.

Lithan…

Lithan lithan lithan. It sounds like the old English word for travel. That word later evolved to laedan in the fourteenth century, which meant to guide and later found its heart in the English word leader. Leader. Is that what he's calling Kenya now?

How he knows she's a leader is beyond my comprehension as is the fact that, even though most of these words are not anything I've heard before, some of these words are most definitely rooted in English and Spanish and others, Arabic. Fascinating. Meanwhile, much of the grammar seems to be Amharic. Incredible.

"Ero, ellama merimerikeganma," another of the giants shouts. I don't understand any of the words, but my focus attaches itself to the first. Ero.

Ero. Ero Ero Ero.

He has a name and it's not Baal, not Azazel, not Hades. And if he has a name, that means he's just a creature, just an animal like the rest of us. He can bleed. He can be gutted.

Ero, the animal, looks back at the woman tied to his throne. He gives an order that prompts another barbarian to release her. Grabbing Kenya violently by the back of the neck, he throws her towards the throne and snaps his fingers.

A single spear is tossed onto the ground and lands directly between Kenya and the other woman. Instincts I know not to ignore tell me that this is Leanna, our general, and that Ero has identified the two highest ranking officers left among our people. But how? And what is his plan? Why did he release Leanna and why is he giving these fighters a weapon?

"Fugcha," he orders and I gasp.

"What is it?" Jia says. "Halima, what is it?"

"He wants them to fight," I whisper back.

Kenya is first to move. She lunges for the spear, but she doesn't attack Leanna. She throws herself at Ero.

Leanna moves a split second later and gathers the loose end of her chain. She spins it around her head like a propellor and wields it like a flail at the same time that Kenya feints and thrusts up at Ero's stomach.

He doesn't move until the last second. Until just an inkling of hope trickles in that these two warriors might be able to beat him.

But even though he's weaponless, he is the weapon. He stands two heads taller than Kenya and one of his hands could easily wrap all the way around her throat. He catches the chain when it comes at him and even though the tail end smashes into his shoulder and a red welt appears beneath it, he doesn't flinch.

At the same time, his other hand catches the spear just beneath its pointy metal tip. He stops its path inches from his ribbed abdomen. His limbs move in perfect sync, his gaze half distracted.

The Devil-worshipping demons around the cave laugh, though it takes me a moment to identify it as such. Laughter. Typically a term used to describe joyous sounds, sounds of mirth. But this sound could not be farther from it. This is a terrible sound, one that reaches into chests and snuffs out all tendrils of hope and happiness like plucking dandelions.

He grins and when he starts to laugh too, I feel my soul whither a little, retreating deeper into my body where it will be safe.

While he laughs, Kenya and Leanna try to retract their weapons, try to attack, try to free themselves in any way, but they're stuck and he's laughing and they're all laughing and Jia's shaking so badly at my side that our sweaty, sticky palms remain locked together through adrenaline alone.

Ero rips back his left arm and Leanna, unwilling to relinquish her weapon, goes flying. She hits the stone ground just twenty feet in front of me and, when she rolls onto her side, I see that her back is covered in brutal welts and slashes. Her grey shirt is shredded. How many times did he whip her?

Tears well in my eyes as I look towards the monster, rage making me sweat even more. My heart kicks like a boot to the chest. I wish I could kill him. I will. But I'm not ready yet.

He drags Kenya in towards him by the spear and catches her by the throat when she falls. Lifting her by the neck, he tosses the spear over his shoulder absently where it's caught by a younger male warrior before Ero tosses her just as easily onto the ground next to Leanna.

"Tekaroella haremu."

Haremu? Like Harem? The thought jolts and I feel shouts of protest surge up into my mouth as two female demons lead Leanna and Kenya away, but then I remember... Don't give yourself away. They cannot know what languages you speak... So I cage angry, violent words behind my teeth.

La'a. No. Nein. Ayi. Bu. Non. Net. I close my eyes, reach for a language that feels distant to me, settling on Turkish, then begin counting to a hundred. Bir, iki, üç, dört, beş, altı...

Very quietly, I hear a soft, shaky voice whisper, "Hana, du, se, ne, daseos..." I'm counting out loud and now Jia's counting with me in Korean. I quickly make the switch. "Yug, ilgob, yeodeolb…"

She laughs lightly and frantically under her breath and squeezes my hand so hard I think she might break my soft bones. Then I'm sure of it when I feel a shadow — a hot, enormous shadow — fall over us. I open my eyes and look up.

A wall of bronze is the first thing I see. It's covered in reflective brown and pink scars. They cover every inch of him. Some thin and fresh. Some old and thick and badly healed.

The thickest one starts at his lowest rib and travels down, disappearing into his dark brown pants. They're woven fibers, but I can't tell beyond that what material they are, just that they're stained. Is that Leanna's blood? Kenya's?

He's twice my height. That's all I can think when I first look up at him. I'm wrong — at least, I hope I am — but it's still what hits me first. And even though I hate him, his size alone gives me pause, makes me shiver, makes me want to lay all my secrets bare so that I don't have to be punished by him when he figures out that I'm here for a rebellion.

And for revenge.

I pull my lips into my mouth and bite down on them. As I do, I notice a downward flicker of his. His mouth is large, almost comically so, and a dark, delirious pink. The wells of his eyes cast dark shadows across his cheeks, which are high and cut like shards from the black and green stones glimmering in the cave walls around us.

Like his heavy eyelashes, his hair is inky black and falls down to his swollen shoulders. Tangled and raging, his curls rush like the River Styx. You are not Charon. You are Ero. You can be defeated.

Jia was shaking before, but now my own tremors are all I can feel as I finally force myself to meet his gaze, only to find that he's not looking at me. He's not looking at Jia either, but at our locked hands.

I shake so badly that it pulls Jia further towards me. Without warning, the disturbed look Ero wore fades and he drops onto his haunches.

His massive body is an occultation of the light trickling down from above. The scent of blood and sweat and salt perfume his skin. He smells like War itself. I want to close my eyes, but I'm riveted to the motion of his bloody knuckles as he produces a dagger from the belt at his waist. Short, it has a leather handle and a blackened blade.

He shouts an order that I can't interpret and a demon approaches with a torch in her hands. Sweat pours from my armpits down my sides, down the back of my neck, and from the curve below my breasts as Ero takes his dagger to the open flame, movements deliberate and slow as he waits for the pointy end to glow bright red.

"Oreyo yasibalu yaruella?" He chuckles and I hate the sound. It's lovely and all I can think of is Lucifer. Lucifer was an angel once.

He holds his blade up before his eyes and, seemingly satisfied, brings it closer and closer to Jia and me. We both cringe away from the heat radiating out of the glowing steel, but in order to escape it we'd have to release each other's hands and we don't. It isn't one of us, or the other, but both.

We don't know each other, but we don't let go.

Ero's mouth twitches, but this isn't a male to make false promises. He brings the blade in closer and closer until it touches the insides of both of our wrists at the same time.

The sight of it burning my flesh comes before the sensation of pain and my fingers lock when I should have spent those precious seconds trying to pry them open and get away.

My brain lurches, but is slow to fire or maybe it's just that the pain in my back makes this fresh agony hard to feel. Jia screams and collapses forward, but she doesn't let go of me. She still doesn't.

And I still don't let go, not even as the smell of burning flesh wafts up to greet me. It clashes with the scent of the blue goop still clinging to my uniform, which reeks of antiseptic, but also with the stranger scents lingering beneath the blood and sweat and salt on his skin.

Woozy, I waver and strangely, I think that he smells like war, yes, but he also smells like Anubis. Just like Hades would in my dreams. He smells like minerals and grass and metal, like salt and like sea. He reeks of survival, of regret, of a paradise lost. He smells like an angel that fell. He smells like ruin.

Where there is ruin, there is hope for treasure.

The thought collides with the pain and pushes it back. Reduces it to rubble. A voice — an actual voice — whispers those words in my head and I know that voice. I know it.

Ebi. Father. Father said that. He was repeating the words of a poet he loved and that poet was called...was called...I stretch further into the memory, but come up short.

"Where there is ruin, there is hope for treasure." I hear the words out loud, but this time in my own voice.

"Woga eh?" He rumbles, but I don't answer or let myself be shocked by the nearness of his voice and his overwhelming presence. So sad. So ruined.

Instead, I close my eyes and let tears leak down my cheeks and I cry for him, for this Anubis, Charon lost at sea.

I cry for this place with its ruined soul and I repeat words that come to me, "My soul is from elsewhere, I'm sure of that, and I intend to end up there." It's the same poet... something...something Jalal...el...something. He was my father's favorite.

"Woga eh?" I open my eyes to see his chiseled face, his brow furrowed.

He must not like what he sees in mine because he bares his teeth at me like an animal, lips peeling back in rage. He yanks the brand away from my skin and Jia's and a surge of breath rushes into my lungs along with the rich, overlapping tastes of pain.

"Kedejiniliste?" His intonation tilts up in a question. I don't understand the word, but I know he wants me to repeat what I've said.

I open my mouth, but as I look up at him and meet his bitter gaze, the words catch in my throat. I shake my head.

Khara. Khara khara khara. I know immediately that I made the wrong choice. It's in his eyes. They're storm cloud grey, reflective of the color of the dark blade he returns to my arm, but my arm alone.

"Just let go," Jia whimpers, pained, but still trying for me.

But I don't let go. I don't speak or answer her or him, but I refuse to let go, just like I refuse to look down and see my skin burning. I just focus on the feeling of Jia's soft hand in mine.

The mistake of my open defiance gets more grim the longer I stare into his eyes. A vein pulses across his forehead. The muscles twitch in his steely neck. His jaw sets and he presses his brand more fully below the wound he already made just below my elbow crease. Harder and harder and harder…

My eyelids flutter. He repeats his question, but I don't repeat myself. And it no longer has anything to do with the fact that the pain has blotted out the memory of the poem, making it impossible for me to recite, and everything to do with the fact that another word creeps front and center, past thoughts of mother and father, past thoughts of ha and jeem, past thoughts of language and who I am or what, and settles calmly in the center of my being.

Together. A reminder that Jia's hand is in mine and even though memories have forsaken me for all the value that they had, there are new memories to be made, new foundations to fight from. I am not here alone.

We're here together.

And if I'm wrong and he is Anubis of this new world, it will be together that our hearts are weighed.

We'll find a way.

"Together," I whisper. "Hamkke," I repeat in Korean.

Jia's hand squeezes mine harder and through the scent of burning flesh and the pain that threatens to eclipse all else, I hear her whisper, Hamkke back.

"Kedejiniliste," he snarls between his teeth.

But my head is foggy. Reality beats a lazy retreat and I rock onto my heels and let my head fall back as I continue to endure.

I endure until the pain gets so overwhelming, I don't feel it anymore. Dizzy, I open my eyes and in Amharic, I whisper, "Anidi laye."

Together.

His nostrils flare and his storm cloud eyes glaze over with fear disguised as violence and they are the last things I see before the dam breaks and the pain trickles in and drowns me.

———————————

Continue reading anywhere print books are sold.

All books by Elizabeth

Berserker Kings - Enemies to lovers. With magic.
Dark City Omega, Book 1 (Echo and Adam)
more to come!

Population - Battles and Heroes that Bite.
Lord of Population, Book 1 (Abel and Kane)
Monster in the Oasis, Book 2 (Diego and Pia)
Immortal with Scars, Book 3 (Lahve and Candy)
more to come!

Twisted Fates - Mafia. Brotherhood. Murder.
The Hunting Town, Book 1 (Knox and Mer, Dixon and Sara)
The Hunted Rise, Book 2 (Aiden and Alina, Gavriil and Ify)
The Hunt, Book 3 (Anatoly and Candy, Charlie and Molly)

Xiveri Mates - Aliens. Heat. New Worlds.
Taken to Voraxia, Book 1 (Miari and Raku)
Taken to Nobu, Book 2 (Kiki and Va'Raku)
Exiled from Nobu, Book 2.5, a Novella (Lisbel and Jaxal)
Taken to Sasor, Book 3 (Mian and Neheyuu) *standalone
Taken to Heimo, Book 4 (Svera and Krisxox)
A Very Xiveri Christmas, Book 4.5, A Novella (Svera and Krisxox)
Taken to Kor, Book 5 (Deena and Rhork)
Taken to Lemora, Book 6 (Essmira and Raingar)
Taken by the Pikosa Warlord, Book 7 (Halima and Ero) *standalone
Taken to Evernor, Book 8 (Nalia and Herannathon)
Taken to Sky, Book 9 (Ashmara and Jerrock)
Taken to Revatu, Book 10, A Novella (Latanya and Grizz) *standalone